TALES OF THE

DANIEL P. MOSKOWITZ

STORY MERCHANT BOOKS
LOS ANGELES
2019

STORY MERCHANT BOOKS

ISBN: 978-1-970157-07-9

Story Merchant Books
400 S. Burnside Avenue #11B
Los Angeles, CA 90036

www.storymerchantbooks.com

Cover art & interior design by IndieDesignz.com

For my mother Gussie who instilled
in me the joy of reading.

For my brother David who impressed upon me
the importance of the meaning of a word.

For the unsung family justice workers and
particularly Assigned Counsel who care as a
matter of practice.

Finally for my wife Jayeme Indira for her
love, her encouragement and her smile.

AN AUGUST AFTERNOON, LATE LAST MILLENNIUM

WEBSTER AVENUE BEGINS IN THE VERY HEART OF THE BRONX. By the borough's standards the avenue was wide, which made it a suitable base for an outer-borough shunt of the Third Avenue Elevated line. For more than a century, the El had cast its dark shadow over Daniel Webster's Avenue, giving the Devil his due. Its stops were mostly local for the yokels. Screeching halts and fitful lurches made the journey an agonizing hour-long, rumbling jaunt to its coupling at Gun Hill Road with the IRT. On the train, would-be voyeurs were frustrated by the boarded-up windows or a pastiche of curtains, blinds, and drapes. On occasion an elderly woman could be spotted resting her head on a pillow spread across a windowsill, staring balefully at the El as its satanic shriek filled her ears.

The El is gone now, torn down twenty-five years ago in an unintended gesture of municipal mercy. Low ridership and high operational costs motivated the Manhattan patricians to bring the El down, girder by girder. In its stead, a labyrinth of clotting traffic lights provided a karmic reminder of the El's former presence as cars flowed sluggishly north to the Yonkers border.

Stuck at a red light, Schwartz waited impatiently for the signal change. Gunning it at the first ray of green proved fruitless, since the light at the next intersection turned red as he approached. And when that light turned green, the signal at the next intersection turned red. Unlike the pattern of green lights that sought to fluidly guide Manhattan drivers up and down gilded avenues, this was a reverse stagger.

Damn this road. Damn this traffic. Damn that judge.

Schwartz struggled to control his diaphragm and lungs. His stomach was performing a loopdeloop. For ten years Schwartz had been an attorney assigned to indigent litigants in Bronx County Family Court, paid from the public coffers under Article 18-B of the New York State County Law. The parade of pathetic souls through 900 Sheridan Avenue had gradually numbed his outrage reflex. Burned out? Schwartz was charcoal, or so he'd thought.

Never before with a newborn. Never. I have to get out of the friggin' Bronx. Just let me make it to the Throgs Neck.

Two hours earlier, Schwartz had sat in a windowless box charitably described as a client interview room. He had just been assigned to represent Leesah Kinard. Ms. Kinard had been summoned to family court because her three-year-old son, Malik, had been in foster care for a year, and child protective services had filed a petition to extend his placement for another year.

While Schwartz reviewed the extension petition on Malik, he asked, "Who's the little lady?"

Secured in a carrier around Ms. Kinard's waist and wrapped in a pink blanket was an infant. The mother was bottle-feeding the baby girl with one hand while fumbling through her bag, searching for various documents.

"Precious Faith. She's six weeks old. You see, I had the baby just after I got off a Rikers. I had to go back to the shelter system. Spent five nights at EAU, sleeping on the floor in somebody's damn office. Nine months pregnant. Know what I'm sayin'?"

"Did you visit Malik when you came out?"

"I called that foster agency. That bitch caseworker was never there. I was being moved every night to a different shelter. There was no number I could leave her."

"Did you start a drug program?"

"Listen, I was due in two weeks when I got offa the Rock. I had to get my Medicaid CIN opened. Tryin' to find a hospital to give birth in, find a place to live. . . Come on, now!"

"Did you give any urine?"

"Man, this baby was born clean. No positive tox. She's my urine test."

Her tone had ratcheted up. Schwartz gestured for Ms. Kinard to settle down.

"Look, these are questions the judge is going to ask. If you're going to go off the rails—"

A court officer rapped on the door and poked his head into the room. He had the pasty white complexion of an Italian mama's boy with the sneer to match.

"Calling this case next after next. Put your client in the well."

Put . . . your . . . client. . . in.. . the. . . well.

Schwartz had heard it hundreds of times. The well was the area between the door that opened from the waiting area and the door that opened into the courtroom. It was a muster station before entering BxFC hell.

Sucking his lower lip against his teeth, he glanced at the certificates and "Dear Judge" letters scattered on the shopworn, bubbled-up desktop. No time to read them. No time to make copies for the judge or counsel. He glanced up at Leesah. Her voice resonated with a low growl of anger, calibrated by men, poverty, and the system. The tawny skin around her eyes and mouth was creased from life's inflicted trauma. How old was she? Her age would be measured not in years but by the wounds winding through her psyche like annual rings of a tree.

She'd finished the feeding and was gently rubbing and patting the infant's back. The baby coughed up a good portion of formula onto the blanket covering Leesah's blouse, suffusing the room with its odor.

"Dammit chil'!"

Leesah composed herself and wiped the spit-up from Precious's lips and chin.

"They want this baby, too. She's all I got. I lose her . . ."

Schwartz forced a grin and gave her a thumbs-up. "Let's see how it goes."

With trepidation, Schwartz made his way into the courtroom. All too often he'd been slammed by the courtroom door swinging open into the well, propelled by disgruntled litigants cursing under their breath: "That fuckin' judge don't know me! "That caseworker's a lying bitch!" "Tell *me* what to do with my goddamn kids!"

The air conditioning in Part I was on the blink. Two fans hummed in diagonally opposite corners of the courtroom. Attorneys milled around the back of the over-lit sterile courtroom that defined the part. Small jokes, smirks, and commiseration flavored the conversation that percolated in the fluorescent wash.

"Got slammed yesterday on intake. Picked up twelve cases. Didn't get out 'til after eight."

"Mom said she couldn't come to court because there was a house fire. But she doesn't have a house—she's homeless!"

"She claims she didn't smoke crack…that the apartment below was a crack den and she must've inhaled it."

"Tell your client to make the admission that she failed to protect her kids from dad. Otherwise, you know she'll never get her kids back. Judge won't return them if she doesn't acknowledge responsibility. It'd be unsafe. Take it to trial, we'll be in court for a year."

Judge Natalie Finkel emerged from the cramped chambers off the rear of the courtroom. A small woman with wiry grey and black hair crowning her head, her witchy Margaret Hamilton countenance was firmly in place. The judge instructed the bridge officer to call the next case.

Schwartz was huddled in a corner, engaged in whispered conversation with the ACS attorney on the Kinard case. NYC-ACS: Administration for Children's Services, formerly known as CWA: Child Welfare Administration, formerly known as BCW: Bureau of Child Welfare, also known as TPTTTDKA: Those People That Took The Damn Kids Away. It seemed to Schwartz that the city agency changed its name every time a child died on its watch.

"We've filed on the newborn. We're asking for a remand."

Schwartz slowly shook his head. "That's a bad remand. Baby was born clean. Mother did parenting skills. She has housing."

"Yeah . . . in a shelter. Where mom left the three-year-old."

Schwartz had just about become oblivious to the condescendingly familiar "mom" or "dad" used to allude to his clients. To rebuke this bright-eyed, bushy-tailed savior of children for the reference would only further sink his chances of cutting a deal for a parole of the infant to his client. He swallowed his protest, and pleaded instead.

"Look, they have twenty-four-hour supervision. That's a Tier II family shelter."

A subtle twist of her neck accompanied the reply.

"Caseworker was told by her manager that it's a remand."

Schwartz felt a ripple in his throat as he shook his head, stood, and said loudly, "She'll lose the shelter. Bad remand."

Judge Finkel had been conducting her examination of a respondent father, a large black man who had the temerity to take the stand in his own defense. She momentarily glared at Schwartz for interrupting the flow of her inquiry. The bridge officer seconded the glare and whispered stridently to Schwartz to take a seat. "You're next."

Resigned, Schwartz joined the Greek chorus of attorneys, seated in a semicircle in the back of the courtroom, awaiting the call of their cases. The modulation of the judge's voice as she circled her prey, from soft to softer to softest, mesmerized the assemblage. The rotating dual courtroom fans swung back and forth with the effect of a gold watch swung by a hypnotist. Schwartz, having witnessed this act countless times before, chomped on his lip.

"Now, you say you've learned from the error of your ways and you want your child returned to you."

"Yeah."

"And you've taken parenting skills classes."

"Got my certificate. Caseworker has a copy."

"Please don't volunteer information. Just answer the question. The last portion will be stricken. Tell me what you learned from your parenting class."

"Oh, use time-outs, take away privileges, you know."

"I don't know. That's why I'm asking the questions. Who taught the classes?"

"There was a Miss Marsh and another person sometimes. I don't remember her name."

"What were their qualifications?"

The man swiveled in the witness chair to gaze helplessly at his attorney.

"Sir, your attorney can't answer for you. What were their qualifications?"

"Their qual—? I don't know. ACS sent me there, so I went."

"So the only reason you went was because the caseworker told you to go?"

"Well, yeah. An' get my son back."

"So you weren't motivated by the desire to learn how to properly discipline your child? How do we make sure that if this child were returned to you, you wouldn't inflict excessive corporal punishment again? You only went because somebody told you to go, correct?"

"No. Yeah, look, Ma'am, I never beat this boy in the first place. Not like you say I did. An' I'll do anything to get him back and—"

"I've heard enough. You're still in denial. You were in denial during the fact-finding hearing, during your interview with the MHS psychologist, and you're still in denial in the face of this court's finding that you struck your child with a belt. I have no confidence that you have gained any insight in the past ten months. The witness is excused. Have a seat next to your attorney."

The sullen man backed out of the witness chair and sank down in a seat at the table. He shook his head and whispered in agitation to his attorney, who stared stiffly ahead.

"Anything further, counsel, for the respondent?" the judge asked sardonically.

"Respondent's counsel seeks to cross-examine the maker of the mental health evaluation."

"You may do so, but that would necessitate an adjournment, and my next available date is in November. Meanwhile, the remand order will stand."

The attorney and his client conferred briefly. They concluded with the respondent shaking his head and gesturing, palms up in surrender. The attorney barely rose to address the court, "Respondent rests."

"At the conclusion of this dispositional hearing—"

"Your Honor, I'd like to sum up briefly."

"There's no need, Counsel. I've heard all the testimony and read the reports. Have a seat. At the conclusion of this dispositional hearing, the court finds that the best interests of the child would be served by placing him with the Commissioner of Social Services for a period of up to twelve months. Having had the unique opportunity to observe the demeanor of the witnesses, I fully credit the testimony of the caseworker. I find the respondent not credible. He failed to make eye contact with the court while giving his answers. His voice wavered when asked about the prior finding of neglect. His testimony was self-serving. Statutory reports to the law guardian. Next case."

Having exiled another family to the post-dispositional foster care Gulag, Finkel rose. All five feet three inches of her made an imperial turn and handed the case file to the part clerk.

The man stood up and glowered at the judge. He took one step toward her. The attorney put a hand on his client's shoulder. The man paused, executed an about-face, and stormed out of the courtroom, twisting his head and cursing under his breath. It was no small wonder that a court officer escorted Finkel to the elevated platform of the #4 IRT station at 161st Street–Yankee Stadium at every court day's end.

Ah, the fear of the Black Man—the jet fuel of the foster care system.

The part had already heard more than fifty cases—a heady diet of familial dysfunction. The bridge officer stifled a yawn.

"Parties in the matter of the Kinard Children. Take the table, counselors."

The ACS attorney slid the Article 10 Neglect Petition across the counsel table to Schwartz. He picked up the document and wryly noted that the papers still had that warm just-off-the-copy-machine, feel.

Newborn petition for newborn baby.

Schwartz scanned the pages. The words slipped in and out of focus.

The door to the courtroom swung open. Officer Mama's Boy entered, sneer intact, with respondent Kinard and infant Kinard in tow. The attorneys noted their appearance on the record.

"Have a seat next to your attorney!" the officer barked.

"Be seated," Judge Finkel ordered wearily.

Her eyes locked with Schwartz's. Schwartz sensed that several court officers had entered and taken a position behind Leesah.

"What's the application?" the judge asked.

"Agency's seeking a remand on the newborn, Your Honor.," droned the ACS attorney.

"Mr. Schwartz?"

Schwartz's vocal chords were double-clutched. He coughed them out of neutral. "We're seeking a pre-removal hearing, Your Honor."

"At five o'clock? Let me speak to the mother. Swear her in."

The bridge officer administered the oath to Leesah Kinard, who nervously promised to tell the truth. Judge Finkel leaned forward in her chair. "Ms. Kinard, do you know why you're here today?"

"Uh, my lawyer said . . . I'm not sure."

"You've given birth, I see."

"Last month, Your Honor. Her name is Precious . . . Precious Faith Kinard. All her shots are up to date. And I got my welfare case reopened. And . . . and I'm gittin' enrolled in a new drug program. And I'm in a Tier II shelter where I can have my own room with the baby.... And-"

The judge has been sifting through some documents when she interrupted Leesah.

"You left your older child—what's his name? Oh, I see it. Malik. You left Malik in a shelter, did you not?"

Schwartz twisted in his chair. He'd known all along where this would be headed. *But never before with an infant in a mother's arms.*

Precious emerged from her feeding haze and looked directly at Schwartz.

"Judge. . . Your Honor, I left him with a friend 'cause I had to take care of some business. Know what I'm sayin'? And I thought the father was goin' to come git him. But he didn't. And I finished my parenting skills class while at Rikers. I got the certificate right—"

"Why were you at Rikers?" interjected the judge.

Schwartz jumped up. His chair scratched against the sticky linoleum. Startled, the baby let out a shrill cry. Schwartz drew a small measure of satisfaction from seeing Finkel's painful twitch as the sound ricocheted off the courtroom walls. He waited for the vibration to dissipate.

"Your Honor what does that have to do with—"

"Maybe nothing, maybe everything. Sit down, Mr. Schwartz." Regaining her momentum, the judge turned back to Leesah. Her voice grew softer.

"Tell me why you were at Rikers?"

"Violation of probation."

Softer still. "All right... and just how did you violate probation?"

"I missed some appointments with my officer because I was going to other appointments. Tryin' to get housing. I also got sick and had to—"

"And what was the underlying conviction?"

Leesah started rocking back and forth in her chair.

"Direct sale."

"Of what?"

"Crack cocaine. But it was two years ago, know what I'm sayin'?"

The judge looked at Leesah and then glanced at the papers before her. She picked up a pen and made a note. She raised her head slowly and whispered,

"I'm granting the application for the child's remand."

"What's a re . . . ? Oh, Your Honor, this baby . . . I'm takin' real good care of her. I'm doin' everythin' I'm supposed to. I haven't smoked a blunt in over a year. It's not gonna happen again. This time I'm not relying on nobody to look afta her."

"I'm sorry. I can't take a chance. This is a newborn. The remand application is granted."

The breadth and width of the groan exiting Leesah's lips rivaled that of any Delta blues belter.

"Nooooooooo! She's all I gots! You can't take her!"

Officer Mama's Boy stepped over to unstrap the child from Leesah's baby carrier.

"Git your hands offa me! Your Honor, pleeeeaaaaase, don't take my baby!"

For the first and last time that afternoon, Judge Finkel raised her voice a notch above cackle level.

"Officer, take the child. Clear the courtroom. Next case."

Schwartz turned his head. He simply could not watch. As the officer jerked the infant away from Leesah, the child let loose with a wail that sounded to Schwartz like, "Moooooom!"

Schwartz's body jerked involuntarily. He jumped to his feet.

"Your Honor, I am requesting a Section 1027 hearing on the in-court removal."

"You just had one, Mr. Schwartz."

"Then I am demanding that this matter be set down within three days pursuant to Family Court Act Section 1028 for a post-removal hearing."

"Demanding? Excuse me? You just waived that relief by having a 1027 hearing, pursuant to statute."

"That wasn't a hearing, that was a—"

The judge responded with a vicious bang of the gavel.

"Clear the table. Adjourned to September 5th for conference."

"But, Judge—"

"Mr. Schwartz, you are done here."

Schwartz stood immobilized. After a stunned moment, he stared down at the counsel table and gathered his scattered file. He turned and walked out of the courtroom with his arm around the moaning Leesah. The attorneys seated in the back averted their eyes.

In the crowded waiting area, Schwartz retrieved a tissue from his pocket and offered it to his client.

"It's crumpled but clean."

Leesah separated herself from his embrace and stared at Schwartz. She didn't make a move toward the tissue.

"Here. Take my card. I heard your child in that courtroom. I heard Precious. She cried out, 'Mom.' You come back to court for her, Ms. Kinard."

Leesah mechanically reached for the card and glanced at it. She wiped her face with it. Dragging the empty baby carrier on the marble floor, the downcast woman headed for the elevator bank.

It was an even bet that Schwartz would never see her again. He followed her at arm's length. Leesah was at the last to step into the packed elevator. The door kept opening and closing, causing the elevator to issue a shrill electronic protest against overcrowding.

As the door opened for the last time, Leesah looked up at Schwartz. "Schwartz, you ain't worth shit," she hissed.

The traffic signal on East 174th Street finally turned green. Schwartz made a right turn, nudging his 1986 red Saab onto the Cross Bronx Expressway's eastbound ramp, headed for the Throgs Neck Bridge. As he climbed the incline, his fears were realized. The expressway was anything but. The gorge that Robert Moses had carved out of Bronx bedrock, disemboweling a slew of stable working-class neighborhoods in the bargain, was choked with traffic. Schwartz inhaled the carbon monoxide deeply and let out a toxic sigh. He began to whistle the Bobby Darin tune "Things."

Stepping into the foyer of his Glen Cove duplex condominium, Schwartz put his shoulder bag down and with a weary voice announced that he was home. He could hear his wife futzing with dishes in the kitchen. She failed to acknowledge his arrival, which was par for the course for the past few months. Julie, the nine-year-old, and Ethan, the five-year-old, appeared. They hesitated to close the gap to where Schwartz was standing. He strode toward them, knelt down, and hugged them hard. Though they squirmed in his grasp, though they cried out for their mother, he would not let them go.

1959

SCHWARTZ WAS A CHILD OF THE BRONX. HE'D GONE TO ELEMENTARY school, junior high school, high school, and college there. Had there been a law school in the Bronx, odds were he would have attended there as well. Instead, his status was elevated some what. He attended law school in an alien territory: Brooklyn. Now he was back in the Bronx, plying his trade. Schwartz was parochial in the most cosmopolitan city in the known universe.

The heroes of Schwartz's youth were, not surprisingly, heroes of the Bronx: Tony Curtis (Bernie Schwartz—a distant cousin, no doubt), Red Buttons (Aaron Chwatt—an even more distant cousin who'd lost the *s*,*r* and *z* and gained an extra *t*), and, of course, Mickey Mantle of no discernible relation. Paramount in this Hall of Heroes was a hip-swiveling, Brylcreem-laden lad· named Bobby Darin (born Walden Robert Cassotto).

There was Schwartz, at nine years old, curled up on the shag carpet of his family's Mitchell-Lama apartment, having yet again lost the battle for the couch to his older brother.

Ah . . . who'd wanna sit on that plastic-covered human fly trap, anyway?

"Mid-century Jewish Provincial" would aptly describe the furniture style of the Schwartz family apartment.

On the after-school menu, the first choice on the family's sole black-and-white television was *The Mickey Mouse Club*. His brother would crack that he'd love to be Spin or Marty helping Annette get off that horse at the Triple R Ranch. Next up, his brother's choice: Dick Clark's *American Bandstand*. Schwartz didn't quite grasp the logic behind some old guy, whom the world would later come to know as the twentieth century's Dorian Gray, showcasing young singers for still younger dancers. The show was broadcast from Philadelphia, but it might as well have been Mars, given Schwartz's narrow frame of reference. Yet Schwartz would watch, hoping his brother would leave the room so he could slip in a couple of minutes of *The Sandy Becker Show.*

On that particular broadcast, on that particular afternoon, Clark began the show with his typical cheerful greeting to the audience, in the studio and beyond. He segued into his typical cheerful introduction of the next performer, with an obligatory reference to the artist's hits and coming appearances, but ending with a sentence that hit Schwartz like a line drive off Mickey's bat (Mantle, not Mouse): "So let's hear it for a young man from the Bronx . . . Bobby Darin!"

At the mention of his borough, Schwartz felt an adrenaline rush. Prancing onto the stage was a regular guy from the street corner, dressed in a sharkskin suit and fancy black patent leather shoes, with a pomp hairdo. He was twisting and swiveling and singing about Schwartz's least favorite activity, right after eating liver and getting polio shots: taking a bath. *Splish-Splash.*

At the song's end, Schwartz's brother shot up and streaked to the bathroom to check his hair and reload the Brylecreem. Schwartz didn't move. He sat there, open mouthed, trying to fathom how a Bronx guy got on TV and did that!

Darin followed up by talking, oh so suavely, with Clark about a new direction for his career and a new song.

"Would you like to hear it, Dick?"

"What do you say, kids?" Clark asked the audience.

Amidst shouts of approval, Darin launched into a swinging yet confusing song about a shark—some creep named Mack who kills people with his knife and these ladies who are running after him. Schwartz couldn't make heads or tails of it, but he knew it meant something—something important. What, exactly, he was determined to find out.

Thus, Schwartz became president of the Bobby Darin Fan Club at P.S.103 in the Bronx. He was also its only member. His classmates were all following either an older sibling's crush on Elvis Presley or their parents' infatuation with the skinny regular guy with magical pipes from a place called Hoboken.

Whazhisname? Oh yeah, uh, Frank something . . . Sinatra . . Frank Sinatra.

That star-crossed alum of the Bronx High School of Science, however, hooked Schwartz at a tender age.

While others still argued the relative merits of the Duke, the Say Hey Kid, or the Mick, Schwartz would take on all comers in the Elvis-Sinatra-Darin debate. Problem was, nobody would pick up the gauntlet.

"Psycho," his peers would taunt, followed by a Hitchcockian *"Eeek eeek eeek!"*

"There it is, rock 'n' roll, the opiate of the masses," his mother, the unrepentant Communist charged.

"It's a phase," his father, the stoic placater, sighed.

His brother treated him like a dead Spaldeen whenever Schwartz tried to engage him on the topic.

When Bobby married Sandra Dee, America's sweetheart, Schwartz felt like the Best Man.

"You see . . . you see," Schwartz said knowingly, nodding in validation.

The British invasion of mop-headed rockers in the early to mid-'60s, spearheaded by a Buddy Holly–Roy Orbison–Chuck Berry tribute band called the Beatles, did little to temper Schwartz's ardor for his hometown hero. His stubborn refusal to join the parade widened the gulf between him and his peers. Certifying his geek status was his insistence on wearing his hair in a Brylcreem-laden pomp, eschewing the now popular mop. Consequently, Schwartz found himself all too available for weekend babysitting jobs.

Lugging his collection of Darin 45s in his book bag, Schwartz would play the records over and over on his unsuspecting employers' Hi-Fi. He was determined to learn every word and vocal nuance of every recorded performance. Of course, this was not solely for his benefit. The enrichment and entertainment of his young charges was a consideration as well. Inexplicably, the ungrateful tykes would soon tire of bedtime lullabies featuring "Dream Lover," "Splish Splash," and, the big finish, "Mack the Knife." Schwartz was eventually compelled to await the onset of their sleep, lower the volume, and only then proceed with his study.

Darin enjoyed a wide range during his career—rock, standards, soul, country/folk. Schwartz's repertoire grew wide and deep as the singer's career evolved. There was only one slight hitch: Schwartz couldn't sing a note in tune. His voice had never quite recovered from a stubborn bout with teenage laryngitis. The only thing worse than hearing young Schwartz talk about Darin was hearing him sing Darin's songs, which he did when properly cued. After a point, to avoid the slings and arrows of outrageous reaction from less-than-thrilled studio audience members, Schwartz would most often sing to himself. At times he would omit the melody and chant the spoken word as if it were his mantra.

In the late 1960s, Bobby shed his sharkskin-suit persona and committed his music and performances to social justice causes: the Civil Rights movement, the anti–Vietnam War movement, the Robert Kennedy for President movement. In 1969 he wrote a folk song, "Simple Song of Freedom," giving voice to his objection to that Asian war and offering a plea for racial equality and peace. A college student during that turbulent era, Schwartz joined Bobby lockstep in those sentiments. While Schwartz couldn't sing a note of Bobby's music on key, he could write and distribute End the War leaflets. He organized demonstrations at the Fordham Road Army/Navy Recruiting Station, where his ability as a speaker against of that war became evident, cowing the war's supporters with logic, stats, and oratory flourishes.

Schwartz had followed Darin's career closely, through its permutations and reincarnations. Schwartz watched him evolve from rocker to Las Vegas swinger, to movie actor, to television variety show host, to blue-denim folkie, and back to Las Vegas hipster, albeit in a blue denim tux. Schwartz had joined Darin in spirit every swiveled step of the way.

On December 20, 1973, Bobby died from complications following corrective surgery to his ravaged heart. Bobby Darin's untimely death at age thirty-seven struck Schwartz harder than the murder of their mutual hero, Robert Kennedy, five years earlier. In the obits, Schwartz learned that Darin had contracted rheumatic fever as a child, causing him to live his life on a hurried timetable. Confronted with the news of Darin's passing via radio, Schwartz reflected on the one time he had seen Bobby live at Freedomland in the Bronx. Freedomland was a Disneyland knockoff, sculpted out of the tidewater wetlands of the East Bronx, intended to resemble the continental United States. Attractions such as the Chicago Fire and The Sante Fe Train Ride transported the denizens of the Bronx to intracontinental locales and experiences.

In 1963 Bobby had performed at Freedomland to the delight of the hometown fans. With pleasure, Schwartz had noted that their numbers had grown. Unfortunately, the outdoor concert was marred by a summer storm. On stage, Darin was curt with his bandleader and sound crew. He made rude comments to audience members who opened their umbrellas obstructing the view for others. His skin was pallid and he appeared to struggle for breath. Darin mopped his brow between songs with a towel or sipped on some tea.

But when Darin sang, when he actually performed his stable of hits or broke into a kick-ass arrangement of an old standard, Schwartz was suffused with joy. Darin overcame the obstacles in his path on that day and lifted Schwartz from the gravity of the Bronx to a musical Nirvana. By the transcendent concert's end, Schwartz was transfixed by a thought: *He knows what he has achieved.*

Several years later in a Psych 101 course at Lehman College in the Bronx, Schwartz learned a phrase that aptly described Darin's state on that day: self-actualized. Schwartz would welcome a dose or two of self-actualization into his unfolding life. His campus advocacy for the oppressed, for justice, for peace, and an assessment of his passions and skills coalesced to inform his decision to attend law school. This brought unmitigated joy to his working-class parents who had come of age during the Great Depression. Neither had attended college, much less graduate school.

"You see, Tessie, this Darin thing . . . it was just a phase like I'd said," his father cooed to his mother.

"He'll serve the People after all." His mother sighed, kvelling.

Bobby Darin talents had lifted him, along with his fans, to a height of ecstasy. All too young, he had been called back to Earth—six feet under to be accurate. But Schwartz's heart would beat double-time in tribute to Darin's memory every time he heard the *ummpah-ummpah* opening vamp of "Mack the Knife." Though he couldn't sing a single note on key and wouldn't be wearing a blue sharkskin suit, Schwartz would persist in carrying on Bobby Darin's good fight for social justice.

At least that was the plan.

MID-NOVEMBER 2000

PRECIOUS KINARD'S TRAUMATIC REMAND AND LEESAH KINARD'S consequential judgment of Schwartz's professional worth had informed his practice and his mood.

He had been tuning out his clients' rants as they prattled on about missed visits with their children or caseworkers' failure to return phone calls. He had been going through the motions of being a husband and a father to the increased peril of his family's domestic tranquility. To paraphrase Gertrude Stein, he was "thereless."

Adding to the sense of "thereless" was the stymied outcome of the 2000 presidential election. Phrases such as "hanging chads" and images of Florida Secretary of State Katherine Harris doing her star turn dominated the national news programs. The uncertain identity of leadership designated to take the country into the next century only confirmed, on a macro level, the rudderless sensation Schwartz was experiencing on the micro.

As he departed family court after another day of BxFC dysfunction, Schwartz shuffled amidst the crush of litigants, lawyers, caseworkers, and clerks exiting the heavy glass doors.

How many times have these windows been broken?

Once outside, he paused to button his coat and search his pockets for his datebook—his compass, roadmap, and North Star for the next three months of his professional life.

Where the hell?...Ahh, got it right—

"We need some whores!" Edgardo Ramos bellowed as he slapped Schwartz on the back.

Surprised by the blow but inured to the greeting, Schwartz struggled to maintain his balance on the grimy sidewalk in front of 900 Sheridan Avenue. Fortunately, his shoulder bag served as a ballast.

"Whores, my friend," Edgardo repeated.

Schwartz narrowed his eyes and drew a breath.

"Are you convening a meeting of the Society of Kindred Spirits, Don Edgardo?"

"I am, most assuredly, Don Schwartz."

"Do we have a quorum?"

"Of two."

Schwartz surveyed his friend. Edgardo Ramos, Esq., six feet tall and broad shouldered, with a punam reminiscent of Jerry Colonna and a delivery that melded W.C. Fields with F. Lee Bailey. Ramos was an old-school litigator. Before a cynical jury, he would cry. Confronted by a lying undercover narc on the stand, he would remove his glasses and thrust them with the purpose of a matador. Crossed by a trial-by-ambush adversary, he relished the opportunity to serve his revenge on a cold plate of "newly discovered" evidence. Challenged by an anal-retentive judge, he'd thunder indignation. His clients wouldn't necessarily benefit, but they'd get a helluva show.

Whether appearing before the bar or drinking at a bar, Don Edgardo knew how to work the room. His patter of words was stocked with corny toasts, jokes, and sayings trotted out as needed. Toasts: "Make new friends and keep the old. One is silver and the other gold." Jokes (after telling one): "That was a time joke; laugh when you have time." Sayings: "See you on the first . . ." (wait for puzzled look, and then), "the first chance I get." To Schwartz, Don Edgardo was a good friend who possessed an abundance of entertainment value coupled with an equally irritating ability to embarrass.

Schwartz's day had shouted for diversion. He'd begun the day with a sixteen-year-old pregnant runaway from Georgia who'd made it to New York by means of stealing—sorry; *borrowing* ("Yo, man, he gave me those keys!")—a car from the twenty-seven-year-old father. It continued with the black man, formerly married to a Jewish American princess, trying to get visitation with his six-year-old daughter. Finally, his day ended with the Vietnamese couple that was ordered to attend three months of a parenting skills re-education camp for disciplining their children with an old-country bamboo-stick whipping.

Schwartz contemplated the phrasing of Edgardo's invitation as they navigated across Sheridan Avenue to the storefront office that the counselor shared with a bail bondsman/process server. In Don Edgardo's cosmology, women were divided into four categories:

His mother ("Santa Maria, may she rest in peace").

His wife ("whose first name seems to escape me at the moment").

His daughter, aptly named Elizabeth ("after the Virgin Queen. May she only have sex with her second husband, if then").

And whores (i.e., every other human female in the universe).

When Schwartz confronted him with the notion that, by definition, Don Edgardo had branded all other people's mothers, wives, and daughters as whores, his reply was concise and bracketed by a caustic snort: "But not mine."

Schwartz settled into a threadbare client chair next to the cluttered desk as Don Edgardo went through his messages and returned calls. Schwartz contemplated the sweaty, anxious asses that had sat in that chair as they doled out cash, check, and/or money order to Don Edgardo in the slim hope of deliverance. The scent of desperation hung heavily from case files stacked throughout the office. Schwartz visualized the exchange:

"Por favor, Señor Ramos. Es mi hijo solamente. Ayúdeme."

In response, Don Edgardo, no doubt, uttered the lawyer's classic admonition as he reached across the desk for payment: "I can't guarantee results—only efforts. *Lo entiendes, Señora?"*

Schwartz, lulled to sleep by the office heat and the shot of Scotch Don Edgardo had offered him, dreamt of a vagina adorned with numbers, with the big and little hands of a clock at its center. Stereophonically, he heard a voice intone, "And the notched marks on the hymen were at two o'clock and seven o'clock."

A young girl's face, contorted in pain, flew into view. Her hand poked through the miasma of his subconscious and pointed a tiny finger in Schwartz's direction. Shaking, he opened his eyes and found Don Edgardo standing over him with his big claw of a hand on his shoulder.

"I know you're dreaming of pussy, my friend."

Schwartz grunted, stretched his arms, and, as he stifled a yawn, wiped some spittle from his lips with the sleeve of his weather-beaten trench coat.

"To your chariot, then!" Edgardo bade.

Schwartz's car was parked several blocks from the courthouse, beyond the Avenues of the Civil War Generals—Sheridan, Sherman, Grant, and McClellan. Enroute, children darted in and out of a bodega, dodging the cluster of men standing in the doorway. A barbershop door swung open and the hard staccato of hip-hop infused the air. A young Muslim woman swathed in a hijab hurried by. With one hand she clutched a young child's coat sleeve while the other held a grocery bag full of Halal meat. Teenage boys playing touch football in the street shouting in protest at the driver of a livery cab that was double-parked in their end zone. In rapid Dominican Spanish, a grandmother shouted from her third-floor apartment to one of the players on the street below.

"Tata, don't bother me now! *Yo estoy con mis amigos!"* came the strident response.

As the two lawyers negotiated their way, Don Edgardo complained about the length of their trek.

"You cheap fuck. Why don't you rent a spot in a lot?"

"And what? Pay $100 a month and lose the best exercise I get all day? And in case you haven't noticed, NYC Assigned Counsel haven't received a raise since 1986. We keep hoping the Mets would win the World Series again because that was the last time the State looked our way."

"Fat chance, with the Yankees ruling the roost. Four games to one, the Mets' tail got waxed this year. Any threat from the Mets and Steinbrenner will just reload."

Schwartz considered Ramos's retort for a moment.

Yet another reason to loathe George Steinbrenner.

Schwartz jumped out of the way of a motorcyclist who was cutting around a van pulling out of a spot.

"Movin' and a-groovin'," he sang to himself.

"What's up with the Valdespino case I referred to you?" Schwartz asked.

Ramos slowed down for half a step and tapped Schwartz on the shoulder.

"That asshole paid me a $1,000 retainer and it's been nothing but promises since. I'm supposed to pick a jury next week, and that piece of shit owes me four grand!" Edgardo erupted.

How does one tell time on a vagina?

That was a question that had haunted Schwartz since he was assigned to represent Carlos Valdespino in the family court child protective sex abuse proceeding. Simply reading the abuse petition had overwhelmed Schwartz with sense of dread and revulsion. He listened queasily to the testimony of the medical expert from New York–Presbyterian Hospital as she described the location and nature of lesions on the vagina of four-year-old Violetta Pichardo. As the testimony was given, he had turned to look at his client, studying the soft eyes that flitted about the courtroom without focusing on anything or anyone in particular.

Did Valdespino's expression signify the deer caught in the headlights or the hand caught in the cookie jar? Did it really matter if the man was innocent or guilty? His goose was cooked, ticket punched, number up.

Schwartz tried to marshal his facts and listen to the testimony as he organized the final touches of his cross-examination. He could not reconcile his client's adamant denials of abusing his pre-school stepdaughter with the mounting evidence to the contrary. The best Schwartz could do was give him a show.

And so he parried with the physician over possible non-traumatic causes of the lesions that marked the face of the child's vagina clock, insinuating that the child had inflicted the marks herself by scratching due to poor hygiene. He accused this medical witness of bias, cited poor medical procedures, and created issues where none existed. When the city attorney called a Sexual Abuse Accommodation Syndrome expert (aka "validator") to the stand, Schwartz attempted to discredit him by charging the witness with practicing voodoo psychology and not following chapter and verse of Dr. Suzanne Sgroi's methodology.

Schwartz's performance failed to sway the judge, who made a finding of sex abuse against Valdespino. Impressed by the assigned counsel's posturing, the clueless client asked Schwartz to represent him at the criminal trial for the rape of Violetta. Schwartz demurred and referred the desperate man to his good friend Edgardo Ramos, counselor-at-law. At least Schwartz would get a one-third referral fee. That was why Edgardo thought Schwartz had mentioned the case.

"When I see some money, so will you, my friend," Edgardo assured Schwartz.

Finally they reached Schwartz's "Saab Story," so named for its inclination to break down. Schwartz cursed as he removed a parking ticket from the windshield. It was covered by a flyer for a psychic.

"I tell you to park in a lot, but nooo," Ramos chastised Schwartz.

Schwartz frowned at his friend. After opening the passenger-side door, he added the ticket to the collection in the glove compartment. He laughed weakly, and then "Aha, I now own a controlling interest in the Parking Violations Bureau," Schwartz declared, the volume of his voice gathering momentum.

"To the whores!" Don Edgardo shouted.

"Yep…to the whores," Schwartz muttered.

They drove through the sleepy suburbs of southern Westchester County. As Don Edgardo chatted up his cases, Schwartz tuned him out. The window of the eight ball lodged in the back of Schwartz's head conjured up his nascent separation from his wife. After twenty years, the marriage tent had folded.

Schwartz and Marjorie had waited ten years before having kids. Their marketing niche would be OPYK: Old People, Young Kids. Starting a family by any means necessary was a phenomenon among contemporaries in their late thirties to early forties. They achieved parenthood through natural means, heroic medical efforts, or Third World adoption. Surely, they believed, financial stability and emotional maturity would equal successful parenting. The toll children would take on the marriages had not been considered in the equation.

It had fallen to Schwartz to explain to Ethan that his dad was leaving.

He wondered how to tell his son that two people meet, fall in love, get married, and have kids and then devote all their energy, time, passion, money, and love to raising their kids and lose sight of why they fell in love in the first place. To wit:

they'd been consigned to society's growing scrap heap of sexless marriages and sacrificed on the altar of the Cult of the Child. All the therapists agreed, "Don't make the kids feel they're to blame," even if, by their very existence, the children shared culpability. Schwartz sugarcoated it as best as he could.

"Where I gonna live?" cried Ethan.

"Look, Eth, daddy and mommy aren't happy with each other, but I'm still happy that you're my son and that Julie's my daughter. And even though I'm not going to be sleeping here, I'll still be coming around a lot. Plus you'll stay with me sometimes."

The tears forming in the boy's eyes signaled that his approach wasn't having the desired effect, so Schwartz took the easy way out.

"And who knows? Maybe mommy and I will get back together."

"That's what I want, daddy. You 'n' mommy together. But not fightin'."

Very slowly, Schwartz had carried the boy to his bedroom, both of them sobbing softly. Schwartz lay down with him until a fitful sleep reigned for the boy.

As he approached his daughter, he realized that Majorie had already broken the news of the separation to her.

"You just don't love us anymore, daddy. We're not good enough for you. That's it, right?" Julie accused.

"Honeybun, don't say . . ."

At that point the child had begun to writhe on the floor, kicking and screaming hysterically for her mother. Schwartz joined the duet for Marjorie, who, through the bedroom door, shouted for him to,

"Get the fuck out of the house."

In the Saab, Schwartz was singing a Buddy Holly tune covered by Bobby Darin "Early In the Morning" and thinking *Yeah, they're gonna miss me. Not.*

"*Oye, chico!* Are you listening to me? I told you to turn left at that light. And *por favor,* whatever you do tonight *con estas mujeres,* promise me, promise yourself, you won't sing. Ho-kay?"

Don Edgardo's rebuke stirred him from his reverie. He had been mindlessly following his friend's directions to the town of Port Chester. The venue for the evening's festivities was located in an industrial part of town near the overpass for the New England Thruway. Port Chester itself was atypical of Westchester. Abutting the Long Island Sound and the Connecticut border, it was a hardscrabble waterfront burgh with an increasing immigrant populace.

"Look for parking. The place is on this block."

On the opposite side of the street was a small storefront with a garish red neon sign that read "El Gallo" featuring the outline of a rooster. A man and a woman stood outside the entrance, gesturing wildly with their hands and arms. The woman's red hair and full figure immediately stirred an autonomic response in Schwartz's pelvis.

Inside, the small dance floor to the right was crowded with intertwined couples moving to tropical rhythms and beats, courtesy of DJ Jef-A. Don Edgardo led Schwartz to the bar and announced himself to the grizzled barkeep.

"Don Felipe, this is my friend. I request that if he should ever return to this fine establishment that you extend to him all the courtesies you would to me."

A balding man with a medium build, wearing a guayabera shirt, Don Felipe laughed heartily, flashing a set of golden bicuspids.

"You weesh dees *por su amigo*? I throw heem out like a drunken bum and put heem in a taxi?"

"*Cono,* Don Felipe."

With that, the two men exchanged an extended hug over the bar and Don Felipe offered his hand to Schwartz.

Don Edgardo put his arms around Schwartz and whispered into his ear as he kissed him,

"I love you, you fuck. Welcome to purgatory. Whether you go to heaven or hell from here is strictly up to you. Oh my God, *mira ese chica*"—he bit his fingers for emphasis—"Uhhh . . . if she ever got her legs around your head, you would suffocate and die—alas, a happy man."

The dance floor had begun to clear, and Schwartz noticed that the women had separated from the men and went to their own section of the room. The men were short and stocky, sporting denim pants and cowboy boots. Central Americans and Mexicans, Schwartz surmised. The women were hard to place geographically. Judging by their language it was obvious they were Latina. Their skin tones ranged from Conquistador white to African black. Though they were dressed lavishly, what struck Schwartz was the uniform color of their hair: flaming red.

Don Edgardo finished his Vodka and Tonic and swiveled on his bar stool to face the emptying dance floor.

"Time to mingle."

He led Schwartz to a table where four ladies sat.

"*Buenos noches, Graciela, Alicea y Senoritas.*" Edgardo tuned in the direction of the other women and addressed them.

"*Como se llama? Yo no la conosco.*"

There was an awkward silence at first, broken by Graciela.

"Don Edgardo. Como esta? Eses chicas son mis amigas Yolanda e Isabel. Y quien es este hombre Americano?"

Schwartz felt Ramos's arm around his shoulders, pushing him slightly forward. Isabel was the woman he had spied outside the club as they drove up.

"Bonitas mujeres, permitame a presentarle a mi amigo, Don Juan."

The ladies began to laugh. Schwartz understood enough Spanish from his junior high school studies to be embarrassed. He smiled weakly, nodded in their direction, and then dug an elbow into his friend's side.

Graciela called for a waitress, who arrived looking at the two men expectantly. Schwartz chose that moment to unveil his anglicized Spanish. *"Que quieren beber?"*

The ladies were amused by the accent and gratified by the offer. The waitress turned and headed for the bar, apparently knowing their drink of choice.

Graciela gestured to an empty table nearby. "Sit down, *Americano. Y usted, Don Edgardo.*"

Graciela prolonged her words into a seductive growl. "Americano" from her lips became "Aaaaa-mer-eeee-canooooo" and "Edgardo," "Eeeed-gaaaaaaar-dooooo." Schwartz referenced Xavier Cugat's lady friend Charo as the phonetic progenitor. The two men energetically moved the table and chairs to join the ladies, Schwartz tipping over his chair in XY chromosome haste. The ladies tittered and one squealed "*Como* Cantiflas, no?"

Schwartz searched his mind for something witty to say in his limited Spanish. The ladies whispered among themselves, occasionally glancing in his direction. The waitress arrived with the drinks, including another round of Scotch and Ginger Ale for Schwartz and Edgardo's requisite Vodka and Tonic. Thirty dollars poorer, Schwartz noticed that the waitress had given each woman a poker chip.

Ante placed. The game has begun.

Schwartz turned in Isabel's direction. She was stunning—blessed with an ample bosom where his head could nestle, smooth light skin with just a hint of mocha, a bright smile of Caribbean coral that promised nothing and everything. Her clothes, an amalgam of orange, red, and yellow, wrapped her body in a tropical sunset. Her eyes were reminiscent of the Rose in Spanish Harlem song. Ben E. King's voice came to him, though he was sure Darin must have covered it.

The music switched from a slow cha-cha to an upbeat number. The ladies shouted in unison, "Baaa-chaaaaaa-taaa!"

Graciela grabbed Edgardo by the belt and, to his surprise and delight, Isabel followed suit with Schwartz.

Having attended his share of parties in the court officers' locker room,

Schwartz was familiar with Salsa/Latin disco. Those functions were wild and wooly affairs hosted in close quarters. The officers would shed their blue-and-whites for tight-fitting jeans. The uptight neophyte city agency lawyers, encouraged by the music, booze, and the occasional smuggled joint, would let their hormones flow and the good times roll. Inevitably, the mix of alcohol, ladies, and guns proved too volatile. After an officer, depressed over a job-ending positive drug screen, discharged his gun into the air, Supervising Judge Natalie Finkel banned such affairs from the courthouse.

The Salsa of Schwartz's experience was a free-stepping, quick-turning *pas de deux*. According to Don Edgardo, salsa migrated to La Gran Manzana from Cuba and Puerto Rico. It dominated the dance floors of the Palladium and the Latin Quarter in the '50s, and the Corso and the Cheetah in '60s.

"See, Salsa is a dance of freedom. But in the '80s, with the Dominicanos coming to New York, the Merengue became the rage. Merengue bore the mark of the slave ship. Conjure two partners in leg irons, attempting to dance. The feet can barely move but several inches in one step. Yet the rest of the adjoined bodies, using the hips as a fulcrum, gyrate and rock with a sexual heat that could capsize the Mayflower. *Ay dios mio!*"

The Bachata, a hybrid of Salsa and Merengue, was the latest craze. Isabel proved a competent *maestra* and Schwartz a motivated pupil. Though she was several inches shorter than he was, Isabel was as strong as she was rhythmic. She proved quite adept at nudging him in any direction the dance required.

Schwartz relished pressing his flesh against her as they danced their lateral two-step. He felt the small of her back as it descended into her full derriere. When her plump breasts grazed his chest, his groin swelled. Rocking like a walrus in heat, hips soldered into place, Schwartz initiated several semi-proficient turns. Isabel's smile gave no hint of whether she approved or was simply amused. After he sang a lyric from "Queen of the Hop," the smile was accompanied by a roll of her eyes.

Mopping the sweat from his brow, Schwartz reached for her outstretched hand and kissed it. She shook her head and laughed. Don Edgardo whispered in his ear, "Pay her five dollars, *cabron.*"

Schwartz clumsily reached into his wallet and counted out five dog-eared singles. He extended them to Isabel, who accepted them with a wink and a pinch on Schwartz's cheek.

Another round of drinks. Another set of poker chips earned. Another dance. Another five dollars paid. Edgardo raised his glass and proceeded to spill Vodka and Tonic on his chest and lap.

"Wha a night, hey com...pa...dray? To the Society of Kindred Spirits. Whores. I . . . love . . . them."

Edgardo's words seemed garbled and his eyes glazed, or perhaps Schwartz's ears were numbed by the blaring music and his own eyes glazed by the Scotch. Either or both. When Edgardo's head rested against the bar counter and he started to snore, Felipe reached for the wall phone and dialed.

"No *precupe*. We get Señor Ramos home. Enjoy."

Schwartz sat at the bar with his friend until the cabdriver walked in and announced Don Edgardo's name. Together they carried the big man to the cab. The driver said he knew where Don Edgardo lived and would see to it that he got home safely. Schwartz slipped an extra two dollars into the man's hand. He walked to the cab's rear door and opened it. Don Edgardo was slumped over on the seat. Schwartz leaned in, lifted his friend's head, and kissed him on both cheeks.

"I love you, you fuck."

Schwartz closed the door and hit the trunk with his hand, signaling for the driver to leave. He looked up at the clear November sky and breathed in the chilly Westchester air. Orion stood poised with his bow, his sword at his side. The red and white lights of a jet crossed the sky—Orion's arrow. Schwartz closed his eyes and listened. A truck zoomed by on the studded Thruway above. The vibration from the tire treads hummed and coursed through him. Rejuvenated, he re-entered the bar.

Schwartz was in a bed, recoiling in his sleep from the image of the vagina clock. He heard its ticktock and a child crying. He bolted upright, barely able to open his eyes. His tongue was welded to the roof of his mouth with a salty paste. Through narrow slits of his eyelids, he made out a form in the bed. He reached for the top of the pink comforter, pulled it back, and revealed an impressive tangled mane of red. Flashes of the previous night and early morning projected off a mirror ball against the walls of his mind.

Isabel. Dancing. Tumbling into bed. Furtive sexing.

Oddly, he still heard the child's cry.

Schwartz stumbled through the darkened apartment cluttered with clothes, shoes, boxes, and bags. Finally he located the bathroom, which was awash in pink. Pink towels. Pink polka-dot shower curtain. Pink toilet paper. Pink soap.

Pink pussy.

Chuckling at his joke, Schwartz lifted the pink window curtain to reveal the pinkish slivers of dawn slipping through the trees and over the tops of the two-story houses. Isabel lived in a basement apartment with an excellent eye-level view of the driveway. Parked in the driveway was a pink and white van with the New York vanity plates "LUV VAN."

Schwartz felt pinked-out.

Isabel had explained that Graciela and she were co-captains of the crew of dancers that worked El Gallo and similar clubs in Upper Manhattan, the Bronx, and Southern Westchester on other nights. The establishment paid the ladies for every drink a man bought them; the poker chips served as chits. The men tipped them for their dancing. In turn, the women paid their crew leaders a percentage of their take and a pro rata share of the transportation costs. Sex with the customers was neither a no-no nor a yes-yes. If it happened, it was a private matter for the lady involved. Payment could come in the form of cash, drugs, car, apartment, or marriage proposal.

What would Isabel's price be?

After the tipping fiasco, she seemed genuinely interested in him, asking personal questions and meeting his gaze with an inviting smile. Intelligence and charm were evident in her halting English and flowing Spanish. Her beauty was comparable to the scantily clad models in the beer posters taped to the windows of bodegas near the courthouse.

Whatever the price, could he afford the bill?

In the dead of night, at her invitation, he had followed the Luv Van through the Bronx and Washington Heights as it returned tired dancers to their homes. Hours later, the ladies would rise for their day jobs as hairdressers, supermarket clerks, receptionists, and factory workers. Some would have children to wake for school and *mangú y huevos* breakfasts to prepare.

Again, the child's cry crept into Schwartz's consciousness. After wrapping a pink towel around his midsection, he ambled toward what he hoped was the kitchen in search of a drink to unhinge his tongue from the roof of his mouth. He felt for the refrigerator in the dark. He found the handle and pulled. The bright appliance light beamed like a supernova. Shielding his eyes, Schwartz rummaged around the sparsely stocked shelves and located a can of guava juice. He shook it, peeled back the aluminum foil tab, and began to drink. As he tilted his head back, he registered a small figure in the corner of the room. He threw open the door of the fridge, and the light illuminated a young child facing the corner of kitchen, crying.

As Schwartz approached the child and knelt down, he felt something hard pressing into his knees. The overhead kitchen light came on suddenly and revealed the back of a girl about five years of age wearing panties and t-shirt, facing the corners of the Formica laden room. She was kneeling on grains of rice.

The child had several red lines across her thighs and back. Schwartz turned to see Isabel advancing toward the child. She lifted the girl by her ear and pushed her into a room, slamming the door shut, Isabel turned to face Schwartz, who was sitting cross-legged on the floor, his back against a cabinet.

"She a bad girl. She no *escuhce*, no lissen. *Yo dice a ella* wha to do. She no do."

Schwartz rose to his feet with appreciable effort. He walked past Isabel silently, deflecting her glare. As he dressed, he debated whether to leave money on the dresser. He lifted the last bills—a twenty and three singles—from his wallet and used an eyeliner pencil to scribble a note on the back of his business card to buy something for the little girl.

As he left, he said, "*Escucheme*. You can't be that way with a child. Nothing good will come of it."

Isabel crumpled into a chair and started to mumble to herself. Schwartz bent down, kissed the top of her head, and headed for the door. The child's escalating cry filled his ears. Once outside, he squeezed past the Luv Van and started cranking up the Saab Story. Finally, on the third try, the engine caught. The vehicle putt-putted down the street as Schwartz dodged potholes with the verve of a skier traversing moguls. He made a left on Soundview Avenue and pointed the car toward Bronx Family Court.

DECEMBER 4: THE KING OF DOMESTIC TRAGEDY

AS ASSIGNED COUNSEL IN FAMILY COURT, SCHWARTZ WAS AN independent contractor earning what every other assigned counsel earned in 2000: $40 an hour for in-court time, $25 an hour for out-of-court time. As independent contractors, 18-Bs, so named because Article 18-B of the New York State County Law created their existence, were not eligible for the usual perks of civil service—healthcare, sick time, paid vacation, pension, tenure, etc. Regardless of how many years of service, whether a case was won, lost or tied, the fee structure remained the same.

One might ask given the lack of financial incentive if Schwartz cared if he successfully represented an indigent litigant. But he did, or at least he had. The accumulation of money had never been important to Schwartz. He was a red diaper baby, lullabied with the folk music of Woody Guthrie, the Weavers, Earl Robinson and Pete Seeger. A favorite Old Left mantra of his mother's, "from each according to his abilities, to each according to his needs," had resonated in Schwartz and informed his career choice.

More affluent members of the legal community regarded 18-Bs as bottom-feeders. The king of the Bronx Bar, Maury Feldman, would openly ridicule Schwartz for his efforts on behalf of "your loser clients." Schwartz would feel a slow burn as Maury rattled off his latest successes on behalf of the borough's Mafioso/Latino Kings drug lords while quaffing cocktails at the Bronx Bar Association's annual soiree. However, when the money ran out and the clients were drained of their resources by *ad infinitem* adjournments at $650 per appearance caused by incomplete court-ordered investigations, pending drug test results, the litigant's child care emergencies, rescheduled mental health studies, supervised visitation logistics, judge's conferences, witness unavailability, attorney's medical emergencies, missing subpoenaed records, court personnel funerals, court scheduling errors, and on and on and on, the Maury Feldmans of the pond that was the Bronx Bar, cut their broke clients loose. Then it was the lowly 18-B that had to step into the morass and try to salvage their appointed client's position and vindicate their rights.

Schwartz rationalized that he was serving the Proletariat his mother so treasured. He would commiserate with his colleagues, frustrated over their relative low status on the legal food chain, that if he had ten dollars in his pocket and his bills paid, he was a happy guy.

"Well, I've got the ten dollars," was Schwartz' self-deprecating tagline.

But sometimes he didn't. The press of raising a family forced Schwartz to cut corners. He drove used cars, purchased suits in thrift shops, took the toll-free bridges if en route, co-opted the court clerk's copy machine, and brown bagged it for lunch. Schwartz exulted in the guilty pleasure of finding a discarded *New York Times*, rationalizing that he saved a tree or two, as well as a dollar or two. What office? Schwartz carried his office in ever-present weather-beaten leather shoulder bag and the date book secured in his suit breast pocket. His support staff consisted of his answering machine and the word-processing program on the home computer he'd previously shared with his wife and children.

Occasionally, a private matter would bring in some spare ducats. Schwartz would furtively pocket the $150 in cash tendered by a father seeking visitation with his offspring. Or he would cover a case for a private attorney seeking an adjournment of a matter scheduled for trial. He would appear on the day of trial like a canary in the mine, absorb the verbal blast from the frustrated judge, secure the adjournment, and submit his bill. This meant a food buy with the extras that his kids loved from Fairways supermarket or a movie and dinner out for the family. Still, it rankled Schwartz to hear fellow panel members like Burton Mitzner openly brag that their efforts on behalf of private clients far exceeded those exerted on behalf of assigned clients. Mitzner would tell Schwartz, just assigned as law guardian to the subject child on a custody matter, that Schwartz should be favorably disposed to Mitzner's client simply because Mitzner was privately retained.

Mitzner was a charter member of the assigned counsel clique and harbored aspirations beyond the panel (i.e., a judgeship). Mitzner was also a fixture on the oversight committee of the NYC Assigned Counsel Panel that presumed to pass judgment on wayward 18-Bs. So Schwartz held his tongue in the face of Mitzner's obnoxiousness.

The clique routinely trashed their poor clients as they sat around the crammed 18-B room, tackling the *New York Times* Crossword Puzzle and waiting for their cases to be called.

"Can you believe how she smelled? And she wants her kids returned."

"Client wants custody of his kids but actually asked me for car fare to court."

"The guy's incarcerated for five years on the Canadian border and he wants visitation with his five-year-old. It's a sixteen-hour round trip. But he's demanding a hearing."

"They beat the kids. They hate the caseworkers. They told the judge to 'fuck off'. Then they call my office every day, 'When are we getting our babies back?' I'm getting relieved from this case."

"I can't wait around all day. I've got a real estate closing at 2:30. I'm leaving available dates with the clerk."

Lately Schwartz spent as little time as possible in the clique's eight-by-ten-foot barely furnished, over-lit lair that smelled of somebody's microwaved fish sandwich.

The vast majority of the attorneys on the Panel were competent and dedicated to their clients' causes. But at the end of the workday, they went home to their children and partners. Their clients, more often than not, did not. Ten years of greasing the skids for the system was further leading Schwartz to the conclusion, which members of the clique had already reached, that his only loyalty was to the voucher submitted to panel administrators at the end of the case. Since the remand of Leesah Kinard's infant, his internal debate had intensified as he struggled daily to find the answer to his question: *Am I a cog in the system's wheel or a brickbat jammed into its gear shaft?*

But in those moments when he contemplated leaving this bottom-feeder law practice, what came to mind was the old joke about the porter in the circus whose job it was to follow the parade of elephants and sweep up the dung. When the porter complained about his lot in life, he was asked why he didn't quit. Indignant he answered, "What and give up show business?"

Schwartz exited the elevator of BxFC on the seventh floor. The case of Jesse Thomas was first up on his calendar. Thomas, seeking visitation with his six year-old daughter, was a tall, strapping black man with a soft voice and demeanor to match. He worked as a computer technician for a local utility. While at Bronx Community College, he had met and eventually married a nice Jewish *goil* from Riverdale, Allison Refkowitz. According to the client, both parties' families never warmed to the union. Schwartz could picture it:

Guess who's coming to Seder.

"Well, I'm glad you asked, Abba, because . . ."

One child, Tabitha, was born of the marriage. After a couple of less than blissful years, the couple began to uncouple. The mother/wife, according to Thomas, began to dabble with cocaine. In addition, he suspected that she was unfaithful to him. The inevitable split ensued, and the mother severely restricted his access to Tabitha. He filed a petition for visitation in BxFC. The mother's response was to cross petition for an order of protection and sole custody.

Hustling to the part for the Thomas case, Schwartz avoided the crowded waiting areas by cutting down secured hallways. He was careful to watch for Captain Dolan, commander of the court officers, who forbade attorneys from taking such liberties. When he pushed open the rear door to the courtroom, the bridge officer gave him a nod. Benny Weinstein sat in the respondent's counsel chair, hunched over an open file of papers. Assistant District Attorney Roger Edens sat in the presentment agency's chair, similarly engaged.

Since the judge was not yet on the bench, Schwartz approached the bridge officer to check in. Schwartz cocked his head toward the litigants' table. "Tom, is this a hearing?"

"Sodomy case with a ten year-old complainant. Could be all morning."

Schwartz walked over to Weinstein. Benny's amiable elderly visage masked a wicked sense of humor. His finest hour was his assignment to a Korean man, Won Sicju, accused of sexually abusing a stepdaughter. Never one to lay off a fat pitch down the middle of the plate, Benny pronounced "Won Sicju" as "one sick Jew" at each and every appearance on the respondent's behalf.

Weinstein was adding up his hours on the voucher, anticipating payment at the end of the case. Schwartz walked behind the aging barrister and gave him a gentle slap on the back.

"Way to review that <u>Rosario</u> material just before trial, Benny."

"Huh? What? Oh. Schwartz. Ach! This piece of schmutz is going down. He *shtupped* some boy at the Y. That kid's a good witness. Very sympathetic."

Edens looked up. "Schwartz, we have Ramirez on tomorrow. I've got the eyewitness coming in. It's a 9:30 call."

Edens was a recent law school graduate and the third ADA to have been assigned to "Kiddie Court" this year. Charged with prosecuting the more serious "A" and "B" felonies (e.g., murder, rape, kidnapping), the DA's juvenile delinquency bureau consisted of one or two ADA's. It was usually a greenhorn like Edens who was anxious to terminate the assignment as quickly as possible in order to move up the pecking order of bureaus, or a grey-beard burnout approaching retirement. Hence, the door to the DA's JD Bureau proved to be of the revolving variety.

"Don't bug me about tomorrow. I'm trying to get through today!" Schwartz said.

Clipboard in hand, the court officer approached Schwartz. "Judge wants to talk to you in the back."

Judge Miriam Velez was sitting at her desk, leaning back in her chair, twirling her stiff auburn hair with two fingers as she read the *New York Law Journal*. Velez, the mother of six, had climbed off the welfare rolls to attend college and then law school. Having served as an 18-B for years, she had been recently appointed to the family court. She was the first female jurist from her country of ancestry, the Dominican Republic. Spread in front of her was standard family court fare: bagels, cream cheese, and donuts.

Seeing Schwartz enter, Judge Velez beckoned for him to sit and partake. Schwartz initially declined. He sensed something was amiss, but his misgivings were overruled by the gurgle in his stomach. Schwartz reached for a bagel from the paper plate on the judge's table. She rose and closed the door behind her. The judge picked up a file, skimmed it, and then asked, "Schwartz . . . you're on the Thomas matter, right?"

"Judge, are you sure we should be talking? I mean, this is *ex parte*. Shouldn't the other counsel be here?"

"Schwartz, don't be an alarmist. I am not going to discuss the merits. But we have ourselves a situation."

God, I hate that word.

In that zen moment before something truly outrageous was revealed, it's as if the moment could be frozen in time and made available on a VHS tape. Preserved, it could be rewound for "where were you when (fill in the blank) happened" purposes, since, after the revelation, the earth under one's feet shifted and life was suddenly more complicated.

"The court clerk just received a call from the 49th Precinct Detective Squad. It's reported that the mother, Allison, was found murdered earlier this morning—her throat slashed. The detectives have reason to believe that the culprit is the father, Mr. Thomas. They are coming here to arrest him. We're going to call the case in and he's going to be taken into custody. Any questions?"

Schwartz sat down. He stopped chewing the wad of bagel in his mouth and spit it into a napkin. He coughed as he blurted,

"How do they know he killed her?"

"Apparently, the little girl said, 'Daddy did it.' I want you to stay in the courtroom and I'm ordering you not to tip him off. I just wanted you to have a heads up."

"Miriam, you've put me in a tough spot here. How can I not consult with my client about this?"

"Because I'm ordering you not to! And don't think that because we were colleagues that I won't cite you for contempt."

Dismissed from the judge's chambers, Schwartz found a seat in the back of the courtroom and wrestled with the impulse to consult with his client. He rose and headed for the exit. At that moment, the bridge officer told Weinstein and Edens to clear the table because a different matter was going to be called. Weinstein protested that he had matters in other parts. With a wave of his arm the officer dispatched Weinstein and bellowed, "Parties in Matter of Thomas v. Refkowitz. Counsels take the table."

As Thomas entered, he was asking the court officer about Schwartz's whereabouts. He brightened when he saw Schwartz standing at the table.

"Schwartz, where you been? I needed to talk to you before the case is called. Why is it being called without Allie? She's not here yet."

Before Schwartz could answer, the bridge officer admonished the litigant to be silent. Schwartz stuttered as he noted his appearance. Thomas stated his name and relationship to the child and swore to tell the truth. Judge Velez gave a little nod and a court officer opened the side door. Two of New York's Finest homicide detectives walked in, each dressed smartly in homicide detective style: sport jacket, colored shirt, tie, slacks, and shiny black footwear.

As they approached Thomas, he jumped up. "What the . . . ?"

One of the detectives produced a set of handcuffs and reached for the man's wrists. Rhetorically he asked, "Jesse Thomas?"

"Yeah! What's this about? I took care of that warrant from the Nassau County."

Thomas struggled against the cold snap of the metal against his skin.

"Judge, may I speak to Mr. Thomas in the holding pen?" Schwartz asked.

"He's now in police custody. Officers?"

One of the sport jacket–and–slacks duo nodded his mousse-laden head.

Schwartz and the wild-eyed handcuffed Thomas were led to the pen. The door slammed and locked behind them.

"Schwartz, what's going on? Did they tell you about this?"

"Jesse . . . Allison was found dead this morning. Her throat was slashed."

Thomas began to cough and stammer, incapable of intelligible sound.

"She was found in her apartment."

The big man spun in a circle emitting a low whine. Finally he came to a halt.

"This is crazy. This is crazy. She's been hanging out with those scumbag druggies, man!" He started to sob and wheeze. "Oh man. Oh man. Allieeee!"

Schwartz did all he could to stem the flow of tears and mucous with lint-laden tissues from his pocket.

"And they think I did it. Oh my Gawd!" He stopped and gathered his breath. "And Tabitha? Where's Tabby?"

"I'm not sure," Schwartz whispered. He took a deep breath and continued, "But I think she witnessed it. She told them, 'Daddy did it.'"

"'Daddy'? 'Daddy'?"

Raising his voice, the big man stood and began to pace the confines of the small holding pen.

"Allie's had this creep coming around for months now, telling Tabby to call him 'Daddy.' Last time I even saw Tabby—what, three months ago?—she was calling that dude 'Daddy.' Schwartz, you gotta find out where she is!"

Schwartz, intimidated in such close quarters, tried to pacify the accused murderer while planning his own exit strategy.

"All right, all right. I'll make some calls. Meanwhile, don't say anything to these detectives until you've spoken to a criminal attorney and discussed your story."

"Man, there is no story. Only the truth. I didn't do it!"

"Fine. Bad choice of words. But good advice. Discuss the case with your attorney before making any statements. Don't be like the fish mounted on the wall plaque. Keep your mouth shut."

Schwartz spent the better part of that afternoon on the phone, trying to track down Tabitha Thomas's whereabouts. From police custody she had been transported to ACS Children's Center in Manhattan, and from there to a foster home while clearances were completed on her maternal grandmother. There was no way to get word to the father. He was being shuffled from the police precinct to Central Booking and ultimately to Rikers Island.

Exiting the courthouse, Schwartz headed to his parked Saab. In his car he organized the next day's case files that were stashed in a cardboard box under the hatchback. At an ubiquitous Chinese take-out joint that dots most urban neighborhoods, he scarfed down a meal of wonton soup and egg roll and washed it down with a cup of tap water begrudgingly served up by the counterman.

Finally, he lumbered into Cliff Johnson's apartment for some shut-eye on a foldout couch where he would count his blessings. He reflected on Thomas's plight and released a low whistle. That case had shaken him out his "woe is me" mood. He softly sang "The Good Life" as a lullaby to himself.

When he reached the end, he couldn't resist going for the crescendo.

"…Gooood-byyeee!"

His effort was met with a pillow landing on his face and a fervent, "Shut the fuck up!" from Cliff as the bedroom door slammed shut.

DECEMBER 5: SIGNIFICANT OTHERS

"DADDY, HOW COME YOU NO COME TO SEE US SO MUCH?"

Schwartz stared at his over-fried, tasteless hash brown patty. Ethan's question was one of many he felt ill prepared to answer. Julie, however, didn't miss a beat.

"Mommy says it's 'cause he's spending time with all his new girlfriends."

The brightly lit orangey-yellow very public dining room was the less-than-ideal venue for a family truth session over breakfast. Such is the lot of the alternate-weekend-and-midweek-meal dad. Schwartz believed that to be a father, in the best sense of the word, he had to be there physically, emotionally, and financially for his children. With all due deference to Meatloaf, two out of three of those factors didn't cut it. He preached this to his father clients as they bitched and moaned about the state of their patrimony. Now he found himself severely challenged on all three fronts.

"Look, mom is angry that we're no longer together. She says these things because she's hurt. She's mad at me. Like how you two sometimes say things to each other when you're fighting, like, 'I'm gonna kill you, Ethan.' I mean, are you really going to kill him? No. You're just really, really mad and you want him to know it. Your mom and I have to go through this angry thing. It's just the way it is. I believe we're going to come out the other side of this and be friends again. Because that's what you two need—both mom and me in your corner. What's best for you two is most important."

Ethan wasn't buying it.

"We want you home, daddy. That's best."

Small wonder I find these visits so tough. Switch gears.

"How's your soccer team doing, Jules?"

"We've got a game this Saturday against the division leaders. Dad, you have no idea. They'll kick you while you're on the ground. You should hear mom scream her head off at the refs. Those girls are such bitches."

"Hey, watch the *B* word. What time does it start?"

Julie shrugged her shoulders at the rebuke. Suddenly her eyes widened. "Oh my God. We have to be at the gym at nine and it takes an hour to get there. And the night before, we have Lauryn Simonetti's sleepover. Dad, can you drive us to the match?"

Spending an hour in a minivan full of cranky, overtired, sugar-saturated lasses on the cusp of puberty seemed an appropriate penance for his sins.

"I'll be there Saturday morning to pick you up. Eth, what do you say help me handle these womenfolk? I could use another man to ride shotgun with me."

Ethan was silent. He nodded slightly.

"It's a deal, then. Meanwhile, Daddy has to get you guys to school and his own self to work."

The mind-body connection 'tis a mystery.

With his files spread on the floor of the bathroom stall, Schwartz pondered his ability to prepare for a fact-finding hearing.

Is there a neuro-portal from the bowel to the brain?

The facts and issues in the case captioned as Matter of Ronaldo Ramirez, a Person Alleged to be a Juvenile Delinquent, were now in sharp focus. Fifteen-year-old Ramirez stood accused of firing a gun at a car driven by Floyd Green. Of course, Ramirez denied it. What was not in dispute was that Floyd Green exited his vehicle and fired his gun down the block at Ramirez. One bullet found its target, hitting the flank of the youngster's midsection. Floyd, being an adult, now awaited trial at Rikers for weapons possession. Somehow he had managed to convince the Bronx DA's office that his account of self-defense had merit. Two detectives from the homicide squad greeted young Ronaldo as he came out of surgery at Bronx-Lebanon Hospital and placed him under arrest.

As the toilet flushed, Schwartz put the final touches on his cross-examination. The case would be called in ten minutes, and the eyewitness to the alleged attempted murder was Shalima Harden, Floyd's girlfriend and Baby Momma to his infant son. Schwartz gathered up the documents and stood. The ballistic field report map fell out of the sheaf of papers, landing face up. Getting an overhead perspective, he noticed something telling about the location of bullet fragments retrieved by the ballistic detectives.

When Schwartz entered Part II, he saw that the table in front of Hon. William B. Williams was stacked with folders of uncalled cases. The seats ringing the back wall were filled to capacity with attorneys waiting for their cases to be called.

Little airtime today. Case'll get fifteen minutes of fame, and then we ah outta heah.

Judge Williams was a white-haired, red-skinned progeny of a Tammany Hall, connected Lil' Ol', New York Irish family. Perceiving a decline in morality and values, the judge routinely castigated youngsters for their failings in behavior, schoolwork, and courtroom demeanor. Woe to the juvenile delinquency respondent who violated the terms of probation by missing a curfew or a day at school. Ronaldo Ramirez had nailed that profile.

"Remand, secure. CJJ!" the judge had thundered when Ronaldo first appeared for arraignment before him.

Schwartz protested that if Ramirez were remanded to lockup, he would not receive the Lithane, Depakote, and Risperdal prescribed by his treating psychiatrist for bipolar affective mood disorder and ADHD. That protest fell on Judge Williams' indifferent ears.

"CJJ knows what it's doing. I'll mark on his papers that he's to be seen by a psychiatrist and evaluated."

With that, the young respondent had been escorted out and taken to the Spofford Avenue Detention Center as a guest of the New York City Commissioner of Juvenile Justice until the next court date.

A week went by. According to the desperate messages Ronaldo's father left on Schwartz's answering machine, no psychiatric assessment had been conducted at Spofford. The father had taken Ronaldo's medication to the facility, but the infirmary refused to dispense it *sans* the assessment. The father related that Ronaldo was acting out after having been tested by the other residents. Schwartz left messages for the counselors' office at Spofford, but they went unreturned.

Schwartz resolved to pay a visit, ostensibly as preparation for the trial. His arrival at Spofford, a prison with all the accouterments (high fences, barbed wire, etc.) caused a stir. Counsel visits at Spofford were a rarity. Virtually all attorneys met with their clients in the holding pen behind the courtroom or the central juvenile detention lockup on the seventh floor on the day of their court proceeding. Spofford didn't even have an allotted room for counsel visits. Schwartz was directed to an empty dining room for his meeting with Ramirez. The privacy would prove fortuitous.

Ramirez was handcuffed when he was brought in. After removing the cuffs, the escort left. The youth was slight of build, his hair alternatively long and shaven in the fashion of the day. Ramirez had lost some of his street swagger over the past week. Between cracked lips, Ramirez mumbled a weak, "What's up?"

Schwartz rose, glanced at the door window, and extended his hand. His client failed to reciprocate.

"Ronaldo, I think it's very important for you to shake my hand when I offer it to you."

Schwartz's hand hung in midair. He looked at the door again.

"Yo. Get me outta this junior Rock and I'll shake all the goddamn hands you want."

Schwartz's hand never wavered. Calmly, in an even tone, he said, "Once again, I insist. It is verrrry important for you to shake my hand."

Cursing under his breath, the teen reached for Schwartz's hand. His sullen expression changed as he realized that the lawyer had placed two capsules and a tablet in his palm. Schwartz reached into his bag, pulled out a bottle of water, and placed it on the table. "Thirsty?"

Shalima Harden had been sworn in and began weaving her tale under the monotonous prodding of ADA Roger Edens.

"Now, Miss Harden, what, if anything, did you hear at the time and place of the occurrence on November 27, 2000, at approximately 2:25 in the afternoon?"

"Yeah, I heard the shots from behind the car. An' I seed him inna side-view mirror, Ronnie with the gun. An' I heard a couple more shots. So I duck down and covered my baby."

"At what street intersection was this?"

Schwartz raised his head.

"Objection. Assumes facts not in evidence. There's been no testimony that this occurred at any intersection."

Judge Williams winced.

"Counsel, when you make an objection in my courtroom, stand up. Sustained. All right let's get to it. Were you at the corner of East 174th Street and Hoe Avenue when the bullets were fired?"

Schwartz leapt to his feet. "Your Honor, I object to this court leading the witness through her testimony."

Williams's face radiated with displeasure. "Mr. Schwartz, I don't need a lecture from you as to the niceties of a bench trial. I am the trier of fact, and if I want to know something, I will ask it. Understood? Now, was this car at the intersection of East 174th Street and Hoe Avenue at the time the shots were fired?"

Schwartz's teeth clamped shut to block an involuntary blast of air that, had it escaped his lips in the form of words, would have ignited the judge's volcano. Down he sat.

"Yeah. We wuz just about to make the left onto Hoe."

Edens resumed his singsong probing.

"How far away would you say he was from the car?"

"I don't know in feet."

"Well, can you point to an object in this room that is about the same distance from where you're seated?"

The witness hesitated and looked up at Judge Williams. "Well, if I'm the car, Ronnie was about where the judge is."

Judge Williams weighed in with, "A distance of about five feet, Counsel?"

Schwartz stood.

"Judge, if I'm the attorney, before I stipulate, I ask what part of the car is my mother, the car? The front, middle, or rear?"

"This is not *The Gong Show*. This is not *Saturday Night Live*. This is a courtroom, Mr. Schwartz. FIVE FEET IS THE DISTANCE! SIT DOWN, MR. SCHWARTZ!"

Judge Williams had little patience for grandstanding by attorneys. He had worked his way up through his local Democratic club, doing *pro bono* election cases for the Bronx machine, challenging the credentials of black and Puerto Rican would-be voters dragged in by reform clubs to the primary polls. Confrontation with a caustic edge was his lance as he jousted with the reform club lawyers asserting their client's right to vote.

Never one to suffer fools gladly, he caught the notice of the bosses and was rewarded with a clerkship for a state supreme court judge. After several years of turning the screws on attorneys and their litigants, pushing them to settle cases before they reached his judge's courtroom, he was given the nod. Instead of the civil court judgeship he was pining for when his name was submitted to the Mayor's Advisory Committee on the Judiciary, family court is where he landed. At BxFC he was confronted on a daily basis with the trials and tribulations of the spawn of the third world.

Edens returned to his direct questioning. "Had you seen Ronnie earlier that day?"

"Yeah. Floyd had rolled up on the block in his car. I was talkin' with Ronnie on the stoop in front of my building. You see, Floyd, a cupala weeks earlier, had sold Ronnie four rims for Ronnie's car for $300."

"Wait a minute, are you saying that Ronnie owned a car?"

"Objection. Basis of knowledge."

Schwartz sucked on his teeth and his tongue adhered to his palate.

"Overruled. You may answer."

"Yeah, well, I dunno if he owned it, but he always be drivin' it. Anyway, Ronnie only paid Floyd half the money. So Floyd saw Ronnie that day and axed him for the rest. Ronnie say he ain't gonna pay. The rims didn't fit his car and he wanted his money back."

"What happened then?"

"Nutin'. Ronnie walked away somewhere. Floyd was washing his car on the street. Then Ronnie came by, walking around the car talkin' shit . . .uh, excuse me, Yo' Honor."

"Young lady, just answer the question. What did he say?"

"OK, Judge. 'Niggers is pussy, niggers is pussy.' Floyd began to walk toward—"

"Objection, Your Honor. The last part is beyond the scope of the question, which was, 'What did Ronnie say?' not, 'What did Floyd do?'"

"Sustained. What did Floyd do?"

Resigned to the fate that his objections would only result in the judge curing the defect, Schwartz sullenly sat back in his chair.

"Well, he started to walk toward Ronnie. But I got in between because Ronnie's father and uncles are always on the street because they be, you know, selling drugs."

"Objection!"

"Yes, that last reference will be stricken."

And I'm sure it will be ignored.

"What happened then?"

"Floyd's like, 'We outta heah!' I got in the car with the baby in my lap and we drove off. We go up 174th Street, to the corner of Hoe, and alla sudden I hear *pow-pow-pow-pow* from behind me. Floyd stepped outta the car, an' he shoutin' and cursin'. Floyd saw Ronnie running down the street with a jammie in his hand."

"What's a jammie?"

"A gun, yo."

"Objection as to what Floyd saw."

"Sustained. Tell us what you saw."

"The same thing, Judge. Ronnie was right behind the car with the jammie, firing away. Floyd took out his jammie and started firing back. Then he jumped back in the car and gunned the gas, and we got the hell outta there. I was coverin' up my baby."

"How many times did Floyd fire?"

"Once, maybe twice."

"No further questions."

Judge Williams rose from his chair, walked behind it, and pushed back the shock of white hair from his head, reinforcing the 1940s-style part down the middle. He stretched with both hands pushing on his hips and pushed his pelvis forward to relieve his back, which had been ailing him since Ancient Order of Hibernians annual golf outing.

"Mr. Schwartz," he grumbled, "any questions for the witness?"

"A few."

Schwartz gathered up his mash-up of a file and stepped purposefully toward the podium.

"Can I hold you to that?" the judge chortled.

Schwartz stopped his forward momentum ever so slightly and then resumed his stride.

"Uh, Ms. Harden, you testified that Ronnie came up to the car you were in with Mr. Green and your baby, right? You called it a 'jammie,' right?"

"Uh-huh."

"For the reporter, you have to answer yes or no."

"Yeah."

"Why do you call it a jammie?"

"I don't know."

"Is it because people who want to shoot people at close range jam it in their faces?"

"Objection. The witness said she doesn't know, and counsel is testifying," clamored Edens.

"Sustained. Next question."

Schwartz was about to take a risk and break a rule of cross-examination: If something helped you on direct, don't look to confirm it on cross.

"And you heard a *pow-pow-pow-pow*, right?"

"That's right."

Whew.

"So would it be fair to say you heard four shots fired?"

I'm pushing my luck, but I want the point nailed.

"Well, yeah."

"Could it have been more like five, six, or more shots?"

Going for bonus points.

"Yeah, it could have been more."

Ka-ching.

"And you said that Ronnie was standing right behind the car, firing at it, right?"

"That's right."

"How many feet would you say he was behind the car?"

"Like I said before, I'm not good with feet. I can't say."

"OK. I am going to walk toward you. I want you to stop me when I'm as far from the car as Ronnie was when he opened fire."

Schwartz slowly took steps toward the witness stand.

"Stop," Shalima said.

Schwartz looked down and counted the tiles from where he was standing to the witness stand.

"Your Honor, I count three tiles. As the court is well aware, these tiles are one-foot squared. Therefore, I would ask the people to stipulate that the distance between Ms. Harden and me is three feet, not five feet as previously testified."

Edens looked at the floor and counted the squares. With a shrug he replied, "So stipulated."

"Ms. Harden, now, you are aware that Floyd Green, the man you love and the father of your young child, is under indictment in Bronx Supreme Court for the shooting of Ronnie Ramirez, yes?"

"Yeah, I know that."

"And you don't want him to go to jail, do you?"

"Not for something he didn't do. He fired at Ronnie in self-defense."

"No further questions."

Schwartz resumed his seat at the counsel's table. Ronnie was slowly turning his head from side to side. His lips were cracked and his skin pale.

Judge Williams glanced at the pile of folders in front of his bench. "This matter will have to be continued."

Ronnie groaned and muttered a curse. Mr. Ramirez shifted in his seat behind Ronnie and poked Schwartz on the back. Schwartz stood and said, "Your Honor, I'm asking that you parole my client. Despite the court's order, he has still not been psychiatrically evaluated at Spofford; therefore, he has not been receiving his medication. He is at risk of harm as a result of this court's remand order. If the problem is school attendance, I ask that this court parole him to the alternatives to detention program."

"I'm denying your parole application. I happen to know, from a matter called earlier in the calendar, that the probation department's ATD school is full and there is a long waiting list. If CJJ won't follow my order regarding the evaluation, as a lawyer, you know you have recourse. Bring a contempt motion against the Commissioner. Is the fourteenth at 9:30 a.m. good for continued hearing?"

Schwartz hurriedly checked his datebook.

"Of what?" Edens piped up.

"December, counsel. This is a continued hearing on a remand. Did you think I was adjourning to January?"

The date looked relatively open for Schwartz.

"No good," the ADA called. "I got a three in-concert robbery with a time certain."

The judge harrumphed. "What about the morning of the nineteenth?"

Every case, whether a hearing or conference, ended with the ritual call-and-shout of the court and between two and six attorneys attempting to find a mutually available date and time slot. Schwartz referred to this exercise as "Calendar Bingo."

All the while aggrieved parties sat stoically, sucking on their teeth, barely masking their anger over yet another adjournment. An adjournment meant another day missed from work, school, or watching television soap operas; another morning in that dreaded line outside the building; another four to six hours sitting on hard wooden benches, waiting for fifteen minutes of judicial fame; another slice of their lives with their children placed in foster care or remanded to a juvenile lockup; another month and a half of fathers on order of protection cases excluded from their homes, or mothers struggling to survive financially as their baby fathers skip out on their support obligation. The glacier like pace of litigation was evidenced by the black line that hovered over the benches perched against the walls. It was grease from litigants' heads as they sought respite with their heads leaning against the walls. The process was the punishment and slow justice was the cruel and unusual sentence.

Edens glanced up from his date book.

"Can't do the nineteenth. I've got a long-standing doctor's appointment."

The judge sighed. "The fifteenth?"

Schwartz's entry for the fifteenth read, "Lincoln—part V, Mendoza—part IX, Cummings—part XI, Krystowicz—HE2."

"Judge, I've got a continued abuse trial in part 5 and a family offense case marked final against me in part 9, a 'willfulness hearing' with a hearing examiner, and some other matters. Can we have another date?"

"Mr. Schwartz, your client is in remand. I'm trying to give you an early date to accommodate him. We're going to be backed up into the Christmas vacation period. This part will be closed for two weeks."

"Judge, you're giving me an early date to meet the requirements of the Family Court Act. You gave deference to the scheduling concerns of my adversary, and I—"

"December 15 at 9:30 a.m., Mr. Schwartz!"

B-I-N-G-O!

The bridge court officer knew a cue when he heard one. "Parties excused. Sir, step out of the courtroom and take your adjourn slip."

Schwartz turned to see Ramirez being cuffed while trying to kiss his father. In the lockup behind the court, Schwartz placed his hands on the shoulders of the despondent respondent. Ramirez leaned his head against the wall as he sobbed softly.

"Ronnie, we're making real progress here. As a young man, you need to gather up whatever strength you have and apply it here. I'm not talking street toughness. I mean whatever it is that makes you, You. Say to yourself, 'I can do this.' You can do this standing on your head. But you are not alone. You have a father and a lawyer who are trying their damnedest to help you. All right, you? You hang in there."

There was a knock on the Plexiglas. It was Cliff. He needed a pen for another prisoner.

Ronnie looked up, and nodded. "I can do this."

Once outside the courtroom, Schwartz made arrangements with the father to visit the scene and interview witnesses. Admittedly, that should have been done prior to trial, but Schwartz had been sidetracked. He would interview the witnesses the father had identified. He would pore over the ballistics reports. He would give Judge Williams no choice but to dismiss the charges. And he would bring that contempt motion against CJJ.

Or, just as likely, he would get sidetracked again.

Schwartz pulled into the parking space allotted to the marital condo. It was at least two hours later than he had told Marjorie he would come. He had hoped to say goodnight to Julie and Ethan when he dropped off the mortgage payment. When Marjorie opened the door, she immediately gave him the "shush" sign.

"Kids are already asleep. Come in."

She led him into the kitchenette.

"I'm not even going to ask where you've been, but you can't be coming this late."

"Look, Marj, I was working late, and—"

"I don't care and I don't need to hear your war stories. But if you couldn't be a responsible husband, at least you can be a responsible divorced dad."

Schwartz's brain fired off an instruction: *Time for a furtive attempt at reconciliation.*

"Look, I'm driving Julie and some of her teammates to the game Saturday. I'm going to take the van, OK?"

Marjorie waved a "whatever."

"About that divorce thing, Marj . . . maybe we're moving a bit too hastily on that one. Why can't we see if we can work this out? You don't want to be saddled with eternal damnation in the eyes of your church, do you?"

"Nice try with the B.I.C. guilt trip. I think the reconciliation ship has sailed."

Detecting a weakness in her rebuff, Schwartz pressed on.

"Think of the kids, Marj."

"That's a laugh. That's all we did, Schwartz! Have you been thinking of me or you in all this?"

"Well, that's what I'm trying to say."

Marjorie had been a paralegal in the public defender's office that hired Schwartz out of law school. Their courtship, if it could be called that, was a stop-start/approach-avoidance dance that took a couple of years to bear fruit. Finally, Marjorie succumbed to Schwartz's motormouth charms and invited him to her home in the Throgs Neck section. Her Bronx Irish Catholic parents were working-class heroes. Her dad was a motorman on the subway and mom a school secretary. After their daughter brought home a kinky-haired Jewish apologist for the City's riffraff, Mr. and Mrs. McMahon joked that they had been transported to the set of *All in the Family*. When, on the tidewaters that connect Long Island Sound to the New York Harbor, Schwartz got violently seasick during an outing on the McMahon family fishing boat, doubts about their daughter's choice for a first mate deepened.

To his father-in-law, Schwartz's only saving grace was his encyclopedic knowledge of the life and times of Mr. McMahon's favorite singer, one Bobby Darin. But Marjorie believed she saw potential in the diamond in the rough that was young Schwartz. As the years passed and the children made their appearance and the income plateaued, her belief transformed into the question, "Potential for what, exactly?"

"Egg-sac-lee, Marj! Like a Cult of the Child. I mean, if it weren't for the kids, we never would have moved to the Island. 'Better schools,' you'd said. 'It's safer,' you'd said. I'll tell what it is: It's boring. And expensive. We shoulda stayed in the boogie-down Bronx."

"Shuuuush! That ship has left the harbor, too. Ask yourself this, Schwartz: Is there anything left of that spark between us? To even make it worth the try?...I don't know."

Her head slumped to the table and she rested her cheek against the cool *faux* granite top. Schwartz rose from his chair, walked over to stand behind his wife, and began to rub her shoulders. He planted a kiss at the juncture of her bare skin and the collar of her flannel housecoat. Marjorie let out a soft moan and then twisted her shoulders, dislodging his hands.

Unperturbed, Schwartz resumed the massage.

"You know what a light sleeper Julie is. We'll wake them up," she protested unconvincingly.

"That's my most ardent hope," he said as he cupped her breast.

DECEMBER 6:
MAKE NEW FRIENDS
AND KEEP THE OLD

ON THE FOLDOUT COACH IN CLIFF JOHNSON'S LIVING ROOM, Schwartz lay awake that early morning. He was roused by the buzzing alarm of the vagina clock. Isabel's anonymous daughter was guest-starring in that version. As the image receded to his subconscious, Schwartz became acutely aware of a sharp pain in his upper back.

Why do they put that damn bar right across the shoulder blades?

Lying there, semi-alert, semi-inert, he replayed the previous night's contretemps with Marjorie.

Who knows where the make-up sex will lead?

It had been mechanical, at best. The visit ended with Marjorie thrusting a paper-clipped batch of unpaid bills at him. Schwartz had given her an awkward peck on the cheek as she averted her eyes and ushered him out the door.

In a booming voice worthy of a calendar call, calibrated to be heard above the din of the seventh floor of BxFC, Cliff Johnson announced his presence. He stepped into the sunken living room that was typical of Bronx apartments of Art Deco vintage.

"Let's do it, my man. Need to get up and at' em. Got to pick up my young' uns 'n' get them to school."

Cliff was also Schwartz's tennis partner. They had met when Schwartz began his stint at BxFC ten years ago. During casual conversation they realized they had attended the same high school, Evander Childs, simultaneously for one year.

New York City in the 1960s was less "melting pot" and more "emulsion jar." Evander reflected that social reality. The stereotypical perception of Evander's student body was that the Jewish kids went there because they weren't deemed smart enough for Bronx Science; the black kids because they weren't considered fast enough for DeWitt Clinton (an all-boys school and an athletic powerhouse); the Italian kids because "hey, that's where they tol' us to go." Each group tended to keep to its own, though all were united in mediocrity.

Highlighting Evander's ne'er-do-well image was the absence of a football team, the legacy of a previous generation of Evanderites. The football rivalry between Clinton and Evander had been an intense, if one-sided, affair. The rough-and-tumble action in the stands eclipsed the confrontations on the playing field. The Clinton boys, sexually frustrated by the lack of girls at their alma mater, strutted their alpha-male powers. Rude comments regarding the relative merits of the Evander ladies in attendance sparked most of the fights.

At the '60 season's opener, unfortunately held at Evander's home field, the Clinton invaders came loaded for bear, or, more accurately, for Evander Tiger. They arrived with bullwhips, zip guns, blackjacks, and brass knuckles. The Evander defenders suffered their own version of the Missile Gap, armed as they were with eggs, shaving cream and peashooters. After the final whistle sounded, with another rout of Evander reflected on the scoreboard, the rival student bodies rumbled and tumbled westward, traveling several blocks on Gun Hill Road to the junction of the Third Avenue El and the IRT elevated station at White Plains Road.

Up the staircase and onto the train platforms, the battles raged, terrifying early evening commuters. When the shaving cream and rotten eggs were wiped from the broken storefront windows of that ignominious day, the Evander Principal declared that from then on, football at Evander would be **VERBOTEN!**

The one boast that Evander could make over Clinton, other than coeds, was its swim team. The Evander Childs' Mermen served as a shining beacon of diversity and competency to which all Evander Tigers could aspire. It was in the chilly waters of Evander's pool, as members of the team, that Cliff and Schwartz first met. Schwartz had proven this to Cliff by producing the 1969 school yearbook with its requisite photos of teams and clubs. At his mother's insistence that he undertake an extracurricular activity to juice up his college application, Schwartz had signed on as the team's assistant manager. Cliff was the only black swimmer on the team. The balance of the squad consisted of sons of the three I's: Ireland, Italy, and Israel.

"Do you know how this black ass learned how to swim?" Cliff had said. "My uncle taught me in the raging waters of the Harlem River. That's right. Unc' told me that when he was a boy, he used to swim from the river's edge in Yorkville to Welfare Island. Couple of kids he knew didn't make it."

Schwartz looked up from the black-and-white photo of bare-chested teenage manhood. "He's like my pops: brave and none too bright. He told me he did the same in his youttt," Schwartz said, affecting a Dead End Kids inflection.

"Cliff, remember that cold Evander pool? Do you remember your first swim class?"

"Shit. Thirty buck-naked boys trying to hide their sad little pubic bush in the four corners of the pool."

Schwartz started to shake his head and laugh. "I mean, what was the point? We had bathing suits at home. We could have brought them."

Cliff rolled his eyes and let out a hearty laugh.

"Personally, I think those gaylord gym teachers just wanted to inspect the fresh meat."

"Damn!" Schwartz shouted.

"Damn!" Cliff called.

They exchanged high-fives. It was then that Cliff asked Schwartz whether he played tennis. Schwartz was a stranger to the game, but on reflection, it seemed to be a life-affirming pursuit and a healthy indulgence to be cherished in the spirit-deadening corridors of BxFC. So play they did, mostly on the courts of Mullaly Park across the street from Yankee Stadium. In the next millenium those very courts would be razed to make way for a new iteration of Yankee Stadium.

They played in the early morning, at lunchtime, and after work. Once Schwartz was bitten by the tennis bug, he even followed Cliff in the middle of the night to play on lit courts in Harlem.

"You do have your gun with you, Cliff?"

"Do not worry, my frightened white schoolmate. I shall escort your scared and tennis-whipped little ass to your sorry excuse for a car."

Gradually, Schwartz assembled a tennis game: serve, forehand, and something that resembled a backhand. The pair claimed their niche in the workplace pond that was BxFC: the Jew lawyer and the Black court officer who played tennis together.

In the car after a match, sweating profusely, they would talk about their kids and their ladies. Cliff had an older boy, Hakim, by his first wife. Schwartz had met him. Hakim had smarts, looks, and his father's self-assured manner. He had justifiable college aspirations to study mathematics and engineering. Cliff also had two younger daughters with a woman he was estranged from. The woman, as per Cliff, was a whack job. The fact that Cliff had stayed around long enough to father two children with her was lost on Schwartz.

One humid eve in late July, after a particularly intense match, they sat in Cliff's Buick LeSabre, model year 1986, guzzling Pabst Blue Ribbons and listening to Dinah Washington growl the blues from the eight-track tape deck. Cliff broke in during the instrumental break on "What a Difference a Day Makes."

"I need your help. Uh, my boy has got himself a situation."

Schwartz sighed. He reached for a sweaty towel from his gym bag, covered his face, and felt the moisture slap against him. He gestured for Cliff to continue.

"Shanice was acting all stupid. And I had to take the kids away from her. Woman gets 25 percent of my adjusted gross income but she wasn't feeding them or taking them to the doctor for their shots. Had no lights in the house. So ACS called me and told me to come get the kids or else it was foster care. Well, I went and got them. They've been staying at my mom's house during the week and with me on weekends."

"When was this?"

"About three weeks ago."

"And you didn't tell me?"

"Look, I'm not one to trot my business out on the street. You know that I keep my own counsel, counsel."

Schwartz allowed a brief grin at the witticism.

Emboldened by the acknowledgement, Cliff took a breath and a first-trimester pregnant pause before he continued.

"But here's the thing. Now this piece of shit is saying that Hakim touched Jahniya, the four-year-old. Shanice's pressing charges against him to the DA. She's saying that because I know everyone in the courthouse I'll get the thing squashed. I need to you to stand up for Hakim. He hasn't even been around this summer. He's taking a pre-college program at Virginia Tech."

It was Schwartz's turn to take a deep breath. Criminal law wasn't his main focus, but he had delved into the field with some success. Intellectually, he felt stimulated by the legal challenge. Schwartz's calling to the law was encouraged by his reading the summer before he started college of *Clarence Darrow for the Defense* by Irving Stone. He had visions of using law to speak truth to power, to clean up the environment, and to push back the fascist state. Darrow's career informed Schwartz that in order to fill the role of a legal crusader he would have to represent his share of criminals. The kismet of similarity between Clarence's and Bobby's last name did not go unnoticed by young Schwartz.

The one problem Schwartz had with criminal law was that he was, after all, dealing with criminals. The stakes seemed incredibly high. He stayed up at night worrying that one false move would send an innocent man to jail or piss off a very dangerous one. Coercion was the name of the game. Take the plea for reduced time with credit for time served while awaiting trial or spin the wheel of misfortune, take the case to trial and risk a stiffer sentence. Maybe it would get tossed or maybe the defendant breaks trial and earns that bus ride to the Canadian border.

Schwartz regarded Cliff. Early-onset worry lines were forming a striated pattern on his friend's broad forehead.

"I'll see what I can do."

Schwartz set out to engineer a minor miracle: nip Hakim's case in the bud.

Because of space constrictions, members of the DA sex crimes unit were being housed in a corridor of offices on the seventh floor of BxFC. Outside her office, Schwartz was able to buttonhole Geraldine Mulrooney, the ADA investigating the allegations against Hakim prior to presentation to the grand jury. They stepped into the closet she called her office for an impromptu conference. The ADA, a veteran litigator of sex abuse cases, was wary of any allegation not supported by physical findings that arose against the backdrop of a custody dispute. Schwartz provided proof of the litgation between the mother and Cliff, the mother's unstable mental history, and her prior history of making unsubstantiated allegations. He documented Hakim's absence from the city for the summer. He questioned the timing of the accusations coming on the heels of the ACS intervention against the mother.

Smelling a loser, the ADA opened her file to Schwartz. Together they analyzed the young girl's statement, made in the mother's presence to an ACS caseworker. Schwartz pointed out that in the worker's case notes, the mother provided the bulk of the statement to the caseworker with the child merely nodding in the affirmative. Mulrooney promised she'd interview the child alone. Schwartz offered to have Hakim come in for an interview by the ADA with counsel present. This latter ploy was risky. It perpetuated a statement from Hakim that could be used to impeach him if he testified at trial. Schwartz saw it as a risk worth taking.

Nip it in the bud.

After several days of telephone tag, the time and date for Hakim's interview was set. On the morning of the appointment, Schwartz met with Hakim at the

Fun City Restaurant across from the courthouse to prep him. Understandably nervous, Hakim declined Schwartz's offer of a late breakfast.

"Your call, Hakim, but if you change your mind, it'll be too bad for you. The specials are over at eleven."

Hakim allowed a wan smile. Once again, Schwartz went through the questions he believed the ADA would ask and the answers Hakim should return. The young man was articulate and likeable, an impression that Schwartz believed Mulrooney and a potential jury would share. Schwartz checked his watch, drained his coffee cup, paid the bill, and asked for his unfinished bagel to be wrapped.

"Lez go."

Hakim answered all of the ADA's questions smoothly and effectively. At the conclusion of the meeting, Mulrooney offered her hand to Schwartz. "We'll talk after I interview Jahniya."

One week later, Schwartz was sitting at his desk in the nook off the living room of the marital condo when he received a call from ADA Mulrooney.

"Schwartz, I've spoken to the child. She still claims that Hakim touched her. She also claims that Mickey Mouse touched her, as did Barney the Dinosaur, and Judge Williams, who's hearing the neglect case against the mother. I've consulted with the bureau chief and we're DP-ing . The young man's arrest record will be sealed and his fingerprints and photos will be returned in eight to ten weeks."

Cliff owed Schwartz big time for the DA's decision to decline prosecution, especially since Schwartz "had done it on the arm". At the moment, payment was being made in the form of a spot on Cliff's foldout couch, complete with the god-awful bar right down the middle of his back. Since separating from his wife, a comfy night's sleep had not been an option.

Schwartz sat with Carmen Fontanez in the interview cubicle at BxFC. It was the very same one he had used to interview Leesah Kinard and a hundred other similarly situated mothers. Schwartz let it be known to the court officers in the intake part that he was looking to pick up cases. His other cases were adjourned early and he needed to justify those magic seven billable hours, at $40 per hour, which constituted the day's rake of $280. The court officer from part X had handed him a neglect petition against Ms. Fontanez.

His new client had given birth to a baby girl, and ACS had preemptively removed the child from the hospital. The reason for the autopilot removal: because of her prior drug use, all three of Ms. Fontanez's other children were already in foster care.

When he first shook hands with his new client, Schwartz immediately noticed her inch-long nails. It wasn't so much the length that caught his eye. Upon each nail, the golden design of an infant or a young child was featured against the dark maroon background. A frail woman with dainty mannerisms, she made it clear that she intended to win custody of the newborn.

Schwartz listened, inhaled, and began the stock speech he had given many times in the room.

"Ms. Fontanez, the judges are reluctant to return a newborn to a mother with an extensive drug history unless she can show she's stable, in a program, testing negative, and has housing and means of support."

"I got 'em all covered."

They were interrupted by a knock on the door. Schwartz called for the knocker to enter.

"Heidi Frias. I work for Shakespeare Hospice Services. I'm the social worker for Ms. Fontanez. She's a resident at our facility."

Despite being dressed in caseworker grunge, Schwartz was taken aback by the simplicity of Ms. Frias's beauty and the assured timbre of her voice.

Tall and tan and young and lovely, the girl from Shakespeare Hospice Services goes walking, and when she passes each one she passes goes "Ahhhh."

Schwartz rose clumsily and gestured toward a chair in the cramped room. With the posture and gait of a runway model, Heidi Frias took two paces toward a different chair. Her Bosco *con leche* skin was poured over a face of disheartening beauty. Schwartz was certain that after administering to the world's needy at her day job she was squired around town by the latest New York Yankee wunderkind. "No, not that one. You'd be taking your life, or at least the life of your hip, in your hands if you sat in that one."

Imitating Groucho Marx, his inner Bobby Darin quipped sotto voce, *"Which I would love to do."*

Schwartz maneuvered a slightly less concerning chair in Ms. Frias's direction. "Hospice services?" he asked.

The mother sat silently. The social worker nodded. Schwartz waited for a verbal response, and then a sharp jab of insight pierced his testosterone-addled brain. He released his grip on the chair that was sliding toward the social worker.

"Oh. I see."

Ms. Fontanez looked up at Schwartz. Her tone was apologetic as she said, "I know you busy and you got lotsa cases. But I've been waitin' two days to get an attorney. You goin' to help me get my baby?"

Schwartz reclaimed his seat behind the sorry excuse for a desk and coughed officiously. He stared down at the petition that identified the child as "Baby Girl Fontanez, a Child Under the Age of Eighteen Years Alleged to Be Neglected by Carmen Fontanez, Respondent."

"What's the baby's first name?" he asked.

"Justina."

Schwartz suppressed a wry smile.

"Was Justina born clean?"

The social worker broke in.

"Look, Mr. Schwartz. Carmen was at our facility for most of her pregnancy. We provided her with prenatal care, drug counseling and testing, and HIV treatment. She's been cooperative and responsible in every way."

"Does the baby have AIDS?"

"Where are you going with this, Mr. Schwartz?" she asked pointedly.

"Ms. . .. ?"

Schwartz fumbled for the beautiful budinski's card since he had blanked on her name.

"Frias. Are you aware of the 'blame the parent' attitude we are up against in this courthouse, trying to get children back to parents? First there is the ACS attorney, fresh out of law school with little or no appreciation for the finer points of ghetto life. Next up, the ACS worker, who, more often than not, is some middle-class climber taking perverse pleasure in grinding her less fortunate brothers and sisters into the dirt. Then there's the law guardian—the attorney for the child. This species of fish eats parents' rights for breakfast. I mean, some of them don't care about what it feels like to be a child removed from his or her parent. Finally we have the person wearing the black robe, earning the big bucks, whose primary motivation is to make sure he or she doesn't see his or her name in the newspaper because some kid they returned to a parent has shown up dead."

Fontanez's pencil-thin eyebrows were moving up and down like indicator needles on a polygraph machine. Frias was ready to lock horns.

"Look here, Mr. Schwartz. I know all too well about the perils of family court and foster care. Had you bothered to attend any of the seminars offered on representing the HIV-positive parent, you would know that a newborn cannot be tested for AIDS until the mother's blood has been thoroughly flushed from the baby's system."

"Ms. Frias, I don't need a lecture from you on—"

The mother suddenly rose.

"It's that foster care agency. The ones that has my other kids. They called

ACS and told them I was due. They haven't done nothin' for me. I found the Shakespeare Avenue program. The agency worker . . . she's in it with the foster mother. All they want is the money for taking care of my kids. You should see the way they show up for visits. Messed-up sneakers. Their hair not combed. I ask them what they had to eat that day. They tell me chocolate candy, lollipops, sugar cereal. They're acting all wired during the visit."

Schwartz's interest was piqued. "Which foster care agency is this?"

Frias answered, "St. Patrick's Services for Children. I've been calling that worker for two weeks, and she never returns my phone calls."

Schwartz jotted down the name on the back of the petition as he spoke.

"I've dealt with them before. This sugar feeding prior to an agency visit is a nasty ploy by a foster mother to get the special rate for ADHD children. It also will make the mother appear as if she can't control her kids during the visit. Sit down, please, Ms. Fontanez. I must explain certain unpleasant realities, and you have to make a decision."

Schwartz waited as she composed herself with Frias's help. Damned if he didn't feel the sudden urge to urinate. Was it the excitement of meeting Frias or the twenty-ounce ginger ale that had washed down his turkey-and-cheese hero at lunch? He began to speak more rapidly.

"It can take six to nine months to complete a trial with these charges. If the judge finds no parental neglect, fine. Baby comes home to you. If the judge finds against us—and most times they do—the case gets adjourned for a dispositional hearing. Disposition is a fancy way of asking, 'What should happen to the child: return her to the parent or place her in foster care?' That phase of the case could take another three to six months.

"So the obvious question is, 'Where should the child reside while the case is pending?' You have a right, under Section 1028 of the Family Court Act, to ask for a hearing within three days from today to have your child returned to you immediately. If the agency can't show imminent risk of neglect or abuse—that means immediate and present risk—the child goes home with you. It's your call, but before you decide, be aware that at a 1028 hearing, hearsay is admissible as evidence. That means the judge can hear things about you that couldn't be introduced in a full fact-finding."

"Such as?" Frias asked.

"Anything and everything that anyone has ever said about the mother to the caseworker, or anyone else, for that matter. Uncertified medical records, incompetent opinions, domestic incident reports, testimony without proper foundation—all manners of prejudicial claptrap can easily slither into the record.

Call it Pandora's box, the kitchen sink, or the big black garbage can. Mind you, the caseworker would probably be the only witness. I won't get to cross-examine the sources of the prejudicial statements made to the caseworker. And what they said to the caseworker will be indelibly marked on the court's mind if, and when, we go to full fact-finding. And, by the way, even if by some miracle we manage to win the 1028 hearing, ACS can run to the Appellate Division and get a stay of the release order. So, Carmen, can I call you Carmen?"

The woman nodded.

"The city has removed your newborn baby. Are you consenting to the remand or do you want a hearing?"

Carmen closed her eyes. The tears began to well up. She turned to Frias, who started to rub Carmen's back in a kind, calming gesture. Schwartz handed her a tissue. It was the one concrete thing he could do for his clients.

"It's crumpled but clean."

Carmen looked defiantly at Schwartz.

"I don't have time to play around with . . .what's your name again? Mr. Schwartz? OK, Mr. Schwartz, I want to hold my daughter in the morning and put her to bed at night. That's what I want."

On the seventh floor, Schwartz turned the key to the staff bathroom. Possession of the key was one of the few perks extended to 18-Bs. As he positioned himself at the urinal, he heard the door open. Despite a slight burning sensation, he managed to get a stream going. Then he heard a low sucking noise. In his right peripheral vision he noted a brown-skinned mass moving awkwardly behind him. He could hear the *whviiip-whviiip* of corduroy pants legs as they made contact.

It was a petition clerk, Andrew Timmons. Andrew weighed over 350 pounds and could barely move about the courthouse. Now he was filling the limited space of the staff bathroom. As Andrew passed behind him, Schwartz found it impossible to maintain his stream of urine. He gulped as the clerk squeezed into the next urinal, boxing him in against the wall.

All he has to do is take a sideways step and I'm done for.

Schwartz maintained his position at the urinal, involuntarily holding back his stream. Finally, Andrew finished, zipped up, and started to lumber out. As he passed Schwartz, he uttered one froggy word that somehow came out in two syllables: "'Bye-eehhh."

Along with other counsel anxious to depart BxFC before dark and beat the traffic, Schwartz sat in part X, waiting for the judge to appear. Burton Mitzner sat next to him, loudly poking fun at Schwartz's three-piece vomit-green linen suit, which hadn't seen the business end of an iron in a week.

"Schwartz, did I ever tell you about the first time I appeared in court as an attorney? I walked into the night arraignment part in Brooklyn Criminal with my $200 fee snug in my back pocket. My case gets called first. I stride up to the defense table, anxious to make a good impression on the judge, my client, and the other attorneys. The court officer says, 'Counselor, note your appearance.' I'm confused. After a moment I look in the direction of the court reporter and say, 'Well, I'm wearing a brown suit with a blue tie.' Schwartz, note your appearance. You look like a million dollars—all green and wrinkly."

The clique members, seated in back, snickered in unison. Mitzner gloated, "Schwartz, I've told you before, I'll give you money for a new suit."

"Burton, you are such a prick. Can you rein yourself in here?"

"Just go to Orchard Street or Syms or wherever it is you go since Alexander's closed and get yourself a new suit. And some fashion advice: three piece suits are passé."

The suit Schwartz was wearing might as well have been his bar mitzvah suit, he'd worn it so long. Even in its better days the garment was ill fitting. Now the front pockets bulged out in the manner of elephant ears, the vest had succumbed to the torque of his midriff, and the cuffs were scuffed beyond repair.

To shut Mitzner up, Schwartz called what he believed to be a bluff.

"You win. Give me the same $200 you earned in that bullshit canard of a story and I'll buy a new suit."

Mitzner's ears twitched as he stammered, "Uh, you'll bring me the receipt?"

"Absolutely."

"And you'll put that monstrosity you're wearing in a garbage bag and give it to me?"

Schwartz ran his fingers across the vest of his old friend.

"You drive a hard bargain."

"I intend to burn it and scatter its ashes on Sheridan Avenue."

Mitzner reached into his pocket, pulled out a wad of bills, peeled off two Benjamins, and handed them to Schwartz.

After Schwartz made his application to Judge Russell Parker for a 1028 hearing in the Matter of Justina Fontanez, the ACS attorney held his head in his hand as he reached for his date book. The law guardian from the Legal Aid Society pursed her lips and moved her head from side to side in an apparent effort to work out a kink.

Judge Parker was a relatively new appointee and one of the few black male judges on the bench citywide. After listening to the litany of reasons why this date and that date failed to work for counsel, he adjourned the hearing date to December 8th. The court officers cleared the courtroom in their never-ending quest to get through the calendar.

Leaving the courtroom, the law guardian, Cindy Grella, confronted Schwartz in the well. "This mother has three kids in placement and a drug and prostitution history that goes back almost ten years. You're wasting my time and the court's."

Schwartz didn't even turn his head toward her. Instead he concentrated on avoiding the onslaught of the next set of litigants entering the courtroom.

"Is there some sort of psychological profile test that gets administered to applicants for the Legal Aid Society? If you want to fight the power, go to the Criminal Defense Division. If you had issues with your parents, go to the Juvenile Rights Division?"

Before waiting for a reply from the open-mouthed law guardian, Schwartz called out to his client and Frias, "Be here early—before 9:30—on the eighth. If you show up late, the judge will rule that you waived your right to the 1028 hearing and adjourn the case for two months for trial. And bring all your program certificates and a brochure from the Shakespeare program."

DECEMBER 7:
INFAMY'S DAY

SCHWARTZ'S MORNING CALENDAR WAS LIGHT SO HE HAD arranged to meet Ronnie Ramirez's father at the scene of the alleged juvie attempted murder. His purpose was twofold: walk the place of occurrence while referring to the field ballistic report and, perchance, locate eyewitnesses who could corroborate Ronnie's innocence.

Schwartz parked the Saab at the corner of Hoe Avenue and 174th Street. When he exited his vehicle holding a Polaroid camera, a group of young Hispanic men who had been standing on the corner scattered. They shouted, "Five-O! Five-O!" as they ran. Schwartz turned to see if there were any RMPs around. Seeing none, he realized they thought he was the cop.

If that buys me a temporary bubble of safety, so much the better.

He laid his copy of the field ballistic report on the hood of his car. The report detailed the location of every bullet or fragment recovered as well as every piece of evidence of bullet impact observed by the ballistics quad. Looking down the hill to the corner of Vyse Avenue and 174th Street, he could see the apartment building where one of Floyd Green's bullets had lodged into a startled occupant's wall.

Schwartz whistled.

"Man, that's almost a hundred yards away."

He checked the camera to see if it was loaded and then snapped a shot of 174th Street in the direction of Vyse Avenue. The Polaroid whirled and buzzed and spit out the film. While waiting for the image to process, he noticed some of the young men who had previously bailed approaching him. Any brief psychological advantage he had enjoyed expired faster than a defective tricked up parking meter. He contemplated retreating to the relative safety of the unreliable Saab when Ronnie Ramirez's father appeared behind him and greeted him warmly.

"Hey, Mr. Schwartz. Welcome to *mi* leettle corner of the world!"

In rapid Spanish he scolded the small posse that had approached. Once again they started to scatter.

"No...No, Mr. Ramirez. I need to talk to them. Bring 'em back."

"Cono. Pendejos, ven atras!"

Reluctantly, the young men gathered around Schwartz and Ramirez.

"Gentlemen, *Caballeros. Yo soy el abogado de—*"

A tall swarthy youth with tattoos growing up his neck like a vine stepped forward. "Hey, you can lose the grade-school Spanish. We speak *Ingleeeees.*"

Ramirez didn't mince words. "Tito, *tiene respecto, muchacho!*"

Schwartz let out a laugh in an effort to diffuse the tension.

"Well, that's convenient because I speak English, too. Look, guys, I'm here with Mr. Ramirez because I represent his boy, Ronnie, in Bronx Family. He's being held at Spofford on a charge of attempted murder of Floyd Green and his girlfriend, Shalima, week ago, Sunday, November 27. That was the first Sunday after Thanksgiving. I'm told there was a shootout between Floyd and Ronnie on that afternoon. Did any of you hear or see any of what went down?"

It was Tito's turn to laugh.

"Ronnie doesn't know which end of a gun fires. But he does have a little bit of a mouth on him. Floyd's a hothead. Ronnie probably flipped him off or said something about Floyd's girl and Floyd jumped ugly with him."

"Listen—Tito, is it?—Tito, 'probably' doesn't work for Ronnie. 'Probably' gets him a five-year stint in a secure Division For Youth facility for a Class B violent felony. So I come back to my question: Did any of you hear or see anything that went down? And . . . and if you didn't, do you know anyone on the block who did?"

The reaction to Schwartz's question was downward faces, shaking heads, and tightened lips.

"OK, I get it. You're all so tough out here on the street, but when it comes to taking a witness stand and standing up for the truth, you're all a bunch of bitches."

"You said whaaaat?"

Tito took two aggressive steps toward Schwartz, only to have Ramirez grab his collar.

"Wha' I got to tell you? Answer the man!"

Another member of the group piped up. He was a short, stocky youth with huge pierced earlobes, with holes rimmed with dark plastic so large one could run a clothesline through them.

"Hey, man, we gots warrants and shit."

"Who on this street doesn't?" Schwartz replied.

"I tell you what," Earlobes continued, "I think my little sister see somethin'. Let me get your card and maybe she'll talk wid you."

"Where is she now?"

"In school, whaddyadink?"

"Well, that's refreshing. OK, get her to call me and mention Ronnie's case. Mr. Ramirez, you know how to reach these peeps?"

Mr. Ramirez nodded.

"Yeah? Good. We'll see where that leads. I'm going to walk the block and take some pictures. Hopefully I won't get myself shot."

"Bery good, Mr. Schwartz. Den let me make you a cup of good Dominican coffee *en mi* social club."

Ramirez's "club" was a converted storage room in the rear of a basement in one of the apartment buildings on the block. In more innocent times, it hosted tenants' baby carriages and bicycles. Ramirez had built a bar and stocked it with rum and beer, which he sold at a healthy markup. Atop the bar was a small glass container. A garish lamp heated the *cuchifrito* and *chicharrones de pollo* contained within. Several older men speaking rapid Domnican Spanish occupied a few tables, playing games. When Schwartz and Ramirez entered, heads looked up, conversations hushed, and the clicking of the Domino tiles stopped.

I might have stumbled into the one drinking hole where even Don Edgardo hasn't been.

Schwartz had read somewhere, probably the *New York Times,* that between six hundred thousand and a million Dominicans had settled in New York City. They had been among the latest wave of wretched refuse from foreign shores, yearning to breathe free of Rafael Trujillo's brutal dictatorship. One group moved in, another moved out. A law school professor of his had labeled this urban dynamic the "Law of Ethnic Succession." The American Indians were pushed out by the Dutch; who were pushed out by the English; who were pushed out by the Germans and the Irish; who were pushed out by the Italians and the Jews; who were pushed out by the blacks and the Puerto Ricans; who were pushed out by the West Indians, Dominicans, and Chinese; who were being pushed out by (in alphabetical order) the Afghans, Africans, Albanians,

Colombians, Ecuadoreans, Koreans, Pakistanis, Russians, and the Vietnamese, as well as true Indians from India and their progeny from Guyana, and Trinidad. The JFK International Airport served as the modern-day Ellis Island. Bringing the influx full cycle, the population of American Indians (aka Native Americans, aka First People) in New York City had doubled since the last census, according to the newspaper of record. As a result there was a boomlet for interpreters of every linguitstic bent in the family courts of the city.

Posters of Puerto Plata and Punta Cana along with photos of Dominican baseball stars graced the walls. Ramirez pushed a steaming cup of java, topped with the white froth of heated milk, across the bar to Schwartz. The white froth reminded him of the chocolate egg creams of his youth. He took a sip and recoiled as it seared his lips.

Ramirez gave a hearty laugh.

"Mr. Schwartz, I like how you handled yourself with those *muchachos* out there. You got *cojones*. Stones."

"Appreciated. Can I ask you a question?"

"Ask *Mas de uno*."

"OK. Shalima, Floyd's woman, testified that one, you are a drug dealer, and two, Ronnie owns a car. That info did not sit well with Judge Williams."

"Mr. Schwartz, don't believe anything that *morena* says. Listen. I run dis bottle club. I have a little money. I lend it out to people and make a little more money. Sometimes *de* people I lend it *hace* a deal or two. Does that make me a drug dealer?"

"Uh. According to several federal statutes, *si.*"

"Haha. You are a funny man, Mr. Schwartz. And Ronnie owning a car? *Mas mierda.* Sometimes I let him drive my Cadillac Brougham up and down the street so he can impress some girls. Dat's it."

"Well, that leads me to yet another question. You obviously have money. Why me? Why am I, a member of the much-maligned assigned counsel panel, representing your son? You could afford the king of the Bronx, Maury Feldman, or someone of that ilk. Why me?"

Ramirez rubbed his chin and nodded. He walked around the bar and spoke rapidly to the other men. They all grunted and then began vacating the premises. Ramirez held the door for them as he ushered them out. He closed the door, walked toward the bar, and sat on a stool next to Schwartz.

"Señor Schwartz, as you guessed, *yo no soy un angel*. I got *mi* hands in dis and dat. I paid thousands of dollars to lawyers over the years. Some are good. Some are bad. Some are ugly. You know, like the movie." Ramirez laughed at his own joke and continued, "But I like you, and more importantly, my son likes you. I mean, what you do for him, bringing da pills. . . and da way you went up against dat white *pendejo* judge for him. I trust you to do da right thing by Ronnie. He no do dis shooting. Yes, he has some growin' up to do. But I tink he can be someone. Maybe even go to law school like you. You do da right thing by him . . . you in *mi corazon.*"

With that, the tough guy, Señor Ramirez, began to blubber. Schwartz, somewhat embarrassed, reached for a tissue from his pocket and offered it.

"It's crumpled but clean."

Schwartz put arms around the man and rubbed his back. Ramirez continued to sob.

I guess even the local Dominican drug lord needs a good cry once in a while.

Past five o'clock, after throwing out the abandoned newspapers, Styrofoam coffee cups, and crumpled take-out sandwich wrappers, Schwartz was able to find space on the table in the deserted 18-B room. He spread out the voluminous pile of case records that Special Assistant Corporation Counsel Barbanel had provided him on the Carmen Fontanez case. The records detailed the foster care sojourn of Ms. Fontanez's other children as well as the mother's inconsistent pattern of compliance with the foster care agency's service plan.

It doesn't look good. With any luck I can give her a show.

Briefly turning from the records, he dialed the phone number of his former home. After six rings, the Schwartz family answering machine kicked in. Schwartz listened to the recording of his voice, accompanied by Julie and Ethan in ostensibly happier days. The message told him that no one was available to take the call and to please leave a message. He found some perverse solace in hearing his voice utter the titular greeting for what was once his family.

"Julie, Ethan, it's Dad. See you on Saturday . . . Marjorie . . . 'bye."

He looked back at the stack of records and then out the open door at the empty waiting area. A single tear slid down his cheek.

DECEMBER 8:
THE MORAL OF THE TWO MARKS

A GREY SQUARE, FASCIST BLOCK OF GRANITE NINE STORIES high occupied half a city block at the intersection of East 161st Street and Sheridan Avenue. Bronx Criminal Court and several civil court parts were located on the lower floors. The basement level featured the pens of Bronx Central Booking, immortalized by Tom Wolfe. Floors six through eight hosted Bronx Family Court. The ninth floor was reserved for family court judges' chambers and the law library.

The social work wisdom had been to keep family issues and criminal issues apart. In homage to this intent, the family court boasted a separate entrance at 900 Sheridan Avenue. Yet the intersection of jurisdiction and common social ills between criminal court and family court are palpable and deep. The line of litigants, children, significant others, and witnesses seeking entry to the Bronx Family Court often extended down Sheridan toward 163rd Street. That line was often lapped by the Bronx County Criminal Court entrance queue that extended around the corner from 161st Street. Roughly parallel, the two groups offered each other commiserations, greetings, and cigarettes as they endured the freezing wind tunnel formed by the opposing palisades of apartment buildings abutting Sheridan Avenue.

Upon presentation of proper ID at the family court entrance; attorneys, clerks, caseworkers, and the like were spared the wait. However, the gauntlet of frustrated, sullen, and frostbitten citizenry had to be run before the double doors of 900 Sheridan Avenue could be reached. In order to survive the trial of stares and mutterings, along with masses' reluctance to stand aside, the strategy was to keep one's head down, eyes averted, and utter a phony yet polite, "Excuse me, excuse me." Resentfully and eventually, a path was ceded.

Once inside the lobby, a conga line of plastic chains and stanchions awaited the public, followed by the obligatory metal detector screening. At that juncture, the ID holders headed down a lane, directly toward the gathering herd in front of the elevator bank.

Schwartz had already negotiated the gauntlet, cleared the double glass doors and was veering toward the elevator bank mob when a voice rang out above the din.

"Mr. Schwartz. Attorney Schwartz!"

He glanced over his left shoulder at Heidi Frias and Carmen Fontanez, who were stuck in the middle of the Conga Line of Misery. Frias was moving out of the line and heading in Schwartz's direction. Stepping over baby strollers, around boisterous teenagers, and between restless young children playing tag in the line, Frias advanced with a graceful athleticism that simultaneously startled and aroused Schwartz.

What is it that causes the male of the species to look around for a club to knock an attractive female over the head and drag her back to the cave for copulation? In 10,000 BC, when the need to propagate was a biological and social imperative, the urge served its purpose. In AD 2000, however, more often than not, having XY chromosomes led to bad decision making. The divorce statistics and the burgeoning family court dockets, if nothing else, bore that out. After all, sex gone bad was the accelerant that launched family court's caseload to the stratosphere.

Schwartz was shaken out of his ardor by the strident tone of Heidi's plea.

"Mr. Schwartz, I'm glad I caught you. Carmen's been in line for over an hour. She took her HZT and is feeling pretty faint. Is there anything you can do?"

Schwartz eyeballed Carmen and confirmed Frias's report.

"Gotcha."

Schwartz headed for the security desk and approached the sergeant in charge of the lobby. Schwartz motioned for Frias to extricate Carmen from the conga line.

"Hey, Bill. Another day in paradise, huh?"

The sergeant nodded.

"Schwartz, what's up?"

"Got a sick client. Need a little of your world-renowned Bronx Family Court VIP treatment."

"Schwartz, stop snowing me. What part you in?"

"Parker's."

"All right. Send her to the front."

Schwartz yelled across the crowded room to Frias, "Go to the part and check in with the bridge officer. Tell them Schwartz is in the building and I'll be there shortly."

On the seventh floor, the bank of elevators opened to a central area flanked by four waiting rooms, approximately 60 by 120 feet each. The seventh floor was the hub, with eight of the twelve court parts housed there. Each waiting area serviced two courtrooms. One could stand next to the seventh-floor security desk and eyeball all four waiting areas. Assigned to the various parts, court officers would hunt for needed attorneys by standing in this central area, shouting their quarries' names. Attorneys looking for clients, witnesses, or other attorneys went from waiting area to waiting area, chanting names. Added to the aural mix was the cursing and screaming that erupted between litigants, the squeals of laughter and cries of the children enjoying a day away from their overcrowded schoolroom just to sit in an overcrowded courtroom waiting area, and clerks reading the names of parties waiting for copies of orders. To describe the seventh floor as the Tower of Babel hosting a commodities trading pit would not be an overstatement.

The elevator door opened for two seconds before slamming shut on Schwartz's shoulder. As he stepped off, several different clients—some on the day's calendar, some not—rushed toward him. A paralegal for the New York City Corporation Counsel's office handed him a thick sheaf of barely legible photocopies of police reports and asked him to sign her copy. A court officer grabbed him by the arm to tell him his case was before the bench in Part II and the judge had been screaming his name. The Corporation Counsel on the Henderson robbery case shouted at him to leave bad dates with Part VIII because the cop scheduled to testify was out on disability. Schwartz needed to get to Judge Parker's part for the Fontanez 1028 but decided that he'd better put out the fire in Part II first.

In the waiting area for parts I and II, Schwartz's head jerked in surprise when he spotted Isabel sitting on a bench, holding her head in her hands. Schwartz sidestepped three people, approached her, and touched her shoulder. Before he even asked the question, he gleaned the answer from her face, which featured a split lip and a blackened left eye.

Schwartz hadn't called Isabel since their tryst. She had called his office number on one occasion and seemed upset, but her message pushed beyond the parameters of his limited Spanish. Sad to say, his reasons for not returning her call could be summed up best by the cohort of angry men who frequented the seventh-floor public bathroom. They held impromptu summits in front of the sinks as they surreptitiously pulled on their cigarettes.

"Man, you put your dick in a woman and you put your dick in her troubles."

"These bitches care about one thing: your goddamn money. Stupid ass thinks she'll get over on me."

"The devil comes to earth in the form of a woman."

"Esas mujeres no tienen respecto. Cono!"

The hiss of cigarettes hitting the basin of the urinal punctuated these sentiments.

Schwartz maneuvered Isabel to a witness interview room. She sat in the cubicle crying and cursing as she related to Schwartz in Spanglish her most recent woes. In contrast to her desperate circumstances, Isabel was dressed to the nines. She wore a pink ensemble that, for Schwartz, resuscitated memories of their one night of passion.

"Mira, me llame a la policia porque mi boyfriend. He mala. He bery bery bad with me and my baby. He *usa* the *cocaina. Pendejo! Hijo de un burro!* The police, dey come. But he not dere. *Pero,* dey see my baby. *Llame* ACS. Dey come and take her away. *Ave Maria. Qué pasa, ahora? Yo no se. Ay dios mio. Ayudeme, por favor. Tu eres un abogadoooooo."*

Schwartz knew he was at a precipice. There was every reason to walk away and let some other attorney be assigned. Isabel unbuttoned the top two buttons of her blouse and gave him two reasons why he should take the assignment.

"Toma, bebe. Toma. Eso es para ti."

Schwartz hesitated and then curled his toes around the edge of the XY chromosome cliff and sprang into a swan dive. He strode over to the intake part's bridge officer and informed him he would pick up Isabel's case.

The Fontanez 1028 commenced inauspiciously. In thickly accented English, the caseworker, a naturalized Nigerian by the name of Ade Adesanya, recounted all of Ms. Fontanez's prior contacts with ACS and BxFC. Schwartz wondered about the disproportionately large number of West African caseworkers employed by ACS. He had no doubt that their ancestors had played a significant role in the slave trade. It seemed like rounding up children of color for the diaspora was the family business.

Schwartz stood up. "Judge, the issue is imminent risk. Not my client's past history."

"Mr. Schwartz, this court must consider all elements of risk. The past is a prologue."

Three months on the bench and this judge is lording it over me.

"Judge, that's very profound, but can we just get to the question of why she can't have custody of her baby?"

Grella, the law guardian, stood and barked, "Your Honor, what Mr. Schwartz has failed to grasp is that Ms. Fontanez's ability to parent is at issue. All her children are in foster care."

"When did the Legal Aid Society start playing God?"

"Mr. Schwartz, do you think my courtroom is a shooting gallery for you and Ms. Grella? I don't have time for that. This matter is adjourned 'til"—the judge looked down at his calendar "the thirteenth of December."

"Your Honor," Schwartz protested, "my client is entitled to this hearing now. It's been three days."

"She's entitled to the commencement of the hearing. We've commenced."

"But, Your Honor, the hearing can only be adjourned for good cause."

"Your bantering has given me good cause, as well as *agita*. Because of the press of other cases, I must adjourn."

Schwartz knew there was little point in arguing.

"Judge, will this be at least a time certain?"

"How's 10:45 until 11:30, Mr. Schwartz?"

"Judge, I have a continued abuse trial, four-in concert robbery with a remanded youth and other matters as well. Can we have 9:30?"

"Mr. Schwartz, the rules of engagement state that a 1028 takes priority. I have other matters on my calendar as well. Very well, the thirteenth at 9:30 a.m."

Schwartz pressed on.

"My client is seeking visitation in the interim. She hasn't seen the child since birth."

"Granted. The caseworker will arrange for it at the foster care agency."

"Why can't it take place at the mother's residence?" Schwartz queried.

Grella's voice rang out.

"In an AIDS hospice? Come on. How can that possibly be in the child's best interest? The law guardian is opposed."

Schwartz glanced in the direction of the ACS attorney, Richard Barbarnel, who was conferring with Adesanya. The caseworker was shaking his head furiously. Barbarnel rose tentatively and said, "Petitioner seeks visits supervised at the agency only."

Judge Parker rubbed his hands together. "Can the mother visit at the agency?"

Frias piped up, "We'll make the arrangements, Your Honor. If the foster care worker would only return our phone calls . . ."

The judge stood up and walked behind his chair. "It's so ordered. Once a week. Mr. Barbarnel, tell your caseworker to get on the horn to the foster care agency worker. We'll see you on the thirteenth. Mr. Schwartz, my court officer tells me your presence is required in intake."

Heidi growled in Schwartz's ear, "Once a week?"

Turning his head, he responded, "How many weekly two-hour Bronx-to-Jamaica Queens, then Queens-to-Bronx subway rides can Carmen tolerate? Let it be."

After exiting the courtroom, Schwartz rushed past Carmen and Heidi and blurted out over his shoulder, "This is how it's going to be. Enjoy the visit!"

He raced off toward the intake part where Judge Finkel was presiding. As he entered the part, he saw Isabel sitting in the respondent's chair at the table. With her were the law guardian and the ACS attorney seated in their assigned spots. The caseworker sat in a chair along the sidewall of the courtroom.

Judge Finkel was addressing Isabel in her smarmy self-important tone.

"And if you can't afford an attorney one will be appointed for—"

Schwartz announced himself loudly. "Judge, she's going to need an interpreter."

"Mr. Schwartz. Are you willing to accept assignment in this matter?"

A gulp and then a beat.

"I am."

"Thank you. Give Mr. Schwartz a copy of the petition. Mr. Schwartz is assigned to represent the respondent mother, Isabel Mojica. How does your client wish to plead?"

What a way to learn her last name.

"Uh, Judge, about that interpreter?"

"I was having a good conversation with her in English before you decided to join us and—"

"Judge, it might have been good for you, but was it good for her?"

Finkel calmly handed the file back to the bridge officer.

"This matter will be recalled."

Having waited all morning to process the case, the other attorneys at the table groaned. For his own sake and for the sake his tenuous relationship with co-counsel, Schwartz opted for the politic.

"Your Honor, I'll waive the interpreter, waive a reading of the allegations, and enter a denial."

"Very well, Mr. Schwartz, it's your case. You know best how to proceed on behalf of your client."

Finkel was biting off every word as if they were nails and spitting them at Schwartz.

The judge's harsh glare downshifted to accommodating as she addressed the ACS lawyer, Holly Benson.

"What's the agency's application?"

"Agency's seeking a continued remand based upon domestic violence and excessive corporal punishment."

"Mr. Schwartz?"

"Respondent objects. The mother is a victim, not a perpetrator. She'll enforce a stay-away temporary order of protection against the paramour."

"I take it from your tone that you're requesting a 1028 hearing?"

"I'm not requesting it. My client's entitled to it by statute."

"Very well, then. December 15th, 9:30 a.m. Tell your client to be in line early that day."

"Judge, the fifteenth is a terrible day. I already have an attempted murder continued fact-finding and several other matters."

"Counsel, I'm on intake on the thirteenth and on the fourteenth the part is closed because I have an all-day meeting with the City-wide administrative judge. It's either the fifteenth or your client comes back after Christmas. Assent?"

Schwartz cursed to himself as he looked at December 15 in his crowded datebook, searching for one more space to scribble the entry, "Mojica, part I, 9:30 a.m."

"Yes? Good. December 15th at 9:30 a.m. Matter adjourned."

"Uh, Judge, about that stay-away TOP?" Schwartz persisted.

Judge Finkel huffed, "Granted. Wait for a copy outside the courtroom."

Don Edgardo confronted Schwartz in the waiting area.

"My man. You are sticking your *pinga* in it. Let someone else take this assignment."

"Eddie, sometimes, rather than sit in her part waiting for my case, I stand in the well leading to her courtroom. I can't stand watching and hearing her do what she does. I avert my eyes. It's like seeing a stray dog in a busy intersection. You know what she does. If the agency has a weak case, she'll twist and distort to fill the gaps. And God forbid you try to mount a defense. She'll take over your cross-examination and undermines whatever attack on an agency witness's credibility you're trying to build. And have you heard her cross-examine a respondent? Torquemada would blush. And she absolutely refuses to conference cases with attorneys to try to work something out. Sometimes litigants open the outer door and ask me, 'Which courtroom is this?' I tell them honestly, 'It's the one where families go to die.'"

Don Edgardo regarded Schwartz incredulously.

"You finished your speech? Feel better? Good. You remember the two Marks?"

Schwartz stared at the floor. Don Edgardo took Schwartz by the arm and led him into an interview cubicle. They had to evict a caseworker doing her nails at the table.

"Hey, schmucko, I asked you a question. Do you—"

"Yes, yes, yes. I remember."

"And?"

"And what? I'm not going to let Finkel kill this family."

"Compadre, some families are meant to die. And you are about to break Don Edgardo's most important rule: 'Never, ever be the client.' Which is what you'll be once the grievance committee sends you that envelope marked 'personal and confidential.'" And for what? A whore and a child abuser?"

Schwartz stormed out of the cubicle.

The two Marks were former members of the panel and charter members of the clique. Seeking passion in the courthouse interview rooms, the two Marks had ingratiated themselves with several court officers by doing occasional legal favors on the arm. In return, the court officers would steer attractive females who required assigned counsel their way. Plying those desperate souls with promises of the quick return of their children and offering to pay livery cab fare prices, they'd make their pitch for sexual favors and salacious photo shoots.

One respondent who had fallen victim to Mark I's entreaties during her first go-round in family court, upset their apple cart of pleasure. Several years after her children were first removed and placed with ACS, she had managed to wend her way through the labyrinth of drug programs, parenting programs, domestic violence courses, and individual counseling to position herself to gain return of her children. For that application, she, of course, required assigned counsel. The court officer's finely tuned women-seeking radar detected her and had sent her Mark II's way.

Unbeknownst to Mark II, the woman had confided in her caseworker following his advances during their initial interview. The caseworker, no great fan of assigned counsel, brought the woman to the Bronx DA's Sex Crimes Unit. The rest was Kel transmitter, tape recorder history.

At the subsequent disbarment hearing, Mark II was hard-pressed to explain the inimitable sound of a zipper unzipping. When confronted with the damning recording, Mark II tried to claim that the zipper sound was merely the opening of his briefcase. In a way, the lawyers on the grievance committee agreed: it was his briefs that were opening and they did indeed have a case.

Mark I's ticket was also punched by dint of the same woman's disclosures of his past sins.

Since he had met Isabel prior to being assigned to her, Schwartz rationalized that he was not barred from representing her. However, as a potential witness to the excessive corporal punishment used on Isabel's daughter, Schwartz realized he stood on shaky ethical ground.

When a man collided with him in the narrow aisle between benches in the waiting area outside Judge Finkel's courtroom, Schwartz was laid out on the hard marble floor.

"Motherfucker, I keel you! You fuck with my woman!"

Schwartz scrambled to his feet as Isabel stepped between him and his newfound friend. Her hands flailed at the guy as she kicked at him. He, in turn, slapped at her and pulled her hair. As the epithets flew, the occupants of the waiting area were on their feet, craning their necks for a view. Cliff and a fellow court officer, belatedly for Schwartz's taste, began separating the combatants. The provocateur, whom Schwartz estimated at just over six feet, was in Cliff's sure grasp and subdued after a brief but violent struggle. While being placed in handcuffs, he spewed threats in Spanish in Schwartz and Isabel's direction.

Officer Mama's Boy had his arms wrapped around Isabel's neck and torso and was attempting to handcuff her while copping a boob feel in the process. As Schwartz stepped toward them, someone grabbed him from behind and spun him around.

"You wouldn't be thinking of interfering with a peace officer in the dispatch of his duties would you, Mr. Schwartz? That's a felony charge, isn't it, counselor?"

That someone was Captain Dolan, commandant of the court officers. Schwartz glared into his shark-grey eyes. More than once, Schwartz had registered on Dolan's radar screen for perceived violations of the Captain's rules.

"And a two-and-a-half-million-dollar lawsuit for false arrest wouldn't look too good on the balance sheet, would it? Let her go, Captain. She's a DV victim and that's her abuser. Judge just issued a stay-away TOP against him on her behalf."

"Has the gentleman been served with the order of protection? I don't have to tell you, counselor, that it has no effect until served personally on him. I let her go, I've got to let him go. In DV cases either they both get popped or no one does."

"Well, can your men hold him until the clerk serves him with the TOP so he is on notice?"

After a pause, the Captain relented. "Vitale, uncuff her."

"Captain, she scratched me. Look. I'm bleeding."

"Vitale, let her go or you'll be searching outside the courthouse for contraband in the garbage cans and bushes on Sheridan Avenue every morning."

Officer Mama's Boy released Isabel, and she immediately started to swing at him. In two quick strides, Schwartz covered the distance between them. He grabbed her arm and firmly led her toward the bank of elevators. Several court officers surrounded the attacker as he was uncuffed and detained. Behind them, Schwartz could hear Officer Mama's Boy whining about needing an AIDS test and Dolan telling him to "bang in" for the afternoon.

Putting his hands on Isabel's shoulders and holding her at arm's length, he could see that she was shaken but nothing more. If eyes were indeed the windows to the soul, Isabel's venetian blinds were down.

Without averting his gaze, Schwartz said, "By the way, Captain. . . "

"What is it now, Mr. Schwartz?"

"It's a Class 'A' misdemeanor."

"Come again?"

"Obstruction of Governmental Administration. Second Degree P.L. Sec.195.05. Class 'A' misdemeanor. Not a felony."

Dolan struggled to suppress a tirade. While repeatedly pressing the elevator button with one hand and holding Isabel's arm with the other, Schwartz sang, "I love a courthouse brawl, howzabout you?" in the tune of "How About You."

The Yankee Tavern on East 161st Street just down from the Grand Concourse attracted two sets of clientele. During the work week, the courthouse regulars— court officers, court clerks, and lawyers—ruled the roost. Come April and through the inevitable October playoffs for this generation of Yankees, on game nights and days, the YT percolates with pinstripe fever. Yankee fans descend upon the bars that border the outfield wall of the stadium, under the #4 El on River Avenue.

The juxtaposition of River Avenue and the El surround the 314-foot right field porch of the House that Ruth Built (or, as some wags have commented, the Ruth the House Built). Unlike the rooftop viewing posts that overlook Wrigley Field, at the behest of the Evil Empire a portion of the station's platform on the Manhattan-bound side was cordoned off to prevent freeloading gawkers from viewing Yankee games.

There was, indeed, a crime problem surrounding Yankee Stadium before, during, and after games, but it had little to do with the denizens of the neighborhood around the stadium. Public consumption of alcohol and controlled substances, disorderly conduct, assault, public urination, and drunken driving constituted the disorders of game day. In the buildings surrounding the stadium, the locals knew to keep a low profile for quality of life's sake.

Decorated in Honeymooner's Raccoon Lodge motif and awash in Yankee paraphernalia, the YT announced itself as the self-anointed mecca for the followers of arguably the most successful team since the Lions dominated the Christians. Featured on the walls were the requisite signed photos of gods and demigods from yesteryear and faded newspapers clippings of past derring-dos. A beer ad from another era was positioned prominently on the wall behind the bar. It beckoned: "What a combination, all across the nation. Baseball & Ballantine."

Schwartz had chosen to have lunch with Isabel here because it was off the beaten path for the midday family court crew. The tavern was suffused with the smell of sauerkraut and the roar of the jukebox. Perusing the photos that competed with a yuletide garland for wall space, he wondered when a Yankee player had last set foot in this establishment.

The days when Mantle, Martin, Berra, and Skowron resided at the Concourse Plaza Hotel, up 161st across the Grand Concourse, were long gone. After the games, players made a beeline for their Hummers, Range Rovers, Explorers, and Escalades, pointed their vehicles toward New Jersey and Westchester, and quickly departed. The fenced-off players' parking lot ensured that casual contact between players and fans was rare.

As they settled onto red foam cushions atop wooden chairs, resting their hands on the Formica table, Schwartz squinted to see the daily specials chalkboard over the bar.

Mantle Meat Loaf. Rizzuto Stew. Babeburger.

"I hope you like red meat," he quipped.

Isabel stared at him, not comprehending.

Schwartz struggled to interpret.

"Tu le gusta carne roja?"

"Oh si, si. Pero solomente quira un hot dog y Coke."

Now, that's what I call a cheap date.

Schwartz walked up to the bar and ordered two hotdogs with kraut for the lady and a meatloaf for himself. On the side he ordered mashed potatoes, corn, and string beans.

"Does the meatloaf come with bread?"

The bartender eyed Schwartz as if he had asked for his girlfriend's phone number.

"Bread's an extra fifty cents."

"Is butter included?"

"Now you're being a dick."

"No, just spreading the Christmas cheer."

The bartender turned in a huff. Schwartz speculated that he was the owner's nephew, marking time as he waited for his name to rise to the top of some civil servants list.

Schwartz couldn't resist the chance to channel his inner Bobby Darin imitating Groucho Marx.

"Well, you certainly have the service attitude down pat. By the way, how is Pat?"

The barkeep turned and flicked Schwartz the middle finger.

While he waited for the poster child for the hospitality industry to return with the vittles, Schwartz ambled over to the jukebox. A Sinatra version of "Luck Be a Lady Tonight" blared out of the speakers on the wall. Standing in front of the jukebox, peering intently at the CD selection list was a gent in a corduroy sport jacket festooned with dandruff on the shoulders. He was holding a stack of quarters. Schwartz thought he recognized the man as a clerk from the matrimonial part over in Supreme. Schwartz offered a greeting and received a grunt in return. The fellow was eyeing a Sinatra CD, obviously considering future play. Schwartz was in no mood to spend the next thirty minutes of his life eating chuck beef and canned vegetables while listening to Ol' Blue Eyes. Alarmed and armed with his tools of persuasion, Schwartz fired his opening salvo.

"You're up in matrimonial, right?"

The man barely turned his head.

"Uh-huh."

Schwartz's nose registered the man's liquid lunch.

"You grow up in the Bronx?"

The man slowly turned and eyed Schwartz, his lips pursed. Turning back to the jukebox, in monotone, he offered, "Kingsbridge section."

"I'm from the North Bronx, White Plains Road area."

"Do I know you?"

"Now you do."

Schwartz extended his hand and the man took it slowly, a tight smile splitting his chapped lips.

"Yeah, I might have seen you in the clerk's office a couple of times," the man allowed.

"Us Bronx boys of a certain age, we have to stick together. Right, uh . . . ?"

"Rob."

"Yeah. Robbie. Schwartz here. So, you like Sinatra?"

"He's the Chairman of the Board."

"Yeah. Sure. What about Bobby Darin?"

"Ah, he's all right. But Sinatra's my main man."

"Robbie, Darin's a Bronx guy like you and me. If he had lived he would have been—"

"Oh, he died? I didn't know."

While absorbing the man's ignorance on the subject of El Darin, Schwartz decided to try a different tack.

"Robbie, you like baseball?"

"Hey. What do you think? Been a fan all my life. Let's go, Yanks."

"Yeah, go, Yanks. How about that designated hitter rule?"

"Look, I'm an American League fan. But—Schwartz, you said your name was?—Schwartz, I think it stinks. Paying some guy two million dollars a year just to bat every other day. Gimme a break."

Schwartz had his opening.

"Well, the way I see it, Sinatra's like a designated hitter, albeit a great one. He did one thing really, really well: sing saloon songs, torch songs, and standards, whatever you want to call them. Like Jose Canseco can hit home runs. But have you seen that clip of the ball bouncing off Jose's head into the stands for a home run? Or Jose blowing out his arm when asked to pitch? Ugly. Same with Sinatra. Could he do a rock song or Motown? Noooo. I mean, have you heard him cover a Beatles tune? Yeeesh.

"Now, Darin, on the other hand, was a five-tool player. Like the Mick. He could swing a standard or cover a show tune with the best of them, whether it was Dean Martin, Vic Damone, or, dare I say, Mr. Sinatra. He could do jazz riffs or skat àla Mel Tormé. When he sang soul numbers, you would swear it was Ray Charles. His folk song covers, 'If I Were a Carpenter'—prime example—topped the charts. And God knows he could do rock. I mean, he cut his teeth on 'Splish Splash' and 'Dream Lover'—which, by the way, he wrote. Do you know he's in the Songwriters Hall of Fame? Got inducted a couple of years ago. And the Rock and Roll Hall of Fame, too. He also got an Academy Award nomination for best supporting actor, and, man, he could do impersonations. I mean, Sammy Davis could, too, but Darin . . . woo-eee. Sammy, by the way, refused to let Darin open for him because Bobby killed it. I mean, the guy could do it all. Here, let me prove it to you."

Robbie was nonplussed as Schwartz reached for the man's stack of quarters with one hand and pressed the CD flipper with the other. Without missing a beat, Schwartz pressed the buttons for "Lazy River," "Artificial Flowers," "I Got a Woman," "If I Were a Carpenter," and "Beyond the Sea."

"To drive my point home, my final selection will be Sinatra singing 'Mack the Knife,' backed by Quincy Jones's band, in which he pays homage, don't you know, to Bobby Darin, as well as Ella Fitzgerald's version. It's been a pleasure, Robbie."

Schwartz stuffed two dollars in Robbie's hand and stepped to the bar to retrieve his cold Mantle Meat Loaf. He could hear Robbie mutter under his breath, "What a fuckin' nut."

As Schwartz approached the table whistling "Lazy River", lunch platters in hand, he assessed them for any retaliatory sabotage of the expectorant variety. Schwartz's sense of musical victory was tempered when he found Isabel crying. Darin's magic was inexplicably lost on her. Isabel attempted to compose herself as Schwartz rubbed her back and offered a tissue.

"Crumpled but clean."

"*Gracias. Tu sabes, mi* come from *ciudad pequeno, Moca. Cerca de Santiago y San Francisco de Macoris.*"

"I've heard of San Francisco de Macoris. Birthplace of the best shortstops and cocaine dealers in the Western Hemisphere."

"*Si, es verdad.*"

Visions of late Sunday afternoon ballgames in parks very different from the behemoth across the street flitted through Isabel's mind. She remembered eating *mondongo, mofongo, y yuca frita* while sitting in concrete stands as hypnotic strains of a nearby *merengue* band reached her ears.

Isabel stared at Schwartz as if making a mental calculation of whether or not to continue. "*Mi padre . . .*"

"*Isabel, yo se tu conosco mas Ingles.*"

"I embarrass. I no speak bery well."

"So my Spanish is any better? *Su escuche, su use, su apprende. Ahora, digame en Ingles que yo digo en Español.*"

"I hear. I use... I... learn."

"By George, I think she's got it!"

With that Schwartz stood and did a mock flamenco dance àla Henry Higgins.

"Now say, 'In Hartford, Hereford, and Hampshire hurricanes hardly...'"

"Een Har...ford..."

"Just kidding. Just kidding. Tell me about your papa."

Isabel stared at Schwartz, rolled her eyes, and took a bite of her hot dog.

"*Mi Papa,* he old *cuando* I born. *Yo...* I . . . I . . . have three sisters and two bra . . . bra . . . *hermanos* in Dominican Republic. We had big house with, *como se llama* . . . uh... uh... helpers. I *de bebe.* Papa, he call me his '*coqui.*'"

"Cookie?"

"*Americano!* No cookie. Co-keey. Lil' *come se llama* . . .Little . . . *yo no se* . . .is green. *Mi amor.*"

Then she made a guttural sound and laughed despite herself. His testicles twitched at her use of the phrase *mi amor.*

"Co-keey. Little frog. OK, got it."

"*Mira su ojoitos azul. Mi Papi, pardone me* . . . my papa, he had dem *tambien,* de blue eyes."

She paused and sipped her soda. Schwartz's stomach was just beginning to come to terms with Mick's meatloaf.

"Oh, I forget. I no have *su tarjeta* . . . your card. I lose it. *Por favor?*"

Schwartz reached into his wallet, retrieved one of his thousand-for-twenty-five-dollars business cards, and slid it across the table into Isabel's hands.

"Don't lose it. Usually I charge thirty-five cents for the second card."

He forced a laugh, though Isabel stared at him wide-eyed, oblivious to his weak attempt at humor. She glanced at the card briefly and then buried it provocatively down her blouse.

"*Mi papa* die when I was *un joven*. He leave his money to *una* lady. *Una puttana*. We lose de house. De helpers. Momma go to work. She changed. Bery bery bad with us. *Yo especialmente.* 'Cause I da *bebe*. I papa's *coqui.*"

"When did you come here?"

"Eh? Oh, *mi hermana, Zoila, y yo en Nueva York para tres anos.*"

Schwartz searched his briefcase for the neglect petition and reviewed it quickly. "Your girl, Zoraida. She's six."

At the mention of Zoraida's name, Isabel's countenance darkened.

"She stay with my mama . . . behind. She jus' came *el año pasado.*"

"Her last name is different from yours. Soriano. That's the father's name, right? Was that the father who attacked us and beat you?"

"No dat's mi *estupido novio*, boyfriend . . . Hector."

"What's his last name?"

Isabel hesitated and looked down at her food. Schwartz pressed.

"If I'm going to represent you, these are things I have to know."

"Machado. Hector Machado."

"Did you give the name to the ACS caseworker?"

The shrug of her shoulders informed and entertained Schwartz. Watching her breasts jiggle, Schwartz endeavored to ask more questions that would engender the same response.

I am such a horndog.

"And the father—Soriano—where is he?"

"He in Moca. He no coming here. He big businessman. *No tiene tiempo.*"

"Well, doesn't he miss his daughter?"

"*Ay dios mio. Muchas preguntas, Señor. Comiste!*"

Schwartz did groundskeeping with his mashed potatoes. He wondered why he had ordered them. His mother, it seemed, had served them for dinner every friggin' night when he was a child. Back then his strategy was to spread them on his plate in a thin layer, place a napkin on top, and attempt to get past his mother on the way to the kitchen garbage can. And if his subterfuge was discovered . . .

Did she make me kneel on rice in the corner when she caught me? No.

No, indeed. Mother Schwartz came equipped with two far more potent tools in her arsenal: the silent treatment and guilt. No teacher or school guidance counselor could discern the inflicted bruises to the ego and the psyche. That was a job best left for psychiatrists and self-help gurus.

"Que tu haces con su papas, mi amor?"

Isabel had grabbed his wrist as he spread a napkin over his plate and she was laughing at him. Startled, Schwartz looked up from his landscaping efforts. Less than forty-eight hours ago, her child had been taken from her, and here she was, sitting in some dive, sharing a hearty laugh and a dirty-water dog with her court appointed attorney and one-night lover.

Is this resiliency or denial? Is it a coping mechanism or tropical blasé? Is it the real turtle soup or simply the mock?

As he negotiated the bumper-to-bumper traffic on the Major Deegan Expressway while driving Isabel to the Yankee Motor Lodge, Schwartz reflected on the word *Yankee.* He thought he had read about the itiology of the word in the *Times.* Apparently it exemplified the dynamic of ethnic succession that ruled the camping and decamping of immigrant groups in NYC over the past four hundred years. The early Dutch settlers, it was said, would refer to recently arrived Brits as "John Cheese," pronounced "Yan-KEES," meaning "cheeseeater." This was an ethnic epithet the Dutch had hurled at the Brits. And that was at the root of the demonizing phrases of Civil War rebels ("Damn Yankees!"), South American Protestors ("Yanqui Go Home!"), and Boston Red Sox Fans (Yankees Suck!). To date, the New York Cheese Eaters had won twenty-six World Series and thirty-seven American League pennants.

The buffet of pleasure that awaited him at the Lodge most likely did not include cheese, but other delicacies came to mind. Schwartz allowed himself a smile.

Isabel crinkled her nose and narrowed her eyes, an expression Schwartz had found peculiar to Hispanic women. It was meant to signify "What?"

Schwartz shrugged. He began to whistle to the tune of "Oh! Look at Me Now" as he nudged the Saab into a narrow parking spot behind the Lodge.

MotelroomdisinfectanttornstripofpaperacrossthetoiletbowelbrokenTVremotefake woodpanelingemptyplasticicebucketoverachievingairconditioningrustcoloredvelo urlampshadesmustardyellowshagcarpetingstrandsofdyedredhairinmouth"tomeba bytome"nippleinmouthbedspringssqueakingohGodohGodcoming,   COMING, COOOMING!

In the hallway, the housekeeper's vacuum cleaner roared, sucking up the dust of lust.

Can't sleep. Must sleep. Three-and-half hours to sleep . . . before . . . must vacate premisessszzzzzz.

Schwartz awoke to banging on the door, accompanied by a shout. "Time's up!" He was alone. Isabel had left a note. She had called a car service and asked him to call her about her case. The TV was on and the newscaster was reporting that the Florida Supreme Court had ordered a recount of the popular vote in the presidential election.

As Schwartz stumbled to the bathroom, his nose contracted at the overwhelming scent of disinfectant. In the mirror, through half-open slits, he took stock of himself. His beard and mustache were just starting to turn grey, the faint impression of crow's feet was emerging around his eyes, and his once-full head of hair was thinning. As he gargled with and spat out the motel's sorry excuse for water, a TV pitchman babbled about a breakthrough product.

"Yes, men, try Skid-No-More underwear shields and get the brown out—"

CLICK!

Once Schwartz returned to the bathroom mirror, he softly sang, "Oh! Look at me now."

SATURDAY, DECEMBER 9: PARDONAME!

SCHWARTZ WOKE TO THE SOUNDS OF CLIFF ADMONISHING his youngest for peeing in the bed. He slowly unfurled his spine from the crouched confines of the couch and attempted to focus on the windup alarm clock perched on the glass coffee table. Time appeared to stand still until Schwartz realized that the clock had stopped. Panic stricken, he fumbled for his wrist watch, which was ensconced in his shoe somewhere under the foldout. As he reached for his shoes, he lost his balance and fell off the sofabed, landing on what his mother called his *koppe*. Hearing his yelp, Cliff and a young daughter came running into the room.

"Man, put some pajamas on. You gonna fall and shit and show your sideways smile to the world."

Both Cliff and Jahniya where laughing at the spectacle of the upended half-naked barrister in their living room. From the head wedged between bed and coffee table came the desperate yet somewhat muffled plea, "Help... me...up..."

"Nah, man. I think I'm gonna let you stay like that and hang a jockey's lantern around your leg."

"Or . . . I...will...kick...your...black...ass!"

"Not from there you won't."

Cliff pulled the coffee table away from the bed and Schwartz tumbled to the ground. Once sitting up, Schwartz grabbed the back of his neck and asked, "What time is it?"

"Time for you to be moving your white mashed-potato ass outta here! I told you when I got the kids here on weekends, you can't stay. That's all those ACS snoop doggy-dogs need to hear from the mouths of my babes—that I'm shacking up with a half-naked white man."

"Listen to me, my schoolmate tennis buddy: 'Schwartz, can you help me out with a little situation?' 'But what have you done for me lately', friend?"

"What?" Cliff's eyes were bulging.

Schwartz started to crack up. Cliff let loose with a baritone laugh and Jahniya joined in. When the laughter had reached a peak, Schwartz suddenly caught himself.

"Oh, shit. What time is it, really?"

"Almost eight. I was getting ready to make the breakfast special: Cap'n Crunch souffle."

"Oh, man, I've gotta pick up Julie for her soccer game."

Schwartz rushed to the bathroom and filled the sink basin with cold water. He then applied "the Treatment": immersing his head in the chilly contents and holding his breath for as long as his middle-age pot-addled lungs would permit. Emerging, he shouted

"All right. Wooooo! Ready for the World!"

He proceeded to brush his teeth with a squeeze from the tube of Preparation H that Cliff had left on the sink.

Overnight, a late fall snow had covered the city. Schwartz hurriedly wiped the Saab's windows clear of the fluffy down. Turning the key in the ignition yielded an ominous silence. Popping the backward-opening hood open, he saw a vacancy where his battery had once resided. Telltale sneaker imprints ran from the front of his car, down the street, and into an alley between apartment buildings. He considered his options.

After half an hour of frantically zigzagging Cliff's LeSabre through Bronx streets and highways and driving by, through, and around the construction bottlenecks endemic to the city's crumbling infrastructure, Schwartz made it to the Throgs Neck Bridge. Half an hour later, he pulled into the driveway of the marital condominium. The layer of snow muted the crunch of the gravel. He raced to the door and rang the bell. Marjorie answered with her disgusted look firmly in place. Schwartz could see Ethan sitting at the table in the breakfast nook.

"Is Julie ready?"

"Uh, Julie left an hour ago, Superdad. What happened to you?"

"What do you mean? She said she had to be at the gym at nine and that it took an hour to get there."

"Not our gym at nine; the *other team's gym* at nine. They were meeting at eight."

"Are you kidding me? How come you didn't tell me when I said I'd be picking her up?"

"I thought you knew. You made the arrangements with Julie, not me."

There it was for Schwartz, a microcosm of the undoing of their marriage: poor communication, blame game, who's right, who's wrong, and who's sorry now?

"Where's the tournament?"

"Somewhere in Valley Stream. It's probably started already."

Schwartz turned, took a furtive step towards Cliff's loaner, and then stopped and did an about-face.

"Can I come in?"

After a brief moment, Marjorie relented.

"OK. For a bit. But Ethan has karate class at ten."

"Karate?"

"His therapist says it'll build self-esteem and help develop motor skills."

"Therapist?"

"Listen, while you're out finding your soul, I'm here parenting. If you have problems with that, have your lawyer call my lawyer."

"Lawyer? Marj, I don't have a lawyer. I mean, other than me."

"Well, I do. Rufus Blumenthal."

"Blumen—what? He's my friggin' classmate. He can't—"

"Well, he can and he is. You want to contemplate your navel and play Hamlet about us, your choice. Now, do we need to do this in front of Ethan? I'll tell you what: you look a little out of sorts. Why don't you sit down? Have a bowl of oatmeal. And then take Ethan to Karate. That should calm you down."

"Haaaaaaayah!" thirteen little voices yelled, simulating a kata of death.

"Oy veeeeey." Schwartz sighed as he watched his sweet, innocent Ethan led blithely down the dark path of broken bones by some ersatz Olympic champion dojo.

What became of Freeze Tag or Red Light, Green Light 1-2-3, or Red Rover, Red Rover, let Ethan comeover?

"Self-esteem issues," his wife had whispered while slipping Ethan's winter coat on the boy. This was her rationale for yet another enrichment experience for their children.

Their enrichment, my impoverishment.

After class, Schwartz drove his ninja-in-training to Mickey D's for a Happy Meal. The main inducement for Ethan's choice was the toy *du jour* promoting the movie *du jour*. That marketing device was akin to Cracker Jack's promise of a surprise in every box. But it went a manipulative step further by tying it to Disney or DreamWorks' latest mega-opus. Presumably that made Messrs. Eisner and Spielberg happy. The "happy" meal was a misnomer.

"I'm the only guy in the house. Julie gets her way in everything."

At least he's talking to me about it.

"Son, there are times you stand up for yourself and times you stand down and say, 'This too shall pass.'"

The boy stared at his father blankly.

"Daddy, I get up to pee in the morning and Julie throws me out of the baffroom to do her hair."

"That's definitely a stand-up."

"I yell down to Mommy. She says, 'Stop whining,' and then Julie's like, 'Tattletale, tattletale.'"

"Don't go to Mom. Work it out with Julie."

Ethan processed the information.

"Mommy wants me to do my homework first thing after school, but I want to watch Power Rangers."

"That's a stand-down."

"I kinda figured. I was just testing you."

Schwartz reached for his son and threw his arm around his neck.

"Come over here, you. You've just earned a dose of Bronx nooggies. Here's the Fordham Road variety."

In a winding path, Schwartz raked four knuckles over the boy's head.

"And the dreaded Webster Ave noggie with all the potholes."

He gave Ethan a staccato of light taps on the boy's head.

With that, the two shared a laugh and the meal turned miraculously . . . happy.

This kid. This kid.

Placating Julie, however, would present a greater challenge. Schwartz pictured it as he drove Ethan home.

Daddy, how could you? I told all the girls that my dad was taking us.

Schwartz was calculating the amount of mall time it would take to placate Julie as he rang the bell. No answer. He rang again. Nothing.

"Daddy, there's a note in the mailbox. Maybe it's from mommy."

Schwartz looked in the box. In Marjorie's immaculate parochial-school penmanship was written, "Meet me at North Shore ER. Julie got hurt."

He and Ethan jumped back into the Cliffmobile. Schwartz turned on his mental siren and bubblegum lights and raced to the hospital.

One blessing of living in the suburbs is that the triage nurse at the community hospital is not perched behind a bullet proof/sound proof partition. Schwartz hurriedly approached her station with Ethan in tow.

"Julie Schwartz? Do you know where she is?"

Barely looking up from her paperwork, the nurse related, "Examination room five."

Schwartz searched the drawn curtains for some clue as to the room numbers. The definitive pitch of Marjorie's voice, combined with Julie's whine, led him to the proper berth. He parted the curtains slightly and ducked his head inside. There was Julie, writhing in obvious pain, with two women, one with requisite white coat and stethoscope, the other his soon-to-be ex-wife, trying in vain to comfort her daughter.

"Marj—"

"Jesus, it's about time. When are you going to get a cell phone?"

"Marj . . . what the hell happened?"

Marjorie stepped outside the curtain.

"She collided with two girls and fell. She was trying to score a goal. The doctor thinks she blew out her ACL. They're going to take x-ray's and an MRI."

"Oh man. Oh man."

"The insurance card I had expired. Do you have the new card?"

"Oh man. Oh man."

"What? You said you were taking care of it. The Child Plus payment?"

Schwartz collapsed on the chair near the nurse's station. "Shit. Shit. Shit. Between the mortgage, car payment . . . the insurance on the condo—"

"Don't tell me this. You couldn't have let that lapse. Well, go do some fast lawyer talking with the registration desk because my baby's getting treatment."

After fifteen hundred seventy-six dollars' worth of the finest orthopedic care that North Shore Hospital had to offer, it was determined that Julie Schwartz had a severely sprained knee but that no irreparable harm had been sustained—to the knee, anyway. The postpartum relationship between Schwartz and his wife was, of course, another matter. Diagnosis: fractured. Prognosis: don't ask. Invoice: to be determined.

Schwartz pulled off suddenly as he drove up the West Side Highway into the 79th Street Boat Basin. He had taken the 59th Street Bridge from Long Island to avoid the $2.25 toll and traversed Manhattan via the washboard bumpy 57th Street. Schwartz could not understand how a thoroughfare featuring the most expensive real estate in the world could morph into a third-world back road. The

Buick's aging springs rocked and rolled as he maneuvered through the minefield.

Parked in the basin, Schwartz popped a CD into the player lifted the lever to recline the driver's seat, and leaned back. The player was Cliff's latest installation to his pride and joy. He had explained to Schwartz how he'd bought the car for peanuts and gradually restored it to its previous glory. The 1986 model was the first LeSabre to have front-wheel power and it was given a radical aerodynamic design by the Dearborn engineering cabal. The hybrid sound system, however, was a particular point of pleasure and pride for Cliff.

It was midnight. The silver hue encircling the moon forecasted more snow. Schwartz gazed at the waters of the Hudson River and at the high-rises that stood where Palisades Amusement Park once beckoned New Yorkers to forget the humdrum and have some fun. Amusement parks and baseball stadiums going the way of housing developments was an evident phenomenon of urban renewal.

Darin's rendition of "All By Myself", courtesy of the Cliffmobile's CD player, fished out from Schwartz's travel pack of Darin CD's, provided background for these reflections. Schwartz searched his wallet for the remains of a joint a client had given him in lieu of cash. Once he located the flattened doobie, he pressed the cigarette lighter. As he waited for it to pop out, he swayed and sang along to the music.

Schwartz lit up and took a hit. He exhaled. The first molecules of THC began the drip-drip-drip into his brain.

I'm sure Darin played Palisades Park.

Schwartz dozed off to the ticktock of the vagina clock. The blurred image of Violetta Pichardo appeared to him on the front of a quarter. Zoraida Soriano's face appeared on the next quarter. The two quarters rested on top of a pile of quarters. Each remaining quarter bore the visage of a litigant, a lawyer, or a louse that Schwartz had encountered in his years in family court. The pile of quarters rotated on a metal turntable.

A metal arm suddenly wept across the turntable, knocking several of the coins off the side and into the turgid charcoal waters of the Hudson. Schwartz was placing coins in a slot, feeding the turntable. He realized in horror that the last two quarters to hit the turntable bore the images of Julie and Ethan. Quarters were sliding off to a separate loud, rapping beat. As the quarters bearing his children's faces inched perilously close to the edge, arriving just under the sway of the metal arm, the rapping sound grew louder. Bright sunlight began to obscure his vision.

Schwartz's body convulsed as his eyes split open. Schwartz was staring into a flashlight. There was a policeman rapping his baton against the window. As he struggled to orient himself, he understood that the officer was motioning for him to roll down the window.

"Uh. . .yes, Officer?"

"Sir, you have chosen a high-crime area for nappy time. Might I suggest you retire to your abode?"

"Sounds like a plan, Officer. That is, if I had an abode."

The officer hovered at the window.

"Can I see your license, registration, and insurance information?"

Schwartz opened the glove compartment and searched in vain for the documents.

"The car belongs to my friend, and I don't see anything. Here's my license."

Schwartz reached into his pocket and pulled out his wallet. He opened it to reveal his driver's license in the wallet's window. In the opposite window, his NYC Corrections attorney photo ID was visible.

"I see you're a member of the bar."

Schwartz grunted in the affirmative.

The officer grabbed the wallet from his hand and inspected it.

"Then perhaps, Counselor, you can explain the smell of cannabis exuding from this vehicle and the presence of what is commonly referred to as a 'roach' in your wallet."

Schwartz chose to exercise his right to remain silent. Then came the words that warm the cockles of all motorists' hearts: "Step out of the vehicle, sir."

For the first time in his life, Schwartz heard and then felt the cold metal snap of handcuffs on his wrists.

"What am I being charged with? Sleeping while under the influence? Come on, you can't be that low on your monthly quota."

He was placed in the rear of the officer's RMP. The officer called on the radio for a tow truck to pick up Cliff's car. The Cliffmobile's destination was the NYPD impound lot in Whitestone. Schwartz's was Manhattan Central Booking.

SUNDAY, DECEMBER 10, 4:40 A.M.: MEA CULPA

"YOU DID WHAT? YOU'RE WHERE? MY CAR IS WHAT?!"

Cliff's roar streamed through the receiver of the pay phone at MCB. Schwartz had just been processed, and his fingerprints and mug shots were making their debut in the States' crime database. He was issued a desk appearance ticket for misdemeanor marijuana possession with a return date sometime in the new millennium. The Buick had been transported to the Whitestone Police Impound for civil forfeiture as an instrumentality in a drug-related crime.

"Listen, Cliff, I'll make a motion. We'll get your car back. Right now I need you to buy my battery back from whatever junkie stole it, put it in my Saab, and come get me."

"No, you listen. No one is selling batteries on the streets of the Bronx this Sunday morning. Break out your wallet and spring for a subway token and get your ass up here so I can kick it!"

SLAMMMMM!

Schwartz boarded the #4 at Brooklyn Bridge Station. He was beyond exhaustion, progressing toward comatose, yet his eyes stayed open. He spied an abandoned newspaper on the floor of the train: "**U.S. Supreme Court Stays Florida Recount.**"

Schwartz rang the bell to Cliff's apartment. Cliff opened the door without a word and motioned for Schwartz to sit on the crushed velour foldout couch.

"Can I see your keys?" he asked calmly.

Schwartz hesitantly lifted the key ring out of his pocket and tossed it on the coffee table. Cliff lifted the ring and inspected the array. He removed one key and lobbed the ring back on the table.

"You'll get this back when I get my car released. In the meantime, you ride with me in the morning. And I don't get to court at no lawyer times. I have to clock in with the Captain at nine. You look like shit and don't smell any better. Grab a shower and get some beddy-bye time."

DECEMBER 11:
INTAKE

"I OWE, I OWE, IT'S OFF TO WORK I GO!" SCHWARTZ SANG AS HE rode with Cliff to court Monday morning.

"And I don't need any of your sorry-ass serenades, neither. Damn, when was the last time you had this vehicle tuned up? It's farting more than my Uncle Willie after Thanksgiving dinner."

"Just be careful with my ride. Watch that lady with the baby carriage."

"Man, this is the Grand Concourse. Mamas push those carriages out first just to get you to slow down. They need to step back. Play chicken with me, huh."

Cliff arrived in the left-hand turn bay at the light at 165th Street. A souped-up SUV, with sound system woofing and bassing at full tilt, pulled up next to the Saab. Schwartz turned his head, seeking to steal a quick glance at the occupants. Having sensed Schwartz's inquiring eyes, the driver's head turned toward him. Schwartz furtively turned his head forward. He knew that looking people in the eyes invited trouble. It had been that way since the days of communal caves, when stares into a neighbor's family fire invited confrontation.

Cliff made the left onto 165th Street and turned the Saab onto Sherman Avenue between 164th and 163rd, a block from the courthouse. He pulled close to a curb and cut the wheel toward a gate. Securing the gate was, perhaps, the largest freestanding lock in the Western Hemisphere. After grunting and groaning for a minute, Cliff managed to twist open the lock with his key.

"They need to oil that baby."

Cliff pulled the Saab into an area that was approximately thirty by one hundred feet. It was half parking lot, half barnyard. Schwartz spotted a menagerie consisting of several ducks and chickens, a couple of chained dogs, a pigeon coop, and a pig. The cars in the area ran the gamut from Lexus, BMW, and Camry to rusted-out wrecks. As Schwartz opened the passenger door to step out, a tall Hispanic man emerged from the coop.

"*Mira*, Cliff! Close the gate before El Diablo gets out."

"Oh, damn! Sorry, Papo."

Cliff ran to the gate but was too late. In a blur of white, a rooster pranced onto the sidewalk and began jumping up and down, chasing two women on the sidewalk into the street. The pair responded with shrieks and curses in some dialect Schwartz had never heard. Cliff was trying to mollify the women and cajole the bird into returning. "Don't make me shoot you, you cock-a-doodle motherfucker."

Papo slipped around Cliff and grabbed El Diablo by the neck. Closing the gate behind him, he walked over to Schwartz. With the irate rooster in one hand, he extended his free hand. "El Diablo, he no like women. *Mi* name is Papo Cuenca. *Cómo estás?*"

"Uh, fine."

Papo threw the rooster in the air towards the yard. It landed while flapping its wings and emitting a shrill protest. Cliff returned to the Saab. "That's Schwartz, my live-in lover. How do you lock the car?"

"Stop pressing the doorknobs. Just use the key; it'll lock them all."

"Hey, pretty advanced for an '86."

"It also has lights that shut off automatically. All in all, it's pretty much idiot-proof."

Cliff covered his mouth with a balled up fist and coughed sarcastically.

"Don't know about that."

Papo walked around to the hood and knocked on it for emphasis. "And, *mira,* it has that backward engine. I think you step on the gas and go backwards."

The men laughed. Schwartz regarded Papo. His skin was the olive shade classified as "trigueno" in the Hispanic racial phylum. His jet-black hair and thick mustache matched the color of his eyes. Schwartz guessed his age at forty-plus.

Papo returned the gaze.

"You a lawyer?"

"I guess a white guy with a suit and a briefcase a block from a courthouse is a tell."

"Maybe you can help with some problem I have with my son. He's on SSI and—"

"Yo, Papo, I'm sure Mr. Schwartz would love to stay and chitchat and hand out free legal advice, but I've got to check in, so I'm ghost. You coming, lover?"

Cliff pursed his lips together and winked seductively.

Schwartz read Papo's revulsion immediately and did his best gay affectation.

"Oh, that Cliffie. He's such a kidder. Anyway, Papo, nice to meet you. We'll talk about your boy some other time. But gotta go. Justice calls."

Schwartz hoped that Papo got the joke. But El Diablo reinforced any doubts Papo may have had regarding Schwartz's gender identity. Just as Schwartz reached for the gate, the bird entered his peripheral vision. El Diablo had his talons extended in castration mode. The startled barrister swung his briefcase and nailed the bird mid-flight.

Papo cheered the move and enjoyed a hearty laugh at El Diablo's expense.

"Señor Schwartz, you *abogado o matador?*"

Catching his breath and safely on the other side of the closed gate, Schwartz answered, "Sometimes a bit of both, Papo. Sometimes a bit of both."

Family Court nourishes like a great blue whale, scooping up the borough's dysfunction in its baleen. Being a Monday, the feeding grounds were well stocked with violated visitation orders and early Sunday morning domestic disputes. There were young mothers who had left their very young children unattended for the weekend in shelters and juveniles who were captured during Saturday night joyrides in stolen cars.

Schwartz was on Intake, meaning every case that put the "dis," "funk," and "shun" into *dysfunction* would be his cross to bear.

Monday, Monday, ready or not, here I come.

Schwartz had already picked up four cases that morning when Cynthia Yellin, special court attorney/referee, bushwhacked him outside the 18-B room. He tried to duck behind a door before Yellin could reach him. Referees handled the custody and visitation cases on the lowest end of the family court food chain. Referee Yellin's part was particularly problematic, since she was palpably bipolar. Her mood swings had earned her the sobriquet "Yellin' Yellin." She was more than capable of savaging a grandmother seeking visitation with a grandchild and then, turning on a dime, offering a tissue and a piece of chocolate to the crying elderly litigant. Woe to the father who sought a change of custody in reflexive response to a mother's demand for increased child support. As her voice boomed, litigants sensed the walls of the already tight quarters start to close in on them. Schwartz referenced Phil Spector's Wall of Sound and would refer to her part as "Studio A."

On that day Yellin' Yellin's mission was to secure a law guardian for a five year-old child in a custody case. Apparently, her court officer had failed miserably in scouring the courthouse for assigned counsel. Once the prospect learned which part was seeking the attorney, the officer and the petition in his sweaty hand were regarded as leperous. Since Schwartz was on intake, he couldn't exercise the most important right possessed by 18-Bs on non-intake days: the right of declination.

Having cornered her prey, Yellin' Yellin thrust the copy of the petition papers into Schwartz's hands.

"Schwartz, you've been ducking my part all morning. I have a case in front of my bench that I need you on right now."

"I didn't know refs had benches, Cyn. Only coaches had 'em, I thought."

"Don't crack wise with me, Schwartz. I didn't like your style when I was on the panel with you. And I like it even less now. But you're on intake and I have a little boy who needs a law guardian very badly. Now cut the crap and let's go."

Yellin stepped between two court officers who were attempting to hand Schwartz petitions for cases that required assigned counsel. Realizing they'd been aced, they called out their part numbers to Schwartz.

"Part 4 when you're done. Got a mother on a PINS case."

"Judge has a prisoner in the back for arraignment on an "N" in part 7. Corrections believes he has TB and wants him out of here."

Schwartz followed Yellin into the windowless cubicle that passed for her hearing room. Schwartz was perpetually amazed that the ref's chair and table, the clerk's table with computer terminal, the court officer's table, and the table for the litigants and attorneys actually fit into that box. The computer terminal with its Medusa head of wires and cables presented a particular logistical barrier to visual due process. If Yellin wanted to make eye contact with the litigants and counsel, she would have to crane her neck to peer around the terminal. That created more incentive for Yellin to raise her voice.

Since Schwartz was to be the law guardian, he would sit in the vacant chair on the extreme right of the referee. Already seated in the petitioner's chair was a rotund white man with a full head of black hair laced with grey streaks. A slight woman with bleached blond hair and black roots sat in the respondent's chair. Though it was early winter, she wore a blouse with a plunging view of her back. Between the petitioner and the respondent sat Gwendolyn Benoit as counsel for one of the litigants. Ms. Benoit, a veteran panel member, was a feisty litigator. She developed her confrontational bones when she worked as a civil rights lawyer in the Deep South during the early '60s. Though her spirit remained strong, her eyesight had deteriorated to the point that she was legally blind. She required the assistance of a seeing-eye dog. The dog had managed to curl into some space at her feet.

Yellin wriggled into her seat as Schwartz tiptoed through the crevices behind the chairs, stepped over the golden retriever, and sat down. Behind her computer screen, Yellin disappeared from his view.

"All right, Mr. and Mrs. Abbatiello, I'm assigning Mr. Schwartz to be your son Paul's law guardian—his attorney. He's going to speak to the child and report back to this court concerning the father's request for visitation. I'm going to adjourn this case for that purpose. In the meantime, the order of protection on behalf of the mother will remain in effect and the previous order of visitation is suspended."

The father boomed, "But, Your Honor, you mean because of the lies she told about me I can't see my son? That's not fair. My boy loves me. He misses me."

The woman was tugging on her lawyer's sleeve and whispering in her ear from the moment the father began speaking. Ms. Benoit cautioned her to remain silent so she could follow the man's diatribe. The counselor then stood.

"Your Honor knows full well why this order was suspended. The inappropriate behavior of the father during visitation is deleterious to the mental health of the child."

"Dela-what? Come on, Your Honor. How come she has an attorney and I don't?"

"You can hire an attorney, Mr. Abbatiello," the referee retorted.

"But I don't have the money for one. My business went bankrupt because of all the lies she told about me, getting me arrested, wasting my time in court."

The mother couldn't restrain herself.

"You don't have money for a lawyer or for your son to have a decent suit of clothes but you can go out all night with your floozies."

Yellin's soprano echoed like a banshee's about the room.

"That'll be enough, Madam! You have an attorney to speak for you. Sir, I've already determined that you don't qualify for assigned counsel. Now, let's pick an adjourned date."

Schwartz fidgeted in his chair. His gaze was fixed on the mother's mole-speckled back. *There was a moment in time when this man caressed those moles . . . planted little kisses on them from the small of her back to the nape of her neck.*

His gaze then shifted to this caricature of a father.

Am I going to be sitting in that chair soon?

From behind the configuration of computer wires, Schwartz suggested, "Couldn't the referee order visitation at a supervised program and order a report on the nature of the interaction between father and child?"

"Certainly, Mr. Schwartz, if you could find such a program. They all have long wait lists, but if that's the law guardian's position, taken without first speaking to the child, I'll order it."

Recoiling from the referee's booming voice, Schwartz responded, "Madam Referee, you can order that I arrange for the program conditioned upon my interview of the child. That way we can have it in place by the next adjourned date, providing I believe it's in the child's best interests."

Benoit, who had remained standing during this exchange, raised her voice in opposition. "Your Honor, I must object. I'm asking that psychological forensics be ordered before there's any further contact between the father and the boy. The father fills his head with nonsense and manipulates the boy against the mother. When he returns from visits, the boy's out of control. His schoolwork is suffering. His therapist recommends against further contact."

It was a shrewd, yet cynical, ploy by Benoit to request forensics as a precondition to visitation. The process of finding a psychological evaluator, arranging the appointments, and preparing the forensic reports could take months.

Schwartz stood at the table so he could make eye contact with Yellin.

"If there's anything inappropriate done or said by the father during any of the visits, the supervisor has the authority to terminate that visit, and then the matter can be advanced for further proceedings."

Yellin hesitated and then spoke.

"All right, Mr. Schwartz, I'll grant your application, but I want you to interview the child by next week. How's January 25th for the adjourned date?"

Amazingly, everyone murmured his or her assent. Abbatiello was effusive.

"Oh, thank you, Madam! Thank you, uh, Mr. Schwartz. I get to see my boy. I get to see my boy!"

Outside the referee's part, Schwartz detected a twinkle in Benoit's eye behind the thick glasses she wore as she reproached him in front of the mother.

"I hope you know what you're doing. Here's my client's number. Call her to set up an appointment to see the child."

"Give her my card. Tell her to call me. And, of course, Gwen, I won't discuss the merits of the case with her."

Benoit leaned forward and whispered in Schwartz's ear, "Schwartz, just do your best to tune her out. I can't stop her from yakking. She's a pain in the ass. But the father? Hoo-boy."

She made the universal crazy sign of twirling a finger near her head.

Now Schwartz knew why Yellin couldn't get anyone for the case. The case jacket on the referee's desk was tattered and swollen with petitions, documents, and reports. The docket number, dating back to 1996, attested to fact that the case had been kicking around the courthouse since Paul Abbatiello was an infant.

Schwartz felt a thud on his back. He turned to see Alphonso Abbatiello towering over him.

"I appreciate what you did in there. These cunts have been trying to run me out of this building for years. But I'm not having it. Can I have your card?"

Schwartz reluctantly searched his wallet for a card. It seemed like a bad idea to give a card with his home office address to this desperate man.

"I'm out of cards at the moment. Give me your paper with the adjourned date. I'll write my office phone number on it. And if you hire an attorney, tell him to call me."

"Why do I need an attorney? I've got you."

"No, no, you don't understand. I don't represent you. I represent your son."

"Sure, sure. I know that. But you're gonna do the right thing by my boy and me. I know it."

As Schwartz's mother would say, *Oy vey ist mir.*

"Have a good day, Mr. Abbatiello. Once I talk to the boy and find a program, I'll call you."

"How long is it going to take for you to find a program?"

"Look, there are long wait lists. Could take a couple of weeks, maybe longer."

"Well, that's no good. I'm not gonna get to see him for Christmas. I got all these gifts for him. I have a great big stuffed lion. He loves lions. When I take him to the zoo, those are his favorites."

"Mr. Abbatiello, I will do the best I can. Just be patient."

"Patient? I haven't seen my boy in over a month. Those cunts suspended my visitation before I even got to court."

"Patience."

Schwartz shook the man's hand, sighed, and turned back toward intake.

The intake part court officer handed Schwartz a copy of a termination of parental rights petition inside the courtroom and nodded in the direction of a bespectacled small man in a grey suit. Schwartz had observed the gentleman sitting silently in the back of the courtroom. Once the petition was in Schwartz's hands, the man rose and approached him. Schwartz glanced at the title page:

FAMILY COURT OF THE STATE OF NEW YORK
COUNTY OF THE BRONX

--X

In the Matter of the Application of
ST. PATRICK'S SERVICES FOR CHILDREN

for the Custody and Guardianship of
HENRY MORRISEY,
A Child under 18 Years of Age,
Pursuant to Section 384-b
of the Social Services Law,

HELEN MORRISEY,
Respondent.

------------------------------------X

"Mr. Schwartz, shall we step outside the courtroom?"

Schwartz acquiesced. He detected the lilt of Ivy League in the man's voice. As he stepped through the door of the well leading to the waiting room, Schwartz flipped the petition to the blueback and read the name of his new adversary. The name registered in his mind just as the din of the waiting room crashed about his ears: Franz Kafka, Esq.

Schwartz tightened his bottom lip and nodded ever so slightly.

"Let's step into the hallway so we can chat, shall we?"

Schwartz followed him into the hallway just beyond the arc of the entrance door while looking askance for Captain Dolan.

"Good. I'm Frank Kafka. Mr. Schwartz, may I have one of your cards? I'd like to send you the case notes and other discovery on this case."

Schwartz rummaged through his dilapidated wallet for a business card that didn't have a handwritten notation on the back. Unsuccessful in his hunt, he picked out a card with a stale notation, crossed it out and handed it over.

"Thank you. Now, before I introduce you to your client, so that you may—"

"Kafka? Franz Kafka?"

"All right, then. Let's get that out of the way. It's my name and albatross. My grandfather was a distant cousin of the author's, which makes me more distant still, so if you don't mind I'd rather not—"

"This is so weird. Your father must have had a perverse sense of humor."

"I'll ask you to withhold your psychological insights for the moment. I need to explain something about your new client and her child. Helen Morrisey is presently a resident of Creedmoor Psychiatric Center with a diagnosis of acute schizophrenia. She checks in and out of the hospital regularly depending on how compliant she is with her meds. She simply cannot care for her year and a half-old child due to her mental illness. Ergo, the foster care agency is seeking to terminate her parental rights."

"Mr. Kafka, I could have read all that in your petition. Why did you call me out here?"

The man took a step closer to Schwartz. Through the glasses, Schwartz could see a yellow hue surrounding the man's dull-green eyes.

"Bear with me, Mr. Schwartz. I know it's intake and it's quite hectic for you. Miss Morrisey was prescribed Cogentin and Haldol while she was pregnant. Her psychiatrist at the Creedmoor outpatient clinic was unaware of the pregnancy until the third trimester; otherwise, he would have discontinued the meds. As a result, the child was born with severe defects, cannot breathe properly, and at best has six months to live."

Schwartz took a moment to swallow the implications.

"The mother visits the child?"

"Once a week, like clockwork."

"Holds the child and bonds with him?"

"In a manner, yes."

"Then kindly explain why she must spend the last six months of the child's life fighting for her rights as a mother? I mean, it will take four months for the Mental Health Services to evaluate her and report to the court prior to hearing. Even if we could finish a mental illness termination case at the breakneck speed of six months and you prevail, you still have to file the adoption petition, which will take another eight months to be approved. Besides, who is your adoptive resource? Who's going to adopt a child with less than six months to live? This whole case will be moot."

"Precisely."

"Precisely?"

"Yes. You see, my client, the agency, has no choice but to proceed expeditiously on the termination case because the child has been in foster care for fifteen of the past twenty-two months. If they fail to move for adoption, then they lose federal funding for the placement under the Adoption and Safe Families Act. Yet the mother will ultimately be spared the legal termination of her rights."

"Because the child will be biologically terminated."

"Yes, to put a point on it, Mr. Schwartz."

"St. Patrick's Services for Children, is it?"

"Yes."

"Didn't St. Patrick drive all the snakes out of Ireland?"

"That's the legend, yes."

"Well, it seems that he drove some them over to this side of the Pond."

"That's uncalled for, Sir."

"No, it's entirely called for."

As the small yellow-and-green-eyed man in the grey suit turned and opened the door from the corridor, Schwartz called out to him.

"Mr. Kafka, wait!"

"Yes?"

"But you didn't have to become an attorney."

"Your point being?"

"Point being, becoming an attorney made you, well, Kafka...Esq."

Schwartz called, "Helen Morrisey!" into the crowded waiting room. A woman in her late thirties, per the petition, who could have easily passed for late fifties, tentatively rose, then sat, and then slowly rose again. It reminded Schwartz of the behavior of the contestants on the TV game show *To Tell the Truth* at the moment of denouement.

"Are you Helen Morrisey?"

The woman sitting next to her, a hospital escort, nodded affirmatively toward her ward. Schwartz introduced himself as Ms. Morrisey's court-appointed attorney. Ms. Morrisey was underwhelmed.

"Madam, we're just going to find a room where we can talk. Please follow me."

Schwartz walked the perimeter of the waiting room, searching for an available interview room. Ms. Morrisey shuffled behind him. They passed a maintenance man banging on an office door. Beside the worker was a shopping cart loaded with fluorescent tubes in boxes. The short, stocky man yelled with his Nuyorican accent, "Liiiiights! If you don open de door, you get no liiiiiights."

He repeated his mantra as Schwartz continued his quest for a room.

"Liiiiiights! If you don open de door, you get no liiiiiights."

Schwartz spied an open door to an interview room and made a dash for it. A husky teenage black girl wearing a red sweatshirt and tan pants was vacating the room. Her arms were manacled to a wide leather belt wrapped around her waist, and her legs were in chains that were also connected to the belt. Two men escorted her out of the room. From their uniforms, Schwartz recognized them as transporters from the innocuously named the New York State Office of Children and Family Services. OCFS managed the facilities colloquially known as juvie hall. Youths found to have violated the Penal Law were placed there after conviction if they did not qualify for probation. As Schwartz waited for the solemn procession of prisoner and guards to pass, he avoided eye contact with the former. Erasing the spectacle of a teenager in chains from his consciousness was a mental exercise critical to daily functioning in the emergency room law ward that was BxFC.

Schwartz beckoned Ms. Morrisey to a chair and sat behind the table. She initiated the interview, calmly relating that she had become pregnant when she was raped. After an awkward moment passed, Schwartz pressed on. He began to explain the implications of a termination of parental rights case. In so doing, he hoped to assess whether the mother adequately understood the nature of the proceedings. If not, he would ask for the court to assign a guardian *ad litem*, ostensibly to protect her legal rights. The GAL's role would be to assist the lawyer in communicating with the client and to discern the client's position vis-à-vis the litigation. Thus, if the ward/client were to become incapacitated or unable or unwilling to attend future proceedings, the GAL assignment would provide the court with a legal straw man who would stand in for the ward/client so rights could be terminated.

There was no sugar-coating it. Schwartz explained that the goal of the termination proceeding was adoption of Helen Morrisey's terminally ill child. Upon hearing the message, the client responded by decompensating in the interview room. The woman's mumbling gave way to cursing and shouting.

The escort from Creedmoor entered the interview room and wrestled with the distraught woman, trying to insert a needle in her arm. Two court officers entered the small room to help. To Schwartz, the woman's reaction to the news that the agency planned to end her parental rights to her ill-fated child was perfectly sane. He was gripped by the irony that her compliance with the medication regimen meant to control her illness was, in fact, what had led to Baby Henry's terminal illness. Ms. Morrisey succumbed to the sway of the drugs and began to nod off.

Schwartz beelined to the nearest bathroom to relieve himself. He wondered about the slight burning sensation at the tip of his little man. Shaking off the last drops of caustic urine, he reprimanded himself for the high salt content of his recent post-separation diet.

THE POST-INTAKE EVENING

"I AM NOT GOING TO REPRESENT YOU AGAINST DONA MARGARITA."
Don Edgardo wheezed between puffs on the cigarette perched on his lip.

"Her name is Marjorie, and I need your help. This is no time for you to turn chivalrous on me, goddamn it! Why won't you represent me?"

The question glided like a twenty-five-cent balsa-wood airplane, circled in the air, and came to rest on Don Edgardo's furrowed brow. Now it was Schwartz's ass squirming in the client's chair while Don Edgardo sat stroking his mustache and running his fingers through his thick salt and pepper hair.

Schwartz had muddled through the afternoon and early evening of intake. Rounding out the balance of his day, he had picked up three more delinquency petitions, a mother/petitioner on a person in need of supervision case, and a father on a neglect petition who allegedly knew or should have known that the pregnant mother was using drugs. He had taken the liberty of Xeroxing his card on a friendly clerk's copying machine and cutting the photocopies with a scissor.

With his larder full of new cases, Schwartz had passed Don Edgardo's office and spotted his friend sitting at the receptionist's desk in the front room. Don Edgardo was waiting he said for a client to surface "at any moment." The client was coming from Central Booking for arraignment in night criminal court, and that moment might not occur for another four hours, if at all that night.

Schwartz repeated his question. "Why won't you represent me?"

Don Edgardo finally responded. "You know there are two classes of people that cross the street: those who've been hit by cars and those who haven't."

"You're speaking in riddles."

"Experience is a great teacher."

"Now it's platitudes."

Don Edgardo stood up from his chair, walked around the desk and leaned against the edge, hovering over Schwartz. He gathered his thoughts, debating whether or not to continue speaking. In a booming voice that startled Schwartz, he began.

"Will you permit a war story, then? I beg your indulgence while I bare my soul, my matrimonially challenged friend. Experience is a cruel but effective teacher."

The tone of his voice modulated to reflective.

"Many moons ago, when my law practice was in its infancy, there was a couple that my wife—whose first name escapes me at the moment—and I were most friendly with. We shared a ski house in Vermont for a couple of seasons. Our kids played with their kids. We'd go to the movies together, eat out . . . get the picture?

"Turns out their marriage soured, primarily because hubby—we'll call him Kevin—the names have been changed to protect the guilty—was finding love in the arms of one of his graduate students. Though wifey, whom we'll call Karen, felt wronged, for the sake of the children, their sanity, and their wallet, they sought a quick and non-acrimonious end to the marriage. Both wifey and hubby approached me, as a friend, with the proposition. They wanted me to draft a separation agreement setting forth their respective rights and obligations. As a friend, I tried to accommodate them. After the first session, I saw that it was futile. Karen's demands were tainted with her venom toward Kevin for his infidelity. Afterwards, I advised Kevin of my assessment. He concurred and asked me to represent him solely. I said yes. BIG mistake. Biiiiig Mistake."

He paused, walked back around the desk, snuffed out his cigarette on an ash tray. And sat back down.

"Two years and Karen's three lawyers later, no accord had been reached. Just when it seemed we were close, Karen would up her demands or fire her lawyer. It was apparent that she had no intention of ever reaching a separation agreement that would lead to the dissolution of the marriage. In the meantime, Kevin and his new love became friendly with both my wife and me. We even shared a summerhouse on Fire Island together. The only proviso was that Kevin's case could not be a subject of conversation. After yet another round of fruitless negotiations, Kevin informed me that he wanted to go in a different direction. So we parted professional company. We lost touch as friends as well.

Edgardo reached over and fumbled for a cigarette from his pack and searched for a lighter. He held both in his hand without lighting. He tapped the cigarette against his head two times and continued.

"Several years later, I was walking along the Concourse and I thought I saw Karen walking toward me. Our paths hadn't crossed in all these years. As she approached me, the pall of recognition descended upon her face—a dark cloud, indeed. We were only a few feet away when I began my awkward greeting—'Hi, Kar—' when she reared back, gathered her saliva, and nailed me in the face with a glob. As I wiped it away, I realized I deserved it. BIG time.

"So thank you, but no thank you, Mr. Schwartz. Once in a lifetime is enough to get spit in the face on the Grand Concourse. Besides—or maybe because—matrimonial is not my thing. Hire a divorce attorney. How about your classmate, whazizname?"

"Blumenthal?"

"Yeah, Blumenthal. He's a real bomber from what I hear."

Schwartz gritted his teeth.

"Because, you pompous a-hole, he's representing Dona Margarita."

"Oh. I see. I guess he hasn't learned my lesson. Well, there are other lawyers in this fair city."

Schwartz sang the refrain of the camp song, "And with what shall I pay them, dear Henry, dear Henry? With what shall I pay them, dear Henry, with what?"

"I see. Well, then get the least expensive lawyer you can rely on. One who'll do his damnedest on your behalf."

"And just who might that be?"

Don Edgardo stared at his friend. Schwartz stared back, clueless.

"You, you whining idiot. You! Represent yourself. At least in the initial stages. Do what you do best. Be a schnorrer. Cut corners. Bug your colleagues for free advice. Drive Blumenthal mad with incompetence and irresponsibility. Do a Lieutenant Columbo on him. And when he least expects it. *Whapada!*"

"Whapada?"

"Yeah, you know. The sucker punch. The *coup de grâce.*"

"What have you been smoking, and can I please have some?"

"Stop pussyfooting. What's his number?"

Don Edgardo searched amonst the files and books on his desk.

"I got the Lawyer's Diary right here. "

Edgardo reached for the phone as he peered at the red tome through his half-lensed reading glasses. He waved aside Schwartz's nonverbal protests as he dialed and then handed the phone ceremoniously to Schwartz and whispered *"Carpe diem."*

Schwartz stuttered into the receiver.

"Uh, is Mr. Blumenthal there? I will hold. Yes. . .Rufus, Schwartz here . . . from law school. I know. I heard. Uh-huh. Well, you're talking to him. I know. I know, Rufus. But I was a fool to get married, so my client is already a fool."

Schwartz grimaced at his self-deprecating joke.

"What? Sure, I play a little. Tomorrow morning. The tennis center in Riverdale. 6:00 a.m. Uh-huh. Why not? OK, see you, Rufus. I'll find it."

Edgardo raised his eyebrows, shrugged, and turned his palms up.

"I'm playing tennis with him tomorrow morning. His regular partner just canceled on him. We'll talk about the case between sets."

"That's good. Be sure to let him win. Give him false sense of security."

"Oh, that won't be hard. He was an NCAA regional champion in college. He never let us forget it in law school."

"Then my only advice is to lose with honor and grace."

"Feels less than *carpe diem* and more like *carpe* Dien Bien Phu."

At the entrance to the three-family house where Isabel lived, Schwartz came upon a rusted-out buzzer box. None of the pieces of adhesive tape affixed to the slots beside the buzzers bore the name "Mojica." Schwartz wondered about the ethnic succession that played out on those slots over the fifty-plus years of the house's existence. He looked up to double-check the address, certain it was the same home where, just over a month ago, he had enjoyed a rendezvous with Isabel.

Using his highly attuned legal mind, he deduced that since Isabel occupied the ground floor, the bottom buzzer would be hers. He pressed it and was gratified to hear a ring inside the downstairs apartment. The gratitude, however, devolved into consternation as repeated rings yielded no response. During the game of telephone tag between Schwartz and his erstwhile client/lover played at various points over the weekend, the appointment had been set for 7:00 p.m. He would leave messages on her cell, she would respond on his new answering machine tethered to Cliff's home number. He would attempt to confirm by calling her home phone. They'd never actually spoken.

So there he stood, his heels cooled by a mid-December zephyr. There were lights on in the apartment. He opted to seek out the most elusive item in the Bronx: a working public pay phone. Since he had already dismissed the livery cab driver who had delivered him to the Soundview section that evening, he began his search on foot.

Despite the darkness and the chill, the streets teemed with activity. Young people of all ages raced around the streets on bicycles, rollerblades, scooters, and skateboards. Basketball was being played on sidewalk courts. Touch football games flourished on the narrow black asphalt ribbons of urban gridiron. Windows and porches trimmed with Christmas lights competed for Schwartz's attention. Dangling icicle lights fluttered in the breeze. Blue, red, and green chaser lights zipped around and around houses. Laughter, cursing, and shouts could be heard on the streets and sidewalks and through open doorways and closed windows. And music—an amalgam of seasonal, Latin, and hip-hop— reached Schwartz's ears from multiple sources. Schwartz was struck by the contrast to the quiet sterility of the suburban neighborhood he had recently departed and the similarity to the Bronx neighborhood he grew up in forty years ago.

There is life here. These children will grow up convinced they had a great childhood and bitch and moan about how the neighborhood has gone downhill. They'll pine for the good old days while the people they're bitching and moaning about will be living their lives, getting along as best as they can in a new world and changing that new world and making it their own.

Schwartz was moved to song, but it wasn't Darin's that came to mind. Rather, it was an Old Left classic, "The House I Live In" popularized by none other then Ol' Blue Eyes in the early stages of his career. Schwartz remembered hearing the song's composer, Earl Robinson, perform it at a worker's colony called Goldens Bridge in Northern Westchester, where his parents had rented a summer home.

As he tried to cross an intersection, a van making a right turn cut him off. Stepping back to save his foot, he recognized the vehicle as the one and only Luv Van. With Isabel in the front passenger seat, the driver was the boyfriend/paramour/person legally responsible respondent whom Schwartz had had the pleasure of meeting in family court. The Luv Van continued on, a picture of pink in motion, its occupants oblivious to his presence.

"Well, I'll be fucked . . . or not, I guess," Schwartz said out loud, punctuating his thought with a whistle.

After an internal debate, Schwartz walked back to Isabel's house. He squeezed by the Luv Van and knelt down next to the bathroom window. Through the slit in the pink curtains and the open bathroom door, Schwartz could make out that Isabel was dancing, half naked, in front of two men sitting on the living room couch. Schwartz recognized one as Machado. With the hypnotic grace of a latter-day Salome, Isabel salsaed, mamboed, bachataed, and merengued. Like Herod, Schwartz was transfixed, but when he saw a half-naked girl, age six or seven, join the dance, his stomach turned inside out.

Schwartz walked to the next corner and flagged a livery cab. He slumped into the back seat.

"Dónde vamos?" the driver asked.

"Espera. Espera. Estoy pensando. OK. *Espera un minuto aqui.* But keep the motor running. Uh, *no cerado el coche."*

Schwartz exited the car and walked as quickly as his nervous flesh would carry him. He was searching for something—anything. As he approached Isabel's house, he spied an old baseball, its leather skin half on and half off, like a snake sloughing off its skin. It had been abandoned and now laid next to the rear tire of the Luv Van. He reached down, grabbed the semi-stitched sphere, and stepped back from the basement apartment's window. It was time to channel his inner Goose Gossage. As if on the mound at the stadium, Schwartz rocked back, raised his hands as high as he could, and brought them together. Then he brought his arms down close to his body, rotated his right shoulder, pivoted thirty degrees clockwise on his right leg and then counterclockwise, pushed off with his right leg, brought his arms forward, and released the ball. The instant it crashed through the glass, Schwartz was off and running, flushed with adrenaline and willing his body to cooperate. As he dove into the cab, he could hear the shouts behind him.

"Driver! *Vamanos!*"

As the cab pulled away he could hear Machado screaming retribution.

Schwartz had delivered a perfect strike.

DECEMBER 12:
THE LONGEST DAY

"MARJ, LET ME TO SPEAK TO ETHAN. DON'T PULL THIS CRAP. Come on, now."

Only Schwartz's exhaled breath colliding with the frigid morning air kept his frozen face from sticking to the pay phone outside the Riverdale Tennis Club,

Why are you calling so early?" Marjorie asked, half awake. "It's not even six."

"Because I'm about to play tennis with your maniac lawyer, who, parenthetically, is my ex-friend, and I promised Ethan I'd call him before his winter concert tonight. Why are you talking to a lawyer?"

"Do you remember that disaster with the health insurance? With Julie? Prime example. Schwartz, I can't be having that while you're busy doing whatever."

"Whatever am I doing?"

"I don't know what you're doing, and that's my point."

"But why Blumenthal?"

"Because I've heard he's very good at what he does from some people I know and trust. And he didn't ask for a retainer up front. He said he'd collect his fee from you."

Would that this tennis racket be an Uzi.

Schwartz swallowed his growing rage.

"Let me speak to Ethan."

"No. Too early. Have fun with tennis."

"You are beginning to act like a real fuckin'—"

With the click of the phone reverberating in his ear, Schwartz slammed the receiver back in place.

He had risen at 5:00 a.m., thrown sweatpants, a t-shirt, and sneakers in a gym bag, and dragged himself to the El station at Jerome Avenue. When the Uptown #4 slid roughly onto the platform berth and its open doors beckoned, he stepped onto the train with a resignation reserved for condemned prisoners. As he had wiped the cornbreads from his eyes and assumed the position of a jaded subway rider—one arm wrapped precariously around a pole—he thought that the last thing he wanted to do that morning was play tennis.

Turning away from the phone pedestal and pushing his way through the revolving doors into the tennis club's lobby, he believed he was a man on a mission. But to where? Battle? Hell? No. The officious blonde waif at the reception desk informed him that he was to go to Court #3.

Rufus Blumenthal, Brooklyn Law School, Class of '77, was in the midst of his kata of death warm-up stretches as Schwartz emerged from the locker room onto the court. The last time they had met was at their twenty-year class reunion at the Marriott Marquis. For legal have-nots such as Schwartz, it was a depressing affair. Riding the elevator up to the View Restaurant, Blumenthal had introduced Schwartz to Bruce Cutler (Class of '74, Evening School Division) of John Gotti infamy. Cutler had inquired about the path Schwartz's career had taken, to which Schwartz said that he was assigned counsel in Bronx Family Court. Cutler had responded, "Neither one of us amounted to much."

Schwartz approached the court and Blumenthal. Dressed in his Ralph Lauren tennis whites, Blumenthal exuded the nose-in-the-air of the Jewish country club. Schwartz knew this species all too well. They went to synagogue only on the High Holy Days, paying $500 a seat. They'd supported the Vietnam War with a passion, until the day they drew a low number in the draft lottery. They went to Brandeis, Syracuse, or Colgate in search of free love and a 2-S deferment. And without shame or guilt, they drove the Nazi staff car, the Mercedes Benz, or its combat cohort, the BMW.

How did the joke go? Oh, yeah. When a Jew drives a Chevrolet, he says, "Young Kipper."When he drives a Cadillac, he says, "Yom Kippooour." When he drives a Mercedes Benz, he says . . . "Merry Christmas!"

Upon spotting Schwartz, Blumenthal straightened from his hamstring stretch, moved toward his opponent, and offered his hand.

"Schwartzie. I was beginning to think you blew me off."

Blumenthal's nickname in law school came to Schwartz's mind.

"*Et tu*, Ruthless?"

"Up or down?" Blumenthal barked.

"Down."

With a chuckle and a narrowing of his eyes, Blumenthal spun his racket on its head with a gyroscopic flourish.

"Down it is for you, Schwartzie. Let's hit a couple. Then give me your best shot. Let's not waste court time, if you get my drift."

Schwartz shrugged off the lame double *entendres*, did some perfunctory stretches, and assumed his position on the court opposite Blumenthal. It had been two months since Schwartz had picked up a tennis racket. Since his sweatpants didn't have pockets, he relied on the pressure from his hip/ass to keep the tennis balls secured to his waistband. As he began a tentative return of Blumenthal's warm-up shot, he felt one ball begin its inevitable journey to the center of his underwear. Ruthless would undoubtedly complain about the possibility of skid marks on his new balls.

C'est la guerre.

"OK. Serve it up. FBI," Blumenthal urged.

"FBI? Where?"

"First ball in, you numbnuts."

"Oh. I knew that. I was just—"

"Serve! C'mon. I've got a massage appointment at seven."

Schwartz retrieved a tennis ball from his underwear for his first offering. The serve found its home in the net, as did the next three attempts. On his fourth attempt, he managed to put it over the net, albeit on a neighboring court. On his fifth try, sensing his opponent's impatience, he lobbed a meatball into the service box. Blumenthal smoked it in a spicy sauce, ticking the baseline at Schwartz's feet.

"Love-Fifteen."

The balance of Schwartz's serves met similar fates. Having already broken Schwartz like a slab of Bonomo Turkish Taffy, Blumenthal cranked up his serve, shooting cannons to the *T* of the box, cannons to the *L* of the box. Schwartz, attempting to return the lasers, resembled a hapless soccer goalie facing the dreaded Brazilians on penalty kicks. Where was the honor and grace Don Edgardo spoke of? Schwartz desperately needed to change tactics to avoid total humiliation.

On his next service game, Schwartz was resolved. He tossed the ball high in the air, swung with all his might, and watched the ball land deep in the service box. With abandon, he charged the net. His racquet frame managed to tick Blumenthal's return over the net for a point.

"Come on!" Schwartz shouted as he clenched his fist and struck a pose worthy of the great Sampras. Blumenthal just rolled his eyes and muttered something to himself.

Anxious to duplicate that Herculean feat, Schwartz double-faulted on his next attempt, conceding a point to his opponent. His next serve yielded a fault, so he changed strategies. For the second serve he tossed in a soft slice to Blumenthal's backhand. Schwartz charged the net, hoping to surprise Blumenthal. Blumenthal returned the serve to Schwartz's forehand. Schwartz, unsure in the serve-and-volley game, failed to put Blumenthal's miscue away. Instead, Schwartz's stroke found its way to his opponent's forehand at the midcourt service line. Schwartz was naked at the net. Blumenthal ripped the ball, intended for Schwartz's midsection. Schwartz flipped his legs counterclockwise in a futile effort to dodge the yellow sphere that was screaming toward his vitals. As the ball struck his baby maker, Schwartz spun like a pinwheel, his legs springing into the air. When he landed on his left side, Schwartz heard a crack and felt his ribs vibrate.

He lay immobile, planted on the green Har-tru. From the other side of the net, Blumenthal's voice of concern masked his aggravation.

"Oh my God. I hope I didn't kill him. I've never killed anyone in a match before. I mean, I've come close. Schwartzie, you OK? Oh, man. This is a pain."

Slowly Schwartz began to turn onto his unbroken side, lifting his head from the ground. With all the strength he could muster, he addressed his adversary.

"Blumenthal . . . has anyone recently told you what a dick you are? Come here. Help me up."

Blumenthal reached down, put a hand around Schwartz's right side, and began to lift. Schwartz gave a painful yelp as he rose. Once they were eye to eye, Schwartz posed the question that had put him there in the first place.

"Why . . . oh . . . why are you representing Margie?"

Blumenthal pursed his lips and hemmed and hawed. Schwartz held his side, breathing laboriously.

"Why?" he asked again.

"Uh, well . . . uh, honestly?"

"No. Tell me a fuckin' lie! Why?"

"Well, I've always thought she was something of a babe."

Schwartz considered the response for a moment. He slowly shuffled his feet several paces to pick up his racquet. He shuffled back to Blumenthal and extended his hand. Blumenthal reciprocated with a nervous giggle. With all his might, which, all things considered, wasn't much at this point, Schwartz swung his racquet at his classmate's right wrist. The blow appeared to shock more than hurt.

"Owww! You bastard! I'll have you arrested!"

"Blumey, blow me. It's a he said, he said. My broken ribs against the boo-

boo on your wrist. Where's your cell? Go ahead. Call 911. We'll both get popped. I'll give you a personal tour of Central Booking."

Blumenthal charged at Schwartz and tackled him. They rolled over and over on the court. Observing the tableau interrupting their games, players on the neighboring courts rushed to separate the erstwhile combatants and bring them to their feet. Blumenthal struggled furiously, demanding, "Lemme go! Lemme go!"

In the arms of the peacemakers, Schwartz sagged a bit. As Blumenthal dusted off green Har-Tru from his white shorts, Schwartz nodded in his direction and called out, "You know what? You give even sleazy lawyers a bad name."

Schwartz collected his gym bag and his racquet and moved laboriously in the direction of the revolving exit doors.

SCHWARTZ SLOWLY WENDED HIS WAY THROUGH THE MORNING crush of hip-hopping holiday shoppers headed to the St. Patrick's office building, located proximate to the Jamaica Avenue shopping district in Queens. Every step reminded him of the fragile state of his ribcage. Over St. Patrick's entrance, a relief of a cloaked male figure—presumably St. Patrick—with his hands on the shoulders of two children led Schwartz to recall a visit he had made years ago to meet with an incarcerated parent at the Elmira Correctional Facility. The main Elmira building had once served as a reformatory for misguided youths. At the reception gate of ECC stood a statue of a naked man with his hand on the shoulder of a naked boy—a vestige from that period—that greeted modern-day inmates as they got off the bus from Rikers Island to begin serving their indeterminate sentences of two to four, three to six, etc.

Welcome to State time!

In the lobby of St. Patrick's, the receptionist doubled as the telephone operator. Her board was lit and blinking as Schwartz approached.

"Excuse me. Hello. I'm here for the case conference on the Fontanez children. I'm the attorney for the mother, Carmen. I have an appointment with Ms. Bentley."

Another demand on the receptionist's attention didn't seem to agree with her immediate plans for the morning. Without saying a word, she cocked her head in the direction of the lobby and gestured for him to take a seat. The lobby was choked with children and adults who were either foster parents escorting their wards or biological parents awaiting supervised visitation appointments. Schwartz attempted a deep breath but the pain from his ribs nipped the effort in the bud. Earlier, he had managed to wrap a wide ACE bandage around his midsection and downed some aspirins. Wincing, he surveyed the posters that adorned the walls of the lobby:

Have You Hugged Your Child Today? Caring=Sobering. Only **YOU** can prevent Domestic Violence!

He found a seat and a resting place for his tennis duffel and shoulder bag. Glancing at his calendar, Schwartz scanned the cases awaiting him in the Bronx this day. It was December 12—a date of no small significance to aficionados of popular American music. It was the anniversary of the birth of Ol' Blue Eyes, the Chairman of the Board, the kid from Hoboken, Francis Albert Sinatra. The penumbra cast by the man's life and career shadowed his heir apparent, Bobby Darin. It was rare for Schwartz to have a conversation about Mr. Darin without Sinatra's name coming up as a point of comparison. Even in his death, Sinatra received top billing over the star-crossed Darin. Sinatra's death and Bobby Darin's birth occurred on the same date— May 14. Eerily enough, had Darin died on December 12 and not several days later on December 20, the ironic circle would have been completed.

As much as Schwartz begrudgingly admired Sinatra's body of work, his birthday stirred up old feelings of diminished self-esteem. His aching ribs confirmed the emotional gnaw in his belly. There was only one antidote.

Softly, Schwartz began to alternatively whistle and sing Darin's swinging version of "My Darlin' Clementine."

A young boy and girl in the waiting area took notice and began to bop their heads in rhythm. Schwartz had been oblivious to them until the girl called out to the entire waiting room, "Hey, the man is singing us a story!"

Some kids rushed over to Schwartz's corner of the room. Confronted with this sudden audience, Schwartz stopped.

Am I being mocked? Could a waiting area at St. Patrick's Services for Children double as a Las Vegas lounge? Am I up for this?

Schwartz thought of the comedian who had flitted about Ed Sullivan's stage atop a bicycle. He had an English gentleman's proper visage and a handlebar mustache and uttered the immortal words, "Why not?" Despite the pain in his ribs, Schwartz delved into a full-throated version of Darin's twist on the old folk song.

It had occurred to Schwartz that these kids had little laughter in their everyday lives. They'd been separated from allegedly abusive/neglectful parents, tossed upon the stormy seas of multiple foster care placements, and referred to a merry-go-round of therapist, caseworker, and attorney appointments. The Best Interest Industrial Complex was having their way with them. He fancied himself the Pied Piper, ready to lead these kids out the front door and into the December sunshine, if only for a few minutes, for a shopping spree on the Jamaica Avenue mall. As he continued singing, he took several tentative steps toward the lobby's front door.

Damned if his little audience didn't move with him. Schwartz snapped the fingers of his left hand and clapped his right hand against his thigh as he stepped toward the door, all the while encouraging his young audience to emulate him. Just as he was about to open the door, audience in tow, he heard a voice boom out across the lobby, "Oh, Mr. Schwartz, you're not leaving yet! We have Carmen's conference."

Schwartz turned his head in the direction of the voice. Heidi Frias, hospice social worker, approached him, applauding. She walked right up to him and whispered, "Are you losing it? This is not the time or place. Carmen and her baby need you now."

The children were applauding, tugging on his sleeve, and asking him to sing some more. Schwartz looked down at their faces and asked their names.

"Ernesto."

"I'm Anil."

"Gloria. An' this is my lil' sister, Violetta."

"Gregory, but peoples call me Flighty."

"OK, Flighty. Listen, guys, I have a meeting upstairs. If you liked my show here, I'll be performing again on the E train for tips and . . ." Schwartz's tongue stopped working. His neck involuntarily snapped in the direction of the little girl, Violetta. A low rumble had begun in his solar plexus. He struggled to form the words of the question.

"Uh, Gloria, what's your last name?"

"Valdespino."

Like Oedipus, he pressed on.

"But your little sister's last name isn't the same, is it?"

"No. She has my mommy's name, Pichardo."

Schwartz swayed. Sensing that he was about to lose his balance, Frias slipped her arm around his to support him. A woman, presumably Gloria and Violetta's foster mother, stepped between Schwartz and the children. She brusquely grabbed the children's arms and admonished them.

"*Mijo*. Wah I tell you 'bout talkin' to strangers. *Vente!*"

"Schwartz, what's up with you?" Frias said. "Come on. We have a meeting now."

She led him to the staircase that would take them to the mezzanine suite of offices. Schwartz gingerly walked up the stairs, looking over his shoulder for Violetta. Now he had a face for his nightmare, and it was marked by sad, shy, little black eyes surrounded by dark circles. He wasn't the only one having trouble sleeping. He also knew the face of the monster starring in her nightmares.

Heidi regarded him with a puzzled expression, crinkled nose and all. When they reached the landing, Schwartz felt her firm hand on the small of his back.

"I think the conference room is to our left," she said.

He barely mumbled a response.

Moving through an open family visiting area, Schwartz spotted Carmen seated near her newborn, and smiling. Sitting across from her was a bespectacled middle-age man. He had a small notepad on his lap. Schwartz caught Carmen's eye and she waved her hand in acknowledgement. Continuing to the conference room, he asked robotically, "How's she doing?"

Heidi raised her eyebrows and shrugged slightly.

"Been better."

He followed her into the conference room. Already seated were the caseworker from the foster care agency, Ms. Bentley and a woman who introduced herself as the worker's supervisor, Mrs. Mastriani, and the ACS caseworker, Mr. Adesanya.

After the round of introductions, the supervisor, a greying doyenne of the foster care system, spoke first. Schwartz would wager that she dated back to the early twentieth century era of Little Orphan Annie orphanages.

"Once Ms. Fontanez is finished with her visit, we'll begin—it's her first since the baby came into care—but let me apprise you that we're not discussing anything—which I hope you understand, but I have my orders from my director—without our attorney here."

The woman spoke with her own commentary, lowering the volume, pitch, and cadence of her speech for her asides.

Heidi was none too pleased.

"Mrs. Mastrini, I informed you on the phone that Mr. Schwartz was coming, and—"

"It's Mas-tri-a-ni. Well, our attorney—a very busy man whom we reached on short notice—wasn't sure he could make it."

Frias' voice ratcheted up a notch.

"And I understood from Mr. Schwartz that a parent is permitted to have their attorney present at any seventy-two-hour post-removal conference or any service plan review. We are here today to find out what the agency's—"

The door opened and Carmen slunk into the room. Frias softened her tone.

"We want to know what the agency's plan is for Ms. Fontanez to reunite with her infant. If you're refusing to proceed because your lawyer had more important things to do, we're going to inform the judge."

Frias turned to Schwartz, seeking confirmation and support. He sat slumped in his chair, his chin against his chest and his lower lip protruding. Heidi had expected that the lawyer's presence would make the agency sit up, take notice, and perhaps play a little straighter. Those hopes were fading.

The telephone buzzed on the conference table, filling the vacuum Heidi's pronouncement had created. Mastriani reached for the receiver, listened for a bit, nodded, and then hung up.

"Our lawyer is here. The reason I asked him to come is—Ms. Frias, is it? I don't think I got your card."

Frias reached into her bag, removed a card from her wallet, and slid it across the table in the supervisor's direction.

"Yes. Ms. Frias…because there's a case in court right now and our worker may be called to testify."

Schwartz stared at her as he thought

Mrs. Mastriani, there's always a case in court and your workers are always called to testify. Does that mean that if a respondent mother at a seventy-two-hour conference, the focus of which is to find out what she needs to do to get her child back, should exercise her right to have counsel present, she can only have the meeting if your attorney is available?

Instead he blurted, "Bullshit."

This rejoinder, which rolled around the table like a wayward marble, coincided with the entrance of Franz Kafka, Esq. Schwartz turned toward the door and sputtered, "Kafkaesq, what are you doing here?"

"Apologies for my tardiness. I was just informed of the nature of this conference. Counselor, so good to see you again. Correct me if I'm mistaken, but before I entered, I believe I overheard an eloquent debate concerning my client's right to counsel"

His adversary's presence had jump-started Schwartz's lawyer motormouth.

"That's a moot point now, Franz, given your belated appearance. Let's just get to the matter at hand. I have a mother here who has a newborn. Her medical condition causes her to be temporally challenged. What's ACS's and the foster care agency's plan for reuniting them?"

Kafka, seated between Mastriani and Adesanya, removed a document from his briefcase and showed it to the agency representatives. After they each perused the document, they nodded.

"It seems, Mr. Schwartz, that Ms. Fontanez has three other children in this agency's care," Kafka noted. "Her rights to the oldest child—a nine-year-old— has already been terminated, and TPRs are about to be filed on the other two."

"Kafka, we know this. But your agency and ACS still have a duty to make diligent efforts focused on returning Justina to her mother."

"Point taken, Counselor. Though the courts could find that no efforts are necessary under FCA Sec. 1039-b, given Ms. Fontanez's extensive history of child neglect. Still, our service plan calls for the mother to complete a drug program, a parenting skills course, and a domestic violence course, enroll in individual family counseling, maintain contact with the agency, and visit consistently."

"Kafka, you forgot sex abuse treatment and electroshock therapy. Ms. Frias, Ms. Fontanez, do you mind if Mr. Kafka and I step outside for a brief chat?"

Adesanya piped up, "Mistah Schwartz, ah have a emergency removal in da Bronx. How much longah for dis meetin'?"

"Calm down, City Child Catcher. Your snares will stay hidden."

Schwartz motioned toward the door and rose. Kafka followed, somewhat reluctantly. Once outside, Schwartz beckoned Kafka to follow him several steps down the corridor. He stopped and faced the small man with round glasses.

"She's dying, you dick!"

"Mr. Schwartz, your use of the vernacular does not move me in the slightest. We're all dying, after all."

"But she's dying very, very soon."

"Sad. Still no reason to throw caution to the wind and place her infant in an unsafe predicament."

"She's in a supervised setting twenty-four seven, a hospice."

"Oh, a hospice, say you? Now, there's a jolly place for an infant to be swaddled. Mater's contraction of AIDS is indicative of her failure to plan for her children."

"Mater? There, you self-important prick . . . you finally said it. She doesn't get the baby because she has AIDS."

"Mr. Schwartz, you can call me every known synonym for the male member that you have in your limited verbal arsenal, but I must say you are acting emotionally and unprofessionally, as well as twisting my words. This sidebar conference is over. Sorry, Mr. Schwartz. From St. Patrick's perspective, no sale."

Schwartz wavered and rocked on his heels. He had already broken the ice with one assault on a fellow barrister. Why not add another to his rap sheet? As Kafka crossed in front of him, Schwartz reached out and grabbed the startled man by the shoulders. Schwartz grabbed the man's bow tie and gave it a viscous twist. In as soft a tone as he could muster, he purred, "You want twisted? Your tie was crooked. There. Now it's straight. But understand this, Kafkaesq: I know the game all too well. Parents are accused of some bullshit charge like failure to maintain welfare benefits by some C.Y.A. social worker, or yelling at a kid in a hospital emergency rooms reported by a do-gooder nurse, or a quarter is dropped on them for smoking pot at the weekend house party by an anonymous neighbor with an ax to grind. A judge signs off on the remand order *ex parte*, sight unseen.

Kafka struggled to break free but Schwartz held him firmly in place, ignoring the screeching of his ribs.

"Soon the referrals start fast and furious. If the parents don't do the dance, they're branded 'uncooperative' or 'in denial.' Next the psych evaluations are ordered and we know how they turn out. Weeks and months fly by, adjournment after adjournment. A year or two passes, the A.S.F.A. permanency clock ticks on, and your foster care agency swoops in for the adoption notch on your belt that allows you to keep the federal cash flowing.

"In the end, it's all about the money. The caseworkers, the shrinks, court officers, judges, you, me . . . isn't it? We are all part and parcel of the Childrens' Best Interest Industrial Complex. These foster care babes are profit centers, aren't they? And these children, in the meantime . . . these children . . ."

An image of Violetta came to Schwartz's mind, derailing his train of thought. Schwartz patted the man's shoulders, turned, and ambled toward the conference room. He opened the door and poked his head in. There was Carmen, sitting and looking at her nails disconsolately. Frias was pacing behind her.

Schwartz took a breath. His ribs were throbbing.

"Ladies, this meeting is over."

Frias began to protest. "But what about the plan?"

"We've heard their plan. Let's go."

In front of the building, Schwartz reminded them of the next day's court date and to have all their program documents in order. Carmen extended her hand and thanked him for coming. Schwartz grabbed the bony collection of fingers and held it briefly in his hands. Each nail had a new sparkling stone mounted next to the golden child design. He took each of her fingers and caressed them.

Frias wiped away a tear and put her arm around Carmen.

"Come, *mi amor*, we've got to catch two trains and a bus back to the Bronx. You have to get your meds before two. Schwartz, we'll see you in court."

Schwartz and Frias exchanged a firm handshake. Schwartz tried to detect whether there was a flicker of chemical attraction on her part.

Inconclusive.

The two women turned and walked toward Jamaica Avenue. The shops were festooned with holiday decorations and holiday shoppers crowded the street. Schwartz glanced at his watch. He was due in front of a family court judge in the Bronx twenty minutes ago. He wondered why he hadn't traveled with Heidi and Carmen to the Bronx, but he knew the answer: he had had his fill of client contact and attorney conference for one morning.

Schwartz suddenly realized that he was hungry. No, more than hungry—ravenous. As he took measured steps toward the subway station, he passed one and then another of the fruit stands of Sutphin Boulevard. They offered a welcome encroachment upon the city's sidewalks, with bins bursting with offerings of varying kinds and quality. What he craved most was a piece of fruit, yet he was pressed for time and dared not stop for even a minute. As he approached the entrance to the station, his eyes opened wide in both recognition and wonderment.

Was it a vision?

On the middle of the sidewalk, ignored by or perhaps invisible to others, lay an apple, brightly striated in orange, yellow, and red. Schwartz reached down slowly, mindful of his aching ribs, and gathered in the offering while extricating himself from his dangled and tangled luggage. He gave the apple a surreptitious wipe on his coat and bit it. He recognized the taste immediately as one of his favorites—a Fuji, which he mistakenly associated with the island of Fiji.

Oh, to be sitting on a beach somewhere in the South Pacific devouring this apple.

The Manhattan-bound E train would have to do.

SCHWARTZ HADN'T TAKEN MORE THAN THREE STEPS OUT OF the elevator on the seventh floor of BxFC when he was accosted by the court officer from Yellin' Yellin's Part.

"Schwartz, oh, man, you have to come down to Yellin's part right now. We have a situation."

"A situation?"

"That's right—a situation."

"I hate situations."

In the tight space where all four elevators converged, people dashed between Schwartz and the officer he was trying to converse with. Several of the passersbys shouted greetings or reminders about various matters:

"Part 2 at 2:30."

"Did you get the case record on Morgan? I sent it last week."

"I'm going down to check in on Bonfiglio. Can you come?"

"Hanukkah party, this Thursday at one."

Schwartz struggled to focus on the court officer's voice.

"In Yellin's part?" he asked over the noise.

"Yeah. Right now!"

"Look, I've got to check into parts 3, 6, and 10, and then I'll make my way down."

Captain Dolan suddenly loomed behind the court officer.

"I believe what the officer is trying to say is that we have a situation in the referees' part and your immediate attention is required. We'll contact the other parts and tell them that you are otherwise engaged. . . in a situation."

"All right. I just want to put my coat and stuff in the 18-B room and I'll be down."

Dolan placed his face not six inches from Schwartz's.

"Thank you, counselor. I would appreciate it."

Schwartz zigged and zagged through the benches in the waiting area next to the 18-B room. Try as he might, his rib pain prevented him from placing his coat on top of the coat tree that already housed an array of trench coats, peacoats, leather jackets, hats, and scarves on its limbs. His trench coat, which his wife had purchased at the Sisters of the Most Precious Blood thrift shop two years before, found a resting spot on the back of a chair. Schwartz thrust the tennis bag under the table. He detected the smell of tobacco leaves and turned to greet Walter Stanton, who had just entered the room.

Walter was mumbling, "Have to file motion. Clients don't show up. Judge . . . judge is . . . who?"

"'Morning, Walter."

"Oh, uh, morning, Schwartz. I left a file on the desk. Did you see it?"

Schwartz surveyed the cluster of half-empty (*or were they half full?*) coffee cups, Dunkin' Donuts wrappers, crumbs, pieces of toasted bagels, egg-stained foil take-out pans, plastic forks, manuals, yesterday's newspapers and directories covering the desk.

"Walter, if you left it there, you'd better create a dummy file."

Walter was in his late sixties, a graduate of Notre Dame, and a former Army officer. His shock of white hair never failed to stimulate an "Is it real or is he the president of the company?" debate. Schwartz would describe his appearance, including attire, as early nervous breakdown.

Daily around 10:30 a.m., Walter could be seen standing in front of the court, sucking down his Camels, staring blankly across Sheridan Avenue. He would take the occasional sip of his black Dominican coffee from the bodega across the street. Oblivious to the passing world, Stanton would have served nicely as a Buckingham Palace guard. A lifer, he'd been on the panel since the late '70s.

"Schwartz, you know the Duhon custody case we have this afternoon? Who do I represent, the mother or the father?"

"The mother, Wally. And don't sweat it. The law guardian called me and said the forensic psych report isn't ready, so it's going to be put over. Just leave adjourned dates in the part."

"You sure I'm not the law guardian?"

"Wally, I've got to run to Ref. Yellin's part. Just leave dates."

Stanton sauntered off, humming a few bars of Donovan's "Sunshine Superman."

To avoid further distractions, Schwartz headed toward the referee's part. It was on the sixth floor. He maneuvered through a maze of secured hallways and back staircases, emboldened by an implied pass from Dolan. As he approached the narrow hallway outside Yellin's part, he began to appreciate the nature of the "situation" that required his immediate attention. There was Alphonso Abbatiello, his face to the wall, surrounded by four court officers and Tony

Napolitano, the warrant squad police officer. Abbatiello was dressed in grey and white pajamas with bunny slippers. His hands were handcuffed behind his back.

Schwartz approached the warrant cop.

"Tony, I'm afraid to ask."

"Not much to say, Schwartz. Mother had a suspension of visitation order. She says she gave a copy to the school, but they lost it. School claims they never got it. Who knows? Father picked up the kid from the school yesterday. He hasn't returned the kid. After getting to school to pick up the kid, Mother ran to court and got a Habeas Corpus writ and a warrant. We found him at his place in his pj's this morning but no kid."

For the second time today, Schwartz's solar plexus shuddered, sending shock waves through his still aching ribs.

"What's his place look like?"

"Nice and clean. There were pictures of him and his boy throughout. Doin' stuff. You know, fishing, amusement parks, ball games. He had a tree with wrapped presents underneath it, so I don't think he took the kid to his place."

Despite having his face squashed against the wall, Abbatiello managed to spot Schwartz.

"Mr. Schwartz, you gotta help me here. I haven't harmed my boy. I've never laid a finger on him. That pot-smoking bitch is lying on me to this court. She wants me out of the kid's life so she and her drug-addict boyfriend can raise him to be a loser like her."

"Tony, is he under your jurisdiction or Dolan's?"

"Well, the warrant hasn't been vacated yet, so he's still mine."

"Can I talk to him in your office?"

Tony nodded. "It's on the eighth floor."

"I know Tony. I've been to one or two of your penthouse barbeques."

"Sure, why not? If you think it'll do some good."

The procession of cop, court officers, lawyer, and handcuffed big white man in pj's and bunny slippers wended its way to the elevators, passing through the waiting room crowd. The spectacle invited comments from the audience.

"Oh man, look like de Easter Bunny done got his calendar mixed up."

"Mira ese maricon."

"Chil', you needs to work on your wardrobe."

Some little kids tried to grab at the bunny slippers, but the officers shooed them away.

As he walked, Schwartz fought to block a fearful image from mind. It was of a catch basin surrounded by a dilapidated chain link fence somewhere in Alabama.

It's the greatest case I ever lost.

Schwartz had been relatively new to the panel and, therefore, more susceptible to the stratagems used by court officers to rope 18-Bs into accepting assignment on cases that fell into the untouchable category. Typically, an untouchable case kicked around the courthouse for several years serviced by a revolving door of attorneys assigned to difficult, problematic clients. Based on a court officer's representation of the case as a straight forward visitation case, Schwartz had walked into the courtroom, petition in hand. When he entered the courtroom and saw the attorneys sitting at the table, shaking their heads and motioning him away with their hands, he suspected he'd been duped. Confirmation was provided by the judge speaking up all too quickly,

"Thank you, Mr. Schwartz, for accepting the assignment. Ms. Wexler, you're relieved."

Jennifer Wexler gave Schwartz the telltale roll of the eyes and whispered, "Good luck," as she dropped her file on the counsel's table and slid it in Schwartz's direction. Schwartz had been inveigled into accepting the assignment to Darwin Goodall, a father seeking custody of an eight-year-old girl from her mother.

"Mr. Schwartz, I'll give you a moment to talk with Mr. Goodall outside. Matter's on recall."

From the very first moment Darwin Goodall opened his mouth, Schwartz realized that he was dealing with an absolute maniac. The cauldron of anger against his wife, the judge, his previous attorneys, etc., had been simmering for years. Schwartz gazed down at the swollen folder so readily transferred by Wexler. Briefly, he perused its contents as he prepared to conduct the initial interview. The sheaf of petitions, cross-petitions, violation petitions, petitions to modify orders of visitation, and petitions to suspend orders of visitation hissed at Schwartz as if he had entered a nest of water moccasins.

"This goddamn bitch is hitting my girl with coat hangers and burning her with curling irons and bribing her into saying she don't want to see me. I've made complaints to the Stern Commission about this judge being racist. Just because I'm an African-American father trying to assert his rights, she gonna shit on me? I don't think so. Now, what are you going to do to get me some visitation while we fight for custody?"

The case wended its way through six months of stop-start hearing dates. Schwartz would dread Saturday nights because of the endless stream of vile messages he would receive from Goodall. He'd complain about some problem with visitation and how he was at his wits' end and was tired of being treated like garbage. Between court dates, Schwartz would occasionally see him walking the streets near the courthouse, speaking loudly in violent outbursts.

To be sure, the man had some valid talking points concerning the mother's ready resort to corporal punishment of the child. She had left the curling iron on once, causing the girl to accidentlly burn herself. Schwartz had brought these facts to the court's attention during the course of the trial. When the court denied Goodall's custody petition and granted him supervised visitation only, conditioned upon his participation in an anger management program, Schwartz breathed a sigh of relief. Goodall insisted that Schwartz appeal the adverse decision, and Schwartz filed the necessary papers to commence the appeal. Most assuredly, Schwartz would see to it that new counsel would be assigned on appeal. He'd served his time on this case. It was time for someone else to deal with Goodall.

One late spring afternoon, several months after the trial's completion, Schwartz and Cliff were rallying at the Mullaly Courts when Schwartz spotted Goodall walking hand in hand with a little girl. Curious, Schwartz called out to the man. Taking a moment to recognize his previous lawyer without suit and tie, Goodall approached the fence warily.

"Oh, it's you, Schwartz. What's up?"

"Who's the little lady?"

"Uh, Kenisha. She's my four-year-old. Her mother's a crackhead, so the judge in Brooklyn, he gave her to me. In fact, we're goin' to be headin' down South. I've got people in Alabama."

"Have you seen your other girl, the eight-year-old?"

"Oh, you know that bitch ain't gonna let go of that child long enough for me to say 'boo' to her. How's the appeal coming?"

"Fine, I guess. I mean, you know that they have specialized attorneys that do the appeals, right? Appellate lawyers."

"Uh . . . huh? No, I didn't know that. So I get a pelican lawyer? It's just another way the system fucks you ovah."

Schwartz turned nervously toward Cliff on the other side of the court. Then he turned back to Goodall.

"Anyway, good luck to you and Kenisha. Make sure you send me your new address so I can forward it to appellate counsel. My partner is getting a little impatient across the net."

"Yeah. A'ight."

Four months had elapsed without a word from Goodall. One morning as Schwartz was dodging the crowds in front of the seventh-floor elevator bank, the very same officer who had sandbagged him into taking the Goodall case hailed him.

"Oh, shit. Did you see the *Daily News* today?"

The officer thrust a copy before him, and there was the blaring headline:

Dad Drowns Self & Daughter: Bx Man and 4-Year-Old Hitched in Ala. Watery Grave

Reading on, Schwartz started to feel numb.

(AP-Montgomery) Authorities retrieved the bodies of Darwin Goodall and his four-year-old daughter Kenisha from a water runoff sump just outside the capital. Goodall, formerly of the Bronx, New York . . .

The paper fell from Schwartz's hand. He knew then and there that was the greatest case he'd ever lost. The eight-year-old girl on his case had somehow sensed the demons afflicting her father and gave voice to it. Her four year-old half sibling wasn't so fortunate.

Didn't the caseworkers, lawyers, or judge in Brooklyn see what kind of person Darwin Goodall was? Couldn't they get a read on him?

Schwartz wondered if he had blood on his hands for not reaching out to the Brooklyn court. Lawyers are not mandated reporters of child abuse, and there was the client confidentially rule. Still, these considerations registered as rationalizations on Schwartz's guilty conscience Geiger counter.

At the door to Napolitano's office, Schwartz drew the warrant squad cop aside.

"Can I talk to him with the handcuffs off?"

"No way."

"Figured I'd ask."

Napolitano led the prisoner into the narrow, cluttered office and sat him down on top of several files on a chair. The desk was barely visible under stacks of files and papers. As he turned to exit, he warned, "Don't be messing up my office."

"And just how would that be possible, Officer?"

"Don't be crackin' wise with me, Schwartz. I've got a delicate filing system. I know where everything is. For example, Counselor, you have your elbow resting on my 'Ignore All Future Requests for Assistance' file. I'm sure you don't want to wind up in that pile. The prisoner, on the other hand, is sitting on my 'Hunt Down and Kill' file. Likewise, he wants to stay out of that file for the immediate future and beyond. So don't take advantage of my good graces, gentlemen. I'll be outside. You have about five minutes before we head back to the part."

Schwartz allowed a tight smile as he collected his thoughts and waited for the door to close. His breath went deep as he surveyed Abbatiello. From the court-ordered investigations in the file, Schwartz had learned that the man was ten years his junior. The wrinkles on his face, puffiness around his eyes, and greying hair indicated otherwise.

What tack to take to get started? Good cop? Bad cop? Both?

He didn't need to decide.

"He's at my sister's," Abbatiello said.

Schwartz was taken aback. He almost asked, "Who is?"

Reading Schwartz's puzzled expression, Abbatiello continued, "My boy, Paulie. He's there. He hadn't seen my mother or my family in over six months. That whore of a mother wouldn't let me take him there. Said they were a bad influence."

The tightness in his stomach released several hitches. Schwartz was going to tread carefully here. *Definitely good cop.*

"Does your son like going to see your family?"

"Of course. They treat him like a little prince. They give him treats from the other side—cannoli, *zabaione*. He likes it there."

"I'd like to speak to Paul. I'd like him to tell me, himself, how much he likes it."

The big man started to blubber.

"All I want is for the lies to stop. This woman acts like she owns this kid. He's mine, too."

Schwartz stood and approached the distraught man. He put his hand on his back and spoke very softly.

"You know, Mr. Abba—can I call you Alphonso? Yes? OK. Alphonso, you made a good point there. You know that many mothers—and fathers for that matter—who are primary custodians of children confuse custody with ownership. The truth, Alphonso, the truth is that nobody owns a child other than the child himself. One of the rights of that child's self-ownership is the right to know and to be loved by both parents and their families. And one of the obligations of being the primary custodial parent is to encourage the child to have a relationship with the other parent and their family. Now, you and I had a conversation just yesterday afternoon in which I said I would be doing everything I could, as Paul's law guardian, to see to it that you had contact with your son under conditions that are safe, appropriate, and in the child's best interest."

Abbatiello focused on Schwartz.

"But when? Two, three months from now? I don't see him for Christmas? After you completed your so-called investigation? What's to investigate? I love my son. He loves me."

"Alphonso, I wish it were that simple. But you and the mother could not settle your differences without the aid of the court. Once the courts get involved, it gets very complicated. Now a judge or a referee is being asked to sign off on whether a parent should have contact with his child and what the nature of that contact should be. They won't do that until everything has been thoroughly investigated. The most crucial part of that investigation is the report from the law guardian. That's me. I'm a father like you. Here. Here's a picture of my girl and boy."

The big man's eyes narrowed as he looked at the snapshot Schwartz had produced from his wallet. The photo was dog-eared from being used as a prop in conversations such as this.

"They're a little older now. Anyway, where was I? Oh, yes, the law guardian's report. The most critical part of that report is the law guardian's interview with the child. From that interview flows the position the law guardian will take—for or against visitation and under what terms. Overnight? Daytime only? Unsupervised? Supervised? If so, by whom? Relative? Family Friend? Professional? But as your child's attorney, I can't begin to take a position unless and until I speak to him. I want to do that. In fact, I want to do that today. So what do you say, Alphonso? Can I talk to Paulie today?"

The big man in the pj's and bunny slippers with his arms locked behind him in handcuffs began to rock back and forth on his rear end.

"I'll take you there," he said.

Schwartz backed away and began to pace inside the small room. Napolitano knocked on the door.

"You gentlemen have two more minutes to wrap this up."

Time for a dose of bad cop.

"No. No. That won't happen. They won't let you out until the child is produced. You're going to have to tell me your sister's address. I will go there. I will talk to Paul. Then I will bring him to court."

"And then what? You're going to return him to that *fattucchiera*."

"I can't answer the 'then what?' Not until I speak to him. You're just going to have to trust me to do right by your son. That's where it's at."

Long pause.

"'Trust me.' Isn't that how they say 'fuck you' in Yiddish?"

For the sake of the inquiry, Schwartz shrugged off the slur.

Napolitano shouted, "Times up!"

Abbatiello grimaced and then grunted, "1865 Pelham Parkway."

"Apartment?"

A pause.

"5D."

"I need you to call your sister and tell her I'm coming."

Silence.

"Make the call, Alphonso."

Schwartz could hear the key in the door. He turned and shouted, "Tony, one more minute!"

The big man's eyes darted around the room as if seeking an escape route.

"I'm going there whether you call or not. If you don't call, I'm going with the warrant officer. If you do call, I go alone and your son doesn't need know you've been arrested. So how do you want to handle this, Dad?"

A beat.

"Dial the fuckin' number for me. 622-9789."

Schwartz dialed and held the receiver to Abbatiello's ear and mouth.

"Di, it's me. I'm OK, but they're holding me at family court. Put Paulie on the line . . . Hey, big guy. I miss you. You'll be seeing me soon, I promise. Listen, Daddy is sending a friend of his to pick you up. He's a nice man. His name is Mr. Schwartz. It's OK to talk to him and go with him, OK, big guy? Daddy loves you, too . . . I don't know where mommy is, but you'll be seeing her, too. OK, put your aunt back on the phone. Give a kiss. Bye-bye . . . Listen, Di, this lawyer from the court is coming to get Paul. It's OK to let him take Paul. . . His name? Schwartz."

Addressing Schwartz, Alphonso asked, "You got picture ID?"

Schwartz nodded.

"He'll show ID. I'll call you and mom later. 'Bye."

Schwartz removed the receiver from Abbatiello's ear and returned it to the cradle with a thud.

"What do you want me to tell him?" Schwartz asked.

"Tell him his gifts will stay under the tree until he can come and unwrap them."

"Alphonso, you don't know me very well, nor I you. Between yesterday and today, we've spent a total of fifteen minutes together. Perhaps I'm in no position to talk to you like this, but take it from one father to another. You don't need to give him Christmas gifts to keep his love. I believe you already have that. What he craves for Christmas is peace at home and good will between mommy and daddy. If you would put that in his stocking, he'd be in your home Christmas Day."

"Tell him I said I love him."

The big man began to blubber. Schwartz produced the ever-ready tissue.

"It's crumpled but clean."

Schwartz gave Abbatiello as much of a hug as his aching ribs would allow. He backed toward the door and opened it. Don Edgardo had joined Napolitano in the hallway.

"Schwartz, you've been assigned to this guy?"

"No. I'm the law guardian."

"Then what are you doing talking to him? That's not right."

"Why? He doesn't have an attorney."

"He does now. His family just called me and retained me."

Schwartz started to say, "That's bullshit because we just spoke to his family," but he caught himself.

"Uh, OK. He's all yours. I have a feeling this case will be called this afternoon. You may want to run across the street to the 99-cent store and get him some XX sweats and sneakers. Meanwhile, I've got to go speak to my client."

Schwartz rode the elevator down to the seventh floor. He walked over to part II and ducked his head inside. A trial was in progress and Cliff was seated behind a juvenile respondent. This meant that the juvenile was in remand and that Cliff couldn't leave his post. Schwartz tiptoed up behind him, careful not to interrupt the proceedings. He whispered, "I need the keys to the Saab."

Cliff shook his head without turning to look at Schwartz.

"It's an emergency, my man."

Cliff turned to look at him. He detected the gimp in Schwartz's gait. Out of the side of his mouth he asked, "What happened to you?"

Schwartz was hesitant to answer. A "shush!" from the bench ended the conversation. Cliff's pissed-off look provided punctuation. Cliff motioned with his head toward the well. Schwartz retreated there and waited for the case to be over and for Cliff to escort the youth back to detention.

When Cliff finally entered the well, he looked Schwartz up and down.

"What's up? You hurt?"

"Uh, I think I cracked a rib this morning."

"How?"

"Playing tennis with a classmate."

"Sounds like rough tennis. See, you go sneaking out in the morning, and I knew you were up to something."

"Sounds like you're more than a little jealous."

"Hey, man, you want to be a tennis slut, go ahead."

"I don't believe this."

"It starts with a little early morning hit and maybe an occasional lunchtime rally. Then, sooner than you can count the hairs on Andre Agassi's balding head, you're playing doubles with him."

"You are a sick puppy, you know that? I've got to go now, man. Are you giving me those keys? 'Cause I've a young client in distress."

As Cliff reached for his key ring, he spit the words out of his mouth, "You best be back by five."

"*No problemo mi compadre.*"

Schwartz winced as he bounded down the back staircase, stepped out on Sherman Avenue, and headed toward Papo Cuenca's yard. He passed the freelance mechanics working on cars in the street and the Christmas tree salesman warming his hands over a fire in a barrel. Even in December, the fire hydrant outside Papo's yard was running freely, icing the sidewalks. Schwartz bent down, cupped his hands, and drank the clear essence flowing from the Catskill Mountains aquifer.

As he carefully navigated the ice floe and stepped into the yard, a warning signal fired in his brain. Instinctively he reached into his pocket for the apple core left from his breakfast. To his left, he could hear the scratching on the ground coming from between two cars in the yard. He whirled and hit the rooster with the core in mid-flight. As the squawking bird fell to the ground, Schwartz ducked out of the way of the flailing talons and ran for the Saab.

As he fumbled for his keys, Papo approached him with his hand around the bird's neck.

"Mister Schwartz. This *gallo*. He no like you."

"You think? Maybe he's heard too many lawyer jokes. Maybe I should learn some rooster jokes to entertain him. You know, get on his good side. If he has one. Like, why did the chicken cross the road? Because some crazy rooster was chasing it. Has that thing had its rabies shot?"

Papo laughed a laugh that swooped down from El Yunque, skipped over the waves of Luquillo Beach, and made landfall in Old San Juan.

"Hey, I like you, Schwartz, even if *El Diablo* no like you."

Schwartz implored the ignition to catch. As he started to pull out, he rolled down his window to shake his rescuer's hand. The hand was a slab of calluses.

"Schwartz, you wan' some *pasteles* for Christmas? My wife, she make dem bery, bery good. Only two dollars each. I'll bring you one to taste, with some *picante*. Mmmm, mmm, mmmmm. "

"Papo, I look forward to it. Uh, *Feliz Navidad.*"

"And I could fix those dents on your car's side."

"OK, I'll think about that, too, Papo. I've got to run."

Schwartz nudged the Saab into the street, circumventing the deep pothole marked by a litter basket protruding halfway out of it. He beeped his horn mildly at some ballplayers in the street and turned toward the Concourse.

The car radio, tuned to WCBS News Radio 88, reported that the United States Supreme Court had effectively elected George Bush as the forty-third president of the United States when it decided *Gore v. Bush* 531 U.S. 98 (2000). In a 5–4 vote, the US Supreme Court overturned the Florida Supreme Court and halted the recount of the Florida popular vote. It was the fifth time in history and the only time in the twentieth century that a President would be elected without a majority of the popular vote.

"Woo-eee. Now, that's judicial activism."

The Pelham Parkway section had been the epicenter of the Jewish community of the mid-twentieth-century Bronx. Schwartz's mother's visit to Lydig Avenue on Friday afternoon meant a Sunday breakfast of smoked white fish, lox, and fresh bagels. The jewel of the neighborhood—a majestic stretch of green grass divided by a wide boulevard and shouldered by twin service roads—was its namesake. Eastbound, the parkway led directly to the Bronx Riviera, officially known as Orchard Beach, and beyond to City Island with its surfeit of seafood restaurants and marinas. Westbound, it bisected the Bronx Zoo and the New York Botanical Gardens and, as it emerged from an overpass, morphed into Fordham Road, the working-class shopping magnet.

While the image of the Bronx had declined during the past half century, a poster child for urban decay and blight, Pelham Parkway continued to hold its head high, sporting some of the finest apartment housing in the Bronx. Furnished with marble mantles and brass banisters with murals gracing the walls, the lobby of the building Abbatiello's sister lived in reflected the neighborhood's charms.

Before ringing the buzzer to the apartment, Schwartz inhaled the exotic ambrosia of Jewish and Italian cooking enveloping the hallway. He glanced at the outline of a Mezuzah secured to the upper-right doorjamb. It had been painted over several times. Once he buzzed, he could hear small feet running to the door, chased by the admonitions of an adult female. The same voice called accusingly through the door, "Who's there?"

The peephole shuttered like the lens of a camera.

"It's Mr. Schwartz, the lawyer from court. Alphonso called before."

Schwartz sensed the deep breath being taken on the other side of the door. Slowly the door chain came unhinged. The deadbolts, which rendered these apartments firetraps, were unlocked. The door opened slowly, and a little blond head stuck through the bottom of the opening.

"Hi," the little blond head said and ran in the other direction as the door opened wider. Schwartz could hear the child's yelps of excitement.

"Grandma! Grandma! We have a visitor! We have a visitor! Just like you said."

In the doorway stood a woman who introduced herself as Abbatiello's sister. She beckoned Schwartz to enter. Her greeting carried an inflection that owed as much to the streets of Naples as to those of the Bronx.

"Come in, Mister. Paulie, calm-a down. Calm-a down or I'm a gonna tell the man to go away."

Duly chastised, Paulie returned to the doorway and took Schwartz's extended hand.

"Hey, Paulie, my name is Mr. Schwartz."

"Come meet my Grandma."

Schwartz was led in hand past the kitchen and into the living room. Still in her housecoat and seated on the plastic-covered Italian provincial couch was an elderly woman puffing on a brown cigarette. A cup of espresso and an Italian newspaper sat on the marble table with gold-painted Romanesque wooden legs.

The woman scrunched up her face and gathered the opening of her housecoat.

"Howza my boy?"

"Alphonso? He could be better. But as far as I can see, nobody's hurt him."

"Ah, nobody but-a that Irish *puttana* wife of his."

Schwartz looked down at the boy whose hand he was holding and turned to the aunt.

"Is there some place I can talk to Paul alone?"

The grandmother rose, snuffed out her cigarette, and picked up her paper.

"Nunge you worry. You talk-a right here. I go to my room. Come here, Paulie. Give Grandma a kiss. I haven't seen you for so long. Uhm-wah! Such a boy."

As she released the boy's cheeks from her two handed pinch, she looked up at Schwartz. "You do the right thing by this-a boy, ho-kay?"

"OK, Mrs. Abbatiello."

Schwartz declined the coffee offered him. The women retreated from the living room. Paulie was a slight youngster, just over five years old, with albino-blond hair. His delicate lips broke the ice before Schwartz could announce the purpose of his visit. In his whiny high-pitched voice, he demonstrated his father's flair for getting right to the point.

"I want to live with my daddy."

Schwartz let this declaration hang in the air for a moment.

"Do you know who I am and why I've come to talk to you?"

"No."

"Did anyone tell you what to say to me when you saw me?"

The boy put a finger to his lips and twisted his body as he shook his head.

Right.

Schwartz found these law guardian interviews to be depressing affairs. The concept of a lawyer interviewing a five-year-old client to glean his wishes or concerns was daunting enough. But to suspect, with reason, that the parents had attempted to brainwash these youngsters in advance sickened him, as well as every judge, referee, lawyer, social worker, and therapist toiling in the Children's Best Interest Industrial Complex.

"So, Paulie, have you started school yet?"

"I go to kinnergarden. My daddy's gonna take me from school and we're gonna go to his farm and ride on the horses. And he bought me a big elephant that I'm gonna feed bananas to."

"What else do you do with daddy?"

"We do boxing and we beat up the bad guys. All the bad people in mommy's family. An' if any monster come into my room, daddy says he's gonna beat them up, too."

"And what about mommy? What does she do with you?"

"Mommy won't let me talk to daddy on the phone. He says he's gonna buy me a phone and . . . and . . . I'm gonna call him and go to his house and play with the dog he got me. But I know mommy won't let me keep it."

Certain red flags guide the Solomonic task of separating the good parent from the bad. For example, if a parent used drugs, he or she was "bad." Little mind, if any, was paid to the type of drug (cocaine, heroin, marijuana, alcohol), the circumstances under which it was ingested (Saturday-night clubbing, stress reduction while caring for toddlers, mainlining in the park), or whether the parent was an addict or a recreational user. In the eyes of the court, if you use drugs, you're an unfit mother or a neglectful father. Schwartz believed, however, that there were loving, functioning, grounded parents who used drugs and lousy, immature, abusive parents who didn't partake. Since the court could test for drugs and alcohol in the urine, blood, cotton swab or hair follicle, it became an objective test for "bad" parents. That was a certainty given the waves of uncertainty that washed over the beaches of family court decision makers every livelong day. The drug test was a "gotcha" crutch leaned on all too heavily.

The "belt question" was another litmus test. "Are you now or have you ever been hit by your mommy (or daddy or other person legally responsible for your care and custody) with a belt, and if so, did it leave marks?" If the answer was "yes," then the conclusion was child neglect, excessive corporal punishment, and unfit parent.

Schwartz was undecided about Doctor Spock's position against corporal punishment. Yet, he did recall two times during his childhood when his mother hit him with a belt on his naked fanny—one time was for throwing rocks at a passing car and the other was for stealing an Oh Henry! bar from John's Bargain Store. He also recalled that the impression it left on him was such that he never repeated those two particular offenses again. Marjorie's and his parenting style was to spare the rod and spoil the child. However, in the face of an extreme dangerous action by either child, such as running into the street or putting a hand in a public urinal, he had doled out the occasional whack on the tush. No belts. No naked fannies. But point made, message delivered.

Was it the right or obligation of the State to remove a child from a parent or change custody from one parent to another because of one or two incidents of using a belt on the child? Schwartz had seen it happen. He had litigated cases on behalf of the offending parent and lost, time and time again. So it was with no small trepidation that he inched up to asking Paul the belt question.

Why ask it at all?

Schwartz knew it was expected. Some therapist, psychologist, social worker, or caseworker was going to ask it at some point in the case. If it was revealed that the parent had chosen belt hitting as punishment and the law guardian didn't cover it in the interview, then the law guardian looked incompetent. When interviewing young and reluctant clients, one needed to be as much Mr. Spock, of the Vulcan mind meld, as Dr. Spock, of the no-belts mind-set.

Schwartz believed he had the gist of his client's position, as well as the source of his negative references to the mother. Yet he pressed on. "Paulie, do you ever make mommy angry?"

"No."

"What if you do something bad? What does she do?"

The boy shrugged.

"Does mommy hit you?"

He shyly nodded.

"Tell me how she hits you."

"She gives me a pow-pow."

"Show me what a pow-pow is."

The boy slapped Schwartz on the top of his hand.

Schwartz felt a sigh of relief at the same time he felt the tiny sting on his hand.

"Is there anything else that mommy does to you?"

"She wash my mouth with soap if I say a bad word."

"I know that tastes yucky."

 "Am I gonna see daddy today?"

"Well, let's just answer one more question. Does daddy ever punish you?"

"No, daddy's always nice to me. He plays with me and buys me things."

Right.

"Can I go see daddy now?"

"I tell you what. You're going to take a ride in my car and we're going to go somewhere and see both your mommy and your daddy. OK?"

Paul's face brightened measurably. He stood up and ran around the apartment, yelling, "Yaaaaaaaay!"

The aunt came out. Schwartz asked her to get Paul's coat and put it on him so that they could leave. Upon hearing the commotion, the grandmother entered the room and tried to restrain the excited child with her hugs, smooshing his face with one free hand. Paul almost knocked her over as he jumped up and down. Sternly she said, *"Ashpet! Ashpet!"*

Then her tone softened. "You go, my little angel, but you come-a back. Grandma will have more little cakes for you."

Schwartz and Paul exited the elevator on the seventh floor of BxFC at the cusp of the lunch break, a stampede of hungry, aggravated BxFC litigants rushed toward them. Schwartz grabbed the boy's hand, and with the verve of an NFL running back, he darted, cut back, and used a great second effort to reach the goal line: the waiting area next to the BxFC Children's Center.

The center served the noble purpose of providing meals, storybook readings, and arts and crafts projects to litigants' children. The staffers were warm and supportive. For most children, it was the best part of the BxFC experience and perhaps an oasis in an otherwise troubled young life. Yet on occasion, it served a more sinister purpose. In the event of courthouse removals, signing a child into the center marked the last time the parent had their child(ren) in their custody.

Schwartz knew the center closed for lunch. He was counting on convincing Miss Abigail, the director of the center, to sacrifice her lunch hour and watch Paul during the break. There was a time, early in Schwartz's participation on the panel, that he regularly brought used clothing and toys for the center. He believed he had acquired some goodwill. However, his view of the center soured as he recognized its role as the disembarkation point for the foster care diaspora, and his as an enabler.

Schwartz knocked on the door. No answer. He knocked stridently. He could hear the shuffling on the other side of the door, and then a voice said, "We closed for lunch."

"Miss Abigail. It's me, Mr. Schwartz."

"Mr. who?"

Slowly the door opened. An elderly woman peeked through the crack.

"Mr. Schwartz, why we haven't seen you much in here lately? How is that lovely wife of yours who used to wrap all those things for the children?"

"She's, uh, just fine, I guess, Miss Abigail. Listen, Miss Abigail, I was wondering—"

"And those kids of yours, they must be all grown up. How old are they now?"

"My girl is nine and the boy is five. Do you think you—?"

"Mr. Schwartz, it's been ages since you brought them around here."

There had been rare occasions when Schwartz brought his children to court, either because his family was picking him up for a vacation, they were going to a Yankee game, or school was out and he had to care for them. Schwartz believed that exposure to social reality would serve them well, but as Marjorie had pointed out, not at the risk of exposure to tuberculosis, lice, and the flu.

Besides witnessing remand after remand of children on relatively minor allegations, Schwartz had a negative fantasy of his own children being remanded. It was predicated on his children making an inadvertent disclosure of his pot smoking or the heated verbal disputes he had with his wife. When his daughter whined about why she couldn't have this or why she couldn't have that, Schwartz would offer her the phone and tell her to dial the child abuse hotline.

"Julie, that's 1-800-TAKMYKD!"

Every now and again, a member of the Children's Best Interest Industrial Complex crossed the thin line from professional to client, from social worker to socially worked over, or from agency representative to respondent. They'd end up with their derrieres placed stoically on the hard wooden benches of family court for a six-hour sit. Some examples were the attorney on the panel from another borough being sued by a caseworker for paternity and child support; the court officer dragged in on a family offense case; and the caseworker whose teenager had been dealing crack cocaine. If Schwartz spotted a Complex member seated in the waiting area, wearing the glazed stare of a deer caught in the headlights of family court litigation, he would cluck his tongue and repeat the mantra, "Never, ever be the client. Never be amongst the seated."

"Miss Abigail, this is Paul. I've brought him to court so he could see the judge today. I'm wondering if you might be able to watch him during the lunch break and give him some of that cheese macaroni I hear all my little clients rave about."

"Well, seeing as I've got some paperwork to do. . . OK, bring the boy in."

Schwartz turned to the youngster and mussed his hair. "Paulie, Miss Abigail is going to stay with you while I go look for your mom and dad. You're lucky because you get all the toys and games to yourself! After lunch, there'll be other kids to play with. When the judge is finished with us, we'll come get you. OK?"

The boy gave a single uncertain nod. Schwartz was thinking of only one thing: the tattered chaise lounge he had squirreled away in a back room on the seventh floor. He and several other 18-Bs had commandeered that room years ago.

Schwartz laid his aching body on the lounge chair, the straps groaning beneath his weight. It was no matter that his ass protruded through several of the broken straps, grazing the floor. Schwartz was headed for Lalaland. Unfortunately, two distractions stood in his way: the yammering of children in the adjacent waiting area and conversations percolating in the offices of the DA's sex crime unit across the hall. It was in one of those offices that he had met with ADA Mulrooney to conference the Matter of Hakim Johnson. As he attempted to sleep, he could hear Mulrooney on the telephone with a witness.

"Doctor, the jury's been impaneled. You have to appear tomorrow. You're my first witness. What? OK. I'll hold. . . OK. You have your examination notes? The hospital record says . . . that's right, lesions at four and six o'clock."

As Schwartz struggled to find sleep, he was confident that he wouldn't dream of Violetta Pichardo and her vagina clock. Between meeting the girl today and hearing the ADA prepare for the trial, he thought the issue was too embedded in his consciousness to reach him from his subconscious. It was a mind trick he'd learned as a child when monster nightmares afflicted his sleep. He found that if he consciously thought about monsters while lying in bed, he wouldn't recall any nightmares upon waking. Falling asleep after that mental exercise, however, proved to be problematic.

*Ah, to sleep, perchance **not** to dream.*

Someone opened the door and turned on the light.

"Oh, I'm sorry, Mr. Schwartz," said a woman's voice.

As Schwartz's mind rode the elevator back to consciousness, he glanced at his watch, shielding his eyes from the overhead light. Sweat had soaked through his undershirt to his dress shirt. It was 3:30 p.m.

"Oh, shit. I've got to get to the ref's part."

With blurry vision, he barely recognized the woman. She was a relatively new member of the panel. He didn't yet know her name. How she had earned admission to the secret back room fraternity was a question Schwartz was not prepared to wrestle with at that moment. Focused on the task at hand, he attempted to rise without success. His ribs were locked into the prone position, and he rolled off the lounge chair and onto the floor. Once on his hands and knees, he rose to his feet with the imbalance of a boxer counted out on a TKO.

"Mr. Schwartz, do you need help?"

"Counselor, note my appearance," he grumbled to himself.

Like a million dollars—all green and wrinkly.

The door to Ref. Yellin's part was locked. An unmistakable *vzumm-vzumm* registered in Schwartz's senses, setting off fight-or-flight adrenaline flares. In the narrow hallway, Andrew Timmons, the petition clerk of wide girth, was walking with a deliberate gait toward him. The substantial stack of case jackets Timmons held in his arms covered his face. Just before force met object, Schwartz leaned against the wall and sucked in his gut, to the acute displeasure of his sautéed ribs. As Timmons passed, he noticed Schwartz for the first time.

Without slowing his inexorable march down the hallway, Timmons said in his low gurgle of a voice, "Mr. Schwartz, if you're looking for Yellin, she's down."

Once again spared a squashing, Schwartz let out his breath.

"But I still have a case with her."

"Try Part 5."

Each referee's part was aligned with a judge's part, the latter feeding cases to the former. Judges despised the "Did not! Did too!" nature of custody and visitation cases and relished the opportunity to dump them on the referees. Occasionally, however, the legal offal would flow uphill, returning to the judge's part in the guise of a return on a warrant with a request for incarceration on an alleged violation of an order of protection, such as in the Abbattiello matter. The referees lacked the power to entertain such applications, so back to the jurist in the black robe went the case

Schwartz walked into Judge Catherine Fitzgibbons's part, but the judge was not on the bench. He had passed the mother and father in the Abbatiello case in the waiting room, so he knew the case hadn't yet been called. Don Edgardo was standing in the middle of the courtroom addressing the clerks, court officers, and attorneys.

"So I says to the Judge, 'Your Honor, you must dismiss this case against my client because the statute he is charged with violating—Section 130.00 of the Peeeeeenal Law, which defines the offense of "deviant sexual contact"—is irreparably flawed. It defines such contact as the touching of the mouth to the penis, the mouth to the vulva, and the penis to the anus. But the statute omits one crucial combination: touching of the mouth to the anus, colloquially known as ass kissing. And do you know why, Your Honor? Because the New York State Legislature knew that if they made ass kissing illegal, they'd all be thrown in jail. So you must dismiss."

The howling in courtroom subsided abruptly as Fitzgibbons entered from her back office.

A former nun, she strode solemnly to her bench. The judge scanned the faces of the gathered for the culprit who dared to riddle her courtroom with laughter just prior to her entry. Failing to discern the guilty party, she settled on an old parochial school solution: everyone was guilty and, therefore, everyone should be admonished.

"Counsels, if you'd like to tell dirty jokes, perhaps we can recall your cases at 5:00 p.m. And at that point you'll be picking an adjourned date with my court attorney. Now, let's cut out the shenanigans and conduct ourselves like lawyers in a courtroom. I know it's a stretch for some of you, but indulge me. Call a case— any case that's ready."

Paul's father and mother were led in from the well, he in handcuffs, she holding a fistful of papers.

"Matter of the Abbatiello Child, counsel, and parties, note your appearance."

The appearances noted, Judge Fitzgibbons cast a withering glance in the direction of the father.

"Kidnapping is a serious matter, Sir. I have a good mind to send you to civil jail for a week to think upon that. If a court order says no contact, there's to be no contact. Understood?"

Abbatiello began, "But, Your Honor—"

Don Edgardo cut him off.

"Judge, we understand the court's order. My client just wants to spend some time with his son. If the court insists, for the time being, on supervised visitation, his mother and sister can supervise."

Gwendolyn Benoit rose ever so slowly.

"Judge, they can't supervise. They can't be trusted. The grandmother and aunt harbored the child for the father and kept him from the mother. Forensics ordered by Referee Yellin need to be completed before we change anything. This man is psychotic. He fills the child's head with nonsense."

"I'll hear from the law guardian."

In this instance, Schwartz chose to apply the Hindu god model for problem resolution. On one hand, the boy loved the father and was at no apparent risk of physical danger in the father's company. On the other hand, the father was a loose cannon capable of running with his son. On the other hand, Schwartz thought of his own difficulties seeing and spending time with his children. On the other hand, the father was playing mind games with Paul. On the other hand, the mother wasn't completely innocent in that regard. On the other hand, if, before forensics, the father disappeared with the child after Schwartz recommended visitation supervised by a paternal relative, it would be his ass in the sling. On the other hand . . . Schwartz was out of hands.

"Law guardian recommends supervised visitation by a professional program until we have the forensics completed."

Edgardo weighed in.

"As the law guardian well knows, such programs have long waiting lists of over two months. How is my client to see the child in the meantime?"

Schwartz searched his heart, his mind, and his calendar.

"Until we find an opening, I'll supervise the visits once per week in family court."

Fitzgibbons knew a resolution when she heard one. "Warrant vacated. Writ satisfied. I'm re-issuing an order of protection under the custody docket. 'Father not to interfere with mother's care and custody of the child.' Mr. Abbatiello, I strongly suggest that you abide by the court's order or you'll be packing a toothbrush for the Bronx County Civil Jail. Take advantage of Mr. Schwartz's gracious proposal. Matter adjourned back to Referee Yellin for the completion of forensics. Parties are to cooperate. Mr. Schwartz, get that forensic order prepared for the referee. How's March 15? Good for everyone? Fine. Seems like an appropriate case for the Ides of March."

Fitzgibbons permitted herself a chuckle and nodded in Schwartz's direction. The court officer instructed the litigants to exit the courtroom. There was a calendar to complete and the start time for the courthouse bowling league at Stadium Lanes was 6:00 p.m. Schwartz had his own agenda: a 7:00 p.m. concert at Ethan's school.

As he hurried through the waiting room, Don Edgardo's voice rang out, "Mr. Schwartz, can I have a word with you?"

Ramos was huddled in a corner of the waiting area with the father, grandmother, and aunt. Schwartz could see Paul in another corner, bracketed by the mother and her lawyer. Don Edgardo beckoned Schwartz to talk with him privately.

"Where are you hurrying to? Somebody handing out half-price coupons for Staples? We've got to set up a visitation schedule. Besides, that whore isn't even letting my client say good-bye to the kid. What kinda *mierda* is that? Don't answer; it's a rhetorical question."

"I have one of the non-rhetorical variety. How'd you get retained?"

"What do you mean? The family called me."

"Bullshit. His family didn't even know he'd been arrested."

"You know, Schwartz, you're a much better lawyer than you are a businessman. And you're a lousy lawyer."

"What's your point?"

"*Schmegegge.* Is that a word? I mean, is it like a *schlemiel,* akin to a *schlimazel,* but not quite as detestable as a *schmuck,* right?"

"Flattery will get you nowhere. How'd you get retained?"

"Do you know why—I see them leaving, Sir. I'll deal with it." He called out, "Ms. Benoit, can you and your client wait one minute, please? Thank you."

Turning back to Schwartz, he continued, "Why do you think I have a ground-floor office with a big picture window right across the street from family court?"

"So potential clients can see your office. I understand, but—"

"You understand only partway, my friend. That window works two ways. If my secretary happens to see cops dragging a white man in handcuffs through the revolving doors of family court, she alerts me. I make inquiries among my friends in the building and *Voilà!* Client has counsel, and, more importantly, counsel has client. Now that I've delivered a lecture from Law Practice Economics 101, I need to collect my fee. Just give me a date and time that the father can see the child in your good company."

Schwartz sighed, took out his date book, and leafed through the pages for the coming weeks.

"Fridays at 1:00 p.m."

"Fine. Do me one more favor: confirm it with Gwen and the whore. And for Chrissakes, let the father say good-bye to the boy. Meanwhile, this is for you."

Ramos thrust a small envelope into Schwartz's hand. Schwartz recoiled. He whispered, "What are you, fuckin' nuts? In a crowded waiting room, no less."

"Relax, Serpico. It's not what you think. It's an invitation."

Schwartz meandered over to Benoit, the mother, and Paul.

"Counsel, how's Wednesdays at 1:00 p.m. for the mother to bring the child for visitation?"

The mother piped up.

"I work during the day. I can't bring him. Besides, is he going to pay my carfare? It's thirty bucks round trip for a cab."

Schwartz grimaced. He knew that Ms. Benoit had a soft spot under her gruff exterior.

"Ms. Benoit, can I talk to you briefly?"

They stepped several feet away.

"Look, Gwen, your client has the upper hand here. But advise her not to overplay it. This case will go on for a while and I have—and, more important— the boy has a long memory. It behooves a mother seeking to retain primary custody to be open to visitation. Does your client have anyone who can bring the child? A babysitter? A relative? Frankly, I think the less the two of them see each other, the better. And tell her I don't want to hear from my client that she debriefed him after the visit."

"OK. OK. I'll talk to her. But he'll have to pony up the cab fare."

"Fine. In the meantime, does your client mind if I take Paul's hand and walk him over to his dad?"

"Give me a second."

Benoit quickly conferred with the mother. The mother's body twisted as she shook her head. Benoit put her hand on her shoulder and whispered something in her ear. She relented with a tentative nod. Benoit motioned for Schwartz to approach.

"Fridays at one o'clock it is," she confirmed.

The mother gently nudged Paul in Schwartz's direction. Schwartz reached down and grabbed his hand.

"See? I told you you'd get to see your daddy today."

The boy looked up at him and stopped walking.

"I don' wanna to see him."

"What do you mean?"

"He scares me."

Schwartz stood with the child in the waiting area equidistant between the two sets of parents and lawyers. The prospect of dragging the boy across the room to the father did not appeal to him. He bent down and knelt on one knee so he was at eye level with the boy.

"Been quite a day for you, hasn't it?"

The boy started to speak but held his tongue.

"Maybe we'll try to see daddy next week. Can you just give him a little wave?"

The boy did as Schwartz asked.

"OK. I'll see you next week. And I'm going to give you a ride in one of the rocket racing chairs that we keep in the back for special kids like you."

He walked Paul back to his mother and shot her a knowing glance. Then he crossed the waiting room to Don Edgardo and Abbatiello.

"The boy's stressed out. I'll see you next week Wednesday at 1:00 p.m. And bring some cab fare."

Schwartz hustled to Cliff's part but it was already locked. He made his way to the court officer's locker room on the sixth floor. He knocked. Officer Mama's Boy opened the door.

"Can I help you, Counselor?"

The tone of his voice suggested anything but help.

"Is Cliff in there?"

"'Fraid not."

The officer started to close the door in Schwartz's face, but Schwartz blocked it with his foot.

"Cliff?" he shouted.

Cliff came to the door half in his uniform, half in civvies. Officer Mama's Boy withdrew, cursing.

"What's up? You got the keys?"

Schwartz entered the inner sanctum, the venue for the longest continuous established lunchtime poker game in the city, if not the tri-state area.

"Listen, Cliff, I need to take the car tonight."

"Another emergency? Look, Schwartz, you said you were bringing a motion to get me my ride back. Have you done it yet?"

"I promise I'll file the papers tomorrow."

"That's not good enough. You've been promising me that all week."

"Cliff, it's my boy's winter concert, and I promised him I'd be there. Where do you have to go? To Stadium Lanes? It's bowling league night, right? I'll drive you."

Cliff's face tightened as if he were passing a kidney stone.

"Man, that's not fair, playing the fatherhood card on me now. All right. Look, you don't have to drive me. I can walk there. But you do have to pick my butt up at eleven. You got it? You got it? Eleven!"

Schwartz clenched his fist and did a two-step and offered a high-five that Cliff reciprocated.

Schwartz beamed as he said "Who loves you, man?"

"All right, cut the corny crap and go listen to 'Jingle Bells' and 'I Have a Little Dreidel.' But I want my ride back!"

Schwartz ran for the judges' elevator in the secured corridor. As he pressed the down button, he kept an eye out for Captain Dolan. Then he ran to press the button for the abutting garbage elevator. Whichever came first, judge or garbage, he was jumping on. It was the judges' elevator that claimed itself the winner with its red down arrow flashing. Schwartz uttered, "May I?" and took a giant step into the empty elevator. Of course, the elevator went up. Schwartz cursed the elevator's randomness. It stopped on the ninth floor, where Judge Finkel boarded, causing the emotional temperature to dip just below freezing.

"Have you received a promotion that I'm not aware of, Mr. Schwartz? As supervising judge, I'm continuously surprised that I'm always out of the loop."

Mercifully, the second-floor elevator door opened and Schwartz made his escape, finding and then running down the stairs to the street. He knew he'd be hearing from Dolan in the morning about taking privileges with the judge's elevator. He hurried to Papo's yard, inserted the key in the gate lock, and warily surveyed the yard for El Diablo. The three-legged dog with the barely audible bark was visible, as were the chicken and ducks. Schwartz knew that somewhere lurking behind a parked car or shed was that friggin' ambushing, castrating rooster, but he was ready.

Just as he inserted his key into the Saab's door, he saw the blur of white coming from underneath his car. He quickly reached into his pocket, pulled out a piece of a pretzel he'd just purchased from the wagon on the corner, and threw it away from the Saab.

What's it gonna be, bird? My penis or the pretzel?

The ever-hungry rooster dove for the morsels, and Schwartz dove into the car.

I hope El Diablo likes mustard.

At 7:10 p.m. Schwartz parked the Saab outside Ethan's elementary school. He knew these concerts rarely started on time, but still he hurried. A wintry mix of snow and rain had made the sequence of bottleneck-traffic light-construction project-detour commute nettlesome than usual. Every second of the journey, he cursed the day he'd moved to the Island.

A bored fifth grader handing out programs at the door greeted Schwartz. Scanning the paper, he read that Ethan's group, the Boys' Chorus, aka the Buckaroos, was scheduled to perform after intermission. He needn't have hurried and could have stopped at the local Chinese takeout and gotten a quart-sized pail full of wonton soup with a side of stale noodles.

Schwartz resigned himself to an evening of off-key clarinets, woefully dragging violins, and cutesy renditions of songs of the season. This was the price he paid to hear his nightingale sing out above all others. Oh, he'd clap for the other kids in all the right places, but he really just wanted to hear his own Pavoratti. He was no different than any other mother or father gathered on that slushy evening. They were all devotees of the late-twentieth-century Cult of the

Child. Put these same parents in the daytime guise of family court judge, attorney, social worker, caseworker, school guidance counselor, etc., and the effect on the poor, working-class, and immigrant families of the inner city was pernicious. Their middle-class assumptions about child rearing colored all too many decisions made in the name of the "best interests of the children."

"You didn't take your child to the hospital when he had a fever?"

"You made your thirteen-year-old daughter watch the younger kids and cook and clean?"

"You let you five-year-old son and three-year-old daughter sleep in the same bed?"

The off-the-record snickering from some judges, attorneys, and court staff disclosed their racism and classism. Their bias seeped out sideways as they referenced the unusual names of respondents' children; the large number of children on a petition, fathered by different men; or the unfamiliar hairstyles or outfits worn by the teens, which their own children would emulate when the urban fashion migrated to the 'burbs a couple of years later.

As if they were sheep jumping over the fence, Schwartz counted the number of performances until intermission and began to doze off. As a result, he committed the most unpardonable sin in school concert protocol, worse than a beeping cell phone and far more catastrophic than a hacking cough. He started to snore.

When the lights came up after intermission, Schwartz received a sharp jab to his sore ribs. His beloved soon-to-be ex-spouse was shaking him awake. Marjorie was flanked by his beloved daughter, Julie, and his not-so-beloved classmate and newfound tennis partner, Rufus Blumenthal, Esq.

Marjorie spoke with her wonderful, sarcastic singsong lilt, "Wake up, Schwartzie. You've just succeeded in embarrassing us in front of the entire school."

"Huh? Huh? Uccchhhhhhhhhh. Hey, Marj, Jules. Blumy."

Still seated, he caressed his face then stretched his arms in the air. As his hands reached the apogee of the stretch, he felt something placed in his right hand. It was a paper. He lowered his hands and, using his still-clearing vision, took a gander. The document consisted of several pages and had a telltale blue legal backing. The first page commenced with a caption:

FAMILY COURT OF THE STATE OF NEW YORK
COUNTY OF NASSAU
--X

In the Matter of Proceeding under

DKT # 0-13789/2000

Article 8 of the Family Court Act

TEMPORARY ORDER,
OF PROTECTION

MARJORIE SCHWARTZ,

Petitioner, Exparte

—against-

He stopped reading.

"Are you kidding me?" Schwartz shouted as he rose from his seat.

The smile on Blumenthal's face was pure Cheshire cat.

"You've been served, Sleeping Beauty, and it's a stay-away order, so I think you'd best be leaving."

"What are the allegations?"

Schwartz flipped furiously, searching for the factual allegations page of the petition. He had held papers such as these well over five hundred times, but in that moment he lost his legal bearings.

Here it is.

"3. On or about December 12, 2000, at approximately six o'clock in the forenoon, the Respondent committed an act or acts constituting Aggravated Harassment in the Second Degree, in violation of Section 240.30 of the Penal Law of the State of New York in that with intent to harass, annoy, threaten, or alarm another person, he communicated by mechanical or electronic means or otherwise, with the Petitioner, Marjorie Schwartz, by telephone, in a manner likely to cause annoyance or alarm in that Respondent did use vulgar language."

"This is bullshit! Marjorie, what the hell is happening here?" Schwartz screamed as he strode toward her. A buffer of social space had formed around them in the auditorium. Blumenthal stepped between them.

"Counselor, I don't think you're pleading your case very well. In fact, I believe you just violated the order with your use of that epithet. As you know, a violation, if proven, can carry a term of imprisonment of up to six months. It's best you leave now. We'll see you on the return date of the summons, December 24th."

Schwartz stared at the paper and then at his wife and daughter. Julie was in tears. Marjorie slowly shook her head. Schwartz turned and walked out of the auditorium.

For ten minutes, Schwartz sat in his Saab, hyper-ventilating. He'd crossed the line. He'd become a despondent respondent. The only thing that separated him and Abbatiello was a pair of bunny slippers.

What would Alphonso Abbatiello do?

Inspiration moved him to get out of the car and climb onto the roof of the vehicle. The wet weather had subsided somewhat. As he had hoped, through the auditorium's window, he was able to see Ethan and the Buckaroos on stage, warbling their songs of seasonal cheer. He could even hear the faint mingling and mangling of the harmonies. He knew that Ethan may never know, but Schwartz had kept his promise to see, if not fully hear, his son's concert.

"Daddy. What are you doing?" Julie asked sharply.

Schwartz almost slipped from the car's roof. Barely managing to control his balance, he climbed down and sat on the hood.

"Attending the winter concert, what else? Hey, your mother and her Doberman will be looking for you. How'd you get out?"

"I told mom I had to use the bathroom."

"Well, I hope you're going for a two and not a one."

"Oh, daddy, you are so gross!"

"I'm nothing if not that."

They both laughed. Schwartz slid off the hood and they hugged.

"Daddy, what's happening to our family?"

"Nothing good, baby doll. Nothing good. Go back inside. Don't worry. I know a pretty good family court lawyer. I'll be seeing you and Ethan soon."

"Take care of yourself, daddy. Happy Hanukkah."

"Yeah, Happy Hanukkah. Oh, listen, here's some gelt for you and Ethan."

He reached into his pocket, and from a wad of papers he retrieved two wrinkly five-dollar bills. He placed them in her hand and gave her a kiss. Schwartz turned her in the direction of the school entrance and gave her a gentle push on the small of her back.

As he watched Julie walk away, his eyes began to well up. Schwartz searched for a crumpled but clean tissue to wipe his freezing tears. Instead he found the envelope Don Edgardo gave him at the courthouse. Opening the envelope, he pulled out a four-color four-by-six card. With the limited light coming through window from the auditorium, he read the flyer from Jimmy's Bronx Café:

Jimmy's Bronx Café
Presents A SPECIAL KARAOKE NIGHT CELEBRATION
THURDAY, DECEMBER 12
A BIRTHDAY TRIBUTE TO

OL' BLUE EYES: FRANK SINATRA

Prizes-Suprizes   Doors open at 9:00 p.m.

"Purrrrfect."

In the background Schwartz could hear his son's faint voice singing a solo on "The Dreidel Song."

HAPPY BIRTHDAY
OL' BLUE EYES

SCHWARTZ HAD ARRIVED AT STADIUM LANES AT 10:30 P.M., IN time to witness Cliff blow a 7–8 pin spare that would have sealed his team's victory for the night. In his foul mood, Cliff had insisted on driving home and demanded the keys from Schwartz.

"Ah'm not going to some dumb-ass karaoke contest. Bunch of vocally challenged wannabees laying waste to the Great American Songbook. You want to hear some music, we'll go to a couple of spots I know in Harlem. Tell me there's a tribute to Coltrane or Bird and I'm there."

"You look like you need to unwind a little. I was just suggesting that you have some fun. Talk to some honeys. You know by that time their kids are in bed with Tata babysitting. They're coming out just to meet you. And after they've sung the evening's third rendition of "Leader of the Pack" or "I Will Survive," you sidle up to them and coo your glowing review of their performance in their ears. My friend, that's an icebreaker that would have saved the *Titanic*."

"Check you out. Since when did you become an expert on strategies for attracting the opposite sex? I've just about had all the fun that one man can stand for one evening."

Cliff was silent for a moment. Then--

"I tell you what. We'll drive over to Jimmy's. If it's whack, I'm a ghost and you're walking back to the crib."

Jimmy's Bronx Café was the perfect venue for a Sinatra tribute. Jimmy's reputation was once enjoyed by Jilly's of the Rat Pack era. The difference-- Jilly's had a Sicilian accent and Jimmy's was distinctly Dominican. Jimmy's was located at a gateway to the Bronx, the junction of western terminus of Fordham Road and the 207th Street Bridge over the Harlem River. It was housed in a converted car dealership that for decades had beckoned to potential customers as they traveled the Major Deegan Expressway.

Jimmy's attracted clientele that didn't flinch at paying twenty-two dollars for a plate of rice, provided the music was pumping. Rubén Sierra, a major league ball player with a good bat and questionable glove, had allegedly been a not-so-silent partner of Jimmy's during his brief tenure with the Yankees in the mid-'90s. Rubén sponsored a post-game delivery from Jimmy's during that time. Chafing dishes filled with *arroz y habichuelas*, *plantanos maduro*, and *yuca con ajo* feted the Yankee clubhouse.

The walls at Jimmy's were plastered with photos of the proprietor joined by athletes, politicians, and musical artists. There was also an impressive collection of autographed baseball jerseys, boxers' shorts, and gloves. For reasons hinted at in the sports pages but never disclosed, Major League Baseball directed players to steer clear of the place and ordered Rubén to divest. As with Joe Namath and the Bachelors III bar in the late '60s, Rubén ultimately complied.

Depending on one's perspective, the occasional shoot-out outside Jimmy's, endemic to club life in the City, added to the luster of the place. Thursday night karaoke attracted an older and highly judgmental crowd that gave the notorious audiences from Amateur Night at the Apollo a run for their money.

In the parking lot, Cliff debated whether or not to bring in his service revolver. "I just might have to shoot you to put you and me both out of our collective misery."

"Be glad I don't pull you up onstage with me."

"I didn't know that Bobby Darin required on-stage security."

"In an audience of Sinatra fans, perhaps. Should I go wig?"

Schwartz reached into the glove compartment and slapped a pompadour rug on his head. Tilting the Saab's mirror in his direction, he combed up the front.

"Oh no, you didn't."

"Never leave home without it."

"You are off the hook!"

"What? Too over the top? Pun intended."

"Where'd you get that thing? At a . . . a . . . chemotherapy patient's estate sale?"

Cliff was able to bring his piece through front-door security since one of the bouncers was a supreme court C.O. and an academy classmate of his. Schwartz spotted Don Edgardo at the horseshoe-shaped bar. A cadre of middle-age damsels surrounded him as the old Ramos wit and wallet wended their magic. Schwartz managed to sneak up behind Don Edgardo and plant a kiss on the back of his neck. The barrister turned and radiated with glee.

"Schwartz, you fuck. You made it. What, you run over a squirrel on the way over here?"

He tried to run his hands through Schwartz's hairpiece, but Schwartz deflected the attempt.

"And I see you brought the *gendarme* with you. Are you applying for membership in the Society of Kindred Spirits, Cliff?"

Don Edgardo shook Cliff's hand. Cliff waved his hand in front of his face to clear the air of the alcohol breath and the residue of tobacco smoke. Don Edgardo was oblivious to the gesture. His slur was in second gear, shifting into third. He whispered into Schwartz's ear, "Whores. I love them."

Raising his voice and turning toward the bar, he uttered the words that warmed the ears of Schwartz the Schnorrer: "Whaddayaguysdrinkin?" Motioning to the barmaid, who was barely above the legal drinking age, Don Edgardo began his shtick. "Madam bartender, these gentlemen are my friends. I ask that if they should ever frequent your establishment in the future that you extend to them the same courtesies that you would extend to me."

With a crack of her gum, the nymph barmaid rolled her eyes as she asked "What can I get you?"

The karaoke tracks was pumping over the sound system. Sinatra wannabes were prowling the bar area, practicing their menacing glares and cufflink thrusts. Playlists containing multiple artists were circulating, as were song slips and short pencils. Schwartz reached for a list and read the offerings presented for the Darin karaoke repertoire. They were the usual suspects.

"Beyond the Sea." Possible. Possible. "Mack the Knife"? Been a long day. Don't have it in me. "Splish Splash"? Nah, too up-tempo.

On a song slip, Schwartz scribbled "Beyond the Sea" along with the corresponding track number and handed it to the karaoke guy, who asked, "That a Sinatra tune?"

"Does it have to be?"

"If you want to be in the contest, it does."

"I'll pass on the contest. That's my song."

"*No problemo.* There are about three people ahead of you."

"Cool, daddy-o." Schwartz cooed, shooting his hands, gun-like, in the karaoke guy's direction. Swiveling on his heel and toe in an about-face, he headed to the men's room. He paid for the move with a throb in his rib.

There was an ubiquitous sampling of combs, aftershave bottles, mousse cans, hair gels, breath sprays, mouthwashes, toothpastes, razor blades, gum, and mints covering the sink countertops. Primping in front of the mirror, sharply dressed patrons crowded the lavatory. They bantered good-naturedly in Spanish with the attendant. The attendant pushed his tie collection as he slid a hand towel in front of each preener. Schwartz angled himself in front of a urinal, unzipped his fly, and waited for the cascading relief. It wouldn't flow. The more he tried, the more blocked he felt. The few droplets that leaked out caused a burning sensation so severe that Schwartz's urethra involuntarily shut down. He feigned the need to shake urine off his peashooter and flushed the urinal.

"Ah'll be back," he growled Teutonically to no one in particular.

Schwartz grabbed a hand towel off the dispenser before the attendant could slide one in his direction, thus avoiding the necessity to tip. He checked his pomp in the mirror, made a few adjustments, cupped his hands under the running sink and gargled warm-up sounds. He headed back to the bar but not before sneaking a mint into his pocket, ignoring the cursing attendant.

As Schwartz rejoined his friends, a contestant was winding up a tortured rendition of "Strangers in the Night." Cliff was shaking his head.

"Brutal. Just brutal. I don't think I can take much more."

"C'mon, man, I'm next after next."

Don Edgardo was engaged in an animated debate with an older black gentleman sitting at the bar about the relative merits of the former's chosen profession.

"Y'all a bunch of liars."

"Let me tell you sump-in'. Behind every stinkin', rotten, lyin', backstabbin' lawyer, there's a stinkin', rotten, lyin', backstabbin' client payin' him to be that way. Jes' wait till your ass is sittin' in Central Booking all night, waitin' for night arraignment. You wont be cryin' for your momma. You be cryin' like a bitch: 'Where my liar?'"

The man grunted while dodging Edgardo's saliva spray.

"Man, I pay lawyas three hundred fifty dollars to show up in court. They waltz in at 11:30, case already be done. An' the motherfucker 'spects to get paid? That's boolshit, I tell you."

The barrister wrapped his arms around Schwartz's shoulders.

"You want an honest lawyer? Here's exhibit A. A member of the most honest bar in the entire court system: the Assigned Counsel Panel. 'Cause it don't matter to their wallet if they win or lose. Not gonna make an extra buck either which way."

Schwartz winced at the sad truth.

Edgardo then addressed Schwartz. "So how'd the tennis match go?"

Schwartz shot back, "Don Edgardo, with friends like you, who needs an enema?"

As the laughter subsided, karaoke guy was introducing the next singer. Don Edgardo proffered a toast.

"To Ol' Blue Eyes. Happy Birthday, Frank."

Momentarily forgetting his bloated bladder, Schwartz took a swill of his Scotch and Ginger Ale.

"To Ol' Blue Eyes," Schwartz repeated and then whined, "But why'd you have to die on Bobby Darin's birthday?"

Cliff shushed them into silence. "Now, this boy can *sing!*"

On stage was a short, skinny Hispanic youth with a chiseled face. He'd been introduced as Marc Muniz. Schwartz thought he recognized the boy from somewhere. He began to croon an early Sinatra standard, "All the Way." Like campfires being doused one by one, the conversations in the large room died and attention focused on Muniz.

He's a ringer.

Muniz finished with an oversized flourish. Amidst the thunderous applause, a lady stood up and started shrieking, "That's Marc Anthony! That's Marc Anthony!"

Soon practically everyone in the room joined her, calling out his name. Schwartz was the lone exception. Instead, he rued his bad luck to follow that act.

The skinny young man was nowhere to be found. The room was abuzz with speculation that Marc Anthony was dining and decided, on a whim, to sing. Schwartz's bladder was bursting. His diffident inclination was to return to the men's room, but as he rose he heard his name being called to the microphone. He quickly combed his pomp, received a pat on the back from Ramos and Cliff, and headed toward the karaoke guy.

"Go get 'em, Bobby D.!" Cliff hooted.

Schwartz ascended the risers, mike in hand, and addressed the crowd.

"I know we're all here to celebrate the life of Frank Sinatra, the kid from Hoboken. But there was another Italian city kid who showed much promise. He grew up a couple of miles from here, in the South Bronx. Went to Bronx Science. Stricken with rheumatic fever when he was eight years old, the doctors told him he wasn't going to live past twelve, then sixteen, then twenty. So he lived every day as if it were his last. He died at the age of thirty-seven from complications after heart surgery."

A voice in the crowd yelled out, "Wha dee fuck is all dis *mierda*?"

Unfazed, Schwartz carried on. "Maestro, if you please." He signaled to the karaoke guy to start the music. "Ladies and gentleman, Mr. Bobby Darin."

A smattering of applause greeted his announcement, along with several voices questioning, "Who?"

Schwartz ignored the word prompt on the television monitor, choosing instead to pace back and forth on the riser and interact with the crowd as he sang "Beyond the Sea".

To his mind Schwartz was holding his own, but he sensed restlessness in in the crowd as he reached for the high notes. Concentrating on his singing, his efforts to control his bladder were diverted and several droplets leaked out. Schwartz felt that acute burning sensation again.

During the instrumental break of Richard Weiss' kick-ass arrangement, as the horns came crashing in, Schwartz pantomimed playing the trumpet. With the violin counterpoint, he moved an invisible bow across his left arm. Just as he was about to resume singing, a man jumped onto the riser and tackled him to the ground, shouting, "*Maricon*, I keel you! I keel you!"

As he rolled on the floor with the man, Schwartz's first thought was, *Man, they take their Sinatra shit seriously here.*

His second thought was to fend off the maniac as best as he could. Unable to hold back his flow any longer, he pissed all over the guy as Schwartz rolled on top. This strategy flushed out not only his swollen bladder but also his assailant's identity.

"Aiiii, Schwartz! I keel you twice! You fuck with my woman and you piss on me!"

The over enthusiastic vocal critic was none other than Hector Machado, Isabel's battering boyfriend. Cliff and Don Edgardo had reached the stage and were trying to separate the two men. Apparently Machado wasn't traveling solo that night. A posse of young Dominicans rushed the risers and joined the melee. Don Edgardo, suddenly sober and energized, removed his jacket, threw punches, and yelled, "Don't let the suit fool you!"

The trio, however, was significantly out numbered. Blows, kicks, and punches were coming from all angles. Cliff was about to reach for his gun when the cavalry arrived. An even larger posse of older Hispanics led by Ronaldo Ramirez's father, stormed the stage and joined the fray against Schwartz's assaulters. The elder Ramirez pulled Machado off of Schwartz, growling in the man's ear "*Qué pasa contigo, cabron*? Dis man works for our people and you try to kill him."

Extricating Schwartz, the elder Ramirez implored him, "You and your friends leave now!"

Schwartz, Edgardo, and Cliff made their way to the front door and stumbled out. Cliff had drawn his revolver and was watching for pursuers as they approached the parking lot. Schwartz inserted the key into the ignition and attempted to start the car. The starter turned and turned but the engine would not catch. The carburetor was flooded. Cliff could see some young Dominicans running in their direction as he stood in front of the car.

"Motherfucka, can you get this lemon going?"

Cliff's voice hit a high note in a range worthy of Little Anthony's that had earlier proved beyond the sea of Schwartz's range.

Schwartz reached down and pulled the hood release. Jumping out from behind the wheel, he unlatched and lifted the Saab's hood. He quickly disconnected and reconnected the computer relay to the carburetor, jumped back behind the wheel, and turned the key. After a nervous moment, the engine caught. Cliff slammed the hood shut and hurdled in just as several of the Dominicans reached the parking lot. Arriving at their own cars, the Dominicans reached into the wheel wells to retrieve the guns they had stashed on top of the tires.

The Saab rumbled out of the parking lot as the first semiautomatic weapons were fired, missing their target. As Schwartz drove past the front door of the club, he could see the elder and younger Dominicans engaged in a full-scale brawl. Curses and beer bottles were hurled in the Saab's direction, the latter crashing against its side.

Schwartz turned left on Fordham Road. One side of his face was wet and swollen. Cliff and Don Edgardo were moaning and cursing. Schwartz made a left onto Jerome Avenue and headed for Montefiore Medical Center. He started to sing to himself, "What a Diff'rence a Day Makes."

He didn't give a rat's ass whether Darin had covered it or not.

DECEMBER 13:
A KING, A PRINCESS
AND A QUEEN FOR A DAY

THE NEXT MORNING, SCHWARTZ AWOKE TO THE SOUND OF Cliff's voice. He was speaking with the BxFC Court Officer Security Office and banging in because of a slip-and-fall in his bathroom yesterday. Schwartz performed a balance sheet appraisal of his present circumstance. On the deficit side: sore ribs, left side of his face swollen, busted lip. On the asset side: three cases on the calendar, including the Fontanez 1028, and the prospect of earning $280 for the day. He thought about Carmen's plight and Heidi's reproach should he fail to appear. He got up, applied ice to his face and lips, and sat on the foldout, dialing his office number to retrieve his messages. One was from Isabel.

"I need to *habla contigo. Mi* case is Fri . . . Fri . . . *Viernes.*"

He deleted the message. It was 9:15 a.m. He was due in court in fifteen minutes.

Somehow he assembled an outfit for the day. He put on the shirt from Monday and the suit from Friday, neither of which had been cleaned nor pressed. To compensate, he put on one of the new ties he had purchased from an Arab street merchant, three ties for ten dollars, the previous week.

Cliff had retired to his bedroom and closed his door. It was Schwartz's turn to call in to BxFC. Half asleep, he called Judge Parker's part and asked the clerk to inform the bridge officer that he was running late and would not be in until 10:30. Schwartz went to the kitchen and opened the cabinet, searching for the box of Cap'n Crunch he had seen before. There was a Post-it with Cliff's writing affixed to the box.

"No more Cap'n Crunch for you. This is your notice of eviction! Just get me back my ride."

Spying the Saab's key on a credenza, Schwartz grabbed it. He reached for a stale hot dog bun on the kitchen counter. While munching on it in considerable pain, he walked out the apartment and toward the elevator.

The King

First on Schwartz's calendar was the Jesse Thomas custody/visitation case, which had devolved into an alleged case of divorce, Bronx Style or, more specifically, Homicide in the Second Degree. Despite the pending criminal charges, Thomas refused to drop his custody/visitation case, insisting on his innocence and his right to see his daughter.

Schwartz relied on client's presumption of innocence in advocating for the visitation case to proceed. Judge Velez, to her credit, concurred. An *in camera* interview, a/k/a a <u>Lincoln</u> hearing, with the child Tabitha, was on Judge Velez's calendar for that day. The child's law guardian and the DA's office had vehemently objected to the interview given the pending criminal court case. Because there was also an application for a stay-away order of protection against Thomas, she granted Schwartz's application to be present for the court's interview of the child and to ask questions.

Before the matter was called into court, Schwartz was determined to re-enter the lion's den and interview Thomas in his holding pen. Though in Schwartz's judgment, Thomas was a wrongly accused gentle giant, nonetheless, he stood accused of a heinous murder. There was no telling how his incarceration and pending charges had affected his mental and emotional state. Once the pen door swung open and Thomas greeted Schwartz with a friendly smile, Schwartz's fears were allayed. The men shook hands and sat down.

"My sister been trying to reach you, but you're never in your office," Thomas said.

"Where do you fink I am? Spending my forty-dollar-an-hour on the French Riviera? I'm in court representing no-goodniks like you. Whaz up wif your sister?"

"She wants to verify my timeline on the morning that Allie was, uh, well, you know. I was nowhere near her place. My sister's probably here today. What's up with your lip? You sound a little like Daffy Duck."

As a result of his nervous chomping, Schwartz's lip had begun to swell again, amping up the lisp.

"You should see the other duck. Never mind. Lithen, I'll call out for your sister. But she should be talking to your criminal lawyer about that timeline."

"That asshole doesn't even come back to the court pens to see me before the case is called. If I get two minutes of conference time at the counsel's table with him, it's a lot. What's going on with Tabitha? How's she doing?"

It was just like this man to be inquiring about his daughter's well-being in the face of his circumstances. Schwartz observed the man restlessly flexing and unflexing the fingers of his hands.

"According to Ms. Hagan, the law guardian, she's doing fine in the care of the maternal grandmother."

"That cow never, ever had a good thing to say about me. You know Grandma's filling Tabitha's head with all kinds of garbage. I can't wait to get custody back!"

"Look, Jesse, you have to thimmer down. You go in there like a hothead and there's no way Veleth will grant you vithitation at Rikers or anywhere else. Maintain an even keel, OK? Now, the cathe is on for Tabitha to be interviewed by the judge. That will take place in the robing room with only the attorneys, the child, and the court reporter present. We will all get to ask her questions. But let me ask you a question: Which came first, the chicken or the egg?"

"What the hell are you talking about?...OK, you got me. Which?"

"Well, according to my daughter, Julie, who, like your daughter, is a very smart young lady, the egg comes first."

"How's that?"

"Julie says it's because we eat the egg for breakfast in the morning and the chicken for dinner at night."

The laughter of the two men was so loud that a court officer gave a reprimanding rap on the door. Schwartz caught himself.

"Tho there are two morals to thith riddle. One, we have to trust in the withdom of children. Two, we have to eat the egg for breakfast before we eat the chicken for dinner. In other words, first visitation, then custody. And you can't get custody until we bust you out of Rikers. Let's thee what happens today. Anything good comes out of thith, I'll get on the horn to your criminal lawyer and light a fire under hith tail."

Thomas extended his hand. Schwartz allowed his to be swallowed up.

"All right, I hear you, man. Do you know why the chicken crossed the road?"

Schwartz shrugged.

"Because it was going to dinner."

"And all thith time I thought it wath because a misogynistic roothter was chathing it."

The Princess

The two attorneys, the judge, and the court reporter squeezed themselves into seated positions in the small robing room. Schwartz gently rubbed the scab beginning to form on his lip. The judge's small desk featured a half-full Dunkin' Donuts box, a plate of sliced semi-stale bagels, a tub of cream cheese, a stick of margarine on a paper plate, chocolate chip cookies, and a variety of cardboard coffee cups at different stages of consumption. Schwartz felt the pangs of hunger sweep through his stomach. Day in and day out, virtually every robing room in the courthouse hosted a buffet of comfort food. Schwartz wondered, was it recompense for the depressing nature of the enterprise at hand? Did swallowing help push down the feelings dredged up by the tragi-comedies unfolding each day?

You betcha.

Schwartz was taking a bite of a stray coconut chocolate-glazed donut he had grabbed when, at that very moment, the door opened, hitting him flush in the funny bone of his elbow, causing him to bite down on his swollen lip, reopening the wound. He quickly reached for his supply of crumpled-but-clean tissues and dabbed his mouth to stem the fresh gush of blood.

As he struggled, a court officer escorted Tabitha into the room. A light brown–skinned imp of six; she wore her wavy sandy-colored hair in pigtails. Her green almond-shaped eyes scanned the occupants of the small room. When she saw Schwartz grimacing in pain with his eyes shut and his mouth wide open, she began giggling, her pigtails jiggling. There was no better proof of the truism that "tragedy is when I fall, comedy is when you fall."

Once the girl's giggling subsided and she was seated next to the court reporter, Judge Velez said, "Good morning, Tabitha. I'm glad you're in a good mood. I have to ask you some questions about some things that happened that are not so happy. Do you think you can answer some questions we have?"

The child had assumed a poker face, but after a moment of consideration, she nodded.

"Tabitha, we have this nice person with a machine who's copying down everything that's said, so it's important that you answer our questions with words, OK?"

The child started to nod again but then, with a slight whisper, mouthed, "Yes."

"And you need to speak up so everyone in the room can hear you, OK? Now, I am Judge Velez, and you know Ms. Hagan, your law guardian. And this man over here is Mr. Schwartz. He works for your father."

Schwartz gave a little wave and slight smile. The girl reciprocated.

"Ms. Hagan, why don't you begin?"

Susan Hagan was a lifer. She carried a been-there, done-that, seen-it-all, know-it-all attitude. She sported an imposing mane of greying orange hair on her head, which probably hadn't been cut since the first day that Hagan stepped foot in BxFC. It was an angry sea of crosscurrents. A huge clip on the back of her head attempted, in vain, to serve as a breakwater to the pounding surf. The color reminded Schwartz of the orangeice–glazed vanilla Humorette pops served by the Good Humor ice cream man.

God, am I starving.

On several occasions since the father's arrest, Schwartz had approached Hagan to discuss the merits of the visitation petition and the details of the underlying homicide. Since, in her own mind, Hagan had already convicted the father, she dismissed Schwartz's entreaties with a toss of her head, forcing Schwartz to duck for cover.

Ms. Hagan turned to Tabitha and performed a masterful sweep of her locks.

"Now, Tabitha, we're going to talk about the day that something bad happened to mommy. Do you remember that day?"

The poker face nodded and said, "Yes."

"Who was there that day?"

"Mommy was there. And then daddy came. And they were yelling."

"Were they in the house?"

"Yeah."

"What did you see?"

"Daddy hit mommy and then she fell. And he stuck her with somethin'."

The poker face folded and was replaced by a saddened one.

"Do you want to see daddy?"

"No. Daddy bad. He hits me and mommy. But I want to see mommy."

The realization that the child hadn't been told of her mother's death permeated the room, inflicting momentary paralysis. Apparently Hagan believed that relaying such tidbits of information was not part of the job description for the $25 an hour out of court pay rate.

"I have no more questions."

"Mr. Schwartz?"

Schwartz collected his thoughts. He wanted to tread carefully and develop a rapport with the girl.

"Hewo. I'm Mithuh Swatz, an it's tho nith to finwy meet you, Tabitha."

His swollen lip had indeed transformed him into a Looney Toons cast member.

Tabitha burst out laughing. "You talk funny. You talk like Daffy Duck."

"Tho I've been told by someone ve-ey close to you. I thaw it maw Elmer Fudd or Slyvester. I got a boo-boo on my wip. Dat's why."

"Can I see?"

Schwartz moved his face toward the girl as she moved closer. When she got really close, Schwartz channeled Mel Blanc as best he could.

"Thufferring Thuccatash!"

The girl sat back in her chair, laughing. From deep in her throat, Velez let out a judicious, "Ahem." Schwartz remembered why he was there and asked his first question.

"OK, Tabitha. Ath best ath you can, try to forget that I'm talking thith way and lithen to my quethtionth. OK, dear?"

The girl nodded and put both hands over her mouth in an effort to control her giggling. Judge Velez reached behind herself and opened a small refrigerator and pulled out some pieces of ice. She wrapped them in a paper towel and handed it to Schwartz.

"Mr. Schwartz why don't you take a moment and address your boo-boo."

Tabitha let out a sigh of sympathy. Schwartz gratefully accepted the offer. After an awkward minute of holding the ice on his lip, it felt somewhat better and resumed his inquiry.

"Now, you thay the last time you thaw mommy, she was arguing with daddy, right?"

"And he was hitting her, too."

"And the man you call 'daddy,' was he black-skinned or white?"

"Oh, that daddy . . . he was white."

Schwartz tried to control himself. He was tempted to ask the question again but feared that the child would change her answer. But he needed this point nailed.

"The daddy that was hitting Mommy wath white?"

"Uh-huh."

"What isth his name?"

"That was Daddy Andy."

"And Daddy Andy was hitting and yelling at mommy?"

"Yeah. I don't like Daddy Andy."

Schwartz paused for effect as he pressed the ice against his lip and assessed the reactions of the room's occupants. Velez was staring intently at the child. Hagan was looking down at her notes while twirling her hair. The court reporter was attempting to remain impassive.

"Now, you know who Daddy Jesse is?"

"Yeah."

"Who is he?"

Schwartz held his breath. The child hesitated and then answered, "He's my real daddy."

"Is Daddy Jesse black or white?"

"Oh, Daddy Jesse . . . he's black."

Bobby Darin looked over the crowd at Freedomland. With a towel, he wiped the rain from his brow. He held a cup of tea in one hand and a microphone in the other. He said something to his bandleader, Dick Behrke, placed the towel and cup on top of a speaker, and then faced the crowd. Then Darin asked, "Did you see Daddy Jesse the day you saw mommy get hurt?"

"Uh-uh. Nope. I saw only Daddy Andy that day."

Schwartz's heart was pumping as the Freedomland crowd stomped and cheered for more.

"Do you want to see Daddy Jesse again?"

With that, the child started to sniffle. "I want to see Daddy Jesse, and I want to see mommy, too."

Judge Velez stood and approached the child. She put her arms around her and wiped her tears with a tissue.

"That's all for now, dear. You are a very brave little girl, and I know that wherever mommy is, she's very proud of you. The officer is going to take you back to your grandmother."

The officer took the child by the hand, and they exited the room. There was silence in the room occupants gathered their respective thoughts. The court reporter shook her head ever so slightly. Velez stood, opened the door, and motioned for Schwartz and Hagan to follow her out.

In the secured hallway, they walked a short distance to a fire exit stairwell. Velez whipped out a pack of Marlboro Ultra Light Menthols and a lighter. Inhaling the smoke as if it were pure oxygen, she tapped her head with her free hand.

"I'm ordering visitation between father and child at Rikers. I'll also be ordering ACS to arrange for grief counseling for this poor child. How long does this grandmother plan to hide the truth from this girl? Amazing. Simply amazing. You know what? I'm ordering a copy of this transcript be made available to the ADA prosecuting the case against the father. I can't believe these hack detectives. All they believed was that Black Daddy killed the White Momma, and they were ready to O.J. the poor fool. And you, Madam Law Guardian, where was your head when you interviewed the girl? Don't say a word.

I don't want to hear it until we go back on the record. Good work in there, Schwartz. Have a donut. And, uh, put some more ice on that lip, for cryin' out loud."

Passing through the robing room, Schwartz glommed a donut as instructed. As he bit into the confection, he felt the rush of sugar share the same pathway as the adrenaline coursing through his body.

I did this. I made this happen. I'm not just greasing the wheels of the system. I'm a brickbat wedged into its friggin' cogs and wheels.

To celebrate, Schwartz planned to head to Fordham Road for some lunch time shopping. But he still had to contend with the continued 1028 hearing on Mojica on his calendar.

The Queen

"Your witness, Counsel!"

Addressing Schwartz, Judge Parker had just issued the classic invitation to commence his cross-examination. His target would be the ACS caseworker Ade Adesanya. As he sat at the litigant's table, he quickly glanced over the allegations in the petition, the notes from his interview with Carmen, and his scant notes from the previous hearing date. He had had no time to review any of his files before coming to court. He turned to look at Carmen, who was seated next to him. Her eyes drooped. Pancake powder covered the blotches on her face. For an instant, he fixated on the dark maroon nails that perfectly matched her lipstick. Heidi, seated in the rear of the courtroom, emitted a nervous, expectant cough.

Adesanya had just completed his direct testimony from the prior hearing date, detailing the neglect findings against Carmen concerning her other children. ACS attorney Richard Barbanel asked the court to take judicial notice of the previous findings of neglect and also to note that Carmen's rights to her other children had either been terminated, or were in the process of being freed for adoption.

"Mr. Schwartz, do you intend to question this witness?" the judge asked.

Schwartz heard Heidi's chair scratch against the linoleum tile floor behind him. He reached for Carmen's hand, gave it a slight squeeze, and offered what passed for an encouraging smile through his swollen lips. She looked at his stitched-up lip and, without saying a word, she asked, *"Qué pasa?"* with her crinkled nose and squinted eyes. He leaned over and whispered, "Slipped in the bathroom."

Carmen's eyebrows sent wigwam distress signals.

"Mr. Schwartz?"

"Yes, Your Honor?"

"Good. Now that I finally have your attention, I'll remind you that the issue in a 1028 hearing is imminent risk to the subject child."

Still lording it over me.

As he rose, Schwartz thoughtfully brought the index finger of his right hand to his swollen lips. He was determined to enunciate each word without the debilitating lisp.

"If that's the case, Your Honor, I would ask this court to grant the 1028 application based on the record thus far. This caseworker has failed to address any of the imminent, present-day facts prevailing in the lives of this mother and child."

Cindy Grella's shrill soprano split Schwartz's left eardrum.

"Objection. Is Mr. Schwartz making his summation or is he questioning a witness?"

The displeasure reflected in Judge Parker's demeanor revealed sudden doubts about his career path.

"Mr. Schwartz! Just . . . ask . . . your . . . questions."

"I'll be brief and to the point."

"That would make my day."

Schwartz inhaled, gathered his collection of notes and documents, and strode to the left side of the table in front of the judge's bench. The table housed the cardboard jackets of the cases on the court's calendar. There must have been fifty or more jackets, color coded for each year of the particular case's origination. The array of pink, yellow, and blue folders reminded Schwartz of Fruit Loops. His stomach gurgled.

The tape recorder memorializing the day's proceedings was also on the table. The progression of red digital counter numbers served as a silent metronome. Throughout the day it would record the fate of fifty or more families as they were sliced and diced, adjourned or burned, litigated and eviscerated, and otherwise Bronx Family quartered. The witness was seated on the other side of the overladen table.

"Mr. Adesanya, to your knowledge, was Justina born with any positive toxicology for any controlled substances?"

The witness answered, "According to the St. Barnabas Hospital social worker, the mother and the child did not test positive for any drugs."

But with his thick West African accent, his response sounded more like, "Ahcordin to da Sane Babbas Hasptl soch waka, da mudda e da chil deed nawt tes pasiteeve for n-ee drug."

Schwartz lamented the plight of the transcriber who might be ordered to prepare a transcript of these proceedings.

"When was the baby, Justina, removed from Ms. Fontanez?"

"An ACS hold was put on da child and da child was discharged from the hospital to ACS."

"How was the baby's health at birth?"

"Ah believe dat da baby had a low birth weight."

Schwartz glanced down at his copy of the oral report transmittal made to the New York State Child Abuse Hotline. The report was typically the only pre-1028 hearing discovery item provided to respondent's counsel.

"Doesn't the ORT state that mother and newborn were doing fine?"

"Ah know ah spoke to da hospital soch waka, Miss Barbuto, and she informed me of a low birth weight."

"What percentile?"

"She deed not say."

"And you didn't ask?"

Barbanel sprang to his feet.

"Objection. Counsel is being argumentative with the witness."

"Sustained as to form," the judge said

"Mr. Adesanya, how long have you been an ACS caseworker?" Schwartz continued.

"Fah years."

"It's your job, isn't it, to investigate allegations of child abuse or neglect and to assess risk to the child's emotional, physical, or mental health, correct?"

"Yes."

"You've been trained for that task, correct?"

"Ah receive training, yes."

"So would it have been important in your investigation of this case to find out whether or not Justina's birth weight placed her in the eightieth percentile, the fiftieth percentile, or the thirtieth percentile, correct?"

Grella could contain herself no longer.

"Objection. Judge, Mr. Schwartz continues to argue with the witness."

"This is not an argument, Ms. Grella. It's called a cross-examination and it's not supposed to be friendly," Judge Parker said. "Objection overruled. Please answer the question, sir."

The tone of Adesanya's voice sharpened and the pitch heightened. "Ah deed not ask da percentile and she deed not tell me."

"But Mr. Adesanya—"

Judge Parker cut in. "Mr. Schwartz, I believe your point's been made to the court. Why don't you move on?"

"Very well, Your Honor. Mr. Adesanya, the ORT states that the mother has no provisions for the child in the form of a crib or clothing. Did you investigate that allegation?"

"In da hasptl da motha admit to me she had not have a crib."

"Mr. Adesanya, does a newborn baby need a crib or a bassinet?"

Grella jumped in. "Objection. Since when is Mr. Adesanya Dr. Spock?"

"I'm thinking more Dr. Seuss, Your Honor," Schwartz countered.

"COUNSEL!" Judge Parker warned. "Let's not go down that path again. I'm long on calendar and short on time."

"Judge, if anyone's short on time here it's my—" Schwartz caught himself. *Back on task.*

"Sir, didn't the mother also state to you that she resides in a facility that would provide her with the necessary items for her and her child, including follow-up drug counseling, health care, and supervision?"

Barbanel erupted, "Objection! Counsel's testifying."

"Sustained." Judge Parker turned to Adesanya. "Did the mother tell you she was in a program?"

"You mean da AIDS hospice, your Honor?"

"I don't know. We're asking you. Counsel?"

Schwartz picked up the thread.

"Did she tell you the name and address of the facility?"

"Yes. Ah tink it was on Shakespeare Avenue."

"You think. Did you ever visit the residence?"

Adesanya looked around the courtroom and mumbled to himself.

Schwartz leaned across the table toward the witness.

"I'm sorry. I didn't hear your answer."

"No, ah deed not."

"How could you assess the risk to the child and the truth of the failing to plan allegation without visiting the mother's residence?"

Adesanya rocked back and forth and then let it blow.

"One quarter of my village in Nigeria is infected with the HIV virus. If you think ah was going to Miss Fontanez's program . . . "

Barbanel was holding his head. Schwartz struggled to control the adrenaline rush.

"Mr. Adesanya," he said, "you've testified that this ORT was called in by the hospital social worker. She did it because you called her before Justina was even born and alerted her to ACS's desire to take the child regardless of whether the child was born clean or not, isn't that true?"

Grella's voice rang out. "Ob-ject-shun!"

"Sustained."

"You were already preparing the butterfly net for Ms. Fontanez's child before it was even born. Isn't that true?"

"Objection. Judge, please admonish Mr. Schwartz not to re-ask questions to which objections have been sustained."

"Ms. Grella, please do not instruct this court in how to conduct a trial," the judge's aggravation was palpable. "Mr. Adesanya, you need not answer the question. Anything further for this witness, Mr. Schwartz?"

"No, Judge, I have no further use for him. But I'll be making application for the court to order a new caseworker assigned to this case."

"I'll deal with that before the end of the day's proceedings. Ms. Grella, any questions?"

"One moment."

Grella stood and walked over to Barbanel. A huddle ensued. Barbanel was shaking his head. Grella appeared insistent. When the conference ended, Grella assumed the inquisitor's position. Since Adesanya was technically not her witness, her questioning of him was considered cross-examination. Hence, under the rules of evidence, she could lead him as a conductor does an orchestra.

"Mr. Adesanya, you've testified as to the mother's extensive drug abuse history and her contacts with the criminal justice system, correct?"

"Yes. Da motha has a lawng history of heroin addiction and prostitution."

"Objection! Relevance and basis of knowledge," Schwartz protested.

Judge Parker responded with a question, "And just how do you know this?"

"She admitted it to me in da past."

"There's your answer. Objection overruled."

Grella went on. "And her three children, other than Justina, have spent most of their lives in foster care, correct?"

Schwartz stood. "Objection. The issue is imminent risk to the newborn."

"Overruled. You may answer."

"Yes, and dey ah in da process of being adopted."

Schwartz was still standing. "Objection. Relevance and non-responsive."

"I'll allow it. Overruled."

"You discussed with the siblings' foster mother the possibility of her taking on the care of Justina?"

Schwartz could sense the quicksand gathering at the feet of Carmen's parental rights to her newborn child.

"Objection. This is not a dispositional hearing. Are we already planning for permanency for this newborn?"

The Judge granted the objection. "Sustained. Move on, Ms. Grella."

"Mr. Adesanya, since you have been the caseworker for the Fontanez children, has the mother ever acted as a caretaker for any of her children?"

"Ah do not buhlieve so."

Grella's locomotive was in full throttle. "Do you have concerns for the health and well-being of an infant being raised in an AIDS hospice?"

"Objection!" Schwartz shouted.

"No. I'll allow him to answer the question. Overruled."

"Ah do. Da people in da program are mostly drug addicts. Deir behavyah is unpredictable. Ah worry about the level of supervision. In addition, there is da fear that da baby will be infected in some way, if she hasn't been already."

Judge Parker perked up at this last comment. "What do you mean, 'if she hasn't been already'?"

"I mean, by motha."

At first, Schwartz could only shake his head. *It's what this case is about after all. Original sin.* He called out, "Objection. Speculative, prejudicial, and just plain wrong. Move to strike."

"Granted. It's stricken."

"No further questions." Grella returned to her seat as a satisfied smirk spread across her face.

Judge Parker rubbed his chin and his neck. "I have no more time for this matter today. This case is adjourned."

Schwartz turned to look at Carmen. Her head sagged at the judge's pronouncement. He glanced sideways at Heidi, who was shaking her head furiously. He gathered his breath and said, "Judge, may we inquire of Mr. Barbanel if he has any more witnesses? Perhaps we can conclude this matter today?"

"Mr. Barbanel?"

"Agency has no more evidence to present."

"Do you have any witnesses, Mr. Schwartz?" asked Judge Parker.

Schwartz knew he had to call Carmen to the stand; otherwise, the court would draw a negative inference against her from her failure to testify. Yet he had to consider the strain of testifying given her fragile condition. He also intended to call Heidi to describe the Shakespeare program.

"I believe I have two: the mother and Ms. Frias."

Grella sprang to her feet. "Judge, if Ms. Frias is going to be a witness, she should have been excluded from the courtroom during testimony."

Schwartz expected this argument. "Your Honor, in the first instance, no one made the application to exclude witnesses. Secondly, I'm surprised, frankly, by the caseworker's testimony that he is ignorant of the Shakespeare program. My application is for a caseworker to visit the hospice to report on its suitability for visitation between mother and child, at the very least, and as a residence to which Justina could be paroled, should my client prevail on the 1028."

"Ms. Grella, will you have any evidence to present?"

"Your Honor, the law guardian may have a witness. I'm not certain."

Schwartz's curiosity was piqued. "Your Honor, by statute, this hearing is required to be completed on an expedited basis. If Ms. Grella has a witness, the witness should have been here ready to testify. Is this a ploy by the law guardian to delay this case?"

"Judge, I don't see why I need to make an offer of proof when I haven't yet decided to even call the witness," Grella said. "And if Mr. Schwartz was so concerned about his client's right to an expedited hearing, he should have been in attendance at 9:30 a.m., when this case was supposed to be called, instead of sauntering in at 10:30."

Schwartz rose to his feet as quickly as his aching ribs would permit. "Judge, I believe Ms. Grella is being disingenuous with this court. Either she has a witness or she doesn't. And if she does, I demand the offer of proof before another adjournment of this 1028 hearing is granted."

Judge Parked turned to his court attorney who had been sitting in a chair near the entrance to the back office. The the two conferred briefly, after which the judge ruled.

"Mr. Schwartz, at this juncture I'm not going to rule on the admissibility of hypothetical testimony. I can only see that given the state of my calendar and the posture of the proof, this matter cannot be concluded today. Therefore, it will be adjourned to the fifteenth at 9:30. In the meantime, Mr. Barbanel, I want a caseworker to visit the Shakespeare Avenue facility and report back to me on the next court date. I will then entertain your interim applications, Mr. Schwartz, for supervised visitation between the mother and child at the Shakespeare program and to relieve Mr. Adesanya from the case. What is the nature of the visitation she is getting right now? Mr. Schwartz, your client is raising her hand. Apparently she has something to say."

Carmen slowly gathered herself up and addressed the court. "Sir, Your Honor, I only get one hour a week with Justina. And I want to tell you that I can care for my baby."

"Well, that's what we are here to figure out, Madam. In the interim I'm ordering at least two hours' weekly visitation."

"Judge, I don't know if I can get a caseworker out there before this Friday."

"Mr. Barbanel, just as your client can get a caseworker to a hospital to execute a removal on a moment's notice, I'm sure the agency has the wherewithal to arrange a visit to the mother's program."

"We'll try."

"Don't try. It is So Ordered, Forthwith. Mr. Schwartz, prepare a short order. I'm sure Mr. Barbanel will accept service. Case is adjourned to December 15th, 9:30 a.m."

Schwartz reached for his date book to check the date and time, but it wasn't in his jacket pocket. He frantically searched his other pockets and then his shoulder bag. No date book. He knew he had the Ramirez continued fact-finding on December 15' and Isabel's 1028, but he wasn't certain of the times. He had painted himself into a corner with his grandstanding on the delay issue and couldn't very well argue for a later date.

With the ambivalence of a Hindu bullfighter, Schwartz gathered his papers. The bridge officer, relieved at the conclusion of another mini hearing, announced, "Case adjourned. Parties, pick up your adjourned slips outside. Counselors, clear the table, please."

The bridge man thrust an adjourned slip into Schwartz's hand.

"Schwartz, give this to your client."

In the waiting area outside the courtroom, Schwartz approached Carmen and Heidi. As gently as he could, he asked Carmen how she was feeling.

"Feeling like I wish I could kick that caseworker in the nuts!"

Heidi rubbed the back of Carmen's neck in an effort to calm her down. As she did so, Heidi turned to Schwartz and pointedly asked, "Where does this leave us?"

"One day and one adjournment closer to a resolution of this case. I'm going to come to your program to eyeball it for myself and to prepare you both for your testimony."

Heidi was reaching for her date book. "When?"

Schwartz instinctively reached for his jacket pocket. Remembering it was not there, he camouflaged his gesture as a reflective patting of his heart. "I'm not sure. Tonight or tomorrow night. I'll call."

"I leave at seven."

"Right. Meanwhile, be on the lookout for a friendly neighborhood, child-snatching ACS worker knocking on your gates. Give them the grand tour."

"Thank you, Mr. Schwartz."

Heidi took his hand and gave it a firm grip. Their eyes connected for an instant. Her grip softened. Schwartz enjoyed a surge of testosterone and then released her hand.

"Call me Schwartz."

"Uh, OK, Schwartz," she said with a sly smile.

Schwartz galloped to the 18-B room. He pushed aside the remains of the assigned counsel breakfast buffet and put his bag on the table. Then he frantically searched the many compartments of the black canvas bag for his oracle, his compass, his road map for the next three months of his life. Schwartz rummaged through the mélange of unpaid parking tickets, crumpled napkins, pens, dog-eared street maps, files, portable office implements, etc. No luck.

Suddenly inspired, he whirled toward the overstuffed coat tree. Schwartz never ceased to be amazed that forty-odd attorneys could coexist in such tight quarters. Through the layers of coats, he found his weather-beaten trench coat. He thrust his hand inside the inside breast pocket and retrieved his little black book. As his heart palpitations began to subside, he opened the book to December 15th. The worst was confirmed: The Ramirez designated felony fact-finding was scheduled for 9:30. Isabel's name, with an encircled "1028 – 9:30," also appeared on December 15th. In Finkel's part, that was a mandatory 9:30 call. With Carmen's case added to the list, he would need the 18-B equivalent of a triple-bypass surgery to survive that day.

Burton Mitzner entered the room to hear Schwartz calling himself a "putz."

"Schwartz, where's the Emperor's new clothes? I'm waiting with bated breath."

Schwartz slipped a spatula under the egg frying on the back of his neck and turned it over easy. He walked out of the room to the sound of Mitzner's chortle.

Schwartz checked his voicemail on the seventh floor pay phone before leaving for Papo's lot and yet another do-or-die joust with El Diablo. The obscenity-laced tirade his good buddy and tennis partner, Cliff Johnson, had left made him wince. He was headed to Fordham Road for that shopping spree. His evening festivities included a visit to a certain hospice and a meeting with a certain AIDS patient and her hospice social worker.

IN THE CAVE OF THE LEPERS

CLIMBING THE STEPS TO THE HOSPICE, SCHWARTZ RECALLED an image from a spectacular movie from his youth, *Ben-Hur*—the scene in which the protagonist journeys to the leper colony in search of his mother and sister. Schlepped to Radio City Music Hall, swaddled in a woolen coat and hat, sodden with sweat from the subway ride, Schwartz fidgeted in his chair through much of the evening's offerings, though the Rockettes managed to make a positive impression. When Ben-Hur dared to enter the caves of the unclean, Schwartz's crew-cut hair felt electromagnetic. As an inquiring seven-year-old, Schwartz wanted to know who were those people and why they were shunned by society.

He rang the bell at the hospice entrance and pushed the door open upon hearing the click in the jamb. A sign inside the vestibule greeted him:

"May all that enter find peace, acceptance, and love."

He pushed the inner door open upon hearing a second click.

"Who are you and why are you here?" a woman behind a desk demanded.

Startled by the hostility of the receptionist's tone, Schwartz fumbled to regain his composure.

"Carmen . . . uh . . . I'm looking for Carmen Sandiego—I mean, Carmen Fontanez . . . uh.. . Heidi . . . Heidi . . . Frias is her worker."

The receptionist, who, judging by the sores on her face and neck, was also a resident at the hospice, slid a pen and clipboard in Schwartz's direction. "Sign in and I'll see if Heidi is still here."

Several of the residents had gathered at the desk, drawn by the interruption of an early-evening visitor from the outside, from the world of the "clean." For Schwartz, the moment of truth had arrived. Would he take the pen that had been handled by the receptionist/resident? Despite his concern, he was aware that it had been proven that AIDS could not be transmitted by casual contact. As he searched in vain for a tissue, a familiar voice called out, "Schwartz, you actually showed up. Good man."

"Hey, Heidi. I'd said I would. I'm going to prepare you both. For your testimony, you know?"

"But Carmen is zzzzed out. Can't wake her after what she went through in court today."

Tall, and tan, and young, and lovely, Heidi Frias took his arm in hers and whisked him past the front desk and the jury of the afflicted.

Who needs Carmen Sandiego when you have the girl from Ipanema?

Schwartz noticed that Heidi was wearing her coat.

"I should have called before coming. Are you headed somewhere?"

"Day is done, gone the sun. I'm headed home. Can I give you the two-dollar tour?"

After a millisecond of hesitation, Schwartz said, "Sure."

Heidi escorted Schwartz through several over-lit corridors. He saw the day room, children's center, dining facilities, and the medical and counseling facilities. He was impressed by the cleanliness and struck by the positive, upbeat tone of the posters on the walls. All in all, it was a nurturing, humane locale for these tormented souls. Schwartz did his best to avoid eye contact with the residents. At tour's end, he asked Heidi if he could drop her off somewhere.

"Sure. We can discuss my testimony on the way."

"Sounds like billable out-of-court time. Where we off to?"

"Co-op City."

Entering the Saab, Schwartz and Heidi exchanged awkward glances. Schwartz began his shtick.

"Listen. The seat belt doesn't work, so just hold onto the strap for dear life."

"Do the brakes work?"

"Last time I tried them. But if not, we could always do a Fred Flintstone through the hole under the mats."

Her laugh had a guttural quality that thrilled and intimidated Schwartz.

"You know, Schwartz, for a lawyer, you're actually a pretty decent human being."

"Well, there's a backhanded compliment. And for a social worker, you're actually pretty . . . well, social."

"Explain that, please."

"Okaaaay. As you can imagine, in my branch of the law, I speak to social workers all the time, usually on the Q side of a Q&A. I'm always struck by the impression that once the veil of social worker–client privilege is lifted, as it is in family court when we're dealing with—dat-tah-da-dah—'the children's best interest,' well, how enthusiastically—with gusto almost—social workers are willing to spill the beans on the very clients they've been listening to bitch and moan about their problems once a week for God knows how long."

"Point being?"

"Point being that most—not all—social workers suffer from the same burnout we attorneys do and consequently take guilty pleasure in sandbagging their clients."

"Whoa!," Heidi hooted.

Schwartz plunged onward. "And that I find you to be a refreshing exception because you actually care. You're committed to your cause of alleviating Carmen's plight."

"Double whoa! Schwartz, this is more than a drive-the-witness-home conversation. Let's get a drink."

"Sounds like a plan."

Heidi suggested that they exit the Cross-Bronx Expressway at White Plains Road near Westchester Avenue. That intersection was known as the Circle because it was one of the few rotary roadways in New York City. Because rotaries require cooperation, not competition, the Manhattan patricians who made these road design decisions probably thought it good sport to place at least one in the Bronx.

One block south of the Circle was another geographic constellation with a somewhat more sinister title: Herpes Triangle. The triangle boasted three bar/dance clubs on three corners of Westchester Avenue. They served as the interface point for the phalanx of cops, nurses, EMS technicians, Con Ed workers, Verizon linesman, data entry clerks, and others denizens of the Bronx working class seeking somebody to love.

Schwartz and Heidi were several scotches (he) and rums (she) into their evening confab when Heidi looked down the bar and said, "I remember him."

On the agenda was the topic of life-defining moments. Schwartz had already trotted out his well-oiled tale of his first encounter with Bobby Darin. Heidi had listened with a tolerant, bemused smile until it was her turn to share.

"I remember him as if he were standing across from us, behind that bar, right now, grinning at me, wearing an apron, serving us drinks. He was my mother's cousin from PR. Just out of the service. Stayin' with us in the projects 'til he got a job. I was—what?—nine? Nine-and-a-half?"

She paused for a moment and took a sip.

"It's funny. When you're young you're in such a rush to grow up, to be older.

I mean, you hang onto that half a year. Make a point of it to people. *'Que chula.*
How old are you now, *mija?'* And you'd tell them, 'Nine-and-a-half.' Especially
when you're still in the single digits. Oh, I'm getting random again. What the
hell was I talking about?"

Schwartz smiled tightly. He felt he knew where this was going, and he was
in no hurry to get there.

"You're just exercising your free association rights under the First Amendment."

Once again Schwartz heard that throaty laugh, and he was grateful for it.

"We called him *Flaco.* But there was nothing skinny about his . . ."

Heidi stopped suddenly and turned away from Schwartz, offering him her
profile. Out of one brown eye, a tear began to ski down her light brown cheek,
bypassing the few moguls of faded teenage acne, negotiating the slight ridge of
her nose, and then circling her coffee bean–colored lips that were contracting
into an ice jam. She glanced down at the glass holding the remnants of her
Bacardi 151 on the rocks.

"Always in such a goddamn rush to grow up."

Schwartz's hand involuntarily reached out to rub her back as if he were
comforting Julie or Ethan. She recoiled, scrunching up her shoulders.

"No, I don't want—don't!"

Schwartz retracted his arm. He waited, staring at his hands smoothing out
the wrinkles in his cocktail napkin. After a few seconds he couldn't stand the
silence anymore.

"Life is about loss. But it's also about gain. Take trust, for example. You
could lose your ability to trust in one individual, but does that mean you stop
trusting everyone else? You couldn't possibly survive without trusting someone
else. I mean, you can't walk down a street without trusting that the driver of that
livery cab isn't going to veer his car onto the sidewalk or that the bartender didn't
spit on this plate of fried calamari before bringing it out. You have to regain trust
in people. Like it or not, if you're living in society, you're in the trust business."

Heidi deeply inhaled and exhaled. She turned to face Schwartz and looked
directly into his eyes.

"Schwartz, I spent two-*and-a-half* years in foster care. That was my reward
for trusting the teacher and guidance counselor after disclosing to them what
went down. My sister and my brothers—all of us were removed because a BCW
caseworker felt that mama knew or should have known about the sexual abuse.
Plus, she couldn't quite account for every little mark on our bodies after my little
brother told them that sometimes we would get hit with a slipper or a belt.

"We were split up into different foster homes, saw each other on the twelfth of never. And my foster brother and sister? What a special pleasure they were. Someone—no doubt my foster mom—must have whispered to them what I was in for. I was 'Heidi Free-ass' and 'Heidi-Heidi-Heidi-*Ho*.' If I complained or acted out, it meant another foster home, and another, and another."

Heidi took a long swallow of her dark rum. Schwartz shuffled the plastic swizzle sticks scattered on the counter.

"Meanwhile, mama wrestled with the child protective bureaucracy. They danced her in and out of parenting skills programs, individual counseling, domestic violence, and anger management classes. Not to mention the judge. Always that same white-haired old bastard. I never got to see him, but that's how mama described him. She would tell us how he looked down his nose at her while signing off on another annual extension of placement. I remember how the foster care workers interrupted her visits with us if she tried to tell us to keep our spirits up by telling us that soon we would be reunited and going home. 'Don't fill the children's heads with unrealistic expectations,' they warned.

She put her hand on top of his and gripped it.

"You've seen it, Schwartz. Foster care is a struggle for a child's heart and mind. The system's constantly hedging its bets. Well, if the mom isn't doing the dance, it's in the kid's best interest to push the child to the bosom of foster care. I don't know how my mother did it, but she got us back. So don't lecture me about loss, gain, and trust. Please. I had a very early object lesson."

Schwartz sighed, hoping the worst was over. Heidi released her grip on his hand.

"Besides, you're wasting your time if you're hitting on me. I don't partake in penile sex. I prefer women. In fact, Carmen and I are in a relationship, albeit platonic."

Heidi punctuated her statement with a more measured laugh.

Schwartz was immobilized as he processed the information he'd just received. Finally his tongue unlocked.

"Isn't that caseworker malpractice?"

Another throaty laugh. "Is that your Scotch talking?"

"To your Rum. Mixing drinks can be risky."

"So is getting out of bed in the morning. OK, in twenty-five words or less, what's your tale of domestic woe?"

"Separated, headed for the big *D* with two young'uns hanging in the balance."

"Why'd you split?"

"I guess one spin would be that I lost who I was in the relationship and now I'm trying to find myself."

"How trite. Have you looked up your ass? Just sayin'."

"Ouch. Does liquor always make you so brutal?"

"Brutally honest. Let's get the hell out of here, Schwartz."

Twenty minutes later, Schwartz pulled the Saab into the vacant parking lot beside the handball courts at Orchard Beach. Through the windshield, Schwartz and Heidi enjoyed a luminous view of the beach, Pelham Bay, and City Island beyond.

On the South Shore of Long Island facing the Atlantic Ocean, Robert Moses created his masterpiece Jones Beach in the 1930's. Akin to his namesake, Moses drew upon his god-like ability to reshape the planet in this achievement. Schwartz had read in Robert A. Caro's The Power Broker how Moses sought to replicate his success in the Bronx in the design and construction of Orchard Beach. Moses raised his staff and summoned barges from New Jersey and the Rockways to bring forth more than a million cubic feet of sand to fill in one third of Pelham Bay, located at the Bronx's frontage on the Long Island Sound.

When Orchard Beach first opened in the 1930s, it earned the sobriquet "the Bronx Riviera." Like much of the Bronx, it had since seen better days. Over the years it had fallen prey to the elements, foot traffic, and municipal neglect. Still, the summer crowds came, and reinvigorated the beach with their *sabor* and soul.

Heidi leaned against the headrest and sighed. *"Ay dios mio* . . . Coming here with my mom, sister, my little brothers, cousins"—she dropped her voice—"my uncle . . . We'd bring *cuchifrito, pernil, plantanos maduros*, and rice. It was a feast. And the *piragua* man would be there, selling that shaved ice sweetened with fruit flavors. Yummm. And the rocks—just in case you got comfortable, just in case you felt a little welcome, the rocks at the shoreline and in the water, mixed with the broken shells . . . oh man, they would cut your feet. Mama would yell at us to stay close. We'd listen. Sorta. But we'd get a little lost anyway. Oh, how'd she panic, sending one of our cousins to find us."

Heidi laughed in a bittersweet way. Schwartz turned his head and marveled at the skin tone of her face as the moonlight touched it. He returned his gaze to the bay.

"I'm a little older than you."

"No kidding? You think?"

"OK, I'm much older than you. Satisfied? Any-hoo, my recollection of Orchard Beach was that it was a great place to get beat up by black and Puerto Rican kids. My family would usually bypass the beach and head to City Island for some fried fish and French fries."

"Do you mean Tony's Pier? That place was the joint! The fried shrimp dinner? To die for. The seagulls dive bombing the place . . . Schwartz, let me ask you something. How did a Bronx boy like you wind up on Long Island?"

He took a breath before answering.

"I guess I sold out. Better schools. Safer neighborhoods. All code words for white flight. Guilty as charged."

Heidi gave him a knowing nod. "I can't blame you. Do you know why they call the Bronx the ghetto? Because people are trying to get-to the suburbs."

"Oh, that's bad pun! I know one when I hear it."

"Look, all I'm saying is this: I live in Co-op City now. Same deal. All those Jewish people moved from the West Bronx to escape us people of color. And look what happened. The black transit workers and the Hispanic nurses moved right along with them. People always want to better their lot. Can't blame them. So, uh, where are you bunking down these days?"

A smile of inspiration creased his face. "I'm glad you mentioned it. Uh, you wouldn't happen to have an empty couch in your crib?"

Heidi let out a whoop and then stroked his cheek with her hand.

"Crib, eh? You've been listening to your clients speak. I tell you what. I like you, Schwartz. So *mi* couch *es su* couch for tonight. But that's it. We both have too much on our plates for anything else, *entiendes?*"

Schwartz gulped and chuckled. "Yes, Heidi Frias, hospice social worker. But you are missing out."

"How's that?"

"Because as a lawyer I am a cunning linguist."

"Ha-ha. And you accuse me of bad punning."

She punched him in the arm and then laughed.

"Besides, if we were going to have oral sex, it would have to be right here in this car.," Heidi teased.

"In my Saab Story? Don't ruin my fantasy. I'm a linguist, not a gymnast."

DECEMBER 14:
DARK MOON ARISING

SCHWARTZ AWOKE ON HEIDI'S COUCH, HAVING APPRECIABLY reduced his sleep deficit. He rubbed his eyes and attempted to focus on his watch. He registered 10:31 a.m. Schwartz sensed something affixed to his forehead and reached for it. It was an envelope. He pulled it off and suffered the sting from the disengaging tape.

Inside the envelope he found a note and a key. In bold strokes, the note simply read, "Breakfast in microwave. Please lock and slip key under door. See you in court Fri. Towel is for you. Heidi F." Schwartz placed the key on a lamp stand and rose from the couch, searching for his date book. The pain in his ribs cautioned him to move slowly. He thumbed the pages to Thursday, December 14 and sighed in relief. He had only two cases, one of them an afternoon call. He searched the bedroom for a phone, finally finding it after a game of hot-and-cold using the paging mechanism on the base. He dialed the part for the case that was an a.m. general call.

"Part 12."

"18-B Schwartz. I'm on the Kaspycyk matter. Represent the mother. I'm delayed on another matter. Be in about twelve."

"I'll let the bridge officer know."

Sometimes BxFC can be a cool place to work.

Ambling in search of the bathroom, Schwartz grabbed the towel Heidi had left on the coffee table. It was a red, white, and blue affair, evocative of the Puerto Rican flag with the logo and call letters of a radio station promoting salsa concerts at Orchard Beach.

He was intrigued by the bullfighter posters adorning the living room walls. In Spain and Mexico, the blood sport was exalted. Once he located the bathroom, Schwartz rolled the towel into a rat's tail and snapped it at his naked image reflected in the full-length mirror on the bathroom door. He assumed the exaggerated posture of a toreador.

"*Oye. Chico. Mira Mira* on *de* wall, who da baddest 18-B of them all?"

Schwartz's answer was to award himself with that sensation he hadn't experienced in many months: a hot bath, and to enhance the experience by singing "Splish Splash."

Schwartz was full out throating it, joined by a *thump! thump! thump!* on the bathroom wall. The thumping provided a nice backbeat until a strident "Shut the fuck up!" disrupted the jam. As Schwartz froze, mid-note, he splished and he splashed. Having lost some of the water onto Heidi's bathroom floor, he opened the faucet and gave the tub a hit of steaming-hot Bronx apartment water to compensate.

Man, those bathroom rugs can soak up water.

To calm himself, Schwartz gazed at the reflection of the light fixture in the bathtub water. When the water was relatively still, the image bounced gently. When Schwartz moved his hand, creating a gentle ripple, the light reacted psychedelically, spiraling into a helix, bursting into stars, and then crashing in waves against the side of the bathtub.

He lay back, arching his neck against the tiled edge and rolling it back and forth, attempting to release the tension. The gesture brought to his mind that moment several months before, when Marjorie decided she'd had enough of him.

At the marital condo on the island, Schwartz had been lying in the bathtub in the dark late one summer night. It was one of the few sensual indulgences Schwartz permitted himself—the occasional hot bath in a room softly lit by candles, with offerings from the Bobby Darin box set collection playing on a nearby cassette recorder. Another indulgence he enjoyed, given the sorry state of sexual inactivity in his marriage, was talking on the cordless phone with a woman in the employ of a telephone sex enterprise. Marjorie had rushed in, cursing, throwing plastic bottles of bubble bath, shampoo, and conditioner as he attempted to rise from his watery den of iniquity. Splish Splash, Schwartz was pushed violently from the warm, dark, watery cocoon into a cold, bright, dry reality.

He stood in Heidi's living room drying himself. Through her living room window, Schwartz could see rays of sunlight, sliced and diced by the cable spires of the Throgs Neck and Whitestone Bridges. Those same rays glistened in the windows of the skyscrapers in the metropolis beyond. On reflection, Schwartz realized he had experienced a rebirth that watershed night in the marital condo.

As he dressed in the midmorning sunlight he wondered where this rebirth would lead.

After removing the obligatory freshly minted parking ticket from his windshield, Schwartz inserted the key in the ignition on the console between the bucket seats, turned it, and gratefully heard the engine start. He paused briefly to reflect on the windmills to be tilted at in the coming days and pulled out of the parking spot.

As Schwartz exited the elevator onto the Seventh floor of BxFC ACS attorney Holly Benson cut in front of him. Benson was only several years out of law school. She spoke in that singsong manner reminiscent of Valley-girl talk, with almost every sentence except the last, no matter how declarative the content, sounding like a question. Schwartz found Benson's speech irritating and her manner cloying. She, in turn, regarded Schwartz as a curmudgeon and gave him short shrift.

"Schwartz, on that Mojica 1028 tomorrow in part 1 . . . well, I'm filing an amended petition today? The case is being upgraded to an abuse? The child was acting out sexually in the foster home? Rubbing her pubic area against a bedpost? Foster care agency had the girl examined at the Montefiore clinic and there are physical, positive findings for sex abuse? Plus, she tested positive for an STD? The girl has not yet ID'd the perp, but she said a friend of her mother did some nasty things to her and that her mother knew about it and didn't report it."

Benson handed Schwartz a copy of the amended petition. Schwartz regarded it as he might a stick of dynamite. He opened to the portion of the petition that pled the new allegations.

"Subject child's hymen had notches at 3 o'clock and 9 o'clock. Furthermore, child was found positive for a sexually transmitted disease, chlamydia. Respondent mother knew or should have known of the sexual abuse and failed to protect child."

"Let me know if you're going forward with the 1028 because I have witnesses on call."

Benson walked off, leaving Schwartz stunned in her wake.

Schwartz's case was called into the part. Schwartz robotically noted his appearance for the record. Judge Ira Kline glanced up from the *New York Times* to give the case less than his undivided attention. The case before the bench was a family offense order of protection case. Schwartz represented the petitioner mother who had allegedly been threatened with a knife by her baby's father.

Given Schwartz's state of mind, it was fortunate for both him and the client that the respondent lover/baby father did not appear.

The opposing counsel was Phillip Braun known for his outlandish wardrobe of pastel sport jackets and slacks, bright shirts and ties, the occasional Bermuda shorts with knee socks, and, on special occasions, a kilt. His more notorious trademark was his irrepressible rogue tongue, which was especially operative when addressing the ladies. Braun's shtick included walking through the courthouse with a bag of hard round candy sour balls and offering them to female attorneys with the invitation to "suck my balls." Braun's saving grace, if there was one, was that he was a skilled litigator who advocated strongly and effectively for his clients. Braun's sartorial choices and his offensive language reminded Schwartz of a cartoon he had seen in a magazine. In it, a clown sitting at a desk with law degrees mounted on the wall behind him said to a potential client, "Well, if I weren't an excellent lawyer, do you think I could practice in a clown suit?"

Braun addressed Judge Kline in a futile effort to be granted an adjournment. "Your Honor, I understand that the woman came and my client did not come . . . to court, that is. But since this is the first time the case came on the calendar, I would ask for a continuance."

Not one to stand on ceremony when an opportunity for a quick disposition of a matter presented itself, Judge Kline denied Braun's pro forma C.Y.A. application.

"In that case, Your Honor, I shall remain mute to preserve my client's right to reopen this matter should he have a legal excuse for not coming," Braun said with a leer.

Judge Kline shook his head. "Your muteness is noted and most appreciated."

The judge then conducted a brief inquest consisting of two questions: Q: "Madam, did you sign this petition?" A: "Yes." and Q: "Are the allegations contained in it true?" A: "Yes."

The judge granted the petitioner's application for a one-year stay-away order of protection, which was extended to cover the child in common. No visitation with the child was ordered for the baby father.

Once outside the part, Schwartz numbly shook the thankful woman's hand and wished her luck. From where she was standing, Schwartz was Clarence Darrow, Perry Mason, and Johnnie Cochran combined. Schwartz managed to mumble to her that for the order of protection to have force and effect, she needed to have the order served on the respondent by someone who was not a party to the case and who was over the age of eighteen.

Braun congratulated Schwartz in his own inimitable style. "Way to shoot ducks in a barrel, mothafucka. Like I always say, every poor lawyer has a right to a client."

Despite the recent eviction, Schwartz's inclination was to find Cliff and try to square things. At the very least, he had filed the omnibus motion on his marijuana arrest, seeking a <u>Mapp</u> hearing on the search and seizure of the marijuana roach from his wallet and the release of Cliff's car from civil forfeiture.

Outside Cliff's part, Schwartz asked the court officer, who was barking out names of litigants, whether Cliff was inside. He responded that Cliff had banged in again. Schwartz headed to the 18-B room and to the communal phone the forty-odd panel members shared.

Clique members, putting the finishing touches on the *New York Times* crossword puzzle or napping, occupied the table the phone was on. Schwartz cringed when he saw Jennifer Wexler on the communal phone. The simple rule for use was that a person could make one call and then the next person waiting used the phone for one call. Schwartz had witnessed the receiver being handed back and forth between 18-Bs for the better part of an hour. Cell phones, for those attorneys willing to splurge, were of variable utility because of the poor reception in BxFC. Though the phone was supposedly for business purposes, Wexler had a reputation for Bogarting it. Decidedly personal in nature, her lengthy conversations revealed intimate details of her life and that of her children, and her husband. All the details became common knowledge to the involuntary audience.

"And I told Stephanie's therapist that I didn't know she'd been smoking pot. Maybe her new school is stressing her out. Meanwhile, I think my husband has been whispering to my mother-in-law about my plans for a belly tuck . . ."

Based on the resigned look of others in the room, Schwartz knew Wexler was in the midst of a monologue, the end of which was nowhere in sight. With resignation, Schwartz the Schnorrer searched his pocket for a quarter and headed to one of the nearby public booths. He was oblivious to Mitzner, who was razzing him about "the suit."

Every court day, those public phones were the conduits for the most caustic, calamitous conversations that occur on this planet. Often times, conversations were terminated with an ear-splitting slam-bam-thank-you-ma'am of the receiver. As a result, the phones themselves deserved combat pay. That any of them they worked at all continued to amaze Schwartz.

After trying several phones, Schwartz finally located one that would accept his quarter and register a dial tone. He searched his date book for the page where he'd scribbled Isabel's number. He flipped back to the page of the early November week when they had first met. There it was in his barely legible, alcohol/sex-sated scribble. Dialing the number, he formulated his approach.

I regret to inform you . . . No, no. Too formal.

Hola, Isabel. Uh, we have a problem . . . No, no. Too cinematic.

OK . . . OK . . . I got it.

When someone picked up on the other end, Schwartz blurted out, "Isabel, *nosotros necisita habla!*"

The voice that answered was decidedly not Isabel's. In fact, it was decidedly male and all too familiar.

"Who de fuck is dees?"

Schwartz slammed down the receiver, adding his name to the long list of phone abusers in BxFC. He turned and gazed out the window overlooking 161st Street, momentarily transfixed by the comings and goings into the building. He decided to call his office number to see if Isabel had left any messages.

After locating another quarter in the bowels of his shoulder bag, Schwartz dialed his number and pressed his access code to retrieve messages. He skipped over several old messages he had neglected to erase. One was a particularly strident plea from Marjorie, reminding him that the mortgage needed to be paid before December 15 to avoid the late fee, and there were two barely comprehensible messages from Helen Morrisey, the schizophrenic mother of the doomed child. Schwartz forged ahead into the crop of new calls. He surveyed the litany of cries and complaints from clients, skipping ahead once he had gotten the gist.

"Mr. Schwartz, that ACS worker is fucking with my head. She referred me to a program but I gots no Medicaids. How I gonna pay for—"

Beep!

"This is Miss Hutchinson. This is the third time I been calling you, Mr. Schwartz, about the father coming late for his visitation—"

Beep!

"Mr. Schwartz, you've been assigned as law guardian in the Contreras matter. Please call my client and arrange an interview of the children. She can be reached at home at—"

Beep!

Schwartz recognized the voice on the next message instantly. It was the voice he had just heard answering Isabel's phone, the voice that belonged to the man who had attacked him outside part I and, most recently, at Jimmy's Bronx Café.

"Meester Schwartz, if you don't take care of de case of Isabel Mojica and get her kid returned to her, you dead. Your whole motherfucking family is dead. I am not fucking around. Do you hear me?"

Schwartz went from numb to panic in a nanosecond. His hand shaking, he was barely able to replace the receiver.

How the fuck did he get my number? Easy, asshole. Isabel gave him your card.

But if he has my card then . . . oh, shit, oh, shit.

"Oh, shit. Oh, shit. What a shmuck. What a cheap motherfucking schmuck I am."

Seeking to save money, Schwartz had never bothered to pay the $100 a month to have a mail drop at some other attorney's office.

If he has my card, he has my home address!

He hung up the phone and searched for a quarter to call his house. No luck. He ran to the 18-B room and found Wexler still hogging the phone in her drama queen turn.

"Jennifer, I need that phone right now."

She turned and gave him an "as if" look and continued right on prattling.

Schwartz grabbed the phone from her and slammed down the receiver. Oblivious to her protests, Schwartz dialed his home number. After it rang several times, he was taunted by his own voice on the greeting. He hung up, bolted from the room, and cascaded down the seven flights to the streets below, with each step jarring his ribs.

After a chaotic death-defying drive from the Bronx to the Island, Schwartz rapped on the door to what was once his condo. No response. It was 5:00 p.m. Once again he tried, frantically. He heard the shuffling of feet on the other side of door.

"Julie? Is that you? Open the door, baby. It's daddy."

Silence.

"Baby, please. I've got to see you, Eth, and mommy. This is important."

Schwartz could hear another set of feet, somewhat lighter, approach the foyer.

"Daddy, mommy said we not to open the door for anyone."

Ethan.

"And if you came we had to call the police."

Julie.

Schwartz struggled to compose himself as he choked on the irony. In that moment he wore the dual hat of protector and predator.

"Where is mommy, Jules?"

"Doctor's appointment. She said she'd be back soon."

That his children had devolved into latchkey kids struck a chord of anger and guilt.

"Look, guys, it is verrrry important for you to let me in. Trust me. Mommy will understand."

Schwartz could barely overhear the whispered debate ensuing between the siblings. Finally he heard the chain slide jiggling and the tumblers of the dead bolt turning. As the door opened, Schwartz was careful not to rush inside. He had already alarmed his children more than he'd wished. Once the door was fully open, he stepped inside and was greeted by Julie and Ethan, hugging him like he'd never been hugged before. Ethan was positively distraught.

"Daddy, where'd you go? You don't call. I think you go away."

Schwartz didn't bother to fight back the tears. Reluctantly, slowly, Schwartz disengaged from the group hug.

"Listen, kids, I haven't wanted to stay away. Julie knows, Eth, what's been going on between mom and me."

In response to Ethan's inquiring glance, Julie looked to the ground, guiltily. Schwartz kicked himself for having outed Julie so blatantly. But he didn't have time for subtlety.

"I've got to check my messages. Then I'm just going to wait for mommy to get home."

"Do you want to eat anything?" Julie asked.

Oh, this kid. This kid.

"In a bit, baby doll, in a bit."

Schwartz sprinted to his office den. Under the strata of files and papers on the desk, he searched for his pocket tape recorder. Once located, he confirmed its operability with the timeless "testing, one, two, three" method. He half expected the recorder to spit back, "Failing, four, five, six." He ran upstairs to the phone with the voice-mail system and searched the messages until he heard that voice. Cueing the recorder, he replayed the message. Cringing at the menace in the voice, he played back the recording to ensure a successful reproduction. Once again, though compressed, the deadly message was delivered: "Your whole motherfucking family is dead. I am not fucking around. Do you hear me?"

Schwartz pocketed the recorder and began to evaluate the security of the condo's entrances and windows. While he was upstairs in the master bedroom, he heard the front door open and then Ethan greeting his mother and telling her excitedly that daddy was home. That disclosure was followed by Marjorie shrieking, "What the—?" and bounding up the stairs.

"Just what are you doing in this bedroom? Julie, call the police! You get out of here now!"

"Margie, listen to me. There's a dangerous man who's going to come here and—"

"You're right, and he's already here. You're dangerous!"

"What are you talking about? Margie, I—"

"What am I talking about? What am I talking about? This!"

She picked up a piece of paper from the nightstand, balled it up, and threw it in his face. He caught it on the rebound before it hit the ground. Uncrumpling it, he read:

OBY-GYN EXAM- 12/13/00
Schwartz, Marjorie
Lab results..............STDs...positive for CHLAMYDIA.

The word *chlamydia* was seared into Schwartz's essence. It described him, defined him, and damned him. Suddenly the burning sensation he felt upon urination made all too much sense. Reeling with the implications of the news, he sat down on the bed. Marjorie had other ideas.

"Now, get the fuck out before the police get called!"

He rose ever so slowly. He couldn't even face her as he walked by. As he passed her he mumbled, "Just make sure you lock the windows and doors, and for Chrissake, don't leave the children alone."

Ethan and Julie were immobilized. Schwartz attempted to kiss Julie, but Marjorie stepped between them.

"And don't be kissing my children until you take an antibiotic bath, you prick."

She opened the door and made an exaggerated motion with her arm in the direction of the street. The last sound Schwartz registered was the door slamming behind him.

Breathing rapidly, Schwartz drove to the first phone booth he could find. He searched his wallet for Sgt. Tony Napolitano's card. Napolitano had jotted down his beeper number for his eighth-floor barbeque buddy in case Schwartz ever needed any help. That time had come. As he dialed Napolitano's number, he prayed that he would get a voice and not the voicemail.

Perhaps Schwartz should have gone to temple on the High Holidays, because the growl from the receiver came in the form of Tony's recorded message. Schwartz could barely contain his *agita* waiting for the obligatory beep.

"Tony, it's Schwartz. A bad guy by the name of Hector Machado is threatening me and my family. He's in his late twenties, just under six feet, black hair, brown eyes, lives in the Soundview section. I know I'm not givin' you much to work with. But anything you can find out about him I'd appreciate. I'll be in family court tomorrow or leave a message at my office number."

Schwartz drove the Saab to the intersection closest to his family's condo development and shut off the engine. He moved the seat back with the intention to surveil as best as he could the incoming traffic.

In a tired voice he began to sing Darin's lonely wail "All by Myself".

DECEMBER 15:
DAY OF RECKONING

WHEN HIS MOTHER TOOK YOUNG SCHWARTZ TO THE RINGLING
Bros. and Barnum & Bailey Circus at Madison Square Garden, he would splurge
on the requisite cotton candy, Cracker Jack, soda pop, and jelly apple. Then he
would try to follow the goings-on in each of the three rings against the backdrop
of hundreds twirling lights. Then he'd hurl the contents of his stomach with the
propulsion of a Saturn rocket.

To Schwartz, the day loomed like a trip to the three-ring circus. His triage
philosophy, gleaned from his poli-sci studies at Lehman College, was fashioned
from the saints, savables, and sinners' method of classifying election districts for
canvassing with limited resources. The saints didn't really need his help; the
sinners, give the damned a show. But the savables were whom he would focus his
limited time and energy on.

That morning Schwartz's dilemma was that all three of his 9:30 a.m. calls
fell into the "savable" category. Carmen Fontanez, having successfully completed
drug rehabilitation, arguably should not be denied the opportunity in her
dwindling days to care for her infant daughter. There was enough reasonable
doubt in the people's case against Ronaldo Ramirez to generate several acquittals.
And Isabel Mojica's case fell into a special savable category: Save my own *tokhes*.

So where to first, Ringmaster?

Uh, the save-my-own-tokhes ring.

Schwartz scarfed down his breakfast special at Fun City Restaurant (two
eggs, toast, hash browns, shot of OJ, and coffee for $1.75) and rode out the
familiar pangs of nausea. He threw his bag across his shoulders, donned his
ringmaster's hat, and headed across the street.

Schwartz hurried down the hall, passing Judge Parker's part and trying to scoot by Carmen and Heidi unnoticed. Heidi brightened when she saw him and darkened when Schwartz shouted that he'd be right back and to tell the court officer that he'd gone to Part I. He quickened his gait to a near trot, dodging litigants and lawyers alike. As he reached the waiting area, he scanned the matrix of benches for any sign of Isabel and, of greater concern, Hector Machado. Not there. The bridge officer announced, "Parties in the Matter of the Soriano Child!"

Schwartz warily entered the courtroom, joining Benson, the ACS attorney, and the law guardian from LAS already seated at the litigants' table. Every time someone entered, Schwartz turned his head toward the entrance. He was half hoping that Isabel would show and half hoping she wouldn't. The bridge officer's tenor wail trumpeted Judge Finkel's arrival from the back office.

"All rise. Counsel, note your appearance."

All complied. Schwartz suppressed the temptation to sarcastically compliment the judge on looking particularly dour today. The judge finished marking her endorsement sheet with the names of those in attendance. She glanced up and trained her vision on the empty seat next to Schwartz.

"Mr. Schwartz, I note the absence of a quorum. Where's your client, Ms. Mojica?"

"I have no specific information as to her whereabouts. There is, however, a rather long line extending out into the street, and perhaps she's in the line."

"Well, shall I send runners out into the street searching for her? It is her application for the return of her children and—"

"Child, Your Honor. There's only one child."

Judge Finkel adopted the soft tone, which played counter point to her rebuke.

"Mr. Schwartz, do not interrupt the court when the court is speaking. Do you understand me? Officer, call the lobby. Ask them to call out the respondent's name."

The officer retreated to the back office. *Awkward* only began to describe the ensuing pause as Schwartz and Finkel stared at each other. *Painful* more aptly fit the bill.

"No answer in the lobby, Judge."

A knowing smile crinkled Finkel's lips.

"The time is 9:40 a.m. There being no appearance of the respondent, the 1028 application is waived. The remand of the child (placing emphasis on that word while glaring at Schwartz) shall continue. Let's set a date for fact-finding. My calendar is booked until late March."

Schwartz rose quickly, nearly knocking over his chair in the process. "Judge, I am asking for a second call of this matter. To deny a mother the opportunity to be heard on the issue of custody of her child for the next six months to a year because she is ten minutes late is unconscionable. This isn't a parking ticket we're dealing with here."

"You're absolutely right. This isn't a parking ticket. All the more reason for your client to be here promptly if she were so interested in the return of her daughter."

"Your Honor, may I be heard?" Benson interjected.

"What is it, Ms. Benson?"

"We've filed an amended petition upgrading the charges from neglect to abuse? This is based upon disclosures made by the subject child of sexual abuse? We would be asking for a short date so we can serve the respondent and have her arraigned on the new petition."

Finkel shuffled the papers in front of her.

"Ah. Here it is. Very well, this matter will be adjourned to Monday, December 18, p.m. calendar. The 1028 is deemed waived."

Schwartz coughed emphatically. "Judge, the court is advised that I will be making an application to be relieved from this case because—"

"Mr. Schwartz, we'll deal with that on the next court date. Ms. Benson, will you approach?"

Schwartz gathered his file and returned it to his shoulder bag. As he turned to leave, he overheard a snippet of Finkel's conversation with the ACS attorney. The judge's phrase "referral to the DA's office" reverberated over the din of ambient courtroom chatter. Schwartz stopped, turned on his heels, and addressed the court in Benson's singsong inflection.

"Excuse me, Your Honor? You wouldn't by any chance be having an *ex parte* communication with Ms. Benson about this case? I mean, if that were so, I would ask the court to at least wait until I've left the courtroom."

All other conversations ceased. Judge Finkel struggled to retain her composure.

"Mr. Schwartz, if you are going to shoot off your mouth in my courtroom, please come prepared with a toothbrush to put in it because I will put you in for future contumacious behavior. Leave the courtroom now!"

Schwartz awarded himself a slight smile as he exited.

I got her goat.

Schwartz headed in the direction of Part II, Judge William B. Williams presiding. The lawyer's intent was to check in on the Ramirez continued fact-finding and then scoot over to Judge Parker's part for the continued 1028 in Carmen's case. Opening the door, he saw the judge on the bench in all his white-headed glory but no sign of ADA Roger Edens. His relief was short-lived. Thunder cracked as Judge Williams admonished Schwartz.

"Counsel, it is now 9:45 a.m. This was a 9:30 call on a continued remand designated felony case. Mr. Edens was here but you were not. I am sanctioning you $250. Mr. Edens left to see if his witness has arrived. Now, be seated."

"But, Judge, how can you sanction me if the ADA was not even ready to proceed? Besides, Judge, I'm straddling two 1028s, which, by the Chief Judge's Rules of Engagement, take priority, and—"

"This is not debate, Counselor. Be seated."

The clerk entered from the robing room and informed the judge that he had a telephone call. The judge left, leaving Schwartz to stew in the curry of his lighter wallet and increasing anxiety. Minutes passed, and the minute hand seemed to race around the clock. The hour hand nudged past ten.

Judges could get surprisingly proprietary regarding the presence of counsel in their courtroom. Schwartz knew of at least one judge who made a regular practice of locking attorneys in her robing room. She would order them not to leave the part, regardless of other calls in other parts, and place a court officer at the rear entrance, thereby eliminating the chance of counsel slipping out the back door *à la* Stevie Wonder and Paul Simon. Schwartz had confirmation from a reliable source (Cliff) that a judge had become so steamed over another judge's court officer retrieving a cross-pressured 18-B that Judge A stormed into Judge B's courtroom and verbally and physically confronted Judge B. ("Don't let the black robe fool ya.") The court officers restrained both judges as the confrontation rose to the level of a Major League Baseball pushing/shoving near-brawl.

It had been more than fifteen minutes—an eternity in BxFC world—since Judge Williams had disappeared. Over the bridge officer's protests, Schwartz rose, grabbed his book bag, and bolted for Parker's part. As Schwartz approached Part X, the court officer outside shouted, "Parties in the Matter of the Fontanez Children!" In close proximity to the officer's mouth, Schwartz received the message loud and clear. Special ACC Barbanel was seated at the litigants' table, alone. Judge Parker was on the bench.

"Ah, Mr. Schwartz. Now, where is Ms. Grella?" the judge asked.

"She's finishing up a probable cause hearing in Part 9 and will be here shortly," the bridge officer answered.

"But this is a 1028 hearing," the judge complained.

He rose from the bench and walked into his chambers. Carmen and Heidi walked through the doors, followed by Adesanya. Schwartz turned to Carmen and started to ask how she was, but her drooping eyelids and skin lesions, camouflaged by pancake powder, provided the answer. Schwartz grabbed her hand and squeezed it. She crinkled her nose, which Schwartz interpreted correctly as a query as to the status of the case.

Schwartz answered with a shrug and said, "We were supposed to start our case but law guardian has asked to go out of turn with a witness."

Parker returned to the bench.

"Ms. Grella will be joining us shortly. Mr. Barbanel, on the last court date you were in the middle of the direct examination of the caseworker, correct?"

Barbanel stood ever so slowly, treating those in attendance to a particularly irksome scratching of the chair against the linoleum tile floor.

"No, Your Honor. My notes indicate that we finished with the caseworker and the agency was prepared to rest. We adjourned for the respondent's case, but I believe Ms. Grella has an application in that regard."

On cue, Cindy Grella pushed through the door carrying an armful of case files and a water bottle.

"Cindy Grella, of counsel to Maureen Sanderson, the Legal Aid Society, law guardian for the Fontanez child. Your Honor, I had this case down as a 9:30 call, but I was told that Mr. Schwartz wasn't here yet, so I got pulled into a probable cause hearing on a remand delinquency. My apologies to court and counsel. I have an application to take a witness out of turn."

"Who's the witness?"

"He's a child psychologist contracted for by the Legal Aid Society."

"Offer of proof, Your Honor," Schwartz said.

Grella turned to Schwartz with a sick little smile.

"Judge, Dr. Merrick Corenthal conducted an evaluation of the mother's interaction with the subject infant in order to assess her ability to bond and nurture."

Schwartz fumed. "Wait a minute. Wait a minute. Where and when and under whose authority did this evaluation occur? We didn't consent to it, nor did the judge order it."

Grella readily responded. "The observation took place during a mother–child visit at St. Patrick's Services for Children. There was no need to obtain prior approval. Notice to the mother would have affected the integrity of the evaluation. The foster care agency permitted Dr. Corenthal on its premises to conduct the evaluation to aid in the formulation of a service plan for mother and child. He never asked a single question of the mother. He simply observed their interaction."

Schwartz trained his memory on his visit for the conference at St. Patrick's. He recalled seeing Carmen sitting in a room, holding her baby. There was a man in the cubicle seated with her.

Right under my nose. I am an asshole.

A burning sensation ignited in his neck, spread to both sides of his temple, and converged at the apex of his cranium.

"Your Honor, the Legal Aid Society has sunk to a new low in its relentless war against parents' rights. To even use the word *integrity* in their argument is an affront. I cannot believe this court is going to permit this . . . this . . . underhanded . . ."

Schwartz's anger choked off any further response. Judge Parker stroked his chin. He called to his court attorney to come out of the back room. In hushed whispers, they conferred for several minutes. Finally, the judge issued his ruling.

"Ms. Grella, while the better practice might have been for you to obtain consent from the respondent and her counsel, since the issue before this court is imminent risk to a newborn, I'm going to permit the testimony."

"Judge, how can you—"

"Mr. Schwartz, you have your exception to my ruling."

"But, Judge—"

"Mr. Schwartz, I have ruled! Counsel, call your witness."

Dr. Corenthal was the shrink from Central Casting, right down to the beard, horn-rimmed glasses, and pedantic manner. As Grella handed out copies of Corenthal's *curriculum vitae*, the good doctor assumed the witness chair and accepted the oath with an air of self-importance. His academic affectation was a curious counter note to Grella's chalkboard-scratching voice.

"Would counsel stipulate to the witness being called as an expert in child developmental psychology?"

Schwartz glanced over Corenthal's laundry list of accomplishments and realized there wasn't much point to challenging his credentials. Still, there was room for mischief.

"Just two questions on *voir dire*. Doctor, on how many occasions have you been called to assess a mother's psychological ability to bond with her newborn child?"

"Actually, sir, this is the first time for a court hearing. But in our clinical work at Schneider's Children's Hospital, we are often asked to assess the ability of mothers to nurture and bond with their newborns."

"So, as I understand it, Doctor, when the state decides to limit the biological imperative of procreation to those psychologically fit, you will be at the frontlines of that campaign?"

Schwartz was already headed for his seat as he finished asking the question.

"Objection!"

Even Parker winced at the crystal-shattering impact of Grella's protestation.

"Mr. Schwartz, was that really necessary? Do you stipulate to the doctor being called as an expert in child developmental psychology?"

"Judge, I will stipulate that he is an expert in deciding who he thinks has a right to parent."

"Mr. Schwartz, I'm admonishing you to can the sarcasm. Having reviewed the doctor's CV, I'm prepared to qualify him as an expert. Ask your first question, Ms. Grella."

"Doctor, are you familiar with Carmen Fontanez and her infant daughter, Justina?"

"Yes. I had an opportunity to observe a mother–child visit at St. Patrick's Services for Children earlier this week . . . on Tuesday, I believe."

"What did you observe?"

"I noticed that Ms. Fontanez seemed uncomfortable handling the child. She wasn't at all at ease in holding the infant in her arms. One notable impediment was Ms. Fontanez's enormous nails. They were inappropriate for holding and bonding with an infant—"

The handle on the detonator at the base of Schwartz's skull plunged.

"Judge, Judge, is this how LAS spends its stipend from taxpayers' money?" he challenged. "On this class-biased, old-fashioned snobbery-quackery? Today we are to decide whether a mother and child can be reunited. Are we reduced to discussing the length of a person's nails?"

"Your objection, if it is one, is overruled. Doctor, other than her nails, is there anything else you observed?" Judge Parker asked.

"Well, the mother seemed ill at ease in bottle feeding. She seemed to quiver while holding the child. Frankly, I was somewhat concerned that she might drop the child."

"Objection! Calls for speculation."

"Yes, sustained. The latter part of the answer is stricken. Ms. Grella?"

"Thank you. Doctor, how did the infant react to the mother?"

"The child was squirming and crying. She was very uncomfortable."

"Dr. Corenthal, have you formed an opinion, to a reasonable degree of psychological certainty, as to whether this infant would be at risk if placed in the care of the mother?"

"I have. Because of the mother's limitations, her history of other children in foster care, and her poor bonding and nurturing skills, I have reached the conclusion that this infant would be at imminent psychological risk if placed in the mother's care."

"No further questions."

Judge Parker turned to Schwartz. "Counsel, any cross?"

Schwartz was aghast. He had never seen the evil in the Children's Best Interest Complex so patently presented. He was raised on good socialist values, believing that all one needs to do is serve the State and the State would look after the people. Now the State, in the interest of protecting children, was steamrolling over the People's rights.

Am I being melodramatic? Perhaps.

But the glint of a tear in Carmen's eye and the downcast frown on Heidi's face informed his mood. He stood silently and stared at the witness for several beats.

"Doctor, do you have any children?" he asked.

"Objection." Grella was intent on defusing Schwartz's attack.

"Sustained."

"Can I see your nails?"

"Objection!"

Another glass-shattering performance by Grella.

"Judge, a little leeway here. This is cross-examination. Subject to connection."

"Counsel, I'm granting you just that—a little leeway. But don't waste the court's time."

"Judge, I believe the law guardian has already achieved that."

"Mr. Schwartz!" Judge Parker barked.

Schwartz approached the witness, who tepidly held out his right hand. Schwartz suppressed the desire to grab his fingers and crunch them together with a vicious twist. He allowed himself a slight grin as he noted, "Doctor, your nails are manicured, are they not?"

"Yes, they are."

"It makes you feel good about yourself, or, putting it in psychological parlance, it enhances your self-esteem to have your nails manicured, does it not?"

"Ob-jec-shun! Relevancy?" Grella was persistent.

"Ov-er-ruled," answered the judge.

The witness allowed "I suppose so."

Schwartz stayed on track.

"You suppose so. Do you get pedicures as well?"

"Your Honor! This is going far afield," Grella whined.

"Yes. Sustained. Next question, Mr. Schwartz."

"Doctor, you're aware, are you not, that Ms. Fontanez is suffering from full-blown AIDS?"

"Yes."

"And that she is ingesting toxic medical cocktails with horrific side effects?"

"I would expect so."

"Would this explain the quivering that you noticed?"

"It could. It might. But the quivering is still there."

"Are you also aware that Ms. Fontanez is residing in a facility with twenty-four-hour staff available to assist and supervise her?"

"Objection! Counsel is testifying," Grella said standing. Barbanel simply sat holding his head in his hands with his eyes closed.

Schwartz replied, "Your Honor, if that's so, it's only because we consented to taking this witness out of turn. We've yet to hear testimony from an ACS caseworker concerning the court-ordered visit to the hospice. I believe that the witness can answer it either subject to connection or based upon a hypothetical."

"Doctor, can you answer Mr. Schwartz's question?" Judge Parker implored.

"Yes. Very well. Assuming the facts implicit in the question, it is indeed commendable and fortunate that Ms. Fontanez is seeking treatment for her HIV affliction, as well as for her substance abuse, in a secure setting. Nevertheless, team parenting is not consistent with this infant's psychological needs. That there is staff that can step in and nurture the child when the mother cannot is of cold comfort."

Schwartz was about to question Corenthal about his observation of the infant's discomfort with her mother. He was going to ask if it could be a result of the infant's unfamiliarity with Ms. Fontanez due to the remand order to foster care. He halted when saw Judge Williams enter from the part's robing room, accompanied by his bridge officer. Judge Parker seemed taken aback by the appearance of another judge in his corner of the pond. Judge Williams mounted the two foot riser where Judge Parker's seat was situated. He whispered in Judge Parker's ear while glaring and pointing at Schwartz. Judge Williams then turned abruptly and exited the way he had entered.

"Uh, Mr. Schwartz, apparently your presence is required presently in Part 2. This matter is on recall."

Resigned, Schwartz closed his file and slid it back into his shoulder bag.

"Ah'll be bock," he promised Heidi and Carmen. Schwartz was escorted by the part II court officer, Schwartz feared the fate that awaited him in the unfriendly confines of part II and would have appreciated a moment or two to plot his defense, if not his escape. He was also afflicted with the burning pain in his groin and ribs. But the three-ring circus dictated that time was of the essence. Striding through the part I waiting area, he scanned the faces, looking for Isabel without success.

Swinging open the door to part II, Schwartz immediately saw ADA Edens, Ronnie Ramirez Sr., and Ronnie Ramirez Jr. seated at the table. Judge Williams was pacing on the podium behind his chair. Upon seeing Schwartz, scowled to the bridge officer, "Let's go. Call the case."

After the parties and counsel gave their appearance, Judge Williams derriere landed on his chair with a boom. The volcano was in full eruption.

"Mr. Schwartz, did I or did I not order you to stay seated in the back of the courtroom earlier this morning? And did you or did you not sneak out at the earliest possible moment?"

"Judge, I have two 1028 hearings as well as this case on my calendar, and each judge, over my objection, calendared their case for 9:30, and I—"

"Counsel, I will tell you that your inability to manage your personal calendar is of no consequence to this court. Your action this morning, coupled with your lateness in appearing, was the most disgusting acts of contemptuous behavior I have witnessed since I've been on the bench. Only because there is a hearing to proceed with will I withhold the immediate imposition of drastic sanctions. Do you have anything else you wish to say?"

Ronnie's father whispered in his ear, "I don tink he like you."

Schwartz whispered back out of the side of his mouth, "You tink?"

"What was that, Mr. Schwartz? I didn't catch that."

"Nothing, Judge. I just said, 'I'm thinking.' I'm ready for trial."

The judge nodded and scrunched his chin up into his lower lip.

"You and I will have further discussion at the completion of today's proceedings. Mr. Edens?"

"Your Honor, the people call Detective John Cassidy. He should be right outside."

"He's coming," was the meek pronouncement made by the court officer who had been sent to fetch the witness.

A giant man emerged behind the court officer. He had blue-grey hair and might have just as easily been a retired power forward for the Boston Celtics as a ballistics expert for the NYPD. When asked to state his name for the record, he answered as if he carried in his larynx his own public address system. There'd be no doubt about the accuracy of the transcript, given the proximity of the witness stand to the court reporter. Schwartz chuckled as the overwhelmed reporter inched her chair away. With the witness having been duly sworn, Edens collected his file and assumed the position at the podium.

"Detective, are you the ballistics expert assigned to the Ramirez investigation?"

"That's right, sir."

"And how long have you been a ballistics expert for the NYPD?"

"For the better part of thirty years, sir."

"What training in the use and identification of firearms and their projectiles have you had?"

"I've completed both the FBI and NYPD firearms and ballistic identification training. I presently serve as a instructor at the Police Academy in firearms identification and am supervising instructor at the NYPD Rodman's Neck firearms range. If you include two tours of duty in Vietnam in Special Forces I'd say I've spent my entire adult life in the field of firearms and ballistics."

Great. Now I get to cross-examine John Wayne.

"Judge, I'll stipulate to the detective's expertise in the use and identification of firearms and what was the word, Mr. Edens?" Schwartz paused for emphasis as he mimicked Edens pronunciation--- "pro-jec-tiles."

"Very well. Move on, Mr. Edens," Judge Williams harummphed.

"Detective Cassidy, did you conduct a field investigation in the Ramirez shooting case?"

"I did."

"And when was that?"

"On the afternoon of November 27th of this year, on the very same day that the shooting was reported to the NYPD."

"Objection to the latter part of the answer. Hearsay."

"Overruled."

Edens pressed on. "Can you tell the court what the field investigation consisted of in this case?"

"Basically, my team and I scoured the streets and sidewalks proximate to East 174th Street, between Hoe and Vyse Avenues, searching for weaponry, bullets, bullet fragments, or physical evidence of bullet impact."

"Did your team make any positive findings?"

"We did, as diagrammed in the field investigation report."

"Objection. Refers to a document not in evidence."

Schwartz wanted the document to be admitted. Yet, he suspected Edens did not share his enthusiasm.

"Sustained."

Edens did not move to authenticate the field report and lay the foundation for its introduction into evidence.

"Without referring to the diagram, report your findings to the court."

Aha. Edens had the opening and passed. Bingo.

"Well, .38 caliber casings were scattered at three different points between Hoe Avenue and Vyse Avenue on East 174th Street. An apartment window and wall was struck by a .38 caliber bullet on the corner of Vyse and East 174th Street. A car struck by an unrecovered bullet was on the north side of East 174th Street, approximately midway between Hoe and Vyse. A .22 caliber shell casing was also retrieved on East 174th Street between Hoe and Vyse—a third of the way down from Hoe on the south side of East 174th Street."

"Were any weapons recovered?"

"Our canvass of the area, including bushes, garbage cans, and the undersides of cars, yielded negative results."

"Nothing further on direct, Your Honor."

As a prosecutor, Edens had the burden of proving the elements of the crime beyond a reasonable doubt, building the case as if it were a boat meant to sail the respondent up the river to a Division for Youth facility for three years. In Ronnie's defense, Schwartz's approach was to use the physical evidence gathered by the People's own witness to capsize that boat. Like Jaws, he circled, searching for the proper angle of attack.

"Detective, how familiar are you with the underlying facts of this case?"

"Well, I was the chief of the field ballistic investigative team."

"East 174th Street, the location of this alleged shooting, is a hill with the top at the Hoe Avenue intersection and the bottom at the Vyse Avenue intersection. Isn't that correct?"

"That is my recollection, yes."

"Prior to testifying, did you review the file in this case, including the DD5s and statements made by the principals?"

"I did."

"Then you are aware that the theory of the People's case of attempted murder against Ronnie Ramirez is that early on the afternoon of November 3rd of this year, Ronnie Ramirez ran up East 174th Street to the automobile driven by Floyd Green in which Shalima Harden and her infant child were riding. The automobile was stopped at the intersection of East 174th Street and Hoe Ave, and upon arriving behind the vehicle, Ronnie Ramirez fired a weapon at close range, discharging several bullets into the automobile and at its occupants. Furthermore, Floyd Green exited the vehicle and, in self-defense, returned gunfire at Ronnie Ramirez, while the latter fled down East 174th Street toward Vyse Avenue. To your knowledge, have I correctly stated prosecution's theory?"

"That is my understanding, Counselor."

"Are you also aware that Floyd Green gave a statement to the District Attorney's office admitting that the weapon he discharged, supposedly in self-defense, was a .38 caliber revolver?"

"Objection. Your Honor, the questions assume facts not in evidence," Edens protested.

"Your Honor, the prosecution has chosen to call this expert witness before all the relevant facts have been presented to this court, the trier of facts. Floyd Green's inculpatory statement admitting that the weapon he discharged was a .38 caliber revolver is well established in the police reports that Mr. Edens has chosen not to introduce. I intend to introduce the documents that prove the statement when I represent the respondent's case. Just because the ADA put the cart before the horse doesn't mean I can't jump on for a ride. If Mr. Edens is not prepared to stipulate that Mr. Green, in fact, made the admission that the .38 caliber weapons was his, then we can pursue two courses: either recall this witness at the conclusion of the respondent's case, or allow this witness, who has been qualified as an expert, to formulate his conclusions based upon hypothesis, as any expert is entitled to do, subject to connection with the facts as proven in the case. Either way, this court needs to have the facts and this expert witness's testimony before it."

Edens looked down at his papers. He turned to look at his supervisor who had just entered the courtroom. He blinked.

"In the interest of judicial economy, the People will stipulate that Floyd Green admitted that he possessed and discharged a .38 caliber weapon."

Jaws takes its first bite.

Judge Williams was relieved that a resolution had been reached without the need for him to rule. "Very well. So stipulated. Move on, Mr. Schwartz."

"Did your teams' search of the area include the street, sidewalks, and buildings at the intersection of East 174th and Hoe Avenue?"

"It did."

"Floyd Green's car was situated at the intersection of Hoe and East 174th Street when Ronnie allegedly opened fire, correct?"

"That is what the eyewitness stated."

"The car had traveled westbound on East 174th Street, which is a one-way street that runs uphill in a westerly direction, correct?"

"That is so, sir."

Schwartz reached in his file for the Polaroid pictures he had snapped when he visited the scene.

"Your Honor, I have four photos that I have pre-marked as Respondent's Exhibits A, B, C and D for identification, and I ask that they be shown to the witness."

The bridge officer looked up from his clipboard and walked over to the podium. He took the photos from Schwartz and handed them to the detective.

"Detective, I ask you to view these four photographs and tell this court whether or not they fairly and accurately depict East 174th Street between Hoe Avenue and Vyse Avenue in the Bronx as it would have appeared on November 27, 2000."

The witness took his sweet time studying the photos.

"Well, there are cars and persons on the street that weren't there on November 27th"

Ok. Try a diversionary tactic. But you're going to need a bigger boat.

"Fair enough, Detective. But in terms of the layout of the streets and the adjacent building do the photos accurately depict the scene as it appeared on November 27th, just under a month ago?"

He looked up and said with a frown, "They do."

Schwartz turned to the judge, "Your Honor, I ask that these photos be entered into evidence as respondent's exhibits A, B, C and D."

The judge directed the bridge officer to show the photos to Edens, who perused them.

The prosecutor offered no objection. The bridge officer then walked them over to Judge Williams. Schwartz paused to give the judge an opportunity to view the photos. After a brief moment the Judge brusquely said "Respondent's A, B, C, and D in evidence. You may inquire."

"According to the eyewitness, Shalima Harden, the car was about to make a left turn onto Hoe Avenue, thereby preparing to head in a southerly direction, correct?" Schwartz asked.

"I believe so."

"You believe so. Well, that's been her testimony so far. So if Ronnie Ramirez was standing behind the car in the middle of East 174th Street, facing in a westerly or southwesterly direction, firing a gun four to five times, would you expect to find evidence of ballistic impact on the streets, sidewalks, and buildings depicted in those photographs in Ronnie's alleged line of fire?"

"Well, you see, Counselor—"

"It's a yes or no question, Detective."

The veteran's eyes squinted a bit. He knew he was being led down the garden path not in the prosecution's favor. He didn't appear to be enjoying the stroll.

"Depends."

"On what?"

"Depends on whether or not the bullets hit some object or person that were removed from the scene prior to my inspection."

"Well, we'll get to that in a minute. But assuming, for the moment, that the bullets did not strike objects or persons removed from the scene prior to your inspection, one would expect to find evidence of ballistic impact on the streets, sidewalks, and buildings on the side opposite from where Ronnie would have been standing, correct?"

"Well, it is possible that there was a ricochet, but, yes, if the line of fire was from behind the vehicle, that would be about right."

From the back of Schwartz's head he could hear Jaws' bass line theme. *Den-dent, den-dent, den-dent.*

Schwartz walked back to the counsel's table and fished around in his file until he found his quarry. He picked up a document and held it in the air.

"I ask that this document be marked for identification as respondent's Exhibit E and shown to the witness."

As the reporter marked Schwartz's copy of the document Schwartz pushed thoughts of Carmen and Isabel from his mind. He knew he had to keep his concentration focused on the task at hand. *Den-dent, den-dent, den-dent.*

"Is this the field ballistic report you prepared?"

"Yes, counselor."

"Can you identify it?"

With a deep sigh, the detective said, "It's the ballistic field investigation report from the investigation into the shooting on November 27th from this case."

"I ask that the ballistics field report be moved into evidence as respondent's Exhibit E."

Judge Williams was anxious to hurry the case along. "Granted. Let's get to it, counselor."

Schwartz, concerned that he was losing the Judge's attention, went for the question that would be the shark's crucial ramming run.

"Detective, were there any findings of ballistic impact on the street, sidewalks, and/or buildings proximate to the intersection of East 174th Street and Hoe Avenue?"

The detective answered with the mien of a man passing a kidney stone.

"No . . . there were no positive findings."

Schwartz paused to let the implications of the detective's testimony sink in with the judge. Williams was writing, but for all Schwartz knew he was signing orders on another case.

"Correct me if I'm wrong, Detective, but two weeks after this alleged exchange of gunfire, Floyd Green surrendered and the automobile he claimed to be driving on November 27th was impounded by the New York City Police Department."

"That is correct, counselor."

"Did you have an opportunity to inspect Mr. Green's automobile for ballistic impact?"

"I did."

"And would you tell this court the results of your inspection vis-à-visfinding any evidence of ballistic impact?"

The detective paused before answering. "The vehicle was negative for ballistic impact."

"And are you aware of any claim made by or on behalf of the occupants of Mr. Green's vehicle—namely Floyd Green, Shalima Harden, or their infant or any bystander for that matter—that they were struck by any bullets fired by Ronnie Ramirez on the afternoon of November 27th?"

"No . . . can't say that I am."

"So, to be clear, Ronnie Ramirez is alleged to be standing five feet behind Floyd Green's vehicle, firing a gun repeatedly, yet there is no ballistic evidence of impact or discharge in the streets, sidewalks, or buildings proximate to the intersection, correct?"

The detective answered with a sigh of resignation. "That is correct, yes."

"Further, there is no ballistic evidence of impact on the target vehicle or on the occupants of the vehicle, or discharge of any weapons, other than the .38 caliber evidence, correct?"

"Well, there was a .22 caliber bullet casing found at the scene."

"Other than the .22 cal shell casing, is there any other evidence of impact or discharge?"

Slowly. "No, there isn't."

Schwartz began circling the podium while glancing up at Judge Williams to see if he could get a read on the jurist's reaction to this testimony.

"So let's discuss this .22 caliber casing. As indicated in the diagram that is part of your field report, it was found one-third to halfway down the block, east of the intersection of Hoe and East 174th Street toward Vyse Avenue, was it not?"

Slower still. "That is correct."

"Detective, do shell casings migrate?"

"I'm sorry, I don't understand, counselor."

"Well, if Ronnie Ramirez fired a .22 caliber weapon, pointed in a westerly direction, at the intersection of East 174th Street and Hoe Avenue while standing within several feet of the intersection, would the shell casing from that weapon be found halfway down East 174th Street, almost one hundred feet east of the intersection?"

Schwartz glanced at Ronnie, who was grinning at the table. Schwartz rebuked him with a glare.

The detective looked at Edens empathetically and returned his gaze to Schwartz.

"The casing is usually found close to the point of discharge. It might bounce and roll several feet, but, no, if the shooter were standing at or near the intersection, one would not expect to find the casing one hundred feet away."

"Detective, are you familiar with this location?"

"Yes, I am."

"And that's because it's a known drug sale location and shootings are not an unusual occurrence?"

"Objection. Speculative."

Judge Williams shook his head as he ruled, "The witness can answer based upon his experience. Overruled."

So the judge is following this cross. Cue the shark music louder.

"That location is identified as a high-crime area," came the witnesses answer.

"So would it have surprised you to find a .22 caliber casing on that street on November 27th"

"No counselor. Not especially."

"In fact, that .22 caliber casing could have been lying on the streets for several days before November 27th, correct?"

The detective ran up the white flag on the mast.

"Well, usually the kids in the neighborhood pick them up as souvenirs, but it is possible that it had been there for several days."

"According to respondent's Exhibit E, the ballistic field report, the .38 caliber ballistic evidence, which was the same caliber weapon used by Mr. Green, was located over 150 feet down the block, toward Vyse, isn't that correct?"

"Yes."

"And that would be consistent with Mr. Green discharging his weapon in that direction. Is that fair to say?"

"Yes."

"Do you know if Ronnie Ramirez was struck by any bullets?"

"Yes. I believe in his right flank."

"Do you know if the bullet entered from behind or from the front?"

"Objection. Beyond the scope of this witness's expertise. He is not a medical forensic expert."

Judge Williams concurred. "Yes. Sustained. Anything further, Mr. Schwartz?"

Schwartz knew he was taking a risk in asking the next question because it gave the witness the opportunity to deviate or dilute what had already been established. But this shark needed to go in for the kill.

"Detective, is my understanding of your report and your testimony correct? That no ballistic evidence of any kind—no shell casings, no bullet fragments, and no bullet impact on buildings or vehicles—were recovered from the intersection of East 174th Street and Hoe Avenue, the very direction from which Ronnie Ramirez was alleged to have fired at least four shots at the vehicle occupied by Floyd Green and Shalima Harden?"

"Objection on two grounds. Asked and answered. And the report is in evidence and speaks for itself."

Edens had provided the opening for the shark's final thrust.

"Yes, it does Your Honor. The field report speaks volumes about my client's lack of culpability. No further questions. Thank you, Detective."

The judge looked skeptically at Edens.

"Do the People have any further proof to present?"

Schwartz knew that Floyd Green, under indictment for weapons possession, should not be available to testify on advice of counsel based upon the assertion of his Fifth Amendment right against self-incrimination. Yet he hoped that there wasn't a bullet in the prosecutor's gun that could explode the shark to smithereens, *ala* Roy Scheider's sheriff character. He exhaled in relief when Edens informed the court, "No, Your Honor. The People rest."

Judge Williams turned his head towards Schwartz. "Mr. Schwartz, does the respondent feel the need to present any evidence, and if not will you waive summations and rest on the record, such as it is?"

The question was unusual for this judge. Schwartz's nostrils detected a rare scent in this courtroom—that of an acquittal.

Schwartz had previously consulted with Mr. Ramirez and then Ronnie, advising them that Ronnie should not testify. Rarely, in Schwartz's experience, had there been a juvenile respondent who actually aided his cause by taking the stand ostensibly in his own defense. Schwartz believed that the People's direct case was mortally wounded. There was no reason to help them by calling Ronnie. Both father and son had agreed.

"Respondent rests on the record, waives summations, and seeks a dismissal for failure to prove my client's guilt beyond a reasonable doubt."

Edens hesitated in answering the judge, then waived summations.

"Very well, then. The court finds that the People have failed to prove their case beyond a reasonable doubt. The petition is dismissed with prejudice."

A yelp went up from the respondent's side of the table. Ronnie was standing with his arms in the air.

"Order! This isn't a free-for-all. The respondent is ordered released."

Mr. Ramirez was slapping Schwartz on his back and shaking his hand. The judge continued to speak above the jubilant noise.

"One more thing. Mr. Schwartz, I am charging you with contempt of court as a sanction for disobeying this court's order this morning. I will adjudicate the sanctions after I have had due deliberation. You will hear directly from the chief clerk of the court with a date to appear."

In that case, I'll be sure to keep my social calendar light.

Outside the courtroom, while Ramirez Junior did a celebratory dance in the waiting area, Ramirez Senior embraced Schwartz.

"Señor Schwartz, wha I ga do for you? Name it."

Schwartz slowly separated himself from the man's bear hug and thought for a moment. He saw Cliff talking to an officer at the security desk.

"There may be something. We'll talk."

Schwartz excused himself and strode purposely to a door that led to the sacrosanct secure hallway, intent on taking the shortcut to Parker's Part. Cliff was approaching from the opposite direction. He coldly ignored Schwartz as they passed. Though Schwartz hesitated, he continued on, making his way through the secured hallway. When he opened the door to the waiting area, Captain Dolan was standing in front of him. Schwartz's reflex to close the door and escape was thwarted. Dolan stepped into the hallway, forcing Schwartz to back up.

"Ah, my favorite 18-B trespasser, Mr. Schwartz. I've been meaning to talk to you about the liberties you've been taking with the judges' elevator. Perhaps you can tell me who gave you permission to use this secured hallway?"

Schwartz had heard the rumors explaining the *raison d'etre* behind the prohibition of attorneys in secured hallways. The story was that a civic-minded, complaint filing do-gooder legal aid lawyer had once observed court officers delivering an overly enthusiastic object lesson to a would-be fugitive juvenile delinquent in the hallway. Schwartz figured he was due, at least, for a tongue lashing when he heard Cliff's voice from behind.

"Uh, Captain? I directed Mr. Schwartz to exit through the secured hallway because I didn't want him disturbing a case in my courtroom."

Dolan eyeballed Cliff and then Schwartz.

"Listen, Captain Dolan, I didn't see anyone beat up anyone while I was back here. Honest. You don't have to worry about me ratting anyone out."

"Mr. Schwartz you're a wiseass. You're in my cross sights."

Dolan stalked off. Schwartz turned to Cliff and said in his best, and only, Southern truck driver voice, "Thanks, good buddy. Thank ya very much."

"Good buddy, my ass. The only reason I got your little heinie out of trouble is because you'd be no good to me in some bullshit lockup. When are you getting me my ride back, you pot-smoking karaoke-crazed slacker?"

"Ouch. I'm going to the car pound on Monday to enjoin the auction. I promise."

"Don't promise. Just do it. I got notice from the pound and went to see it. Man, they busted up the front fender and one of the wheel wells when they towed it. You have to make this right. Plus, somebody tried to lift my sound system from the console and did some terminal damage."

"I know. I got the same notice of damage as the operator. I'm on it."

"Yeah. OK. Just get me my ride back. In one piece. You hear!"

"How're you feeling?"

"A little sore in the neck and a lot like an asshole."

"Why's that?"

"Because momma gave me two pieces of advice, and I didn't follow either one of them."

"What were they?"

"Number one, don't get the first girl you fall in love with pregnant. And number two, don't go to nightclubs with crazy Jewish men obsessed with dead Italian crooners."

"You know I'm not really Jewish."

"How's that?"

"I'm really a black man trapped in a Jew-Boy's body."

Cliff cracked up. "What you are is an off-the-hook whack job. My nigger."

He extended his hand for an upright clasp

Schwartz joined the clasp and gave salutation, "My African brotha."

Cliff held Schwartz's hand tightly and brought it back and forth with such gusto that it alarmed Schwartz.

"Go ahead, man. You gonna be my nigger, then you've got to say it. Come on, now."

Schwartz balked, stuttered, and stammered as his liberal, politically correct tongue unhinged and he said the unsayable. "Nig . . . uh. . . Nig . . . Na . . . Nig . . . Nig-ger . . . Nigger."

"There. Was that so hard?"

Cliff pulled him close.

"Just get me my damn ride back. I pimped that ride from scratch with Papo."

"I feel you, my nigger."

"Uh, don't be pushing that 'nigger' thing. That was a one-time pass."

"Oh. Right. Gothcha."

Schwartz veered toward Parker's part. Passing the waiting area for part I, he scanned again for Isabel. There she was, standing outside the part, engaged in heated conversation with Officer Mama's Boy.

"What you mean, dey call my case? I be on de line."

"Listen ma'am, the matter is adjourned."

"Adjourned? Dat's no good. I got to get back my *bebe*."

"Oh, good. Your knight in shining armor is here. Schwartz, tell this respondent what happened."

Isabel turned to face Schwartz. The turmoil of the past two weeks was evident. Her reddened eyes were accentuated by mascara runoff, black roots sprouted at the base of her ginger mane, her shoulders were slightly hunched, and tightness circled her mouth. In defiance, she maintained the fashion front, wearing a fire-engine red blouse with a plunging neckline and hip-hugging black slacks. Her nostrils flared as she demanded, "*Qué pasa con mi caso?* Wha I do? Wha I do?"

Schwartz tried to take her hand but she jerked it away. He beckoned her to follow him as he searched for an empty interview room. They walked silently into the next waiting area, which, unfortunately, served Parker's part. Heidi and Carmen glared at him. He waved, lamely, as he closed the door to the interview room.

Once seated, Isabel began to wail with drama of an overacting telenovela star. Schwartz bided his time as her torrents of grief gradually subsided. He dug in his pocket for the crumpled-but-clean tissue. She accepted the meager offering and attempted to repair her makeup. One of her false eyelashes had come unglued. Schwartz regarded Isabel skeptically, as if he had just met her for the first time. Then he felt a flush of shame for judging her.

"You missed the 9:30 call, and the judge has deemed your 1028 application waived."

Isabel scrunched her nose and forehead. "*No entiendo.*"

"*Usted no esta aqui a las nueve y trienta. Por ese, Señora Juez dice no quire eschuchar su application por... por... uh . . . da su hija atras.*"

"*Ay Dios mio. Yo estoy en frente de ese* fuckin' place, man. De line go round da block, man."

Once again the tears flowed.

Might as well give her the rest of the bad news.

"Also, ACS has filed new charges, *nueva allegacions contras tu.* They say that your daughter Zoraida was sexually abused by someone. *Abusadora sexual.* That you knew about it and did nothing to protect her. *Tu sabes pero tu haces nada.*" Schwartz fumbled in his bag and produced a document. "Here is the petition."

As Schwartz translated the allegations in his pidgin Spanish, his eyes became transfixed on one word: *chlamydia.*

"*Mentira! Mentira!* Dat's bullshit, man. *Quien dice ese? Ay increible!*"

Isabel was out of her chair, pacing and mumbling to herself in pressured Spanish.

Schwartz's thoughts were briefly derailed by the chlamydia reference. Slowly, he got back on track.

"Listen. *Escuche* . . . This matter is adjourned to this coming Monday, the eighteenth, for conference. I suggest that if you believe someone abused your daughter, you tell the authorities who he is before they find out on their own. It will demonstrate that you are cooperating in the best interest of your daughter. *Entiende?*"

Isabel shook her head.

Schwartz tried again to explain. "*Si tu sabes quien hace mala con su hija, di le quien esa el trabajador social.*"

Schwartz tried to read Isabel's face. Was she shocked at hearing that her daughter had been abused or that the disclosure of abuse had been made? She started to leave, but Schwartz beckoned for her to remain.

"One question: Did you give anyone my card? *Da mi tarjeta a alguen?*"

Isabel stopped pacing and looked at him. "*Porqué* you ask me dat?"

Schwartz removed the microtape recorder from his pocket and played the hateful message.

"*Quien es ese? Di me.*"

Isabel blurted "*Yo no se.*"

Schwartz grabbed her arm and put his face an inch from hers.

"Bullshit! Who is that and where is he right now?"

Isabel broke free of his grasp. She laughed cruelly.

Pendejo. Maricon. You are no man. *Tu eres* bullshit *abogado.*"

At that moment, Heidi Frias opened the door.

"Schwartz, the entire waiting room can hear what's going on. Who is this Iris Chacón wannabe?"

"Well, it's sort of a long—"

Isabel understood enough to know she'd been insulted.

"*Quien es esa chica?* Dis bitch."

As the two women rushed towards each other Schwartz launched himself between Heidi and Isabel.

"Ladies, that'll be enough! I don't think either one of you wants to risk a disorderly conduct arrest."

As Isabel stormed out, she stepped on Heidi's foot with vengeance. Heidi, hopping in pain, began to follow Isabel, but Schwartz grabbed her by the arm.

She stopped in the doorway, glowered at Schwartz, and limped back to her seat next to Carmen.

Schwartz closed the door, sat down, had a conversation with himself, and checked his watch. 11:40 a.m. With trepidation, he opened the door a crack. Heidi and Carmen were staring right at him. He closed it again and sat down at the desk. Since there wasn't enough room to curl up in the fetal position, he laid his head on the table, just as he'd been instructed to do in elementary school after being caught misbehaving. After taking several slow, deep breaths, he got up, secured his bag on his shoulder, and exited. He headed toward part X.

"So, Doctor, based upon one observation, you believe that you are in a position to assess Ms. Fontanez's ability to nurture her baby?"

"I spent the better part of forty-five minutes with Ms. Fontanez and the child."

"Wow. You scared me for a moment! I thought you were going to say you spent only ten minutes with them."

"Mr. Schwartz!" Judge Parker interrupted. "If you think you're scoring points with this tactic, let me assure you that you are not. Ask your next question and ask it straight. Do you understand me?"

Schwartz feigned a hangdog expression. "My apologies to the court." He turned back to the witness. "Doctor, don't you believe that before reaching the monumental conclusion that the infant would be at imminent risk if returned to the mother, it would be prudent to observe the mother and child on different occasions, in different settings?"

"Not necessarily."

"Aren't there multiple variables that need to be weighed before reaching your conclusion? Doesn't the child's mood, the unfamiliar sterility of the supervised visitation environment, and the mother's energy level impact the interaction observed and present confounds to your conclusion?"

"Yes, and in an ideal world I would have attempted observations at different times and places. But the exigency of this hearing did not allow enough time for that. Based on my observation, I am satisfied that my conclusion is sound and consistent with the best interests of the child."

"But, Doctor, are you aware that the issue here is not best interest but whether or not the child is in imminent danger of neglect if placed in the mother's care?"

"Mr. Schwartz, is it? I can tell you, Mr. Schwartz, that I would rather place that child in the middle of the street than place her in the care of this mother."

"Really? Huh. Doctor, I see from your CV that you served as a psychologist evaluator for the New York State Mental Health Services in New York County Family Court from 1993 through 1997. During that time you were conducting forensic evaluations of respondents on neglect and abuse cases, termination of parental rights cases, and juvenile delinquency cases."

"That is correct."

"Doctor, how many evaluations did you conduct during that time span?"

"I'm not sure I can fix an exact number."

"Over a hundred?"

"Certainly."

"Over a thousand?"

"I'd say four to five hundred would be an approximate value."

"And in those approximately four to five hundred evaluations, you were required to make recommendations as to whether a respondent parent should be allowed to resume custody of his or her child or whether a juvenile respondent should be allowed to return home to his or her parents, correct?"

"Yes, that was my function for the bulk of evaluations. I was also called upon to perform occasional expedited evaluations. These were conducted to see whether a litigant before the court was a danger to him or herself or to others. Colloquially, these are sometimes referred to as 'short *E*'s.'"

"Tell me, Doctor, of those evaluations that were not short *E*'s, what percentage would you say you recommended a child be returned to the parent's care?"

"Objection!"

"Sustained."

"You know the answer, don't you, Doctor? Answer it."

Judge Parker was curt. "Mr. Schwartz, you have crossed the line."

"No, this court has crossed the line by allowing this testimony. The answer is next to zero, isn't it, Doctor? Because you're part and parcel of this whole cover-your-ass system, aren't you? You have as much objectivity as an NRA lobbyist. I'm embarrassed to have to ask you a single question."

"Mr. Schwartz, you are now in contempt of this court, and I will not tolerate anymore—"

"Doesn't the court see what is happening here? We are handing the family court decision-making over to the psychologists and therapists. I get sick and tired of hearing judges and attorneys say, 'If the therapist approves family therapy, it's OK,' or 'Visitation can start when the therapist feels it's appropriate.' As legal professionals, we have abdicated our responsibility to use our training in the analysis of facts and interpreters of the law to reach a just result. Instead, we've empowered the shrinks without even bothering to learn what they are about."

"Mr. Schwartz, I am out of patience with you. Counsels, this hearing is adjourned to Monday the eighteenth. Mr. Schwartz, I am issuing an admonition to you. Bring your toothbrush and towel next time you choose to cross the line and speechify. Do you hear me?"

Schwartz was about to reply that given his current state of homelessness and the constant threats of contempt, he was going to start carrying his toothbrush in his vest pocket, when he felt a tug on his arm. A strained whisper urged, "Schwartz, answer the man nicely and slowly back away."

It was Heidi Frias, hospice social worker.

Swallowing the bile that had risen up from his stomach, Schwartz complied. "Yes, Your Honor," he uttered while catching his breath and steadying his heartbeat.

Parker got up, left the bench, and headed for the back room. The bridge officer loudly announced the end of the morning's proceedings. Schwartz stood at the table watching the red digital display of the tape recorder counter fade out. This earned him a rebuke from the bridge officer.

"Counsel, the matter is adjourned. Please clear the table for the next matter."

Outside the part, Heidi was leaning over Carmen, consoling her.

Schwartz approached. In a gentle voice, he asked, "Carmen, was there a psychologist watching you during a visit with the baby?"

Carmen shrugged her bony shoulders. "I just thought he was supervising my visit. They didn't tell me anything."

Schwartz reflected for a moment. "This happened the other day, just before our conference, right?"

Carmen nodded ever so slightly.

Schwartz sucked in some air through his teeth. "Those bastards. No wonder they opposed visitation at your residential program. That clown never would have gotten past the front door."

In a hushed but urgent tone, Heidi reproached Schwartz. "You were off the hook in there. Now we have another adjournment. When are you going to stop grandstanding and start lawyering?"

Schwartz attempted to deflect Heidi's accusation. "Did Adesanya or any ACS caseworker ever show up at the hospice?"

"Don't you think you should have asked me that before we went inside, instead of flirting with that *putana*? What do you think?"

"Damn, I could have nailed the agency for contempt of the court's order!"

"Damn right. You were so steeped in your righteous anger pose. And at the agency you were in a walkabout. You saw that pompous prick talking to Carmen but didn't think to do anything about it."

Schwartz could only respond with, "I'm sorry. I'm sorry."

"Sorry doesn't cut it for Carmen. Now, get your act together for Monday. By the way, you look like shit, even for you. *Mira tu.* Did you sleep in that or what?"

"Or what?" resonated in Schwartz's ear as Heidi and Carmen made their way toward the crowded elevator bank. Schwartz felt his larynx roll over. He was exhausted and stressed from the morning's festivities. He wondered what the afternoon would bring. After checking his date book he realized that he was scheduled to supervise the Abbatiello father-son visit at 1 p.m., which he now regretted. Resigned, he turned away from the elevator bank. An elevator door opened and Warrant Squad Officer Napolitano stepped out, worked his way through the rush of humanity filling the vaccum of the now empty elevator. He ran right into Schwartz.

"Schwartz! I got your message. I've been trying to find you."

"After all, that's what warrant officers do. Well done."

Napolitano offered a weak smile and a still weaker handshake. "Let's walk away a little bit."

They walked behind the security desk, finding an eddy in the flow of the lunchtime crowd streaming toward the elevator. If, as Mao said, a true revolutionary swims in the Sea of the People, Schwartz was in his element. The court officer who was on the lunchtime watch was at the desk, his newspaper and brown paper bag at the ready. Napolitano raised his voice to be heard above the din.

"Schwartz, I have some bad news and some bad news."

With a tight smile Schwartz forced a joke. "Well, I'd prefer to hear the bad news first."

"OK. I got a line on this Hector Machado fella from the detective squad over at the 43rd Precinct. If he's the same Hector Machado harassing you and yours, you're confronted with a certified bad guy. He's a known drug dealer with several crews working the Soundview section. According to the detective squad, he's wanted for questioning in connection with a homicide from three weeks ago. He's suspected of having thrown a compadre by the name of Livan Soriano from a roof."

Like a Times Square marquee zipper, the name "Livan Soriano" traveled across Schwartz's brain. To the chagrin of the court officer, he put his shoulder bag on the desk and proceeded to rummage through the tangle of papers and files. With an "Aha!" Schwartz reeled in his catch: the newly minted amended petition in "the Matter of Zoriada Soriano, a child under the age of eighteen years, alleged to be abused by Isabel Mojica and John Doe." Inserted within the boilerplate was a paragraph that began, "The father of the child is" was "LIVAN SORIANO."

"Lying bitch from the beginning," escaped from Schwartz's lips.

"What's up, Schwartz?"

"Nothing. Maybe everything. She said the dad was still in D.R. Do you have an address for Machado? I know his girlfriend's address. Can he be picked up for his phone call to me?"

"As if wanted for questioning for murder isn't enough motivation? Like an aggravated harassment charge would finally release the hounds. If they can, the detectives will. Give me the address. We'll check it out."

Schwartz knew the way to Machado was through Isabel. He planned to lie in wait for her that afternoon and, with Napolitano's help, use her to lead them to Machado. Before he could explain his grand scheme, Napolitano said, "And now for the other bad news."

Napolitano reached into his back pocket with one hand and turned Schwartz to the wall with his other, pressing his body against the shocked man. Metal cuffs pinched Schwartz's left wrist and then his right wrist.

"This hurts me more than it hurts you, my friend. Well, maybe not. I just received a fax from the warrant squad officer in Nassau County Family Court. Your wife has filed a Petition for Violation of Order of Protection, and the judge out there issued the arrest warrant. Sorry, man."

For the second time in a month, and in his life, Schwartz felt the humiliation and pinch of handcuffs.

The Nassau County Sheriff, the operator of the Nassau County Jail, was a full-service hotelier. At taxpayers' expense, an all-inclusive package of room, board, clothing, sheets, linens, towels, ground transportation, and medical screening were provided, but, alas, no toothbrush.

One free call to the family member or barrister of your choice was also included. Schwartz, a firm believer in multitasking, sought to communicate with his family by calling a barrister, albeit not one of his choice. Though it was after six o'clock on Friday evening and the prospect of contacting his quarry was iffy, Schwartz hoped against hope that he wouldn't have "reached the voicemail of Rufus Blumenthal. I'm not in the office. Please leave a detailed message including the date, time and purpose of your call. If this is an emergency, my pager number is 917-CALLRUF. Have a great day."

At the prompt Schwartz said rapidly, "Rufus, listen, this is Schwartz. You win. I say "Uncle." But Margie and the kids are in danger. There's a man named Hector Machado who may be trying to hurt them. Please warn them. Call Officer Napol—"

Beep!

"Damn it."

Schwartz looked over his shoulder at the impatient line of fellow guests seeking to use the limited telephone facility. Resigning himself to paging his classmate-turned-adversary later, he shuffled back to his cell.

A LOST MID-DECEMBER WEEKEND

SINCE NASSAU COUNTY FAMILY COURT WAS CLOSED FOR THE weekend, Schwartz would not be processed until Monday. Schwartz would have ample time to contemplate the navel of his life, how the overt/covert, conscious/subconscious/unconscious choices he had made had led him to his current circumstance. Stealing a page from his ambivalent Jewish upbringing, he decided too fast, to empty his vessel, to atone. That, he felt, offered him the slim hope of achieving enlightenment/salvation/connectedness to his center while dropping a couple of pounds around the waistline in the bargain.

Schwartz recalled how the "good" Jews of the Bronx celebrated the High Holy Days by purchasing high-priced family tickets to the local synagogue. For most of them, it was their annual jaunt to temple. Dressed in their finest, they offered prayers, using the harsh, ancient desert language of the Chosen People in a bid for forgiveness for past sins. After the day of prayer and fasting, most of the observants would retire to a huge food orgy either at their homes or at the local Chinese restaurant, cleansed of their sins, primed for a new year of sinning.

As a pre-teen, Schwartz attended classes weekly at Hebrew School. He did so mainly because his mother was determined to pay homage to her long-departed socialist/religious zealot father. Should a Jew picket on *Shabbos?* That was but one topic of debate that raged in the household of his mother's childhood.

Each week in Hebrew school Schwartz would learn of a different dictator, despot, or demagogue who had tried, and failed, to eliminate these chosen people from the face of the Earth. To Schwartz, it seemed that every Jewish holiday could be summed up thusly: "They tried to kill us all. They didn't. Let's eat."

As a result of that education, Schwartz had the distinct impression that his "people" certainly were "chosen." They were chosen for history's punch in the nose and kick in the ass. He thought if the Jews had only soft-pedaled that "chosen" designation and maintained a slightly lower ecclesiastical profile, perhaps a pogrom or two could have been averted. To believe that any one "people" sat at the right hand of God was to invite unwanted intervention from those at the perceived left hand. Even if it were assumed that to be "chosen" was a reference to doing God's work and being of service to mankind, the use of the word still elevated the "chosen" to a prideful position of moral superiority.

Schwartz had come to distrust all forms of organized religion. He believed that religious institutions were much more about power and money than spirituality. All that the people of the world truly needed were some mutual acts and thoughts of compassion.

Still, at the end of the Day of Atonement in his younger years, Schwartz enjoyed the sensation he shared with his fellow fasters. The lightheadedness lent itself to insight into one's essential being. It was that same state of enlightenment, through denial of food and beverage, that he was hoping to achieve this cursed weekend. Besides, the food at the jail was *ha-ha* god-awful.

Schwartz achieved a number of insights come the early hours of Monday morning:

I am a self-righteous asshole. A tad harsh, but close to the mark.

I need to stop following my dick around as if it were a divining rod. Well, that states the obvious.

I need to take voice and tennis lessons. Hey, I could have figured that one out without fasting.

I need to get out of my own way if I'm going to be a self-actualized human being, whether as a lawyer, a parent, or a mate. That's more on the mark.

He realized, accepted and embraced what truly made his heart sing, made him feel good about himself, and place him on the path to self-actualization...

Go ahead; say it. It is to help my fellow human beings. "The simple art of being kind."

As an attorney representing the poorest of the poor, the lowest of the low, those tossed from the stormy seas of family life marooned on the shores of family court, Schwartz was in a perfect position to help people. Being in lockup was an object lesson. He realized that he was no different from his clients. He, too, was subject to the same passions and susceptible to the same follies that could cause him to cross the line separating lawyer from respondent. It was a slippery slope from standing in the halls of family court to sitting on its hard wooden benches.

No one fact brought home that point more forcefully than the positive results showing up on his jailhouse medical screening for *sonofabitch* chlamydia and *no surprise here* cannabis. Schwartz was struck by the notion that the only difference between Carmen Fontanez and him was the identity of their respective STD infections and drug of choice.

Then the question he had avoided for a trimester loomed up in the eight-ball window of his mind: *Was I kind to my own family by abandoning them?*

A dual rarity ensued. Schwartz started to cry. Then he prayed for forgiveness.

DECEMBER 18:
FROM FRYING PAN TO FIRE

MONDAY MORNING SCHWARTZ WAS HERDED INTO A SHERIFF'S van with two fellow inmates. The van was pointed toward Nassau County Family Court. His perspiration had adhered the green linen suit to his skin.

One of his fellow passengers piped up. "You a lawyer?"

"That I am."

"Can I ask you something?"

With his resurgent empathy Schwartz resisted the reflex that rejected giving randomly solicited legal advice. "Sure."

"My wife filed for an upward modification of support and I . . ."

Schwartz listened patiently to the man's tale of woe. At issue was that the man had been paying support for his children but the mother was living with another man and he hadn't been able to see the kids, so he stopped paying support and was in jail for failure to pay arrears.

"My friend, you and the wife no longer have sex, right?"

The man nodded.

"And she's probably having sex with baby-daddy-to-be number two?"

"That scum bag."

"But you're still being ordered to give her money, right?"

"That cum bucket."

"And I know this pisses you off. But you know what? They're still your children and she's the one caring for them. So pay the friggin' money, if you can. If you can't, be prepared to prove it. Or drive a taxi at night. Either way, file for visitation. You can do it from jail. Make sure you're seeing your kids so that they know their daddy is still in their life."

The man asked Schwartz the age-old icebreaker between inmates. "Whaddya in for?"

"Loving my kids too much and yet not enough."

Schwartz was taken into the Judge Stewart Simon's courtroom. Blumenthal and Marjorie were seated at the litigants' table. After being sworn, Schwartz sat at the table. A court officer stood ominously behind him. Judge Simon informed him of the nature of the petition and asked whether he wanted time to consult with counsel or to speak for himself. He was about to answer that he'd represent himself when the courtroom door opened and Schwartz heard a booming yet familiar voice behind him.

"Your Honor, Edgardo Ramos, 907 Sheridan Avenue, Bronx, New York, appearing for the respondent. May I please have a copy of the petition?"

"Counsel, have you filed a notice of appearance?"

"If the clerk would be so kind as to provide me with the form, I will do so, Your Honor."

As Don Edgardo sat next to Schwartz, reviewed the petition and scribbled notes, he whispered, "Nice threads."

"How did you—?"

"Your good buddy Tony Nap called me. Listen, were you served with the underlying TOP?"

"Yeah. By Blumenthal."

They exchanged a knowing glance. Simultaneously, they covered their mouths and coughed, "Traverse."

"Now, I'm gonna work the room." Don Edgardo snickered.

The barrister rose and addressed the court.

"If it pleases the court, may I inquire whether the court is in possession of proof of service of the underlying petition and temporary order of protection whence this violation is said to have sprung?"

Judge Simon searched the folder without success. He directed his comment to Blumenthal.

"Counsel, do you have proof of service?"

"I do, Judge."

Blumenthal self-assuredly reached into his neatly bound file. He lifted the ACCO clasp, removed a sheet of paper, and handed it to a court officer, who handed it to the judge.

"Seems to be in order," Judge Simon said after scanning it.

"May I see it, Your Honor?" Don Edgardo asked.

With a judicial sigh and a dismissive flick of his wrist Judge Simon handed it to a court officer.

Don Edgardo placed the proof of service on the table, and he and Schwartz began to read it. Indeed, the document was Blumenthal's affirmation of service. A non-attorney would need to give an affidavit sworn to before a public notary. Since an attorney is an officer of the court, he need not swear before a notary. He simply affirms, under the penalties of perjury, that the written statement is true. In his affirmation, Blumenthal stated that on December 12, 2000, he served the petition and the temporary order of protection on Schwartz at Granley Elementary School.

Don Edgardo stood. "Your Honor, before we proceed to a hearing on the violation of the temporary order of protection, I am asking for a traverse hearing on the service of the underlying petition and the TOP. As this court is well aware, due process requires that notice of the existence of the TOP be given to the respondent. If there was no notice of the order to the respondent, then he cannot be said to have willfully violated it. This violation petition of the TOP, which carries with it a maximum sentence of incarceration of six months, would then fall."

"Are you disputing service?"

"We are."

"Very well. Mr. Blumenthal, call your first witness in support of service."

Branches of crimson sprouted across Blumenthal's face as he rose to speak. "Uh, Judge, that witness would be me."

Sporting a cat-that-ate-the-canary grin, Don Edgardo addressed the court.

"Well, you see, Your Honor, Mr. Blumenthal is on the horns of a dilemma here. The Canons of Professional Ethics are very clear. Ethically, an attorney may not serve as trial counsel in a matter in which he knows he may also be called as a witness. He cannot wear the hat of an advocate whose function it is to zealously advance the cause of his client while wearing the hat of a witness whose function is to speak truthfully to the court. It places the attorney/witness in an irreconcilable conflict. If Mr. Blumenthal takes that witness stand, he can no longer represent Mrs. Schwartz, either in this proceeding or in any related matrimonial actions."

The judge rubbed his chin and turned his head in the direction of Blumenthal, who was irate. "Mr. Blumenthal?"

Blumenthal was holding his shoulders and twisting his torso back and forth. He stopped twisting and hurriedly conferred with Marjorie. Then he turned back to the judge.

"Your Honor, after conferring with my client and considering the arguments of counsel, she has advised me that she will withdraw the violation petition if counsel and his client would stipulate that there is now a valid full stay-away temporary order of protection in effect running to her benefit and that he will abide by its terms."

It was Don Edgardo's turn to huddle with Schwartz. Then Edgardo addressed the court.

"We will do so if the temporary order can be modified to read 'except for visitation with the parties' children every Saturday from 10:00 a.m. until 6:00 p.m. and every Wednesday after school until 7:30 p.m."

Schwartz tugged at Don Edgardo's sleeve and whispered furtively into his ear.

Don Edgardo continued, "And, uh, telephone contact every day between the hours of 5:00 p.m. and 6:00 p.m."

Yet another huddle between Marjorie and Blumenthal ensued.

"So stipulated. Pick-up and drop-off in front of the Glen Cove Police Department."

Schwartz felt a wave of anger well up in his belly. He started to rise, but Don Edgardo's firm hand forced him down.

"If that's what counsel and his client believe is in the best interests of the children, then that is on their heads. We consent."

With the cadence of a tobacco auctioneer, Judge Simon made it official. "So ordered. The respondent is released."

Schwartz gave Don Edgardo a hug after they stepped out of the courtroom. Don Edgardo pulled away. "Señor, you need a bath."

"As if I was going anywhere near the showers at NCC lockup. Get me to a diner for takeout. I need to wrap my lips around a bagel, lox, and cream cheese. Or maybe some french fries with brown gravy. Then I'll shit, shave, and take your favorite: the Puerto Rican Shower."

"Eh, watch it, *cabron*! And you screwed the pooch by missing that supervised visit the other day with the Abbatiellos."

"Apologies. Mea culpa. Tell your client I will do a make-good. Also, please convey to Blumenthal my condolences on his loss and my suggestion that Marjorie get out of town with the kids for the Christmas school break with this maniac Machado running loose."

"Anything else?"

"Yeah. I've got a 1028 hearing to get to."

Schwartz reached the seventh floor of BxFC just before the lunch break. As he approached Parker's part, the court officer was closing the door. While in transit, Schwartz had used Don Edgardo's cell phone to try to notify the part that he had been detained on a matter in Nassau Family Court. Alternatively, the phone to Part X was busy or Don Edgardo's cell phone had fallen victim to its imperfect technology.

All the court officer would say was that the matter had been adjourned and that he knew neither the reason nor the date of the adjournment. Schwartz sat on a bench outside the part, disconsolate. He brightened when he saw Heidi walking out of the woman's restroom.

"Heidi, what happened this morning?"

"No, Schwartz, ladies first. What happened to *you* this morning?"

"Would you believe me if I told you that my soon-to-be ex-wife dropped a bogus violation of a TOP on me and I spent the weekend as a guest of Nassau County?"

"Oh, great, I was providing temporary shelter to a DV perpetrator."

"Charged but never convicted."

"I suppose that counts for something."

"Where's Carmen? Still in the bathroom?"

"No. She didn't make it to court. She's not feeling all that well."

"Hmm. So it's adjourned. What date?"

"Thanks for your show of concern. Adjourned to this Wednesday, the twentieth. Adesanya finally showed up on our doorstep over the weekend, swaddled in gauze to limit his exposure. He looked like the Black Mummy. We gave him the grand tour. When we offered to show him the basement where we told him we perform the autopsies, he bolted. I don't think mummies like autopsies."

"You're a real kidder, Frias."

"Well, I'm not kidding about Carmen. Her T-cell count is dropping. And I..."

The proud voice cracked. Schwartz put his arm around her and hugged her. As Heidi exclaimed, "Shit, shit, shit!" Schwartz absorbed the blows of her fists on his chest and then the torrent of her tears with his suit.

"Cry. Cry on the suit. It's crumpled but clean."

Through her tears, Heidi sniffed at the suit. "I'll give you crumpled."

After a moment, she separated from him. Schwartz held her face with one hand and wiped away what remained of her tears with the other. Suddenly, he grabbed Heidi by the hand and marched back toward Parker's part.

"We are getting this case recalled."

Schwartz begged Judge Parker's bridge officer to recall the matter before the lunch break. He went so far as to promise to pick up the next untouchable case that found its way into the part, be it a PINS matter with a perpetually absconding youth or a willfulness hearing with an incarcerated deadbeat dad. Then Schwartz stalked Barbanel and Grella by means of a courtroom-to-courtroom, office-to-office canvass.

They located Grella in her office. She was reluctant but succumbed to Schwartz's amalgam of threats and cajolery.

Next they sought to find Barbanel. With a tip from Barbanel's office mate, Schwartz found him in the sixth-floor stairwell behind the secured hallways. Barbanel looked up sheepishly as he pulled on a cigarette. Barbanel suffered from the Nuremberg Syndrome: the otherwise decent man following morally offensive orders. A youngish man, only several years out of law school, Barbanel carried himself with a "why me?" demeanor.

Well, why not you?

Without a word from Schwartz, Barbanel snuffed out the cancer stick. Schwartz informed him of the nature of his application. Barbanel promised to meet him in Part X in a few minutes.

Given of the nature of the application Schwartz was about to make, Barbanel had alerted Franz Kafka, Esq., who was in the courthouse on another matter, to appear. As the case was being called, Kafka entered the courtroom and sat down at counsel's table next to Barbanel. Heidi winced when she saw Kafka enter the room.

Schwartz addressed the court first. "Thank you for recalling this case and to counsel for appearing. I have a simple application to make on behalf of Carmen Fontanez and her infant daughter, Justina. The court has already heard that Carmen was unable to appear due to her illness. I am asking that I be able to bring Justina to her hospice for a visit, forthwith."

Grella was the first to stand. "Your Honor, how appropriate is it to bring this infant into the hospice and expose her to all kinds of germs?"

Schwartz responded quickly. "Judge, if memory serves me correctly, this child was born in a hospital and somehow managed to survive that hotbed of germs and then was transferred to the ACS Children's Center—an even more toxic germ pool—awaiting placement."

It was Barbanel's turn to object. "This child is in ACS's custody by order of this court and cannot be released to Mr. Schwartz. This application should have been done on papers with adequate notice to counsel."

Schwartz answered the objection in a huff. "This court issued the remand order to ACS without a written application, and this court can temporarily rescind it by paroling Justina to my care. It's at this court's discretion to do what is in the child's best interest and to vindicate the rights of a mother who is living on a shrinking time frame. As far as notice is concerned, this is an exigent circumstance. The agency has their notice."

Next it was Kafka, Esq. "Mr. Schwartz has no special qualifications to take temporal custody of this infant. He's not a social worker with training. My agency would object and ask this court to deny this request as it is highly irregular and puts the child at risk."

"Well, you see Judge, I anticipated that objection, which is why I've asked Heidi Frias, MSW, who is present in court today, to accompany me with the child. She is a mandated reporter for child abuse and neglect, and I am an officer of the court, duty-bound to follow this court's order. So, Judge Parker, will the court grant respondent's application?"

Judge Parker shuffled some papers and motioned for his court attorney to approach from his seated position on the judge's right. The two men conferred, and Schwartz could see the court attorney shaking his head. The judge broke the confab and then turned to address counsel.

"Mr. Schwartz, I am denying your application. I have yet to hear from the caseworker about his visit to the hospice."

"Judge, have some *rachmones*—some mercy here."

"I'm sorry, Mr. Schwartz, but my responsibility is to the best interest of the infant."

"That is only partially correct. My client's rights as a parent are being trampled on by ACS, the law guardian, and this court."

"THAT'S ENOUGH, COUNSEL! Case is adjourned to December 20."

Schwartz stopped to catch his breath once he got outside the part. He sat down on a bench in the waiting area and stared at the tile floor. Heidi sat down next to him and rubbed his back.

"You did good in there. You tried. With your heart."

"To hell with trying." He stood up. "I'll call you later."

"You'd better."

"I mean, about Carmen."

"You'd double better."

She clasped his hands warmly, slung her bag over her shoulder, and walked slowly toward the elevator bank. Schwartz made his way toward the lawyer's lair, where a broken chaise lounge awaited him in a darkened backroom.

Schwartz eased his body into the sagging aluminum frame. Through the walls he heard ADA Mulrooney's bullhorn of a Bronx Irish Catholic voice working her cases on the telephone. Though he struggled not to listen, he couldn't avoid it as she blared, "All right, Detective. So you reinterviewed her. Has she ID'd the perp or not? So who was it? The boyfriend? No. You're not serious. No fucking way! Come on. He what? Sonofabitch. What about the paramour? You say he tested clean for STDs? Well, fax over both lab reports to me. You got the number, right?"

Mulrooney's words receded into the background as if they were an anesthesiologist's countdown. Schwartz was laid out, too pooped to pop, dead asleep.

Schwartz was in Bobby Darin's dressing room during the Freedomland gig. Bobby was stretched out in a chair, breathing from an oxygen tank. Sandra Dee was mopping Bobby's brow with a kerchief she had removed from her platinum-blond hair. Bobby was asking Schwartz to sub for him on the second show because he wasn't sure he would make it. Schwartz was shaking his head, and his neck, torso, arms, and legs followed suit.

The sudden blaze of the spotlight woke him up. Committing the cardinal sin of seeking to interview a client in that four-by-eight bastion of privacy, another 18-B had flicked on the light. Schwartz shielded his eyes, brought his wristwatch close to his face, and registered that it was 3:30 p.m. Yet another layer of sweat had been added to his clothes. Mindful of the penchant the chaise lounge had for imitating a kayak in rough waters, he gradually shifted his body weight onto the floor. The intruding 18-B apologized as his client backed out of the doorway. Schwartz waved his hand, saying, "No problem, no problem. Just give me a moment. OK, OK. I'm on my feet, ready to make justice happen."

Having made this declaration, Schwartz fell against the wall.

Kneeling in front of the toilet on the tile floor of the seventh-floor men's restroom, Schwartz's digestive and excretory systems were staging a protest demonstration. As a novice hunger striker, he had made the rookie mistake of gorging himself at the fast's end. Remarkably, french fries with brown gravy tasted almost as good on the way out as they did on the way in. Wiping the last of his recycled breakfast from his lips, he heard two men talking at the sink.

"He do nothing but fuck my woman. I gonna fuck him up. Na, na. Not dat way. Not yet. First, I gonna get dis *muchacha atras para mi novia.*"

Through the crack in the bathroom stall, Schwartz could see Machado staring into the metal bathroom mirror, combing his thick processed hair with a metal pick.

Schwartz's ego sent a memo. *I think it's time to get off this case.*

To which his superego responded, *You think?*

Discretion being the better part of valor, Schwartz traveled the back alleys of the secure corridor to the 18-B room, keeping an eye out for Dolan as he slunk around corners. Miraculously, he found the 18-B phone available. He dialed the number to the marital condo. Julie picked up.

"Julie, it's dad."

"Daddy, what is going on? Where have you been? Ethan is crying himself to sleep every night. Mommy is . . ." her voice trailed off.

"I know. There's a lot going on. And I don't want you kids in the middle of it. I'm trying, baby doll, to do the best I can. You know I love you guys . . ."

As he struggled to compose himself, he could hear Marjorie in the background telling her to hang up. Julie rushed out the final words. "Anyway, Mom is taking us away for the Christmas break to—"

Click.

Schwartz replaced the receiver and slowly walked out the door. He reached the waiting area of Finkel's part as court officer shouted, "Parties in the Matter of Mojica-Soriano!"

Schwartz entered the courtroom and bellied up to the table for what he knew would be a bumpy ride. Since the day before, he had been stewing over the ethical implications of his application to be relieved from this case. Given the breadth of the charges against Isabel, especially the newly minted sex abuse allegation, the chance of success on the merits was nil. Thus, the threat that Schwartz and his family would suffer violent consequences should he not prevail in clearing Isabel and having her daughter returned to her, was, indeed, real. If he revealed the basis for the application—the violence threatened by his client's paramour—it would prejudice his client on the merits because it would confirm that she is residing with a bad *hombre*.

While the crosscurrents flowed through his mind, Isabel entered the courtroom and appeared beside him. Dressed to kill, she wore a pink halter with a plunging neckline. Her crimson hair and beauty-shop makeup were accessories to the crime. The windows to her soul were now closed with an iron gate.

"Señor Schwartz," she hissed.

Finkel had not yet returned to the bench. Nonetheless, the court officer turned on the tape recorder and invited the parties and counsel to note their appearance. To an empty bench, Schwartz stated his name. The echoing drone of the Spanish interpreter was heard in the background. After that process was complete, Judge Finkel made her entrance. Once the judge was seated, the court officer instructed the parties to be seated.

Judge Finkel tilted her head in the direction of the ACS attorney. "Counsel?"

Benson stood. "We filed an amended petition alleging sex abuse, Your Honor, and the respondent mother needs to be arraigned?"

"Do you have proof of service?"

"Well, we served Mr. Schwartz and made several attempts at the mother's place of residence to no avail?"

Finkel trained her attention to Schwartz. "Mr. Schwartz, will you accept service on behalf of your client?"

"Judge, before my client takes a position on service or is even arraigned on the amended petition, I must make an application to be relieved on the grounds of conflict of interest."

Her voice softened. "Mr. Schwartz, kindly share with the court the nature of your perceived conflict."

Warning! Danger, Will Robinson! Danger!

"I fear, Your Honor, that I cannot do so without prejudice to my client on the merits in the court's eyes."

"As you are well aware, Mr. Schwartz, this court finds it difficult to get 18-Bs to step into my courtroom and it's nearly impossible when asked to substitute for another attorney on a difficult case. Furthermore, I wear two hats: trier of fact and applier of the law. They are two separate functions, and the court has the ability, by dint of training and experience, to maintain the firewall between the two."

Schwartz nodded in mock appreciation for the judge's claim to impartiality. "I am mindful of the court's dual function. I remain concerned that the client will not appreciate the subtlety and will perceive my stating the basis of my application as a personal attack, prejudicial to the merits of her case. As for the reluctance of 18-Bs to enter your lair, I think you have to start with the judge in the mirror on that one, Your Honor."

Judge Finkel's voice grew softer still. "For the time being, I will ignore your impertinence. As for your client, Mr. Schwartz, I will explain the nuances of the law to her. Are you doubting my ability to do so?"

Isabel strained to understand the interpreter's version of the exchange. The interpreter was leaning forward, working hard to catch each of the judge's words. Machado had entered the courtroom and was sitting in the back.

"Your Honor, I am an officer of this court. I can assure the court that I am making this application in good faith. Is this court questioning my good faith?"

"Mr. Schwartz, are you going to tell me the basis of your application or not?"

"Not."

Judge Finkel rocked back and forth in her chair. "Sit down, Mr. Schwartz. I am going to reserve decision on your application until after I've spoken to the respondent. Ms. Mojica, please stand."

Without waiting for the interpreter, Isabel stood. She turned ever so briefly to glance at Machado. Machado nodded in her direction.

"Ms. Mojica, you understand that the Administration for Children's Services has filed an amended petition charging you with knowledge of the sexual abuse of your daughter Zoraida and failure to protect her despite this knowledge? You are entitled to legal representation, and since you cannot afford counsel, counsel was appointed free of charge. I had assigned Mr. Schwartz to represent you, but now he says he can no longer represent you. What do you want me to do— relieve Mr. Schwartz or keep him on the case?"

Isabel's bosom rose and fell as she inhaled and exhaled, taking in the interpreter's words. Then she let it blow. "Señora *Juez*, I wan Señor Schwartz be put in jail. He is *el pendejo* who abuse *mi* Zoraida. He hava sex *conmigo*. An den, I no know dis den, he do it *con mi hija*."

With a hysterical yelp, she charged at Schwartz, her lacquered, rhinestone-festooned talons reaching for his face. Recovering from the shock of her accusation barely in time, he narrowly avoided permanent disfigurement. Machado was out of his chair and moving toward him.

The judge screamed for decorum to no avail. A surprised court officer managed to recover and flung himself between the combatants. His partner strode toward Judge Finkel as she headed for the asylum of her inner office. For the second time in less than a month, Schwartz was able to extricate himself from a jumble of court officers, Isabel, and Machado. He headed for the door to the well. Before he could reach it, ADA Mulrooney entered, accompanied by two detectives.

"That's our boy!" Mulrooney shouted.

Realizing that they had been waiting for him, Schwartz did an about-face. Making his way through the courtroom fracas, he moved swiftly toward the side entrance that led to the secure hallway. Mulrooney and company were in hot pursuit. Schwartz raced through the maze of back corridors, passing startled court personnel on cigarette and cell phone breaks.

Just before he ran into a particularly narrow bend in the corridor, he heard a loud "Psssst!" in his ear followed by a sickeningly familiar sucking noise. Schwartz whirled around to find Andrew Timmons ushering him into his clerk's office. Schwartz sidestepped the large man as he accepted the invitation. The clerk closed the door, leaving Schwartz alone inside.

Through the closed door, Schwartz could hear the collision of Mulrooney—no lightweight herself—the detectives, and Timmons, followed by a muffled mix of groans, curses, and Timmon's unrequited demand for an apology. Fifteen seconds later, the door opened and Timmons stuck his massive head into the room. He was sporting the joyful visage of an NFL nose tackle that had just stuffed a run on fourth and inches.

"Mr. Schwartz, I think it best that you leave this building now. I will escort you to the garbage barge elevator. Walk fast but don't run. Running would attract unneeded attention."

"Who are you and why are you helping me?"

"Objection, Counsel. Compound question. I'll answer the first part first. I'm a doctoral student of psychology at NYU. I'm conducting field research for my thesis, 'Synergy of Social Stress Sequentials: Quantifying Emotional Overload in Prediction of Violent Behavior.' I use my provisional position as a petition clerk to evaluate external and internal stressors impacting first-time filers of petitions. I utilize a one-to-seven rating scale to calculate various factors. I'm attempting to predict, quantitatively, which subject of inquiry will lose his cool. I'm applying for grants from the Department of Defense, Federal Aviation Administration, Transportation Security Agency, the Ford Foundation, and others to develop a field application for quantifying personality profiles in order to identify the 'terrorist within.'"

They had just about reached the barge.

"And you're helping me, because?"

Timmons reached for the elevator button and pressed it emphatically. "I've witnessed your work in the courtroom. I find your passion on behalf of these poor dysfunctional souls compelling and heartfelt."

Schwartz felt a gush of gratitude and attempted to hug his savior.

"Nah, you don't have enough time or arms to try to reach around me. Your barge is leaving. *Pax ex.*"

"Come again?"

"Peace out."

The door to the barge opened, half filled with black bags of refuse. The judge's elevator, which was right next to the garbage barge opened a second later. . As luck would have it, Captain Dolan was in the judge's elevator, saw Schwartz, and let out a "Hey!" followed by some expletives. Schwartz stepped gingerly into the available space on the garbage elevator, oblivious to the stench, and pressed the button for the second floor as hard as he could. The door closed abruptly on Dolan's cursing face.

On Sherman Avenue, Schwartz ran from payphone to payphone. One had no dial tone. A second had a dial tone but wouldn't accept his quarter. Schwartz had scraped skin off his finger while wresting his lone quarter back from the armored coin box. He finally found a phone that actually accepted his quarter and gave him a dial tone. Schwartz frantically flipped through the scribble-laden pages of his date book seeking the number he needed to dial. He squinted at his notations, making a mental note to pick up a pair of cheap, +2.0 magnifying reading glasses. Finally, he located his quarry and dialed the cell number of the ADA.

Come on. Come on, goddammit.

"This is Mulrooney. Whadyagot?"

She sounded as if she was running.

"Mulrooney, this is Schwartz. What the hell is up?"

"Schwartz! Look, where are you?"

Schwartz feared that Mulrooney would begin a trace on the number displayed on her caller ID, so he made it short and sweet.

"Mulrooney. It's not me you want. It's Hector Machado. The boyfriend's the doer."

"His negative test and your positive test for chlamydia say different."

He held the receiver without saying a word for a few seconds. Then he said, "Don't believe everything you see in a petri dish. Gotta go."

Schwartz could hear the shriek of his name from Mulrooney's lips as he hung up.

I need a plan.

Schwartz raced to Papo's yard. Papo was sitting outside, shooting the breeze with several *compadres*.

"Papo!"

"Oh, I have a leetle bone to pick with you. Señor Cliff know this spot is not available on weekend. Your Saab was sitting here all weekend."

"Papo, I need your help, big time. I'm sorry about the weekend parking thing. I'll make that up to you, but I need a huge favor 'cause my ass is in the sling."

"OK, Popi, OK. Slow down. How can this broken-down *jibaro* help *el gran abogado del* Bronx?"

When Schwartz parked the Saab on University Avenue, it was close to nine o'clock in the evening. He'd been driving, planning, and thinking. He'd stopped in various stores to purchase various items, the last being a sixteen-ounce can of Budweiser and a large bag of barbeque pork rinds. If he was going to hell in a bucket, he would grease the skid. Entering the main gate of Bronx Community

College, he reflected on the time he'd attended his brother's graduation from what was then NYU's uptown campus.

The graduation was in May 1968, and America seemed headed to hell in a bucket with one spring time assassination of a leader and another soon to follow. Schwartz was finishing his sophomore year at Evander Childs. He had worn his "Kennedy for President" button on his vest, much to the derision of his brother, who had campaigned for Eugene McCarthy in New Hampshire. Schwartz took it in stride. Bobby Kennedy was Darin's man, and that was good enough for him.

The two brothers had traveled together to Washington, DC, the previous fall, with the high hopes of levitating and liberating the Pentagon in an effort to stop the Vietnam War. For their trouble they were tear-gassed and chased with nightsticks and bayonets by the United States Army, MPs, and National Guardsmen, as chronicled by Norman Mailer in *The Armies of the Night*.

Schwartz was back on the old NYU campus to visit the Hall of Fame For Great Americans colonnade, to meditate in the semicircle of bronze busts of one hundred of the greatest American white thinkers and doers George Washington Carver and Booker T. Washington being the only exceptions of color, and their input would gladly be accepted. He would commune with their spirits and formulate his final plan of action. He would also smoke a joint to settle his nerves.

Leaning against the bust of Henry David Thoreau, he lit the doob and inhaled the sweet smoke. He looked at the Daniel Boone bust facing him and wondered about the nighttime conversations that passed between the two gentlemen. Schwartz chuckled as he paraphrased a debate that was inscribed on the walls of Frankie & Johnnie's Pine Tavern on Bronxdale Avenue:

Henry David Thoreau: To do is to be.

Daniel Boone: To be is to do.

Sinatra: Do Be Do Be Do.

As the drug percolated through his brain, Schwartz reminisced about his first night with Isabel and how they'd drunk and smoked and fucked all night and into the early morning. Once again he heard the cry of a little girl.

Was it possible that in that hedonistic haze I violated Zoraida?

Schwartz felt a pang of nausea.

True to form, the pot intensified, amplified, and front and centerized whatever mood, emotion, or sensation Schwartz was experiencing. At that particular moment, potential guilt was on the menu.

Schwartz's first course: A slice of teenage babysitter experience. One of his wards had been a precociously cute six-year-old girl with a obvious crush on Schwartz. At least that's what Schwartz thought. Then he recalled a Saturday night when she sat down on his lap and jumped up and down like a jockey in the saddle. As he inadvertently placed his hands on her chest, exactly where her boobs would one day develop, Schwartz got the hardest boner of his young life. With horror and shame, he had thrown the startled girl off his lap.

Was the crush mutual? Did it go deeper than that?

Suddenly Daniel Webster jumped off his pedestal, ambled toward Schwartz, and, pointing accusingly, questioned, "When you defended the Carlos Valdespinas of this world, had their transgressions vicariously fulfilled some dark desire in you? Are you a child molester in spirit? Did you abuse Zoraida Soriano? To be more specific, counselor, did you have sexual intercourse with her? Did you touch her for the purpose of sexual gratification? Are you capable, psychologically and physically, of sexually molesting a child? Did the mother put the child in bed with you on that November night? Are you in deep denial of your actions, yearnings, and feelings?"

"No . . . no . . . no . . . no, and no!" Schwartz screamed into the frigid Bronx air.

The Jury of Great American thinkers and doers retired to consider their verdict. Schwartz closed his eyes and began to pace. The jury appeared, deadlocked, and requested a recess. He muttered a line from Don McLean's "American Pie," reference to the Chicago Seven Trial:

"The courtroom was adjourned, no verdict was returned."

Schwartz continued to pace with his eyes closed. To find his way through the darkness, Schwartz needed to suspend the illusion of seeing. In order to cast light on his personal path, he had to acknowledge his blindness first. Schwartz wondered out loud, "If the road to hell was paved with good intentions, was the opposite true?" Because if the road to heaven was paved with bad intentions, he had plenty to spare.

The Saab Story was parked outside Isabel's basement apartment when the Luv Van pulled up just before midnight. Hector Machado pulled himself from the driver's seat and stood unsteadily. In slurred Spanish he barked at Isabel to wake up, get out of the van, and go inside the house.

Machado approached the Saab and put his face to the window, his hands framing his eyes to reduce the reflected glare from the streetlights. He tried the door and it opened. As Machado stuck his head into the vehicle, El Diablo shrieked his "Cockadoodledoo!" and leapt onto the man's head, entwining its talons in Machado's hair. The rooster did a *rat-tat-tat* with his beak on Machado's scalp. Machado was cursing at the top of his lungs, wrestling frantically with the homicidal cock.

With a stickball bat in his hands, Schwartz stepped from behind a nearby vehicle. Releasing a feral grunt, he whacked Machado across the back of his knees, sending the man to the ground, face down. He delivered another whack to Machado's back for good measure.

Schwartz jumped on the stricken man, held him to the ground, and pulled his shirt up, enough to reveal his flesh. Wearing handball gloves, Schwartz produced a blood sample stick, inserted it into the top of Machado's buttock, drew the sample, and then put it in his pocket. He grabbed El Diablo around the neck in the precise manner Papo had shown him. Schwartz removed the bird from Machado's head, using a pocketknife to free the bird from the man's hair. Machado was yowling curses in Spanish.

Schwartz whispered in Machado's ear, "You shouldn't drink and drive. You could spill your drink."

He made a dash for his Saab. The hair sample tangled in El Diablo's talons was a nice bonus. Schwartz fired up his red rocket. The backward engine coughed twice, ignited, and proceeded to zoom down the desolate slushy streets of Soundview.

DECEMBER 19:
YOU CAN'T HANDLE THE TRUTH!

EDGARDO RAMOS, ESQ. PICKED UP THE TELEPHONE RECEIVER in his office and dialed ADA Mulrooney. Schwartz sat across from him, collapsed in a chrome-and-imitation-suede chair.

"Mulrooney. It's Eddy Ramos. Listen. I have Public Enemy Number One, the lothario of Bronx Family Court, sitting across from me. Can you come to my office? That's right, the one between the bodega and Fun City. We want to show you something. Uh-huh. I understand. He will. He will. Just do me two favors: have the detectives wait outside and bring your copy of the lab report on Hector Machado....Why ask why?....Good."

With a tilt of his head, wrinkling of his face, and shrug of his shoulders, Don Edgardo returned the receiver to its cradle.

"What'd she say?"

"That she wants to kick your ass for running. But she bit the bait."

Fifteen minutes later, Mulrooney and her entourage were buzzed into the waiting room from the street. Schwartz watched on the office security monitor as she directed her detectives to remain on the well-worn chairs in the waiting room.

As she entered the inner office, Don Edgardo greeted her, "Geraldine. Thank you for coming. Won't you sit down?"

"Save the charm for the jury, Ramos. I told my boys that if I'm not out in five minutes to come in with Tasers blazing. Whatcha got other than this poor excuse for a lawyer over here? Schwartz, you look like shit."

"So I've been told. Salutations to you as well, advocate for the People. The People. I wonder if that's why hardcore criminals adopt aliases. Maybe they think it evens the odds a little bit in their favor, at least in the heading. You know, instead of the People v. Joe Blow, it's the People v. Joe Blow, aka Joe Shmoe, aka Joseph Blowsa, aka Joey Blowme."

Mulrooney curled her hair with one finger and gazed at the ceiling. "I see your flight from justice has not dulled your rapier wit. You're down to four minutes."

Don Edgardo glared at Schwartz and turned to address Mulrooney. "Do you have the copy of Machado's lab report?"

The ADA handed a paper to Don Edgardo.

LABTEX SCREENING
CHLAMYDIA REPORT
Lab Report #Specimen SourcesPatient:
245578DFA-CT URETHAHECTOR MACHADO

Date Drawn	Date Slides Examined
12/15/00	12/18/00

INTERPRETATION
Crotrak DFA Test-Negative for Chlamydia Trachomatis.

Edgardo rubbed his eyes and placed the report and his reading glasses on his cluttered desk. "I have a question about the timeline here. Schwartz, when did you say you first saw Isabel in the courthouse?"

Schwartz flipped through his date book. "It was over a week ago, on a Friday. Here it is, on the eighth—Friday, December 8. There's her name and the part."

Edgardo thought for a moment. "So you figure they did the removal of the child, like, say, the day before?"

Schwartz nodded in agreement. "And that would give our boy enough time."

"Enough time for what?" asked Mulrooney with more than a slight salting of annoyance.

"Enough time, dear Geraldine, to be warned by the mother to get treatment," Edgardo answered.

"What are you talking about?"

Edgardo searched around his desk for a document.

"Give her my copy, numbnuts," Schwartz urged.

"Fine! Fine! *Carajo!* You see, thanks to Mr. Schwartz channeling his inner Ninja Turtle, we've obtained a specimen this morning from Mr. Machado. And thanks to Mr. Schwartz for driving excessively fast in his questionable coupe, we've obtained lab results which show—"

"Which show what? Come on, Counselor. The clock is ticking here on this dog and pony show, and don't ask me who's who."

Edgardo stood, took off his glasses and gestured with them in Mulrooney's direction. "Which show traces of Azithromycin, the antibiotic of choice when seeking a one-shot knockout punch for chlamydia, though it takes seven days to work its magic. Which brings us to the December 15 collection date."

"Uh-huh." Mulrooney curled up her lower lip till it collided with her top lip.

"That's right. 'Uh-huh.' Your lab didn't look for antibiotics because no one asked them to. But you had to wonder how Machado could be banging that whore and not be infected, right? Our lab was asked and . . . voilà!" Edgardo performed a torredor's pass with the report.

"Voilà, huh? Let me see that report." Mulrooney snatched the report from the barrister's hand. "Hmmm. OK. But the mom didn't know there were sex abuse allegations until Schwartzie here informed her a week later."

Schwartz interjected, "Yeah. She didn't know there were allegations until December 15. That was the date Machado's sample was drawn. Probably by some Urgent Care quack. But she knew that there had been sexual abuse. She knew that ACS had announced its presence in her life by the remand of Zoraida on December 7th. And she warned the perp to get an antibiotic bath so that when the shit hit the fan, he'd come up clean. Now, isn't it interesting that I meet with her on Friday the fifteenth to inform her of the new sex abuse allegation, but the girl hasn't yet IDed a perp. Isabel no doubt went for a visit with Zoraida over the weekend. Then—boom!—the girl points the finger at me. What does that tell you?"

Mulrooney got out of her chair and nodded her head in thought.

"All right. All right. I'll call off my bloodhounds. Besides, I have some new info. Forensics has been going through the clothes the mother brought to the foster care agency for the girl. Turns out we may have a positive semen stain on her nightshirt."

Edgardo let out a whoop. "Holy Monica Lewinsky, Batman! Now, that's a really big voilà!"

As Mulrooney stood she turned to face Schwartz. "But, Schwartz, we have secured your sample from Nassau County lockup. So stay in town. At least until we get the results of the DNA match on the semen sample. And for Chrissakes, get yourself a dose of—what was that cure-all? Azithromycin—before you make the scene at Herpes Triangle tonight."

"It's on my to-do list, Mulrooney. But just for my peace of mind, how long will it take your hack lab to reach a conclusion?"

"Oh, you mean the FBI lab in Washington? Two to four business days. We sent it out over the weekend. I'll put a rush on it and see if they comply. But before you start feeling your oats again and crack wise with me, I have some questions for you that I don't want you to answer straight off. I want you to think about it. Let it sink in a bit. When you were having your tryst with this mother of the year, did you even see this little girl? And if you did, did you see any bruises, marks, or welts on her or any evidence of maltreatment? And if you did, did you lift your finger to help her in any way? Because if the answers are 'yes,' 'yes,' and 'no,' then therein lies the real crime here. Unfortunately, lawyers are not mandated reporters of abuse, given lawyer-client confidentiality issues. So it's beyond my jurisdiction. But it's not beyond someone else's."

The ADA pointed her finger upward and made the sign of the cross.

"Now, if you'll excuse me, gents, I've got to go throw my boys some Dunkin' Donuts before it gets ugly in your waiting room. See you in the morn." Mulrooney headed for the reception area.

"Whew!" Don Edgardo exhaled in the ADA's wake.

Guilty as charged worked for Schwartz. Don Edgardo regarded his downcast friend.

"Schwartz, why don't you come home with me tonight and let 'she, whose name I seem to have forgotten', lay out a spread of *carne guisado, plantanos madura, arroz con gandules, yuca con ajo*?"

"She'll really make all that for me?"

"No, you putz. We're probably just having Boston Market. But I can dream, can't I?"

"You're such a tease. Nah. I've got a lot to mull over between now and the morning. I want to stay close to court. Has anyone heard from Marjorie or the kids? Do we even know where she's taking them?"

"Blumenthal says they'll be going to an aunt's house in the Poconos for the school break. But before you rush out there in one of your self-help impulses, remember the stay-away TOP." Sensing his friend's darkening mood, Don Edgardo asked, "So where are you going to bed down tonight?"

"I'm not exactly sure."

Schwartz was looking out the door toward the suite's conference room. Don Edgardo laughed. "When you say 'close to court,' you don't kid around. All right, I'll clear it with my suitemates. I'm sure they won't mind. After all, it's Give a Homeless Lawyer a Home Week."

"Duly grateful."

MIDNIGHT IN THE
GARDEN OF PAPO

THE BONDSMAN WAS ON A DINNER BREAK BEFORE NIGHT
court started, and the process server was making his rounds. Schwartz was alone
in the office suite. He sat at Don Edgardo's desk. The family photos stared at
him.

He reached for the office phone and dialed his former home.

With his little man's voice, Ethan answered, "Yes? Who is this, please?"

"This is the Boogeyman Removal Company, calling to see if there are any
Boogeyman that need beating up."

"It's Daddy!" the boy screamed.

"Hey, big guy. You have a vacation coming up soon, don't you?"

"Yeah, Mommy's taking us to Uncle Bernie's house in the Poconos. We're
going snow tubing."

"Sounds really cool. Hey, listen, Daddy's going to come see you and Julie
after school tomorrow, OK?"

"I know. Mommy already told us. But how come we're going to the police
station? Are you in trouble?"

"No . . . yes. Put Julie on, Buddy."

"She's not here. She got invited to a holiday party."

Schwartz struggled to modulate his voice.

"Then please put your mother on."

Those were the moments he needed to breathe through, to transform the
anger bubbling up from his gut into energy that healed rather than tore apart.

"What is it?" Marjorie asked.

"Why isn't Julie available for my call?"

"She didn't have time to clear her social calendar to meet your visitation order."

Don't let that button get pushed.

"Are we on for tomorrow?"

She hesitated before answering. "Yes."

"Both?"

"Yes, Schwartz, both kids. And bring a check for $400. Julie's having a consult with an orthodontist."

His turn to pause. "Between now and then, help me think of a good explanation for why I'm picking them up at the police department."

"How about, for starters, the Bronx DA's sex crime unit has been out here looking for you?"

Schwartz gulped and exhaled. "That's been squashed."

A brief calculated silence followed. Then she said, "Well, that's certainly reassuring. 'Bye."

Schwartz depressed the receiver button, waited for a dial tone, and dialed Heidi's number. It rang four times and then her answering machine kicked in. Schwartz left a lame message inquiring about Carmen's health.

Restless, Schwartz decided to take a walk. Considering the hour and his ethnicity, that was a dicey walkability choice. As he headed up Sheridan Avenue toward 163rd Street, he thought about the Twentieth Century as its days dwindled. The wars. The genocides. The assassinations. The bombs: nuclear, chemical, and biological. The social and political turbulence. The economic upheaval. The religious fanaticism. The epidemics. The natural disasters and global warming. The famines. The rise and fall dance of fascism and communism. He wondered about the horrors of the next century, stored like floats in some demonic parade, waiting to be inflated and unfurled.

Maybe it could be horror-lite. Like Y2K. Why not 2K?

Schwartz looked up to find himself outside Papo's gate. Through the open door of the shed he spotted Papo hunched over the engine of a car, the back of his head illuminated by a mechanic's light hung from the hood. Schwartz rattled the gate and called to him. Papo emerged from under the hood and called out, "Who dat?"

"Who dat who say 'who dat'?"

Walking toward the gate and wiping his hands, Papo smiled as he picked up the thread of the old minstrel bit.

"Who dat who say 'who dat?' when I say 'who dat'?"

As Papo unlocked the gate, Schwartz glanced around anxiously.

"El Diablo? N*o precupe.* You 'n' he are friends now. You fight shoulder-to-shoulder with heem. He no bother you no more."

"I never thought of roosters as having shoulders."

Schwartz offered his hand. Papo, self-conscious of the grease on his hand, extended his forearm for an awkward touch and led Schwartz the lawyer over to a portable firepit. After some stirring, the embers sparked. Papo placed the legs of a broken wooden chair on top, rebuilding the fire. He motioned for Schwartz to sit on a nearby chair that had seen better days as a member of a disbanded dinette set.

Papo walked into the shed, wiped his hands on a rag laden with solvent, and returned with a bottle of light brown liquid. He handed Schwartz a small paper cup and filled it. Filling his own cup, he crouched down close to the fire and added a small log.

"151 proof rum. *Mi compai* works in the distillery, near Ponce. *Cada* Christmas, he sen us a bottle. *Salud!*"

"*Le'chaim!*" Schwartz answered as he drained half his cup in one swallow and then asked, as he coughed through the burn "Do you miss P.R.?"

Papo picked up a tire iron and stirred the embers. The ambient light revealed the wrinkles encircling his eyes. He sat back down and stared into the fire.

"*Mi padre,* he work on the sugar plantations. I work alongside him since I was ten. Den dey close the plantations. It was starve or come here. So I no miss starving. America, as dey say, been bery, bery good to me."

"Been back?"

"No. *Y porque?* To see that shack, no bigger than that shed over dere, where I live with *mi familia*? Nah. What the point? *Yo recuerdo* bery well wha it look like. *Cada* inch."

"But what about *La Isla del Encanta?*"

With a derisive snort, Papo waved his hand. "Hah! *Mierda por los touristas.* Now I live on the mainland, US of A. *El* Bronx. No more *Islas Encantas para mi.* I work hard. Feed *mi familia.* Feed *mi pio-pios y mi perros.* And get to share a leel rum with *El Gran Abogado del Bronx.*"

He pointed the bottle in the direction of Schwartz's empty cup. Schwartz gratefully accepted the refill.

"*Salud!*" they toasted.

Schwartz stared reflectively at the fire. "Do you know what an IRS agent once told me as she graciously accepted my check? It was in satisfaction of a lien for back taxes. She said, 'If your only problem is money, then you have no problems.'"

"Hah! That agent never in her life go a day *sin comer.*"

Schwartz crumpled his paper cup and threw it into the fire.

"Papo, I thank you for the rum, the rooster, and the words of wisdom, though not necessarily in that order."

He stood and stretched.

"OK, *El Gran Abogado del* Bronx. Someday I show you dose SSI papers *para mi hijo.*"

Schwartz offered his hand.

"It would be my pleasure. You bring the papers to the yard next week and I'll give them a gander."

Papo extended a closed fist in the direction of Schwartz's hand. His eyes glistened as he nodded. "You OK, Schwartz. *Mi* barnyard *es su* barnyard."

Schwartz reached out with a fist and touched Papo's. Unsteadily, he turned and headed back to Don Edgardo's office. He hoped that his restored faith in humanity would remain through tommow's half a day's session in BxFC.

DECEMBER 20:
THE DAY THE MUSIC REALLY DIED

IT WAS THE EARLY MORN OF TWENTY-SEVENTH ANNIVERSARY of Bobby Darin's death. Annually, Schwartz fell into a funk that began December 12th, the anniversary of Sinatra's birth, and had deepened to black hole status by the 20th. It was an eight-day observance, the same duration as the Jewish New Year and Passover. It was a pre-winter funk, and this year he had funked things up royally.

His predicament was summed up perfectly by the fact that he was stretched out on a conference table, using appropriated couch cushions for comfort and legal files for a pillow.

Next year will be better. At least I'll have a better pillow. Maybe one of those buckwheat pillows I read about in New York Magazine at the dentist's office.

As he rotated his neck searching for comfort, a pointed pen, letter opener set pricked him. Rubbing the wound, "Mack the Knife" came to mind.

What would Mackey do? Eliminate his enemies with the flick of a stiletto.

Were he so inclined. Schwartz had more than his share of potential victims. Like Nixon with his enemy list, Schwartz visualized each face and their last expressions. He imagined the tone of their voice and what their last words would be.

One wouldn't think that homicidal musings were the stuff of lullabies, but Schwartz's macabre mind game gradually garnered him sleep.

The shrill grind of the hydraulic lift on a commercial garbage truck servicing the bodega and Fun City woke him early. As a groaning dumpster was raised and emptied, the defender of the poor and downtrodden reached for a file to place over his face. Realizing the futility of his attempt to reconnect with sleep,

Schwartz rolled off the conference table. He stumbled toward the office lavatory and then made the crucial mistake of turning on the light and catching his unwashed image in the unwashed mirror.

"*Oy, gevalt.*"

Schwartz left Edgardo's office and headed for his mobile home. Opening the hatch of the Saab, he rummaged through the box containing his current files. After locating the files of the cases *du jour*, he got into the front seat. He twisted the knob to set it to recline and began to review the file contents. Counting respondent parents jumping over the hurdles of the Children's Best Interest Industrial Complex was the perfect prescription for sleep. He dozed off.

When Schwartz opened his eyes and glanced at his watch, it was already 9:30 a.m. He got out of the car, opened the hatch, and pulled out some fresh underwear. While monitoring the streets for passersbys, he changed while reclined in the front seat. He dabbed himself in strategic spots with a damp brown paper towel, courtesy of Don Edgardo's office bathroom.

A young girl of about ten approached the car while walking her dog. Schwartz, of course, was at the pinnacle of nakedness when the Yorkie lifted its leg on the Saab's front passenger hubcap. Schwartz dared not move. An arrest for indecent exposure would, unfortunately, round out his rap sheet nicely. The girl looked right through Schwartz as if he were invisible. The dog finished its business and they continued on their way.

Once he'd gathered his files and placed them in his shoulder bag, Schwartz sprinted to the courthouse, his ribs vibrating like a tuning fork. He dodged the litigants' line outside, skirted the conga line inside, and squeezed onto the elevator, earning hostile stares from those his maneuverings had aced out.

Just before the elevator door opened on the seventh floor of BxFC, Schwartz felt palpitations in his chest. Once on the seventh floor, he bolted through the crowd and headed toward Part X. There was Heidi, standing by the window of the waiting room with her back to him. Schwartz rushed up to her and breathlessly asked, "Did they call the case yet?"

Heidi turned to face him. Her reddened eyes and grim demeanor startled him. Schwartz quickly scanned the nearby benches.

"Where's Carmen?"

Heidi shook her head and turned back toward the window. Schwartz took several involuntary steps backward and leaned against the ledge of the window, holding his head.

"Bitch, bastard, bitch, bastard, bitch, bastard . . ."

Schwartz's voice got softer until it was inaudible but his lips still mouthed the words. A court officer stepped out from Part X and shouted, "Parties in the Matter of the Fontanez Child!"

Schwartz slowly straightened himself. He grabbed Heidi's elbow and guided her into the courtroom. Judge Parker was on the bench. Grella and Barbanel were standing in front of their chairs. Caseworker Adesanya was the last to enter.

"Counsel, note your appearance for the record."

Schwartz gazed at the empty chair to his left. He attempted to force air through his larynx but no sound would come forth. Judge Parker glanced up from his writing on the endorsement sheet to ask, "Mr. Schwartz, are you all right?"

Schwartz found the will to speak.

"For the respondent Carmen Fontanez, I have a motion, Your Honor. On behalf of Carmen Fontanez, the mother of the infant Justina, I hereby . . . I hereby withdraw her 1028 application. It has abated, as has she. It's moot, as is she. I wish to congratulate the Commissioner of Social Services and the Legal Aid Society for having successfully protected Justina from her mother."

Schwartz turned and walked out of the courtroom, pausing only to put his arm around Heidi. Outside the courtroom, awash in the auditory collage of the waiting room, Schwartz and Heidi sat on a bench holding each other's hands and staring into space. When Schwartz began to rub her back, Heidi jerked away and stood abruptly. "Funeral arrangements. Gotta go."

At 1:10 p.m., Schwartz sat in a near-empty waiting area. Several yards away, Alphonso and Paul Abbatiello were playing tag in the labyrinth of benches. At first Schwartz was oblivious to their laughter. However, their joy penetrated his cloud of mourning, and his thoughts turned to his own children. When was the last time he'd engaged them in a game of running bases or touch football? It felt like eons instead of months. Tonight he was scheduled to pick up Julie and Ethan from the Glen Cove Police Department and was emotionally ill-prepared for this court-mandated encounter. He dialed the number to the marital condo and left a message for Marjorie to cancel the visit with some bogus work-related excuse.

After the lunch break was over he instructed Abbatiello to check Paulie into the Children's Center to await the pickup of the child by the mother. He then stumbled to the respite room and the wellworn chaise lounge. As he passed Mulrooney's office door he knocked seeking an update on the semen lab results. No answer.

Schwartz rang the street entrance buzzer to Don Edgardo's office suite. The evening exodus of court personnel and clients from Sheridan Avenue was well underway. People headed off to holiday shopping, parties or home. Schwartz was stewing. His stomach growled with hunger and dread. An office door opened toward the back of the dimly lit hallway, and Don Edgardo Ramos, Esq. emerged. He walked slowly down the hallway as he perused a file. Glancing up, he identified his visitor, shook his head upon recognition, and unlocked and opened the door.

"*Hombre*, you have screwed up my entire afternoon. I was summoned to the seventh floor to calm that idiot Abbatiello down because Mommy Dearest wouldn't let him take the kid home without you. I had to intercede with Judge Williams on your behalf because he wanted you to appear for a contempt hearing. And then take the calls from Blumenthal about you blowing it and failing to pick up of the kids. And then the DA gets back to me with the results of the DNA test. What am I, Tom Hagen in *The Godfather* and I represent only one client: you?"

Schwartz collapsed in the client's chair.

"I'm sorry. I've been in a trance this afternoon. Carmen Fontanez died."

Don Edgardo's eyes narrowed as he considered the statement. "Carmen Fontanez? Who? That whore you were bent out of shape over because they took away her kid? That's what has you so upset? She's a whore and a junkie. She's supposed to die. From what? AIDS, right? It's the way of the world."

Schwartz shook his head. "You are a cold-hearted motherfucker, you know that? I remember walking down the street with you once. A one-armed beggar came up to you. Before you gave him anything you asked him if he was a righty or a lefty. That's you, Don Edgardo. Always looking for the angle. Well, I'll tell you the slant on this: Carmen Fontanez was a mother, just like your mother and my mother. And all she wanted was to hold her baby in her arms. But somebody with a title said, 'No. It wouldn't be good for the baby to bond with you. You're garbage. And if we just string this court thing out, you'll be dead.' And as it turns out, they played their hand perfectly. Pur-fect-ly . . ."

Schwartz's voice trailed off. In the ensuing silence, Edgardo's face contorted. Schwartz got up to leave. Don Edgardo snorted. "You're going to compare my mother to that whore? Sit down. I'm not finished with our consultation. Don't you want to know about the DNA test? That's right, you'd better sit. More bad news. The semen on the girl's dress was a DNA match for you, lover boy."

Schwartz's face began to burn and he started gasping for air.

"Holy shit. Are you . . . ? That bitch! She set me up. At out rendezvous after the YT. I'll bet she took my spunk home and spread it on her girl's clothes. That evil bitch! Doesn't Mulrooney question why that bitch would bring the clothes to the agency without washing them? The clothes are corroboration of her complicity. This was a setup from the get-go."

Ramos was on his feet, gesturing as if he were simultaneously conducting an orchestra and a cross-examination.

"She's a whore right? Go ahead say it. This mother you were trying to reunite with her child is a whore. C'mon, say it!"

Schwartz was awash in revulsion, anger, and fear. "Damn right she's a whore. A lying, scheming, motherfucking cunt whore!"

"Good. I just wanted to hear you say it. I was jerking your chain about the DNA test, you prick. It's not yours. But check this out. It didn't match up with Machado's either." Don Edgardo paused dramatically. "The match was with the recently murdered father, Livian Soriano. The cops believe that Machado killed him in an exercise of street justice. There's a warrant out for his arrest."

"What? Soriano? Machado? You bastard. Oh, man. I mean, how could you make me think—"

Ramos laughed caustically.

"Because you needed to be knocked off your own pedestal so you could stop placing these whores on a still-higher pedestal. You needed to stop with your messianic-savior-of-the- masses pose. Your Christ complex. This woman, Isabel, was trouble from day one, and I tried to warn you. But, nooooooo, you were going to follow your dick and white knight pose into battle. A lethal combination. *Don Schwartz de la Mancha*, you are guilty of delusion, not sex abuse."

Schwartz took a deep breath. "But if they're all whores, then why do you bother with them?"

"Ah, you've articulated one of the great conundrums. All I have to say is that they are the very breath of life. Just understand that some have blinking red neon lights that say, 'Walk on by.' If you fail to see the sign, be prepared to do the time. At least don't forget the condoms."

Schwartz sat immobilized, staring at Don Edgardo. After several seconds he said, "You are some piece of work."

"So I've been told. I just know how to work the room, that's all. Now, I accept your apology for inadvertently insulting my mother and bid you adieu. She whose name escapes me at the moment is meeting me at La Maganete for a night of Salsa. *Orquestra* Broadway is playing. Once in a while, just to throw them off the scent, you have to do the right thing. Ah, yes," he remarked as he stroked his mustache and winked.

At the Bay Plaza shopping center in Co-op City, Schwartz rocked back and forth on his heels, clutching a five-dollar mix of carnations, baby's breath, and pompons. The pre-holiday evening bustle of off-duty office workers, EMT technicians, police officers, subway motormen, and medical assistants that populated the massive development passed him with scant acknowledgement. Schwartz slowly spun his body around, shielding his eyes from the setting sun. He noted a few nervous glances from the passing populace as he knelt down in the middle of the Plaza, placed the bouquet at the base of a bench, and held the position for several minutes.

Schwartz began singing the first few bars of Darin's cover of "Artificial Flowers", about a poor girl who froze to death early in the last century. A crowd began to gather. Critiques were offered in the form of derisive comments, which could be accurately described as Bronx Cheers. Heidi stepped out of the semi-circle surrounding Schwartz, softly applauding and approached him. She reached down and gently placed one hand on his flower-holding hand and another over his mouth. Accustomed to have his singing interrupted, Schwartz stood.

"I think this is the exact spot where Bobby Darin performed at Freedomland here back in '63."

Heidi's mood shifted from slightly amused to slightly exasperated. "What am I going to do about you, man?"

She put her arm in his and led him toward one of the brick-and-glass towers. The buildings were constructed atop the Bronx tidal wetlands some thirty years ago. Their design seemed as if it had been run off an East German architect's mimeograph machine,

"Heidi, did it ever occur to you that the Bronx is the only borough of New York City that is not an island? That the Bronx is connected to the continent? When I was in college, I would meet girls from Queens at house parties who would stick their noses up in the air and pronounce that they were 'from the Island.' To which I would respond, mimicking their snotty tone, 'Well, I'm from the Continent.'"

"Great. A pickup line that's also a geography lesson. And check you out, you still wound up on the Island."

Schwartz hung his head ruefully. "'Tis true. 'Tis sadly true."

Reaching the lobby of one of the mimeo buildings, Heidi placed several packages on the ground and began fumbling for her key. Several elderly white people sat in beach chairs on the other side of the lobby glass. It was evident that they were engaged in a heated discussion. Behind Schwartz and Heidi, several people of color mumbled impatiently. Heidi finally located her keys and opened the inner door. Schwartz caught a snippet of the lobby confab conversation.

"What ya gonna do? The *schvartzas* and their kids have taken over and—"

"Morris, shush! People are coming."

The conferees offered amiable smiles to the rainbow coalition entering the lobby. Schwartz, recently of Long Island, could hardly judge them for their attitudes. In the early 1970s, entire neighborhoods of West Bronx Jews made an exodus to Co-op City, leaving their rent-controlled havens in search of the land of milk and honey.

Intraborough white flight.

To the assembled elderly, someone else's promise was being fulfilled in what used to be their Promised Land. When tired of the race-versus-class debate at CP meetings, Schwartz's mother would sigh and say, "I guess people just want to be with their own kind." If that were so, he wondered who was his own kind?

Schwartz followed Heidi's lead, entered her apartment, and removed his shoes. Heidi smirked upon seeing several of Schwartz's toes making their presence known through holes in the socks.

"Darn it," Schwartz whined in mock surprise.

"Schwartz, you're so hard on yourself."

"No, I mean, 'Darn it' is what I said to my wife before she threw me and my holey socks out."

Heidi laughed her first throaty laugh on that dismal day. She motioned for Schwartz to sit on the couch. She headed for the kitchen, returning with two chilled El Presidentes beers, shaking her head.

"You . . . are . . .a. . . trip."

"Hop on board."

She sat next to him on the couch and handed him a bottle of beer, which glistened with condensation. "And a shameless punster."

"Guilty as charged. I used to be the punster for the Giants."

Schwartz knew as the words escaped his lips that he had pushed the "lighten up" motif beyond its limits. Heidi's glare confirmed it. Contritely, he raised his bottle. "To Carmen. *Salud!*"

Heidi fought to maintain her composure. She softly offered her toast. "*Le'chaim!*"

They clinked their bottles. The frothy brew soothed Schwartz's taxed vocal chords.

"What's up with the funeral arrangements?"

Heidi's expression darkened further. "Sunday. At 10:00 a.m. St. Patrick's is footing the bill. The one diligent effort they made on Carmen's behalf is the referral for her funeral. Because now her children are truly freed for adoption. And they just saved several thousand in agency attorney fees not having to file a TPR."

"So young, so beautiful, and so cynical."

"I'm not so sure about the young part, but two out of three ain't bad."

"Hey, I know a song that goes like that. Would you like to—"

"Schwartz! What is it with you, man? Do you have some jukebox stuck up your ass? Shut the eff up."

Heidi took a pull on her brew, swallowed, and put the bottle against her forehead. Schwartz reached for her free hand and rubbed the top of it. She turned and stared at him but didn't withdraw her hand. As she spoke, she waved the bottle emphatically, like a conductor's baton.

"The sad truth is, Carmen's mother had been trying to get custody of her grandkids for years, but the agency wouldn't work with her because she didn't have a white-on-white clearance. I think the grandmother had an indicated case for educational neglect twenty years ago. Some bullshit . . . I'm not sure. And her apartment size didn't meet agency regulations. So St. Patrick's wouldn't certify the home. Last year, the grandmother died. Carmen said she had a sister in Florida, but she hadn't heard from her in years."

Schwartz took a long, thoughtful swallow. "Do you know that Bobby was adopted?"

"Schwartz, I don't want to hear—"

"No, no. Check this out. I mean, not in the formal sense. But his mother and father raised him, along with his older sister. Older by seventeen years, that is. His mother died when Bobby was—what? About thirty. After a gig, his big sister came to see him in the hotel where he was staying. Bobby had been thinking about trying his hand at California politics. Maybe a run for Congress. And his sister, I mean, I'm not sure what her motivation was. I guess she wanted him to hear it from her first and not the press or a possible opponent. Anyway, she goes to the hotel room. I can imagine how that went:

"'Hi, Bobby. How are you?' 'I'm fine, sis. How are you?' And then she says, 'Sit down. I've got something to tell you.' Just like in the soap operas or the last scene in Chinatown. 'I'm not your sister; I'm your mother.' Bam! Just like that. Bobby freaks out. I mean, he knew who Bobby Darin was because he'd created him. But suddenly he had no clue who Walden Robert Cassotto was. He asks, 'Who's my real father, then?' But sister/mom refuses to tell. After that, Bobby dropped out, did the Big Sur hiatus thing for a year or two, and re-emerged as a folk balladeer in a denim tuxedo."

Heidi took a deep breath and shook her head. "Well, your Bobby and my Carmen share a death day."

"That they do. But I have to say it. Heidi, you are a hospice social worker. Given the sorry state of HIV treatment modalities, you bury most of your clients. No?"

Heidi shifted her weight on the couch and stared directly at him. "Where are you going with this, Schwartz?"

"I mean, what was it about Carmen that drew you to her?"

Heidi allowed herself a moment. A fire truck's siren blared from the street below. A child's cry could be heard from down the hall.

"As flawed as she was, as beaten up by the world, Carmen had this light in her. A spirit that said, 'I can still love. I can still give. Against all odds.' I don't know. Maybe I transferred too much of my own struggle to reunite with my mom onto her. But in the brief time I knew her . . . I loved her."

Heidi hung her head and let out a soft moan. Schwartz shifted his weight on the couch and put his beer on the coffee table. He put his hand on Heidi's shoulder and started to rub her back. Heidi didn't pull away. She laid her head against his shoulder and started to cry.

Both to lighten the mood and to soothe her grief, Schwartz began to sing "If I Were A Carpenter", Bobby Darin's folk hit.

She laughed a little bit and picked her head up. "Schwartz, close your lips and kiss me."

Schwartz knew an audience request when he heard one.

As their lips bowed and curtsied, the kiss was hesitant at first. Gradually, good manners gave way to saliva as their tongues joined the fray. With a jolt, Schwartz felt Eros course through his body.

What better way to greet death than the act of lovemaking?

Apparently, Heidi concurred because she welcomed Schwartz's hand at the top of her zipper. He slowly unfastened it. His fingers carefully but firmly massaged her vulva through her cotton panties. From deep inside Heidi's lungs, a guttural gasp escaped like a smoke ring headed for the ceiling. Schwartz's middle finger pushed aside her panties and entered her slippery vagina as Heidi spread her thighs. Schwartz undid her belt buckle with his free hand and proceeded to remove her slacks. Heidi shifted her weight in concert with his movement. Heidi reached for Schwartz's zipper and reciprocated by stroking him. Schwartz positioned his head at the intersection of Heidi's Y, eliciting a deep breath.

Heidi reached out for Schwartz's head and pushed the base of his neck toward her upper body. Schwartz was mystified, but the answer was forthcoming.

"Please come inside me," Heidi cooed in his ear.

He mentally gave a three-fingered salute to the Boy Scout within him who had been prepared. After testing positive for STD he had sought treatment. But as a fail safe move he had thought to purchase a three-pack of condoms at the bodega. He retrieved a foil-wrapped balloon from his wallet and dressed his little man. Schwartz lay ever so gently on top of Heidi, careful not to place all his body weight on her as he began to insert Tab A into Slot B. Heidi began to moan and cry simultaneously.

"Am I hurting you, babe?"

"No, I was hurting me. Go on, Papi."

Given her history and his recent brush with the law, Schwartz found the "Papi" reference unsettling. Consequently, his erection softened slightly. Gradually he felt the inner muscles of her vaginal wall accept him into her, reinflaming him.

Breathing rapidly, Schwartz placed his hands under Heidi and rotated their conjoined bodies so that he was on his back and Heidi was on top. After they rolled over, Heidi began once again to find her rhythm, her pussy-tears dripping onto his thighs. Schwartz felt his own orgasm building but struggled to hold off for Heidi's sake. Her hips moved ever so swiftly, gaining momentum. With their arms wrapped around each other, their united orgasms achieved a perfect Venn diagram. They remained in each other's arms, panting softly, gazing into each other's eyes, accepting their mutual surrender. Her breath tickled his chest.

"Hmm," was all he could immediately muster. Then he added, "I guess I can cross simultaneous orgasm off my bucket list."

She punched him in the arm and feigned a protest. "Is that a bucket list or a 'fuckit' list?"

That cracked Schwartz up. "I guess the latter is a subset of the former."

She laughed a little, sat up, stretched her arms above her head, and then brought her arms behind her head. She covered her face and rubbed her eyes.

"Where do we go from here?" he asked, dewy-eyed.

"Where do you think? Ortiz's Funeral Home," Heidi answered.

DECEMBER 21:
WINTER SOLSTICE

WHILE NOT EVERY DENIZEN OF THE BRONX PAYS TAXES ON time, if at all, many succumb to the other eventuality, early and often. The Ortiz Funeral Home, with four convenient locations throughout the county, was the *jefe* of the "burial to meet all budgets" business in the Bronx.

Carmen Fontanez was laid out in a modest salon. When Schwartz and Heidi arrived, several of her housemates from the Shakespeare facility were already there, having been brought by the hospice van. They greeted Heidi warmly and gave Schwartz a shy once-over. Four young children, two boys and two girls, including an infant, were in the company of the foster care worker, Ms. Bentley, and three other women. Schwartz assumed that they were Carmen's children and their respective foster/adoptive mothers.

Heidi knelt at Carmen's casket for several minutes and then joined the seated hospice residents in meditation. Schwartz slowly ambled up to the open casket.

Thanks to the undertaker's efforts, the waxlike husk of what was once Carmen Fontanez wore a mask of serenity. Looking at her hands crossed peacefully over her chest, Schwartz was pleased to note that her nails were resplendently decorated, each with the image of a child of different age. Carmen would appreciate that. He bent down and kissed each fingertip. He started to cry tears of anger mixed with sorrow. He stormed off and sat in the back of the room. A priest from a local parish who knew nothing of Carmen began the service. He waxed passionately homilies about life, death, resurrection, and the Holy Trinity, while barely mentioning Carmen.

Ms. Bentley eulogized Carmen for her efforts to reunite with her children and for loving them. She remarked that the assemblage need not worry because the agency had found foster mothers to adopt all the children. The assistant funeral director, a small nattily dressed man, made some end-of-service logistical remarks and asked if anyone else wished to pay their last respects. Schwartz stood and, deep in thought, slowly made his way to the front of the room.

"I was Carmen Fontanez's lawyer in family court. I represented this mother in her efforts to live with her newborn child, Justina. Carmen was a failed human being. No doubt. But aren't we all failed human beings? Every one of us sitting in this room, next door at the nail salon, at the bus stop in front, at the bodega on the corner, on and on, are failed human beings. I'm not a Bible expert, New or Old Testament. But I do recall, somewhere, something about 'judge not lest ye be judged.' What was the other one? Oh, yes. 'Let those of you who are without sin cast the first stone.' All her life, I'm willing to bet, people threw stones at Carmen. People who should have known better and taken stock of their own transgressions.

"Well, as her attorney, I feel obliged to throw a stone in her defense. The judges, lawyers, and social workers are focused on the protection of children. A lofty goal, no doubt. But the name over the entrance of 900 Sheridan Avenue reads 'Family Court.' In contradiction to that name, the court has become an altar upon which families are sacrificed in worship of the Cult of the Child. Not just mom and dad are sacrificed, because we all know what wretches they can be. But aunts, uncles, grandparents, brothers, sisters, and cousins get shoved aside unless they are willing to do the adoption-permanency dance. See, there's little federal money to help families care for families. There are big bucks supporting foster care agencies and foster parents, foster therapists, foster social workers, and foster lawyers. It's a huge industry, supporting many members of the professional middle class, including myself.

"In the name of protection, children are separated from siblings and relatives and jettisoned into the foster care gulag, becoming strangers in a very strange land. Overmedicated with psychotropic drugs, they set off on the road to continued dysfunction: drug abuse, sexual abuse, delinquency, crime. They become respondent parents themselves. Those who manage to climb out of the system"—Schwartz paused to catch his breath and to look in Heidi's direction— "do so with an inner strength that is amazing to behold.

"This foster care agency, St. Patrick's, by whom Ms. Bentley is gainfully employed, made Carmen jump through hoops. They required she take parenting skills classes, go for drug treatment and counseling, obtain proper housing, and endure psychological evaluations. She complied as best she could. Still, the agency hemmed and hawed, stalling the return of her children, supporting, and nurturing the artificial bond created with their foster parent clients. I'm speaking of the very children sitting right here."

Schwartz walked over to the children, surprising the foster mother holding Justina in her arms as he bent down and picked up the sleeping infant. He walked back to Carmen's open casket.

"I want you kids to know what a fighter your mother was, how beautiful her spirit is, how much she wanted you in her care, and how much she loved you. Her sins caught up with her physically, and the system played a game with her. It reminds me of a game that was played on these streets when I was a boy: Red Light, Green Light, One-Two-Three. Carmen would see a green light, start to go, and then the light would change to red. Just like the traffic lights on these streets. Every time your mother took meaningful steps to have you with her, she was stopped and sent back to the start line. Maybe she lost her housing or tested positive for marijuana or her Medicaid lapsed so she couldn't go to therapy or she had an argument with a foster care worker and was labeled incorrigible, mentally unstable.

"Well, staggering through the foster care system is over for Carmen. But the fight for these four children to be with family can continue."

Schwartz held Justina higher. "These children are scattered amongst four different foster homes. If anyone in this room knows of a relative of Carmen Fontanez who would be willing to step forward and care for these children, I volunteer my legal services to represent that family member in court. My phone number is written next to my name in the sign-in book."

Schwartz placed the infant on top of Carmen's still bosom and held her there for a moment. The baby began to cry.

"Hear that, Carmen. Your child is crying for you. Justina. *Es su madre. Ella tiene mucho amor para ti. Siempre sabe eso.*"

Schwartz took a deep breath, walked back to the foster mother, and handed her back the crying infant. He touched the cheeks of each one of Carmen's children. He resumed his seat at the back of the salon. He covered his face and softly cried. Heidi came over and rubbed his back with her hand and kissed the back of his head. Through his hands, in a low voice, he said, "I'm walking in the dark, searching. Yet I can't find my way. I must close my eyes to see. Surrender to the darkness, drop the illusion of seeing. Then I will find my way."

DECEMBER 25:
THE MAGI APPEARS

SCHWARTZ WAS DRIVING WESTWARD ON PELHAM PARKWAY from Co-op City headed toward Fordham Road. He passed the Bronx Zoo, the New York Botanical Gardens, and then Fordham University,

Fauna to the left. Flora to the right. Jesuit Liberal arts straight ahead.

The reptile house dominated his memories of childhood visits to the zoo. At the exotic snakes exhibit, Schwartz would press his hands and nose against the glass, hypnotized by the undulating serpents. Inevitably, his father would ignite the young boys fear/flight warning system by demanding, "Can't you read the sign? 'Don't lean against the glass!' What would you do if it broke?"

One summer, he had taken Julie and Ethan to the Botanical Gardens. They had strolled through the colorful gardens and gone off the beaten track by doing a Yogi Berra coin-flip tour. When they approached a fork in the path, they took it. Schwartz would flip a coin. Heads, they turned right, tails, they turned left. Their random trek took them into the middle of a deep forest, the likes of which Schwartz had never seen in his home borough. Julie saw a plaque and read it out loud:

"Welcome to the largest original old-growth forest remaining in New York City. Explore these forty acres and experience the landscape as it existed four hundred years ago."

The three of them started hooping, chanting, and performing dances in tribute to the Manhattan tribe that had once roamed those woods.

Schwartz's most vibrant memory of the Fordham University Rose Hill Campus, which abutted Pelham Parkway as it transformed to Fordham Road, was as the terminus for the Mobilization to End the Vietnam War March in 1969. Schwartz's mother, the old Leftie, had joined him. The march had wended its way eastward from the Lehman College campus on Bedford Avenue. On either side of the Grand Concourse underpass, supporters of the Vietnam War welcomed the demonstrators with eggs, bottles, and obscenities. At that point, the march had become a sprint. Mama Schwartz showed she still had wheels.

On this Christmas Day, Schwartz headed to Cliff's apartment in the Highbridge section. When he got there, he parked and as someone left, made his way through the iron-gate. He climbed the stairs to Cliff's floor and knocked on the door. Cliff opened it, dressed in his briefs and court officer navy blue t-shirt. He growled, "Schwartz, what the hell are you doing here?"

"I'm here to make a trade."

He reached out his hand to Cliff.

"Now shake my hand."

"I'm not shaking your hand, you sorry excuse for a lawyer, tennis player, and friend."

"It's verrry important for you to shake my hand. I repeat, shake my hand."

Cliff slowly raised his hand and extended his palm toward Schwartz's. When their hands met, Schwartz passed the key to the 1986 LeSabre Cliffmobile to his friend.

"Look out the window."

Parked on the street was the Cliff-mobile, restored to all its glory.

"Oh no, you didn't."

"Let's just say I had a leetle help from your friendly neighborhood drug dealer. Just give me back the keys to the Saab, which you'd insisted I return to you, so that I might be on my way. And uh, Happy Baby Jesus's birthday."

The two men embraced, made tentative plans to play some indoor tennis, and parted company. Schwartz located the Saab Story, fired it up, and headed back toward Pelham Parkway.

On that Christmas Day, he was picking up Paul Abbatiello for a lunchtime visit with the boy's father, aunt, and grandmother. After that, he was headed to the Poconos for a Christmas/Hanukkah dinner with his children and soon-to-be ex-wife.

JANUARY 2, 2001:
HAPPY NEW YEAR

THE DAY AFTER THE DAWN OF A NEW MILLENNIUM CAME, IF one follows the Gregorian calendar. If one were Hebrew, Hindi, or Hong Kongese, or a member of the more than one hundred cultures or scientific communities that mark the beginning of the world from a different reference point, it was just another day.

For Schwartz it was a day of reckoning. He had been summoned to appear before the Appellate Division, First Department Assigned Counsel oversight committee. Due to an array of alleged transgressions, he was to show cause why he should not be disqualified from the Panel. His rap sheet read as follows: sexual relations with a client, willful contempt of court orders, disruptive courtroom behavior, possession of marijuana, alleged domestic violence, and, the biggest offense of all, failure to appear timely on his assigned cases.

The meeting was set for 1:00 p.m. in the ninth-floor library of BxFC. Significant among the committee members were Judge Natalie Finkel, Burton Mitzner, Esq., and Franz Kafka, Esq. No witnesses would be called. Letters of complaints would be entered in the record, and Schwartz would be given an opportunity to respond orally to the allegations.

Schwartz exited the elevator on the ninth floor carrying a plastic bag containing the old vomit-green wrinkly linen suit that so offended Mitzner. He entered the library, approached the table where the committee was seated, and tossed the bag in the air toward Mitzner.

"Burton, I believe this is yours."

Mitzner reached for the bag and pointed at Schwartz. "Schwartz, is that your new suit?"

Schwartz pointed to his brand-new suit. It was the suit he had purchased with the $200 Mitzner had given him. His new suit was also vomit-green and crafted from wrinkly linen, yet it exuded a certain sharkskin sheen.

"Off the rack at Fordham Road's finest men's shop. I think it says 'me.'"

Judge Finkel cut in. "Gentlemen, can we end the fashion critique and begin? Mr. Schwartz, are you aware of the allegations against you?"

"I am."

"How say you?"

"Judge, 'How say you?' That is so Star Chamber proceeding formal. I'm impressed."

"Mr. Schwartz, perhaps you haven't quite grasped the seriousness of this proceeding."

"If it's so serious, why am I denied the right to counsel, the right to cross-examine witnesses, and the right to a fair and impartial tribunal?"

Mr. Kafka interjected.

"Mr. Schwartz, the rules of the committee, as drafted by the Appellate Division, do not provide for the considerations raised by you because your very membership on the assigned counsel panel is a privilege, not a right. You serve at the whim of the panel. As a courtesy, this opportunity to respond is afforded to panel members whose fitness to serve has been called into question. Now, how do you wish to respond, in writing or orally?"

"Orally will do just fine. I've decided that it should be in song, with apologies to Kurt Weill and Bertolt Brecht."

With that, Schwartz began to sing his version of "Mack the Knife," with his hips swaying and finger snapping.

"Oh the shark, babe, has such teeth dear
And it shows them pearly whites.
Just a quick tongue, has old MacSchwartz, babe
And he keeps it for the fights.
When that shark bites, with his teeth, babe
Scarlet billows start to spread.
Crumpled tissues has old MacSchwartz, babe
So there's never, never a teardrop shed.

There's a sidewalk, ho, ho, around a courthouse, uh huh
Crammed with people just losing rights.
Who's that coming,' round the corner?
Could that someone be Schwartz the Knight?"

Judge Finkel raged, "Mr. Schwartz are you out of your —"
Schwartz raised the volume on his singing and trained his attention on Finkel.

"And there's a jurist, huh, huh, huh, down by part 1, don'tcha know,
With a gavel just banging on down.
Oh, that gavel's justice done wrong, dear
Five'll get you ten, babe, some family's gonna drown."

Finkel sat back in her chair and managed to inch her hand into her purse to retrieve her cell phone. She called the security desk and alerted the drone court officer. Upon arriving in the library, the officer, usually relegated to the difficult task of reading three newspapers a day while sitting at a table in front of the elevator door, decided that a singing lawyer would require more than he had in his package to handle. He called the main security office for backup.

Mitzner's response to Schwartz's meltdown serenade was a broad grin and a snort. Schwartz did a pirouette and ended it with his finger pointed at Mitzner.

"Didja hear about Burton Mitzner, he done gets relieved, dear,
After draining out his client's cash.
Now he berates them for their failures
Could it be our boy's talking trash."

Kafka piped up. "Really now, Mr. Schwartz, this is totally uncalled—"
Turning to Kafka, Schwartz continued his singing as he raised his hands above his head.

"Now Foster care lawyers, administrators
Look out you social workers, both white and brown.
The line forms on the right, babe,
For the greenbacks from Washingtown!"

Captain Dolan, Officer Mama's Boy, and several other court officers arrived through a side entrance. Finkel scowled. "Mr. Schwartz, I'm sending you up to the MHS clinic for a Short E."

Schwartz, not feeling like a danger to himself or others, submitted his non-concurrence with her proposal by voting with his feet. He bolted out yet another side door and ran down a hallway, with Dolan and company in pursuit. He made it to a back staircase and headed for the sixth floor—the next floor that permitted re-entry. He bounded up the staircase that lead to the seventh floor toward the merge area of the four waiting rooms. Dolan and his posse had entered the floor from all four directions and were rapidly closing in. At the top of his lungs, in the crowded convergence of waiting areas Schwartz offered his final verse.

"Now all you Mamas and all you Papas, you need to hear this sound.
Form some lines now, rise up strong and loud now.
Claim your rights in New York Town.
I said, form some lines now, rise up strong and loud now.
Claim your rights in New York Toooooooown."

As Dolan and his minions closed in, Schwartz gave 'em the big finish:
"Look out, Ol' Schwartzie's go-o-o-o-o-one."
Schwartz bowed and mopped his forehead with tissues that were crumpled but clean.

A LATE JANUARY AFTERNOON
IN THE NEW MILLENNIUM

AKIN TO THE TREATMENT OF POLITICAL DISSIDENTS OF THE former Soviet Union, Schwartz was remanded to the psychiatric ward of Bronx-Lebanon Hospital. Schwartz had insisted that he was not a threat to himself or others. After thirty days of observation and interrogation, the treatment team concurred. On discharge, his diagnosis was "Narcissistic Messianic Syndrome with Histrionic Features."

Subjected, *ad nauseum*, to Schwartz's performance of the Darin songbook during his stint, the treatment team recommended cognitive therapy and voice lessons. When his treating psychiatrist suggested Schwartz seek another trade or profession he would be more emotionally suited for than family law, Schwartz's response was swift,

"What? And give up show business!"

Behind the wheel of the red Saab 900, Heidi met Schwartz on the street in front of the hospital. She slid over to the passenger seat as he approached the driver's side. She kissed him gently on the cheek when he got in. As he pulled away from the curb and steered toward the Grand Concourse, she asked, "So what's next for you, Schwartz?"

"I still have two kids to feed, so I'll put up a shingle and try to hustle up some clients. I'll be my first client, since I will be filing a false imprisonment lawsuit against Judge Finkel, Captain Dolan, and NYC Health & Hospital Corp."

He made a right turn, maneuvered into the center lane, and headed north. Heidi gazed out her window thoughtfully. She turned to Schwartz and tapped her hand on his lap. "I might have something that would interest you."

Schwartz's interest was immediately piqued. *"Qué pasa?"*

"I've been writing grant proposals on behalf of the Shakespeare Hospice. We're trying to fund an alternative-to-foster-care program, a residence for mothers at risk of having their children removed by ACS. The residence would provide preventive services, such as counseling, GED tutelage, childcare, vocational training, parenting skills, and—ta-da!—legal representation in family court matters involving custody, domestic violence, child support, and Article 10 cases."

Schwartz considered her words as if they were musical notes being played on a xylophone. In his best imitation of the German soldier played by Artie Johnson on *Rowan & Martin's Laugh-In*, Schwartz said, "Verrrry interesting." He was lost in thought for a moment. "I think I have a great name for it: Carmen's House."

Heidi smiled. "I like it. I like it a lot."

Schwartz continued to drive the Saab up the Grand Concourse toward Fordham Road. Wouldn't you know it, he made every green light.

THE END

Made in the USA
Monee, IL
04 May 2021